A JACKETING CONCERN

Praise for
A Jacketing Concern

" ...a vividly drawn cast of characters from all walks of life...Lovers of Regency novels and of classic historical fiction will love this well-researched novel, a story with overtones of mystery and a hint of romance."

Susan MacDuffie, author of award-winning Muirteach McPhee Mysteries

"Margaret Southall imagines a richly detailed world ... her story is filled with complex characters, suffused with humanity from every social caste."

Adrienne Dillard, author of *Cor Rotto*, a novel of Catherine Cary

"A wonderful romp through 19th century London...wonderful descriptions and characters for this intriguing tale of danger, betrayal and odd companionship... "

Christy Nichols, author of *Legacy of Hunger* (Druids Reach Series) and *Better to Have Loved*

"In this debut novel Margaret Southall's strong evocative writing brings the Regency era before our eyes as we travel alongside the characters involved."

Historical Novels Review, a publication of the Historical Novels Society

A JACKETING CONCERN

Margaret Southall

KNOX ROBINSON
PUBLISHING
London & Atlanta

KNOX ROBINSON PUBLISHING

34 New House
67-68 Hatton Garden
London, EC1N 8JY
&
3104 Briarcliff Rd NE 98414
Atlanta, Georgia 30345

Copyright © Margaret Southall 2017

The right of Margaret Southall to be identified as author of this work has been asserted by her in accordance with the Copyright, Designs and Patents Act 1988.

All rights reserved.

ISBN 978-1-910282-54-0

Typeset in Bembo

Printed in the United States of America and the United Kingdom

www.knoxrobinsonpublishing.com

To

Bill, Shirley, Roy and Stella

"**jacket, v.** ...this term–*jacket*–is more properly applied to removing a man by underhand and vile means from any birth or situation he enjoys, commonly with a view to supplant him; therefore, when a person is supposed to have fallen a victim to such infamous machinations, it is said to have been *a jacketing concern*: 1812 J. H. Vaux; 1823 Egan Grose etc..."

Eric Partridge
The Wordsworth Dictionary of the Underworld (1995)

PROLOGUE
Sussex, 1811

Slowly, very slowly, first a mop of thick brown curls then two large brown eyes rose above the mountain peak. The eyes shone with excitement as their owner peered down the mountainside at the French army camped in the valley. A lock of hair fell across his forehead; impatiently he brushed it aside. So eager was he to prove himself in battle, he could hardly wait to begin a surprise attack on the enemy.

Addy took several deep breaths, for if the attack was to be successful he must stay cool and calm; after all, he was the officer who would lead it. This command and his promotion to colonel were Lord Wellington's rewards to him for the success of his previous mission: among all the army scouts, it was he who had discovered the enemy's hiding place. He took one last look at the French. All was as it should be in the enemy camp; the French had not reinforced their perimeter or placed extra pickets because they were not expecting an assault. Quietly he began to guide his men down the mountains slopes and crevices.

The French were in a sorry state. There were so few of them; and they must have been short of supplies, for instead of French uniforms they wore old British ones. Napoleon Bonaparte, himself, the Emperor of the French, the Conqueror of Europe, was in the saddest state of all: his left hand and right foot were missing, lost, of course, in a previous battle with the British.

The day was too beautiful for war. The sun shone down from a cloudless blue sky, its heat tempered by a soft breeze that wafted the scent of late summer flowers. But intent on the attack, Addy was oblivious to these delights and the accompanying calls of the wheateaters and skylarks. When a chalkhill blue butterfly fluttered past his head, instead of chasing it as he usually did, he ignored it. His only thought? Destroy the enemy! Eyes glowing, he knelt above the toy soldiers of the opposing armies. The British were new tin soldiers grandpapa had given him on his last birthday. These he carefully guided over the mounds and through the creases he had created in the blanket to make it look like a mountain. His old worn and broken soldiers were the French; the most worn of all was 'Boney'.

There was never any doubt about the outcome of the battle.

The British won, of course–*he* made sure of *that*.

That was the way it should be for 'Boney' was a bad man. Bette, his *gouvernante*, often told him so, and she must know for she was from France. If 'Boney' and the French invaded England they would do dreadful things, Bette said. They would rob all the women of their 'most precious possession'. As he was not quite eight years old, he had not understood what she meant by this. When he asked her to explain, Bette threw her apron over head and sobbed, so he was left none the wiser. What bothered him most about 'Boney's' was when Bette said–as she often did when he was naughty–that the French emperor ate naughty English boys for his supper. Little boys just like him, she said, who didn't always do their lessons, who wouldn't go to bed at bedtime and who often wandered too far from the house as he had done today. But Bette's threats did not frighten him as much as she hoped, for he was a daring little boy who intended to fight the French when he grew up. And more often than not, when told of his misdeeds, grandpapa would smile affectionately and say, "Boys will be boys." To which Bette would sigh, "Your *grandpère*, he always spoil you."

When he told grandpapa what Bette said about Bonaparte, the old man just laughed. "Eh, lad, 'Boney''s French. Those Frenchies eat frogs and snails, not little boys. Now in my day 'twere chimney sweep who took away naughty boys." This, coming from someone as old and wise as grandpapa, who seemed to know everything, did frighten him. So each night before he went to sleep he looked under his bed just in case a sweep or Napoleon was hiding there ready to pounce on him.

The battle on the blanket over, the French lay where they had fallen. But, he reminded himself, you could never be too sure of those Frenchies! He stood up and looked about him. They could have reinforcements hiding in the bushes waiting to counter attack. A cavalry charge would flush them out! He would lead a charge just like the one he and grandpapa had watched at a military review. How he had loved the review: hundreds of soldiers and cavalry marching and counter-marching, cannons booming, bands playing and crowds cheering. And when the people shouted, "God Save the King," he did so, too. The king's name was George III—grandpapa had showed him the king's picture on a coin—and he lived in a castle, just like grandpapa and he did.

What he had most liked at the review was the soldier who rode on a big white horse at the head of the cavalry. A colonel, grandpa said, and such a fine sight he was in a red coat with shiny gold buttons and a black hat with white feathers. There and then he decided he would be a colonel when he grew up and ride a white horse. His mamma and papa in Heaven would look down and see him and be very proud of him.

He had never known his mamma and papa and could only imagine them. He was born too early, Bette said, which was why he was small for his age. Mamma died not long after he was born, while his papa was in a faraway place. His papa, too, had died before he could return home, Bette said. In his childish way he had created a fantasy of a gentle, beautiful mother and a tall, brave father. But although an orphan and sometimes lonely because he had no other children to play with, grandpapa and Bette filled his small world with love and warmth. Of his two dead parents, his mother seemed more real and closer to him than his papa, even though all that he had of her was a miniature of her in his bedroom and a lock of her hair braided into the gold mourning ring grandpapa had had made as a keepsake for him when she died. The ring was too big for him to wear yet, but because it made him feel his mother was near to him, he wore it on a narrow chain around his neck under his clothes. Of his papa, he knew only what Bette told him in secret. That was because although grandpapa loved him and made much of him, the mere mention of his papa, even by him, made the old man very, very angry indeed, Bette said.

Perhaps his mamma and papa were watching him now from Heaven. He hoped so. He would show them just what a fine colonel he would be one day. He put on the pointed colonel's hat he had made from one of grandpapa's old newspapers, gathered his horse's bridle and leaped into the saddle. He raised an arm and pointed his sword.

"Chaaaaaarge!" he yelled, and with this defiant scream he set off at a gallop towards the large clump of bushes behind which, he was certain, the French were hiding.

He never reached the bushes.

Unseen hands threw a rough cloth over his head and plucked him from his horse.

He had been wrong about the French! They had not been hiding in the bushes but in the trees behind him. And now they had captured him–*a British Army colonel!* Well, he would show them that a British officer did not surrender easily. With fists and legs he struck out again and again. The cloth over his head smelled of fish and sweat and he almost retched. It muffled the yells and curses with which his attackers responded to his kicks. Struggling hard to free himself, he did not notice that the enemy's curses were in English not French. He gasped for air and his head swam as he felt himself hoisted high and thrown over someone's shoulder. His body sagged. Exhausted, he could fight no longer and slowly he drifted off into oblivion.

When Bette came to look for him, she found only the aftermath of battle: toy soldiers tumbled on a rumpled blanket, and a wooden sword and a hobby horse each broken in half.

The servants of Addy's grandfather searched for the boy until darkness fell but without success. Not until dawn would they resume their efforts, for even though a person might carry lanterns, the downs with their chalk pits were a dangerous place for people to walk. They were glad to leave the dark and empty land to itself, the only sound the distant *ssssssh* of the waves upon the beach carried by the ever-present breeze. The servants were newcomers to the area, but the locals had yet another more sinister reason not to be abroad on the downs at night. They believed the tales whispered among themselves about the restless spirit of the man who shot himself at *The Beeches*, the house built like a mysterious fairytale castle. There was no place in Heaven for someone who killed himself, they said, so his spirit haunted the house. Some claimed his ghost lured unsuspecting folk to fall over the cliffs to their death on the rocks below; still others swore he aimlessly wandered the downs at night, moaning like the wind. It was only a few years since his death and fear of his ghost remained strong among the locals, so strong that day and night they avoided the house, even though recently it had acquired a new occupant.

Had anyone dared to be abroad late that particular night, they would have sworn–just before he or she fainted with fright–that the eerie light bobbing across the downs in the dark was the dead man's ghost. There was, however, nothing supernatural about the light: just a small lamp carried by a solitary rider on horseback. The lamp gave little light, so the rider was forced to lean over the bundle that lay across the front of his saddle to see his way ahead.

He was in no hurry. Secure in the knowledge that local superstition and darkness would keep prying eyes at bay, he had waited until after midnight to begin his journey. And if by chance someone did see him? He chuckled at the thought. Fear would be his ally. Anyone who encountered him would do what they always did when a smuggler like himself rode by: turn away and pray *he* had not seen *them,* for they knew smugglers dealt viciously with those who could identify them.

Although an indifferent horseman, the rider knew this part of the South Downs well; he crossed it often enough with teams of packhorses loaded with spirits, tobacco and silk. One such horse was his present mount, a docile but sure-footed beast, used to finding its way in the dark.

At last the rider reached his destination: a natural fault in the land that time and weather had eroded to expose the underlying chalk for a depth of several feet. He dismounted and for want of any trees entwined the horse's reins in a large clump of gorse. He lifted the bundle from the saddle, slung it over one shoulder then, with the lamp in his other hand, picked his way cautiously to the edge of the chalk pit.

The bundle was light. Hardly surprising. Scrawny little bastard! Always ill. No wonder it died. A weakling like that couldn't be his, though the woman swore that it was. He had told her so, too, when the bitch tried to stop him from smashing the brat's face into the wall. As if it mattered: the brat was already dead. Of course she made a fuss when he made her undress her dead son and exchange his clothes for those of the unconscious child. After he beat her, he kicked her out. There was no fear of her going to the authorities. By removing the kidnapped boy's clothes, she had committed theft: a hanging offence. He'd had enough of her whining. He'd been with her long enough. A woman was good for only one thing–as long as it didn't result in brats! He could always get a woman when he wanted one–not for his good looks, for he had none–but because he always had plenty of something more seductive than a handsome face: money.

He raised the lantern and peered into the chalk pit. The light was too feeble to penetrate its deepest recesses, a sure indication that it was more than deep enough for his purpose. He put the bundle on the edge of the pit, undid it and let the weight of the little body unroll the cloth as it tumbled into the pit. A rattle of loose chalk and stones marked its descent.

He rubbed his hand with satisfaction. He would make even more money than the large sum the fancy 'swell' was paying him to dispose of the other boy. The 'swell' was a passenger aboard an East India Company ship homebound from China, one of several vessels he and his gang regularly intercepted on moonless nights in mid-Channel to trade with its crew. The ship's cargo was tea, and the crew, like many of the company's employees, did business with it on their own account; in this incidence, selling it to his gang much cheaper than it cost to buy on shore because of the heavy duty on it. The smugglers carried it ashore strapped to their bodies beneath their clothes, or wrapped it in oilskins and weighted it down in the sea, returning later to retrieve it in the guise of innocent fishermen trawling their nets. The 'free traders', as they liked to call themselves, then sold it locally or inland at a profit but much cheaper than it cost to buy from a merchant who had paid duty on it.

Except for the stranger who had come up on deck for air, the Indiaman's passengers were abed. He watched the exchange between crew and smugglers and even spoke to several of the latter. A few weeks after the Indiaman docked in London, the stranger returned to Sussex, sought him out at a local smugglers' haunt and made him a proposition: money, and lots of it, to kidnap and kill the young boy who lived at *The Beeches*. Having killed more than once, he had no qualms about doing so again, and he readily accepted the offer. But, unbeknown to his client, he unexpectedly found himself in a position to make even more money from the scheme. The sickly boy whom the woman claimed was his son took yet another fever, and this time he died. Having neither paternal feelings nor moral scruples, he had no wish to saddle himself with child's funeral costs when he might make money from its death. He would dress the body in the clothes of the boy he was supposed to kill, smash the child's face to hide its identity and throw him into a chalk pit some way from *The Beeches*. The grandfather would believe his boy died in an accident, while the stranger would think he had carried out the task for which he was hired. Tomorrow, when he went to deliver tea in London, he would take with him the heavily drugged kidnapped boy, for in the city there was a ready market for the sale and purchase of children for labour–and sex.

All in all a great day's work. No wonder he felt pleased with himself. He laughed and the sound echoed eerily across the dark empty downs. Anxious to be gone, the horse whinnied and pulled at its reins.

The smuggler remounted, and horse and rider slowly made their way back the way they had come, their passage through the darkness marked only by the lantern's faint bobbing light.

A few days later, a small group of mourners dressed in black with touches of white, gathered in the shade of ancient trees beside a newly-opened grave in the parish churchyard. The solemnity of the scene belied its cheerful surroundings. Beneath a bright sun, red squirrels scampered in play among moss-covered tombstones, praying marble angels and stone crosses. In the trees, birds called to each other, and one or two, no doubt attracted by their shrill voices raised in a hymn, swooped low over four fresh-faced village girls in white dresses as they lowered into the grave a small coffin attached to the white bands they held.

The mourners were not the only ones in the churchyard that day. Unseen by them, a young woman in worn clothes, her face a picture of grief, watched the interment from behind a nearby marble mausoleum.

"*Earth to earth, ashes to ashes, dust to dust…*"

At the parson's words, the chief mourner, an elderly man with a white crepe band around his hat, bent to take up a handful of soil. Overcome by emotion, he tottered and would have fallen, had not the young man beside him put out a steadying hand to help him. The earth trickled through the old man's fingers and fell with soft thuds on the coffin. At this, one of several servants at the graveside, a plump middle-aged woman, burst into tears and was led away by a younger woman. For the rest of the committal service, the old man stared into the grave with unseeing eyes, tears rolling down his cheeks, his thoughts elsewhere.

With a quick, *"The-grace-of-our-Lord-Jesus-Christ-and-the-love-of-God-and-the-fellowship-of-the-Holy-Ghost-be-with-us-all-evermore. Amen."* the parson ended the service. But the old man continued to stare down into the grave, oblivious to all else.

The other mourners appeared unsure what they should do next. The young gentleman took charge. He took the elderly man by the arm and said gently, "Allow me to escort you to your carriage, sir."

"All gone. All gone. A judgment that's what it is," the old man muttered as he allowed himself to be led away.

The young man helped him into his carriage.

"It grieves me, sir, to leave you at such a time," he said, "having only so recently made your acquaintance. Unfortunately, urgent business—business that I can no longer put off—awaits me in London."

The old man reached out the carriage window and grasped one of young man's hands between his feeble ones.

"Ee, lad, how can I ever thank 'ee for all you've done for me during this sad time? 'Twas much more than Christian duty. I'm only sorry that you and he did not meet."

The young man made a self-deprecating motion with his hand.

He waved as the carriage drove off followed by the one carrying the old man's servants, then walked to a waiting post chaise. Once inside the vehicle his mournful expression changed to one of triumph. He yanked the white crepe band from his hat and threw it to the floor.

"To London!" he shouted to the lead post boy.

1

Angels were smiling down at him.

Several of them, in fact.

Through half-open eyes, unfocussed and still bleary with sleep, he saw them: rosy-cheeked cherubs, each one alike, smiling as they came and went in a confused pink blur above his head. Still engaged in that tug-of-war between sleep and full consciousness, he was only vaguely aware of them. He closed his eyes and languidly stretched his naked body. The pink silk sheet that partly covered him slithered softly over his skin as he did so, creating delicious *frissons* of pleasure in his lower body. He sighed. He was in no hurry to wake up; he wanted to return to the dream from which he was just waking: a dream of a lush garden, its air redolent with the perfume of exotic blooms, where he and a woman cavorted naked.

Unwilling to stir, he shut his eyes tight. Shouts from outside made him open them. He swore aloud. How could a man sleep in peace with that commotion going on? He looked up, his eyes still heavy with sleep. Above him the angels were still there, still smiling.

Angels?

Good God! Had he died and gone to Heaven? What could he, of all people, be doing there? Heaven was for the good and virtuous, qualities that no one would attribute to him: Roderick Giles Edward Fortescue Davenant, sixth Baron Davenant. No. He could not be in Heaven.

Slowly he took stock of his surroundings. He was in a bed—but it was not his own—in a bedroom decorated in a profusion of pink satin and lace, a room redolent with the perfume of his dream garden.

Where the hell was he?

He rubbed his eyes and looked up again. The smiling angels had now coalesced into one winged being high above the bed: the god of love. Not the God of Love of Sunday sermons but a plump Cupid of painted bisque with a naughty twinkle in its eye, a quiver full of arrows on its back, one hand holding a bow, the other clutching the festoon of pink silk draped above the bed.

The god of love!

Now he knew where he was.

What more vigilant sentinel could there be than Cupid for the bed of Harriette Wilson, London's most popular and fashionable courtesan? There she sat at her dressing table, sensuously stroking her chestnut curls with a silver-backed hairbrush, her perfume–that of his dream garden– scenting the room. Davenant leaned up on his elbow to watch her and savour the tantalising sight of her partially clad body visible through the diaphanous wrapper she wore.

Harriette caught sight of Davenant's reflection in the mirror and sighed. He quite left her other admirers in the shade. Such a man! So dark and brooding! His body so-o-o-o strong, so-o-o-o athletic. Those dark eyes so cool and penetrating.

She favoured him with a wink and a saucy smile. "I hope you slept well," she said.

"That goes without saying," he replied.

Any man slept well after a night with Harriette, he thought. A man who enjoyed her favours received more than value for his money. She knew how to please a man both in and out of bed. Last night she had delighted him sexually, exhausted him physically–and lightened his pockets substantially, for she put a high value on her charms. Admirers paid dearly, but willingly, for their time with her. Last night's debauch would cost him a hundred guineas, but he thought it well worth the cost.

Still brushing her hair, Harriette turned to him. Davenant gave one of his rare smiles. Beneath the wrapper she was naked from the waist up, her only other garment a pair of lace-trimmed drawers, two bags of silk covering her legs, tied at the waist with nothing below. Because they resembled men's drawers these latter feminine unmentionables were still considered indecent in England. For Davenant, the novelty of this indelicate French fashion lay not in seeing them worn but in removing them from the wearer. This he had done last night–to the mutual pleasure of them both. Watching her, Davenant saw that she was ready to offer more of what she had given him last night–for another hundred guineas, of course.

She rose from the dressing table and faced him. She smiled, a wicked twinkle in her hazel eyes. She gave a shrug and the wrapper slithered to her waist to reveal the pearly pink skin of her naked shoulders and breasts. Still smiling, she stood silent for a couple of minutes tantalising Davenant, before she let the wrapper glide to the carpet. Clad only in her lace-trimmed drawers, Harriette began to sashay towards Davenant. Inflamed by the promise implicit in her performance, Davenant's desire mounted. Halfway towards him, she stopped and gave a defiant toss of her head that set her curls dancing.

Davenant could wait no longer. "Come here, damn you!" he said, his voice hoarse.

"No," Harriette whispered. "*You* come *here!*"

"You little devil!" he cried as he leaped from the bed and pulled her into his arms.

2

Addy winced and moaned in pain as the rough walls of the narrow flue scoured the tender skin of his elbows and knees for the umpteenth time since he began his climb up it. The soot in his nose and mouth set him off on yet another bout of coughing and sneezing that strained his small body so much he felt as if he were on fire. Unable to move because of this onslaught, he stopped to rest. His arms and back had to take most of his weight: it was too painful for him to bend his cut knees against the other wall. Instead, he put his feet against the wall so that he was lodged at an angle in the flue.

All around him was black.

He could feel but not see the wet blood from the repeated scraping of his skin against the bricks as he climbed. Bodger, the oldest of the climbing boys, and Addy's only friend at the sweeps' yard, had warned him what would happen to his elbows and knees.

"The master rubs salt on 'em. They gets real 'ard after awhile," Bodger said, displaying the thick scaly crusts of skin on his own elbows and knees. "After a bit yer feels nuffink. An' don't rub yer eye with sooty fingers if yer gets soot in it… cos it'll go bad. That's how master lost his eye. One day, we'll both look as ugly as the master," Bodger added cheerfully. "We'll have missin' eyes, bandy knees an' a limp, like him. Yer knees give out cos a-climbin' and a-carryin' bags o' soot. Mine's getting like it."

Addy didn't want to be a climbing boy! He didn't want to look like the master or Mick, the journeyman. He wanted all the dreadful things that were happening to him to stop; for it all to be just a bad dream, a bad dream from which he would wake up safe in his own little bed at home, with grandpapa and Bette to care for him.

Although there had been no fire in the fireplace below for a long time, the chimney was airless and stuffy, making him sleepy. He was physically tired, too. He had been up since five o'clock that morning. That was when Malloy, the one-eyed master, roused him, Bodger and the two other climbing boys from the damp bags of soot on which they slept. They had had little to eat; just a piece of bread that Nell, Malloy's wife, dipped in the fat in which she had fried bacon for her husband and her four-year old son, the vague-looking Eddy, whom Bodger said was 'loony'.

While stuffing the bread in his mouth as fast as he could, Bodger explained, "Starve us… they does…don't want us fat…cos then… we wouldn't… be able… ter go… up chimleys."

None of the boys washed. Except for the white circles around their eyes, their faces were black, encrusted with the soot of months past. Addy's face, although grubby, was clean compared to theirs, but he had only been in the yard a couple of days. Everyone and everything in the sweep's yard smelled of soot and was speckled with it: Malloy, his wife and son, Mick the journeyman, the climbing boys and the shed in which they slept, Malloy's hovel and the three white geese he used to clean chimneys.

All the climbing boys hated the mean and vicious Mick. They saw little of Malloy—he spent most of his time in taverns—but Mick was always there. He kicked and cuffed the boys, took what little money they earned, either by stealing it or forcing them to play pitch-and-toss. When servants at houses where they swept chimneys gave them food, he took that, too.

That morning, after their scanty breakfast, Addy and Bodger went with Malloy and his geese in search of customers. All morning they trudged the neighbourhood surrounding the yard; but to Addy's relief, for it was to be his first time up a chimney, no one answered Malloy's persistent call of "Sweep O!"

Lack of business that day didn't stop Malloy from doing what he did every afternoon. Taking his three geese with him ("Thinks more of 'em birds than is old woman," Bodger said), he went off to spend the rest of the day in a tavern. Mick, Addy and Bodger were left to seek customers while the two other boys remained working in the yard under Nell's watchful eye.

To Addy it seemed as if they walked forever, Mick yelling "Sweep O!" When no one answered the call, Mick took out his anger by cuffing Bodger and Addy. After plodding the length of a long and busy street Mick called Tottenham Court Road, they reached a broad and well-travelled highway. Only after they crossed it and entered a place Mick said was Somers Town did they find a customer among a row of houses. A servant came out of a house and asked them to sweep the chimney of an empty bedroom.

Addy's coughs and sneezes finally stopped but he stayed where he was, afraid that if he moved too soon they might begin again.

"If yer don't urry up, I'll fetch Bodger a muzzler!" Mick's yell up the chimney set Addy's heart thumping wildly.

What was Mick doing to Bodger?

Bodger was rough and dirty but since the time a few days ago when Addy woke up from a drugged sleep and found himself in Malloy's yard, Bodger had been his friend and protector. Mick knew this and used it to hurt both boys. He tried to get Bodger to stick a pin in Addy's foot to make him go up the chimney.

"Nah!" Bodger spat, "not even if yer kills me!"

"An' that's what I'll do!" Mick shot back. And he grabbed Bodger and threw him hard against the wall of the empty bedroom. Bodger had lain so still, his face bloodied, that Addy was sure he was dead.

"Don't die, Bodger! Don't die!" Addy sobbed over him. "You're my only friend."

Bodger opened his eyes and whispered, "Did me best young un…did me best."

"No Mick, no!" Addy begged as he struggled to free himself when Mick pulled him away from Bodger and hauled him to the empty fireplace. "Don't make me go up the chimney, please! Oh please! I'm scared!"

Mick's response was to thrust a brush in Addy's hand, grab him by the neck and the seat of his trousers and shove him head first up the chimney. Shaking with fear, Addy remained where he was until a sharp pain in his foot made him scream.

"Move yer bastard!" Mick snarled, as with grim satisfaction he inspected the blood on the long, thick pin he had just yanked out of Addy's foot.

With no choice but to obey, Addy began his climb. With scarcely an inch of space between the wall and his shoulders, he could only move slowly. The air was stifling; he could hardly breathe. Soot got into his eyes and mouth and up his nose, setting off fits of coughs and sneezes that racked his aching body so much that he had to stop and rest just as he was doing now.

A shriek came from the empty bedroom below.

Addy shuddered. Mick had carried out his threat to hurt Bodger. He must hurry to the top or Mick would hurt Bodger again, and maybe light a fire in the grate. That was what Mick often did to make the boys work faster. His breath coming in gasps, he began his upward climb again, sweeping as he went. Every move hurt him. His body was by now slippery with sweat from exertion and fear, making it hard for him to hold the brush and maintain hand and footholds. He stopped a few seconds to catch his breath and looked up. What at first had been a tiny patch of blue above had grown much bigger. He sighed with relief; he was nearing the top of the chimney. The further up he went, the bigger the blue patch became and the fresher the air. Then suddenly his head popped out of the chimney and he was surrounded by blue sky.

For the first time in days, Addy smiled. As frightening and painful as the climb had been, he felt proud of what he had done. He had never been on the roof of a house before! He rested his arms on the chimney's rim and took a deep breath. The sun warmed him; the breeze ruffled his curls. He forgot fear. He forgot pain. He forgot stinging eyes. He forgot soot. He even forgot Bodger. He was once again the curious little boy who was always getting into mischief at home.

The chimney was one of a stack of four between two adjoining houses. Emboldened by the adventurous curiosity of a seven-year-old, Addy struggled out and on to the sloping roof. Perhaps he was not far from the little castle in which he lived with grandpapa. He squinted against the sunlight. Not too far away were green fields, cattle and hayricks—but no houses.

Holding fast to each of the chimney pots in turn, he slowly circled around them. Nearby in the other direction, beneath a smoky haze that always surrounded them, were the many steeples, roofs and chimneys of London. Addy's eyes widened. On grandpapa's map London was a black dot —a big dot, to be sure— but still a dot. The real London was *so* big!

He looked down at the people on the ground. Everyone looked *so* small. If only he could get down there, he could get away…if only…if only…

A loose tile gave way beneath one of his feet and rattled down the roof into the backyard below. His foot slipped and he almost lost his balance. To prevent himself falling, he clung to one of the chimney pots with both arms.

"You lily-livered bastard!" yelled a voice he had temporarily forgotten.

Mick had gone into the yard to see if Addy had reached the top of the chimney. "Come down, yer little turd!"

At Mick's voice, Addy, the curious little boy became once more the boy in the bad dream.

He did not want to go back down inside the chimney; but there was no escape for him across a roof of loose tiles. He had no choice: he must obey.

"Yer 'eard me!"

Addy shuddered. Mick was angry. Addy was certain he would beat him once he reached the bottom of the chimney. Tears welled up in his eyes; he could scarcely see where he was going. Slowly he pulled himself up the side of the chimney and braced himself to go back into the narrow, dark flue. He took one last look at the blue sky. Up there in Heaven were his mamma and papa. How he wished they were with him now to help him. He sighed, took a deep breath and began his descent.

About halfway down he stopped to rest. It was black, of course, and he could see nothing, but he sensed something was wrong. He coughed. The flue was full of soot. How could that be when he had swept it on his way up? There was a bend in chimney that hadn't been there before. The walls felt different, too: some of the bricks were loose and crumbled at his touch. He stopped and braced his feet and shoulders against the walls. Pieces of brick and lumps of soot rattled down beneath him.

This wasn't the chimney he had just swept.

Panic overtook him. Mick would beat him for this mistake. He *must* climb back up to the roof again and go down the other chimney. Frantic, he tried to move upwards, but the loose bricks gave way beneath his hands and feet. Unable to maintain his balance, he slipped.

He screamed.

And then he was slithering and sliding, feet first, down the chimney's rough walls, taking pieces of brick, and soot with him.

3

With a long, low chuckle Harriette slid her arms around Davenant's neck, pulled down his head and kissed him. Breathless, Davenant drew back and looked down at her. Without taking his eyes from her face, he teased loose the ribbon of her drawers and gently slid the silk down over her hips to fall to her ankles.

She closed her eyes and moaned softly as Davenant carried her to the bed. So completely absorbed were they in each other that neither Davenant nor Harriette heard the first trickle of brick and soot that came down the chimney. But there was no ignoring the very human-sounding wail, or the torrent of bricks and soot that next roared down the chimney, bringing with it a billowing cloud of soot that filled the room, and a filthy bundle of what looked like rags that knocked over the fire screen and irons before coming to rest on the carpet.

"Bloody Hell!" Harriette shrieked when a startled Davenant lost hold of her and she fell on the bed. Panting with fright, she lay there with her drawers down around her ankles.

The bedroom was a mess. Davenant and Harriette were red-eyed and coughing, the two of them speckled as black as the hangings and curtains were, the scent of Harriette's perfume replaced by the sulfuric smell of soot.

Davenant recovered first. He yanked one of the pink silk sheets from the bed and wrapped it around his body. Harriette scrambled to her feet, pulled up her drawers and clutched them tightly about her waist, all the while staring in horror at the bundle of rags, which had begun to move and groan.

"It's moving! It's an animal!" she screamed.

She screamed again and went on screaming, even when Davenant shook her. Only when he slapped her hard across the face did her screams subside.

Davenant knelt and gently rolled over the bundle of rags. Two terrified eyes, red-rimmed and filled with tears looked back at him: the eyes of a child. Its face and matted hair were so black that for a moment Davenant thought they were those of a blackamoor. He moved the tattered rags aside and found himself looking at a small boy, his body a mass bloody scrapes, and bruises.

"It's not an animal, Harriette," he said. "It's obviously a climbing boy." He paused then added, "Although I dare say there are those who consider them one and the same."

Harriette lay prostrate among the cushions on a sofa in her dressing room while her French maid dabbed *eau de Cologne* to her forehead. Wrapped toga-fashion in a pink silk sheet, Davenant sat by her side holding her hand.

Her behaviour had surprised him. When told the heap of rags was a climbing boy, she fainted only to have a fit of crying when she regained consciousness, behaviour he would have expected from a more timid and demure woman. But Harriette? Worldly and confident Harriette? Unlike most women of his acquaintance, she had never been one for tears, palpitations and swoons.

"There is no cause for alarm," he reassured her yet again. "The boy is a child. He can do you no harm."

Her eyes wide with fear, Harriette reached up with both hands and grabbed the sheet he wore.

"For God sake! He *can* do me a great deal of harm," she wailed. "No one—*no one*—must know. There must be no scandal! Oh, how people will laugh...and sneer...if they hear that, that... that thing...fell down the chimney while... we...we were..." She covered her face with her hands. "My reputation!" she wailed, "my reputation!"

Davenant lips twitched in amusement.

Harriette did have a reputation, it was true, but not for the virtuousness and propriety expected of most women. *She* was renowned for physical charm and her ability to entertain men in more ways than one. As a courtesan, her income depended on this, and she entertained only the wealthiest and powerful of men. Should it become known that a climbing boy had fallen down her bedroom chimney during one of her sexual encounters, there would be no end of malicious gossip and taunts. What spicy caricatures of the incident would appear in the print shop windows! What jokes would be told in the clubs of St. James—jokes about *coitus interruptus* and *ménage à trois*, and Harriette's admirers would be the men telling those jokes. And while laughing mercilessly at her embarrassment, they would think twice about soliciting her favours for fear a similar interruption might happen to them while in her bed. Meanwhile, any one of her several rivals among the *demi-monde* would be only too happy to step into her shoes. In no time at all Harriette would be destitute of admirers–and money.

There remained Davenant's own involvement in the incident.

The raffish society to which he belonged was not concerned with a man's morals or lack of them. It was an accepted norm that wealthy men of fashion like Davenant would enjoy the favours of women like Harriette. And he himself cared little for society's opinion of him, anyway. But ridicule of his sexual liaisons and prowess? In that, Davenant ruefully admitted to himself, he was no different from other men. He knew the sort of caricatures that would be drawn and printed of it if the incident became known; he had witnessed the salacious delight shown by the crowds gaping in print shop windows at caricatures of the amorous *affaires* of the Prince Regent and his brothers, the royal dukes. To be the subject of such public ridicule would be worse than being put in the stocks.

The irony of his present situation was not lost on the cynical Davenant, and he did something he rarely did: he smiled. He was about to play knight-errant to a whore, as much as to maintain his own manly pride and dignity as her dubious reputation.

"You have my word as a gentleman," he promised. "I will certainly not speak of the matter to anyone."

This assurance proved even more effective than *eau de Cologne* in restoring Harriette's composure. She relaxed and even managed a cheeky grin. But her respite was momentary. She clutched him again. "That…that…boy! What about him? He knows what happened!"

Davenant gently removed her hands. "Calm yourself, Harriette! He is unconscious." He shrugged his shoulders. "I'll deal with him. You have my word on that, too."

She sighed. Such a gentleman! And so, *so* attractive. Were it not for that awful creature in the bedroom, she would have liked him to stay longer. Instead she said, "*And* I give you *my* word, that I will not tell a soul, either. *Je le jure.* Oh, and have no fear for my maid. Her English isn't good…and besides, she is the keeper of a great many of my secrets."

A glance in the mirror told Davenant she referred as much to his appearance as to what had happened earlier: Lord Roderick Davenant clad in a pink silk toga, liberally smudged with soot.

"My valet would be mortified," he said.

Despite his impromptu costume, Davenant managed an elegant bow.

"If I were you, Harriette, I should have that chimney swept," were his last words to her.

He was gone before she could reply.

Was that the time? Henry Rollins stared at his pocket watch and shook his head. It was well past noon. His freckled face crinkled into a grin. Davenant's departure after his night with Harriette Wilson would be much later than was usual after such a visit—much, much later. As Davenant's personal groom and tyger, Henry was an authority on such matters, his loyalty and discretion having made him privy for years to many of his master's most personal activities.

Henry had been waiting more than two hours to drive Davenant home in a vis-à-vis, a small two-seater vehicle, devoid of the family coat-of-arms that Davenant used when he wished to travel incognito. Henry knew better than to knock the front door and announce himself. 'Is Nibs—as Davenant's servants referred to him behind his back—would emerge in his own good time, so it could be a while yet before he left.

There was little for Henry to do or see to relieve his boredom. Somers Town was very familiar to him: he had been there so often to Harriette Wilson's house with Davenant. For a short while he had amused himself by trying to identify from among passers-by former *aristos* who had settled in Somers Town after escaping the French Revolution twenty years before. This pastime proved difficult and did not last long, because he had no idea what outward distinguishing marks set apart a former French *aristo* from the rest of London's citizens.

Undaunted by the paucity of French *noblesse*, Henry then attempted to identify French spies from among the area's residents, reasoning that Somers

A JACKETING CONCERN

Town's French community was the ideal place for them to hide. But although he carefully scrutinised everyone who walked by, no one appeared the least bit furtive or in disguise, so he gave up that, too. There was nothing else for him to do except walk the horses a couple of times and take them to drink at a public trough in a neighbouring street. The only real excitement–if it could be called that–was what looked like a chimney sweep dragging a ragged apprentice from a neighbouring house. Chastisement of apprentices by their masters was a common practice, especially among sweeps. Henry gave them but scant attention.

Although he found the waiting tedious, Henry bore it cheerfully enough because it indicated that 'Is Nibs was enjoying himself. "A night wiv a mort doxy like 'er will do 'im a power good," he said to the horses in the Flash tongue of the underworld he habitually used, and of which neither Davenant nor Henry's adopted parents had ever been able to cure him. As if in agreement with him, one of the horses tossed its head a few times.

"Damned if he ain't been more blue-devilled of late than I ever know'd 'im be," Henry went on, "snappin' at me fer no reason at all…"

"Damn your eyes, Henry Rollins! And damn your impudence!"

Henry started, arrested in mid-sentence by Davenant who, unseen by him, had heard what Henry said. Davenant towered over the diminutive Henry, who had to crane his neck to look up at him. Not the least disconcerted by 'is Nibs haughty stare and abusive greeting, Henry grinned. The sudden twitch of Davenant's lips told him he was forgiven.

"Mornin' guv…er, I mean…good afternoon," Henry said, remembering the time.

Davenant merely nodded.

After night and a morning with Harriette Wilson, Davenant looked the picture of health; but then, thought Henry, he always did. Davenant's excesses had no effect on his physique, countered as they were by hard riding, fencing, and weekly sparring sessions at Gentleman Jackson's Gymnastic Academy. Unlike some gentlemen of fashion, he needed no corsets to narrow his waist and enhance the width of his shoulders. Despite a night with a doxy and the absence of his valet (Harriette provided razors for her guests), his *toilette* left nothing to be desired. Among the *ton*, he, like his friend George Brummell, was regarded as the personification of male elegance, favoring the superbly-tailored austere style made famous by Brummell. His evening dress of the previous night–a coat and breeches cut by a master craftsman–fit his body like a glove, his only jewelry a diamond cravat pin. And the cravat itself? A sartorial *tour de force* of his own creation–the Davenant Drape–was the envy of every *beau* in St. James.

Nothin' wrong with im bodily. But I 'opes as how he's in a better humour now than he's been these past weeks, Henry thought to himself.

His freckled face wrinkled into a sudden grin.

There was a flaw in the otherwise elegant perfection of his master's *toilette*.

"Beggin' yer pardon, milord," Henry said, trying hard not to laugh, "but… but…there's soot… on your nose."

"How observant of you, Henry," Davenant drawled. He took out a handkerchief and removed the offending smudge. "Let us test your powers of observation, further, Henry. You see that house behind me?"

"Miss Wilson's 'ouse? Course I do!"

"Excellent."

Henry beamed.

"You will enter that house, Henry."

"Yes, guv."

"Inside, you will find a staircase. You will ascend the aforementioned staircase… and there, in the first room to the right of the landing…"

Henry nodded.

"…you will find a boy…er…ahem…a climbing boy."

Davenant took his seat in the carriage, stretched out his legs and closed his eyes.

"Close the door, Henry. I have no wish to take a chill"

Henry remained standing where he was, on his face a puzzled frown.

Davenant, sensing that he was being watched, opened one eye.

"Well?"

"When I finds the boy…my lord…then wot does I do?"

Davenant sighed and shrugged.

"There appears no other alternative," he said. "The boy goes home with me."

4

Henry Rollins prided himself on being a thinking man, a person who reflected deeply on life's great mysteries. For Henry the greatest of those mysteries was Lord Roderick Davenant. Devoted as he was to his employer, Henry often found himself pondering the eccentric behaviour of 'Is Nibs. And he did it yet again as he drove the vis-à-vis carrying Davenant home from Somers Town.

A climbing boy! What did 'Is Nibs want with a dirty, smelly creature like that?

As there existed between him and horses an affinity that to others seemed almost mystical, Henry proceeded to reflect on this question, confident the horse needed little guidance.

Is Nibs hadn't taken the boy because he liked children, of that Henry was very certain. He grinned and shook his head. 'Is Nibs couldn't stand nippers and thought them a nuisance. Nor had 'Is Nibs taken the child because of an unnatural interest in boys. Henry's grin widened. No. Definitely not. Liked the ladies did his lordship, or rather 'twas the ladies who chased after him, 'Is Nibs taking them up or discarding them at his leisure.

Perhaps 'Is Nibs had taken the boy out of a desire to see justice done. After all, it wasn't the first time he had rescued someone from the gutter; he, Henry Rollins, was living proof of that. When he was a boy, Henry, decked out in a furry monkey costume and mask, had been an attraction at a circus sideshow: The Pugilistic Ape. There, members of the public boxed with him in hopes of defeating him and winning a cash prize. Although a small man, with arms that seemed too long for his body, Henry was a skillful boxer and often won; but when he lost and a challenger received a prize, the show's owner beat him unmercifully. Out for an evening's fun away from his tutor, a young Davenant had fought Henry and won; then he rescued Henry from the beating that followed. Davenant took the orphaned Henry home to his Sussex estate, where his former nurse, Sarah Rollins, and her husband, adopted him.

No one–least of all Henry himself–knew his exact age because his parents had abandoned him before he was taken into the circus. Physically, although he was small and ill formed, he had the vitality of a young man. His cheeky freckled face, beneath a shock of red hair, was no indication of years; although when thinking deeply, as he was now, his face furrowed like that of a wizened gnome. For his part, Henry repaid Davenant for his compassion with unquestioning loyalty, complete discretion and a lively and proprietary interest in matters affecting 'Is Nibs.

After some reflection, Henry concluded the climbing boy's predicament bore no comparison to the trials and tribulations he suffered at the fair. *His* distress had been by far the greater because it lasted so much longer than that of the boy, Henry being much older when rescued. That such reasoning by a thinking man might be flawed never occurred to Henry, he having an exaggerated idea of his own importance and understanding. The basis for this belief was that Henry's adopted ma was also 'Is Nibs former nurse. "Almost blood brothers," Henry often said, a boast that served not only to bolster his self-esteem but his standing in the servants' hall.

Having considered and dismissed possible explanations for Davenant's strange action, Henry reluctantly concluded that it must be yet another symptom of the malaise that dogged 'Is Nibs so often of late. Most people had not noticed these moods, only *he,* being so often with his lordship, saw them.

"Proper shame it is, them happening to him cos he's such a swell cove wiv bottom. Not to mention being a fly devil with a full knowledge box," Henry said aloud, reminding himself in the Flash tongue of 'Is Nibs' courage, ingenuity and intelligence. It was then that Henry had one of those sudden flashes of enlightenment that thinking men have been known to experience when pondering a subject deeply. What ailed 'Is Nibs was that he lacked an outlet for these abilities which, not so long ago, he had had to use to the fullest when fighting to restore his family's fortunes.

"Newgate seize me!" Henry said to himself. "The things 'e did and never got caught," he chuckled. "It's true wot they say, Devil looks after is own…an Old Nick looked after him all right! They don't call the Davenant's the Devil's Brood for nuthin.'"

Henry had no time for further nostalgic reminiscences. The vis-à-vis had reached the busy Paddington-Islington highway that ran east to west across north London, dividing Somers Town from the city. All his attention was then needed to guide horses and carriage into the steady stream of traffic that would take them west to Mayfair and home.

Below in the carriage, Davenant lay slumped against his seat, his eyes closed although he was not asleep, his mind restless with thoughts about himself in similar vein to Henry's own on the subject. His night with Harriette Wilson had been but a temporary diversion from his strange moods of late; that deep-seated *ennui* he seemed unable to rid himself of no matter how much he tried.

For want of anything better to do the previous evening, he had gone to an 'at home' at the house of Amy Wilson, Harriette's sister, in hopes of riding himself of yet another of the blue-devilled moods that beset him of late. One glance at the guests crammed into the little house when he entered sufficed to tell him he would find no diversion there. He saw only one or two new faces. The rest were the usual crowd of guests to be found at one of Amy's 'at homes.' Held once a week, they were famous for their raucous carnival atmosphere. That evening was no exception. Lights shone from every window of the small row house. Outside the street was lined with carriages, phaetons and curricles, the coachmen and footmen shouting and gambling, their voices swelling the noise from the house's open windows. Amy's neighbours must be very tolerant, Davenant thought as he entered.

Inside the little house people were pressed together in every nook and cranny, leaving little room to move. They thronged the hall and downstairs rooms, the staircases and landings, the continual babble of their conversation punctuated by ribald masculine guffaws and feminine shrieks and giggles. Davenant sighed. It would have been bad manners to leave so soon after he arrived, even among the *demi-monde* with which he found himself, although he saw no reason to remain. So he shouldered his way through the hall into one of the downstairs rooms, where amused guests were sampling the novelty of a supper of working-class delicacies: jellied eels, and tripe and onions. With aloof nods, Davenant deigned to acknowledge a number of male guests. Drawn from the ranks of the aristocracy, politics, the army and the navy, they were acquaintances, not friends: he had few of those.

He raised his quizzing glass and cast a practiced eye over the women in the crush: women with professional names such as The Blonde Venus, Thais, Lilith, Amorous Astarte, as well known as many of the men—but for different reasons. Lively, attractive, often beautiful, they were the courtesans, Cyprians, bits o' muslin of the *demi-monde*. Clad in form-clinging, high-waisted gowns with necklines low enough for more than a hint of rouge-tipped nipples, they chatted, flirted, laughed and drank champagne, their male escorts fondling them in ways that would not be permitted in polite society.

"Lord Davenant! *Quelle surprise!*"

It was not an exclamation but a command from the reigning queen of London's demi-monde Harriette Wilson. She, like the members of fashionable society, liberally sprinkled her conversation with French words and phrases. Britain might be at war with France, but society still viewed that country as the true home of style and fashion.

Dressed all in white, with little jewelry, Harriette graciously waved away her circle of male admirers and favoured Davenant with a saucy smile. She was not beautiful, but she had a liveliness, gaiety and saucy wit that men found attractive. Harriette and her sisters, Amy and Fanny, held sway over the *demi-monde,* but Harriette was its leader. Among men of fashion, 'Harry' or the 'Little Devil', as she was affectionately known, was *de rigueur* as a companion both in and out of bed.

"As charming and lovely as ever," Davenant murmured and kissed her hand. "A delight for jaded eyes."

"Jaded?" Harriette looked surprised. "Well, I am sure *I* can aid your recovery," she said. "However…"

"However?"

"…the Duke of Ryedale. " With a nod Harriette indicated a distinguished-looking, middle-aged man with silver hair who was watching them from across the room. "A sad and lonely man," she went on, "who also seeks my company this evening. Still looking for a wife, I hear. Needs an heir."

"He seeks your company with a view to matrimony?"

"*Mon Dieu!* Of course not," she replied with a chuckle. "Wouldn't have the likes of my sort anyway. Besides, I don't like the notion of having only one man for life. Like to pick and choose do I!"

She tapped Davenant's chest with her closed fan. "Now shall it be Ryedale, or…?"

He glanced at the duke and then looked down at Harriette. "It's the lady's choice, of course."

Harriette's eyes sparkled. "I'll get my cloak," she said.

Left alone, Davenant took a glass of champagne from a tray carried by a passing waiter. His friend, the Honourable Lionel Willoughby, a former schoolmate at Eton, struggled through the crush, one arm around a young woman, his hand cupping her breast.

"Just as I thought—no one interesting here, tonight," Davenant greeted him.

Willoughby grinned. "Allow me to present the fair Helöise…my one and only love. Helöise, *ma belle,* Lord Roderick Davenant."

Davenant's lips twitched, the closest he usually came to a smile. Every few weeks Willoughby acquired a new 'only love.'

Helöise smiled. Davenant bowed. Young as she was, he could tell by the bold way she appraised him that she was not inexperienced. Willoughby whispered to her and she disappeared into the crowd.

"I hear your passion for a certain lady has waned" Willoughby said. "That means I owe Alvanley some blunt. Damned inconsiderate of you, Davenant! I wagered him the lady's *tendre* for you would last at least until Christmas."

"Alas," Davenant yawned, "her *tendre* for me may well last until Christmas. 'Twas I who wearied of her. But enough of that. I'll wager *you* fifty guineas the fair Helöise will give you the Covent Garden ague and milk you of your entire blunt before the month is out."

At the suggestion his 'only love' would give him a venereal disease and steal his money, Willoughby held up his hands in mock horror. "She is but seventeen! Pure as snow! Straight from the country." He winked. "So she tells me!" He grinned. "Tonight I'll initiate her into the delights of Venus' couch."

"I wonder, now, who will initiate whom?" was Davenant's parting shot as Willoughby went off in search of his amour.

He was about to raise the glass of champagne to his lips when a sudden shove from behind jolted it from his hand, spilling the liquid down him. He turned slowly and raised his quizzing glass on a fair-haired young man, well in his cups who swayed before him. But for another slightly older man who was holding him up, the young man would have fallen. Both men had drunk a good deal; but the wine that had made one belligerent, elicited only inane smiles from the other.

With his usual aplomb Davenant said, "Pray sir, have you no notion what you are about? To splash a coat of mine is to desecrate a work of art."

The perpetrator of this grievous act tried unsuccessfully to focus his bloodshot eyes on Davenant. "D-d-d-damn…y-y…your…hic…im…imp…imp…"

"Impertinence?" Davenant suggested.

The man nodded. "Yer…yer…yer in my…w-w-w-w…"

"Way?"

An even more vigorous nod was followed by, "You…you…cox…cox…"

Bloodshot eyes implored Davenant for help.

"Coxcomb?"

The man nodded.

"Really, sir, I must protest," Davenant said with a haughty stare. "If you will insist on beginning a sentence then, I pray you, do have the goodness to complete it–*yourself!*"

"I…I…"

"I think you should take your friend home, Mr. Basingthwaite," Harriette Wilson interrupted. She smiled at the young man's friend, who struggled to maintain his companion in an upright position.

Hardly aware of him before, Davenant turned his attention to Basingthwaite. A pleasant-looking man of middle height, he had a strange yellow-brown complexion and sun-bleached hair. Unlike his friend, Basingthwaite's *toilette* left little to be desired, and his clothes were obviously the work of an excellent tailor. The only fault Davenant found with it was an excess of baubles: several rings, a large diamond cravat pin, and a number of fobs hanging from his waist. Was he unaware of Beau Brummell's dictum—and one with which Davenant concurred—that the wearing of any jewelry was too much jewelry for a man of fashion? That flaw in the fellow's appearance was easily remedied, Davenant thought, for in every other way—even his restrained behaviour while drunk—Basingthwaite, unlike his friend, had the manners and the quiet air of consequence of a gentleman.

"Yes, yes…" Basingthwaite said, "high time I was abed. Not used to all this gallivanting." He smiled sheepishly. "Tom, here," he continued, indicating his friend, "has been kind enough…to take me…under his wing…show me the town. Thank your sister for her hospitality, Miss Wilson. 'Scuse Tom. Too much champagne."

Arm-in-arm the two men stumbled off together.

"Impudent puppy! But the other one? A decent sort," Davenant remarked as he watched them go. "Odd complexion, though. He should dispense with the walnut juice. Pale and poetic like Byron is all the rage, now, I hear." He looked down at Harriette. "Basingthwaite? A northern name. Is he in trade? An ironmaster? A manufacturer?" he teased, well aware of her snobbish aversion to anyone in trade entering her social circle or her bed.

"No, indeed!" she said. "Of very good family. No title, but aristocratic connections. *Prodigious* fortune! The Regent's taken to him as well as his friend."

"Then what more need one say?" Davenant said dryly.

"And he adores me!"

"As indeed we all do," Davenant said, giving her his arm.

They made their way through the crush of guests to the door. With a mocking glance, Davenant inclined his head to the Duke of Ryedale. The latter, his lips compressed, gave only the briefest of nods.

Davenant stared unseeing out of the carriage window. Last night's diversions had been just that: diversions, temporary distractions that had not dispelled the latest of his blue-devilled moods. These moods were new to him. When being dunned by creditors and only a hair's breadth away from debtors' prison, he had been full of energy, motivated by his self-imposed challenge to restore the family's fortune and by anger at the father who had so recklessly gambled it away.

He had now more than recouped his family's wealth, but his anger toward his father remained, hidden deep beneath the habitually distant façade he presented to the world. The rest was an inner void, a listlessness that had nothing to do with fashionable *ennui*.

Ironically the only means by which he could restore the family's fortune was by the same way in which it had been lost: gambling. Moneylenders were out of the question; their exorbitant interest rates would have increased his debts; and his estates being mortgaged, he had little to offer as security. As for going into trade? There could be no question of that, even though the war with France was making many in trade rich overnight. He was, after all, a gentleman and an aristocrat: trade was not for him! For that reason and an even more personal one–a fiancée–he had not sought marriage to an heiress of one of those *nouveaux riches* merchants eager to acquire a title in their family.

For young men on the town gambling was a sport. But as it was a necessity for him to restore his family's fortunes, his manner of play, with what few assets remained, was very different to that of his dead father and other gamblers. In the clubs and gaming hells of St. James, he soon gained a reputation for being lucky; but his gambling successes owed more to common sense than to chance. He quickly realised that a cool, studied manner at the tables and a brain not befuddled by alcohol improved his chances against richer more reckless opponents. He did not drink when he played, learned to remember which cards had been played and closely studied the behaviour of his fellow players for every blink and twitch that might indicate their intentions at the table. He adopted a similar approach to wagers he made away from the card room, such as walking backwards along Pall Mall from St. James Palace to Carlton House, swimming the Serpentine in winter, or racing a loaded stagecoach along the Brighton Road in his curricle. He did not always win every game or every wager, but he won many more than other players did.

In those days his pockets had been to let, his debts enormous, his escapades scandalous, and his company shunned by respectable people–but what days they had been! Days when he lived by his wits.

Davenant sighed. And now? Now life was one damned, long bore! He still gambled and young bucks still tried to best him at the table and at those other pastimes for which he was renowned: boxing, fencing, horsemanship—and womanising. But such challenges held little excitement for him now. They were as meaningless diversions as those of last night.

A low moan from the opposite seat of the carriage reminded him he was not alone. The climbing boy, his eyes shut, lay in the horse blanket in which Henry had wrapped him. ("Don't want him to dirty the upholstery, do we now, my lord?" Henry said.) Davenant stared at the boy. He was small and young; *too* young to be in a harlot's bedroom. Scared, red-rimmed eyes gazed back at Davenant from the sooty mask that was the boy's face.

Davenant leaned across and patted the child's shoulder. "Don't be afraid. You are safe," he said, his hawkish face unconsciously softening.

The boy closed his eyes.

Davenant continued to study him. Poor devil! For more than an hour after his fall the climbing boy had been at Harriette's house, but no one had come to claim him. What a life he must lead! In constant danger of falls, burns and asphyxiation. Davenant had read about such mishaps in the public press. Other than what little he had read about them, he knew nothing about climbing boys. His curiosity was piqued. He would have Dingley, his always eager, always efficient secretary make enquiries about them. An admirable fellow, Dingley: he could always be relied on to handle even the most tiresome details of his employer's life. And after the boy recovered from his fall, Dingley would arrange to make suitable provision for his future. In the meantime the child would be cared for at Davenant House.

At last the vis-à-vis turned into Grosvenor Square, the centre of fashionable Mayfair, and slowed to a stop before the elegant stone portico that graced the stucco exterior of Davenant House.

Whenever he entered his London home Davenant always experienced a feeling of personal accomplishment. During the years when family fortunes were low, the house had been closed and had fallen into disrepair. What pictures and furniture that had not been sold had been hidden under holland covers. But once his fortunes improved, Davenant had begun buying back the items that had been sold; he had also engaged Mr. Nash, the Prince Regent's architect, to refurbish the house's interior. Prominent among these repurchased art works was a set of marble statues of the Nine Muses of the arts and astronomy, originally obtained in Herculaneum by an ancestor while on the *grand tour.*

"Why spend my life with one woman, when I can spend it with these nine–metaphorically speaking, of course?" he was fond of saying when family members urged him to marry.

Davenant was met by Dingley, a bespectacled young man clutching a sheaf of papers, and Venables, the butler. The latter with the inscrutable face of a well-trained servant, looked like a much larger version of one of the jade Buddhas in Davenant's collection of Chinese *objets d'art.*

Scarcely stopping to hand his hat and cane to a footman, Davenant marched across the marble hall past the row of Nine Muses, Dingley and Venables hurrying after him. They caught up with him just as he began his ascent up the horseshoe-shaped, marble staircase that lead to the upper floors.

"My lord," Dingley gasped, "several letters…letters that need your…urgent attention,"

"I am sure there is nothing you cannot handle in your usual efficient manner," Davenant said over his shoulder.

"A last minute invitation…from the Prince Regent…to dine with him…this evening."

"Send round an acceptance *at once.*"

"Yes, my lord. Also several request from charities seeking your support. The Committee for the Betterment of Climbing Boys, in particular, has written several times."

Davenant stopped halfway up the stairs and looked down at Dingley. "Ah, yes," he said airily, "that reminds me. There's one in the carriage."

At Dingley's puzzled look, Davenant explained somewhat impatiently, "A climbing boy. Needs food. A doctor. A bath. Henry Rollins will explain."

Astonished by this announcement, Dingley and Venables could only stare. Only the movement of the butler's Adam's apple beneath his unfathomable visage betrayed his real reaction to the notion of a climbing boy taking up residence at

A JACKETING CONCERN

Davenant House.

"Oh, and after the boy recovers from his injuries, Dingley, arrange a future for him. You know the sort of thing…with a family on the estate," Davenant said, as if the reception of climbing boys was a regular occurrence in his home. "By the way Dingley, what knowledge do you have of climbing boys?"

Dingley looked even more bewildered than before. The answer was obvious, wasn't it? "They…er…clean chimneys…my lord," he ventured.

Davenant's tone was biting. "What need have I of encyclopedias, Dingley, when I have you? That committee you mentioned may be more forthcoming. Write to it! Arrange an interview!"

Then without more ado, he dismissed all thought of climbing boys from his mind and took the remaining stairs two at a time.

5

"Aaaaaaaagh!"

Jabbed into consciousness by the fingers probing his body, Addy screamed when they sent pain from his cuts and bruises radiating through him as if he were on fire. The fingers were those of the white-haired man in a black coat bending over him.

For a moment Addy thought he had woken in his own bed from a bad dream he was having about chimney sweeps. The pillows were soft, the sheets clean, the quilt warm, and grandpapa had sent for a doctor, for that was who the man must be. But the pain from the doctor's final prod reminded him that his fall down the chimney and all the other bad things that happened to him had been all too real.

"Bruises and cuts? Yes." the doctor said. "Broken bones? No. Stake my reputation on it, ma'am. Look! Signs of life, already."

An elderly woman in a white lace cap and a black dress, a large bunch of keys at her waist, peered around the doctor and smiled at Addy. She must be a housekeeper, Addy thought; but she was not grandpapa's housekeeper.

Where was he?

The doctor packed his bag. "Keep the cuts clean. Bacilicum powder on the bruises. Rest. Food. A few drops of laudanum to help him sleep." Then with a brisk "Good day," the doctor was gone.

The housekeeper plumped Addy's pillows, smoothed the sheets and left. A housemaid entered the room with a bowl of soup, the aroma of which reminded Addy just how hungry he was. Between the spoonfuls the maid fed him, he took stock of his surroundings. He was not in his own bedroom with its tiger skin rug. This room was small and plainly furnished with a bed, chest of drawers and a washstand. Flower-patterned wallpaper covered the walls, and the ceiling sloped to the floor on one side of the room. It was an attic room, like the ones in which grandpapa's servants slept.

The soup finished, the housekeeper reappeared. From a bottle, she poured a spoonful of dark liquid, which she made him swallow; the taste made him screw up his face. "Sleep well," she said and left.

Addy lay back against the pillows, doing his best to keep still so he wouldn't feel his cuts and bruises. From there he could see himself in the washstand mirror. Someone must have washed him and removed his rags while he was asleep, for his body was free of soot and he had on a linen nightshirt that was too big for him. He stared at his reflection: he looked so white, so sad and so very lonely.

Grandpapa had been only half right. It was sweeps *and* the French who carried off naughty boys. They had both taken him because he was naughty. At the thought of his grandpapa, tears welled up in his eyes and spilled down his cheeks. Grandpapa would be *so* worried about him, and Bette, too. If he could only go home, he would be, he promised himself between sobs, the bestest, bestest, *bestest* boy there was…and never, never, *never* be naughty again!

But how could he go home?

He dare not move because it hurt so much to do so. He didn't know where he was. He didn't know how far he was from home. He was lost and alone in the great big world.

The realisation of this brought on another bout of sobs and tears that drained him, but strangely left him feeling more like his old self. He gave a long sniff, licked away the salty tears that had reached his lips and wiped away the rest on the sleeve of his nightshirt. He was a colonel, he told himself–or would be one day. Colonels were brave: they didn't cry. And he was no longer in the sweep's yard; kind strangers were caring for him.

But where was he?

Seeking an answer, Addy stared around the bedroom again. He saw nothing that told him where he was.

His head hurt and his mind was a muddle of fleeting dark images that came and went, jostling with one another as he tried to remember how he came to be there. Sleep beckoned, but he fought it, because he was afraid that if he fell asleep he would wake up in another strange place. That was what had happened before. The first time he woke up after a long sleep, he found himself lying on a sack of soot in the shed with the climbing boys. And after his fall down the chimney, he had woken up in this strange room. If he fell asleep now, where might he wake up next?

In an effort to stay awake, he set himself to try and remember all that had happened to him since he was grabbed from his hobbyhorse. This was no easy task because his kidnappers had given him something that made him very sleepy, making it hard for him to recall much of what happened. He had been vaguely aware of a woman taking off his clothes, dressing him in others, and gently tucking the ring on the chain around his neck inside them. Try as he might he could not remember her face, only that she said as she sobbed, "I won't let him find it."

His first clear image was of a black face staring down at him when he woke up on a pile of empty soot sacks in the shed with the other climbing boys.

"Yer musta been asleep a long time, young un. Reckons they give yer somethin' ter make yer groggy," said the black-faced boy.

He held out a hand to Addy. "Tip as yer daddle! I'm Bodger an' you an me is gonna be mates." With his thumb he indicated the two other boys staring at him, "Them an' Eddie is daft."

And for the few days that he was in the chimney sweep's yard, Bodger had been his friend: his only friend, there.

Bodger was very grown up: ten years old, he said, but Addy thought him even more grown up than that. He knew so much that Addy didn't know: strange things that puzzled him although he didn't like to admit it.

"Nell and Mick goes at it like rabbits when ever Malloy ain't about, Bodger said, but Addy had no idea what 'it' was. And when Bodger told him about daft Eddie, the son of Nell and Malloy, a little boy who spent his time staring at nothing in particular, Addy did not understand what he meant.

"Malloy reckons Eddie is 'is kid, Bodger said, "but he isn't cos Malloy ain't up ter doin' it anymore." What did he mean? "It's on account of is drinking," Bodger explained. Used to getting his own way with grandpapa and Bette, Addy told Mick, "I want to go home to my grandpapa!" The journeyman's reply was a cuff to the head that floored Addy. Surprised but undaunted, Addy got to his feet and made the same demand again, but this time he leapt deftly to one side when Mick went to hit him.

"Good for you! You'll do young un," Bodger said, slapping Addy on the shoulder

And when, one night, Addy's sobs for his grandfather kept them both awake, Bodger told him funny stories about Malloy and Mick that made him laugh.

Each night when Addy said his prayers Bodger watched him, mystified.

"What's a grandpapa?" Bodger said when Addy asked God to send his grandfather to fetch him.

Pleased he knew something the clever Bodger did not know, Addy said, "Everybody has a grandpapa. Everyone has a mama and papa, too, even if they are in Heaven, like mine.

"Don't you have a grandpapa? A mamma? A papa?"

Bodger shook his head. "Nah. I'm from the workhouse."

"You must be very lonely."

"Nah," Bodger said with a grin. "'Sides, I got you for me mate."

Pleased, Addy grinned back at him. He was even more pleased when Bodger promised to get back the ring and chain with his mama's hair. "Then I'll look after it for yer. Malloy snatched it off yer, 'e did, when yer got 'ere. Saw 'im do it, I did."

"How will you get it back? I don't think he will just give it to me," Addy said sadly. "He is not a kind man."

Bodger held his hand in the air and wriggled his fingers.

"Wiv these, of course!"

Addy's heart sank.

Bodger's stealing was the only thing the two of them fought about; or rather Addy did the fighting. Bodger just laughed. Stealing was a way of life to Bodger. He stole things all the time, mostly food from bakery shops, pie men, market stalls and houses where he swept chimneys, because Malloy kept the climbing boys half-starved so they stayed thin enough to climb narrow flues. Bodger also picked pockets, an activity that had provided him with a small cache of odd coins, silk handkerchiefs, cheap snuffboxes, and pearl and silver buttons.

"Its wrong to steal," Addy told him. "You must stop or you won't go to Heaven."

Bodger just chuckled and offered him half of the pie he had taken unseen from a strolling pie man's tray. At first Addy refused, but then the gnawing hunger that had been his constant companion since he arrived in the yard got the better of him. Deeply ashamed and wondering what grandpapa would say of such behaviour, he accepted Bodger's offer and ate what remained of the pie. At last he understood why Bodger and the other boys stole: it was the only way they could get more food than the sweep fed them.

"Good at it, I am," Bodger said of his stealing. "Ain't never been caught."

Dear Bodger, always laughing, always joking. Lying there in the attic bedroom, Addy struggled to remember his friend's face but found he could not. Sleep was fast overtaking him and he could no longer fight it. Just before his eyes closed he remembered why he could not remember Bodger's face: he had never seen it because it was always covered with soot.

6

Davenant's long gallop across the downs had brought colour to his cheeks, and the strong breeze blowing in from the sea ruffled his dark hair. He closed his eyes and filled his lungs with the salty air. He was alone–a solitary figure on horseback atop the cliffs at Seaford Head–alone to enjoy the panorama of the undulating South Downs with their close cropped grass, thanks to generations of sheep, covering their white chalk.

The late summer day being too pleasant to spend indoors, Davenant was enjoying one last ride before his departure for London next day. The downs were his favourite retreat whenever he was at his Sussex estate, Downsley Priory. As a boy he had spent hours roaming them on foot, exploring the remains of Iron Age forts and barrows, and smugglers' haunts, yarning with shepherds, or digging for fossils. From these sorties he had carried home enough flint arrow and spear points, Roman coins, pottery shards, birds' eggs and fossilised ancient marine life to fill several glass cabinets in his library.

Davenant opened his eyes and looked about him. From this spot he could see east as far as the village of East Dean. Just beyond it and out of sight was Beachy Head, where the South Downs met the sea with a great wall of chalk. West, the River Cuckmere slithered seaward through its valley, and away in the distance were the windmills and church spires of Brighton, otherwise known as 'London-by-the-Sea.'

Before him, the green waters of the English Channel–for once clear of mist–sparkled in the afternoon sun. Across that narrow strip of water lay France with which England had been continuously at war for almost twenty years. To combat the threat of a French invasion, the Kent and Sussex coastline had been fortified: martello towers looking like upturned flower pots lined the beaches at regular intervals, together with a large redoubt at East Bourne, all armed with soldiers and guns. But now, in 1811, there was little fear of a French invasion: Nelson's victory at Trafalgar had settled that, making British sea power supreme. Besides, Napoleon had other concerns. It was but a matter of time before France and Russia went to war. Although Wellington's army was poised to push the French from Spain, it was rumoured Napoleon was already withdrawing troops from there for a Russian campaign.

War between France and Russia was the main subject of conversation at Carlton House when Davenant dined there after he rescued the climbing boy. Talk quickly turned to lighter matters, for the Prince of Wales, nearing the end of his first year as partial regent, was feeling the weight of his new responsibilities. His Highness declared he was in need of some sea air. He and his guests must all drive down to Brighton that night and breakfast with him at his pavilion next morning.

Much to Henry Rollin's chagrin, it was Lionel Willoughby, and not he who accompanied Davenant to the seaside. After a hearty breakfast at the pavilion, Davenant took a respectful leave of his royal host and, on a whim, drove off to Downsley, the site of a Carthusian Priory that Henry VIII gave one of his ancestors for his efforts in aiding the king dissolve the monasteries. There, for a week, Lord Davenant, the fashionable Corinthian, the *habitué* of Mayfair salons and the clubs of St. James, led the life of a country gentleman as landlord, farmer and good neighbour. He had discussions with his agent, inspected his lands, visited his tenants and dined with neighbours. Evenings he spent quietly, either reading, or poring over his archaeological and fossil collections. And each afternoon he rode across the downland.

He was in no hurry to end his present ride. He wanted to enjoy the freedom and beauty of this place once more before he left. Here was home. For three hundred years Davenants had been born and raised here by the sea. No wonder some of his ancestors had been privateers, one even a pirate. The sea was in the Davenant blood, and no doubt explained his half-brother's choice of career. Somewhere out in the English Channel, Lieutenant, the Honourable Peregrine Davenant was aboard a Royal Navy vessel blockading French ports. Perry, who had begun naval life as a midshipman at Trafalgar, was now an experienced, energetic officer of one-and twenty, who likened the boredom of blockade duty to a stay in purgatory.

As there seemed no likelihood of Davenant marrying in the foreseeable future, or ever for that matter, family members had implored him to forbid Perry, heir to the Davenant estate and title, from joining the navy, because to do so in wartime was to risk an early death. Nevertheless, the wily Perry managed to get himself expelled from Eton, so Davenant, his guardian, had little choice but to let him join the navy.

Perry would come through the war unscathed, of that Davenant was sure; his half-brother's actions to date were testament to that assumption. And in the course of time —and Davenant hoped it would be a *very* long time—Perry would become the next Baron Davenant and carry on the family name.

Davenant stared unseeing at the sea sparkling in the sunlight. His family was mistaken in their fears for Perry; but they were right about his own marriage prospects. It was unlikely he would marry now—or ever. Once, a few years ago, he had been passionately in love but…

He sighed.

That was a long time ago and best forgotten.

Reluctant though he was to leave the bracing beauty of Seaford Head, there was something he must go and see before he returned to Downsley, so he turned his horse and rode inland.

Davenant's lip curled in disgust at the sight before him. As if Sussex did not have enough castles already!

Unlike those other castles at Pevensey, Arundel, Herstmonceux and Bodiam, no knights had ever ridden forth from this Gothic monstrosity, no arrows been shot from its walls and no siege machines battered its ramparts. This eccentric-looking edifice was an insult to good taste: his good taste. It obtruded on land he considered part of the Davenant estate, no matter the law said otherwise. But as matters now stood, no future Davenant heirs would inherit it. Years ago his father had sold this unentailed part of his land to help settle some of his debts. On his father's death Davenant had found himself heir to these debts, impoverished estates and guardianship of the twins, Perry and Georgiana, the children of his father's second marriage.

His father's untimely death followed an evening of heavy drinking that so addled the late baron's brain, he took it into his head he was the highwayman Dick Turpin and set out to repeat the highwayman's moonlight ride from London to York. He never reached his destination. Instead, his journey ended at a turnpike gate on the Great North Road, when, in true highwayman fashion, horse and rider attempted to leap over it–to the eternal detriment of both. There was no wife to mourn the baron's demise, both of them having predeceased him. His children hardly noticed his passing: father and heir were not close, and his younger children hardly saw him when he was alive. Only the members of the dissolute set to which the baron belonged grieved, and they more for the loss of fine horseflesh than for the death of a friend.

From behind one of the beech trees that surrounded it, Davenant studied the strange little castle. Of course, it was not really a castle but a house built to look like one, a *cottage ornée* with a central tower, spires, buttresses, arched doors, slit windows, and crenellated walls covered with creeper.

"It is just like every castle, in every Gothic novel my governess forbade me to read," his half sister Georgiana said when she first saw it. "Can you not imagine a rascally villain with twirling mustachios living there? A beautiful princess locked up in its tower? A lovelorn swain serenading her from below on his lute?" she teased, knowing his dislike of the Gothic style and the picturesque, both of which were popular.

Davenant's taste was for the classical Greco-Roman and the new French style it had inspired. But this monstrosity? *This* villa was covered with a muddle of curlicues, spandrels and finials better suited to a wedding cake than a house. It was another fault to lie at his father's door; but for his father's prodigality, this tract of land would not have been sold and this house built on it.

Davenant had never met the wealthy grocer who built this castle. That had been in the days when he was striving to recover the family fortunes. Unable to afford the upkeep of his London home, Davenant stayed with Lionel Willoughby in his London lodgings. He was rarely at Downsley Priory, so there had been no opportunity to meet the grocer socially, not that he would have wanted to anyway. Unconventional as he was in many ways, Davenant, like the other members of society's elite, thought those in trade beneath them, no matter how rich they might be. That such a person legally owned what he considered was rightfully his, Davenant regarded as a personal humiliation.

The grocer was one of the *noveaux riches* the long war with the French had created. Made wealthy almost overnight, he sought to acquire class and status just as quickly with the building of his castle. But his business collapsed almost as fast as it had grown when it was discovered that to increase his profits he had adulterated his merchandise. His China tea was thorn leaf painted with verdigris; and the greenness of his pickles was achieved by the addition of copper. The ensuing scandal resulted in the loss of his lucrative victualling contract with the navy. This, and the failure of a country bank, ruined the man. He blew out his brains, leaving his family and creditors to fight over what remained of his estate.

Determined to reacquire the land and demolish the pretentious architectural folly, Davenant instructed his agent to buy back the property, whatever the price, as soon as it came on the market. For several years the house stayed empty while executors and creditors argued about its disposition. Then a month ago his steward informed Davenant by letter that unbeknown to him the house appeared to have been sold privately.

Now Davenant saw for himself that the house was indeed occupied. There was a gardener raking leaves, horses in the stables, a gig waiting at the front door, washing hanging on a line at the rear and dense black smoke belching from what must be the kitchen chimney.

It was then that Davenant recalled the climbing boy.

He shrugged. An odd thought.

The smoking chimney must have prompted it; obviously it needed to be swept.

With one last look at the now occupied castle, he turned his horse homeward, determined to take his agent to task for failing to act swiftly.

During the ride home his horse cast a shoe, forcing Davenant to stop at the blacksmith in the nearby village of Lower Twitten. At the forge he found blacksmith Ned Ticehurst in the middle of a noisy exchange with a weather-beaten man of indeterminate age. The man, who wore shabby clothes and a hat pulled low, had with him a worn-out looking packhorse.

"I've told yer afore not to come here and…"

Ned stopped when he saw Davenant. "Be off with yer!" he added in a quieter tone.

With a muttered curse, the scowling stranger led his horse from the forge.

It was only when he emerged from the shadows in the back of the forge that Davenant become aware of another person there. He could not see this man's face clearly because it was in profile, but this individual was taller and younger than the first, though just as shabby in appearance. Arms folded, this stranger stood and glared at Ned for several seconds before he, too, turned to go.

Hissssss!

The man spat, sending a gobbet of saliva into the forge's fire. Then he pushed past Davenant, leaving in his wake an odour of fish, stale sweat and rum.

"Devilish queer friends you have, Ned."

"Friends! The Conways?" said Ned. "No friends of anybody. Bad lot, they are. Do anythin' for money. Pimp for their own mother, they would. And murder? A day's work to them."

Beneath Ned's contemptuous words Davenant detected an undertone of fear. Naked to the waist, the heavyset blacksmith with his powerful muscles appeared well able to defend himself and not easily frightened. Who were the Conways to make him so anxious?

"I hope I don't meet them again," Davenant said.

"Probably not, my lord. Does their business at night they does…if yer gets my meaning."

Davenant gave a knowing nod.

The two men were smugglers. No wonder Ned was wary of them.

"Not from these parts, are they? I don't recall seeing them before."

"From along the coast," Ned said. He lowered his voice. "Big gang. Tryin' to move into this part of the world. Rumour is there's a rich swell inland somewhere puttin' up money for 'em."

"Really?"

"Prefers to deal with the local lads, myself. People I know." Ned smiled. "That reminds me. Forgetting my manners, I am. I hopes as how yer lordship finds himself in the best of health—*and spirits?*"

"Thank you. *Excellent spirits,*" Davenant said with mock politeness.

This supposed enquiry about Davenant's health referred to Ned's recent delivery of contraband French wine to Downsley Priory. Like generations of his family before him, Ned was involved in the smuggling trade, which was an inherent part of daily life along England's south coast. A skilled craftsman, churchwarden, husband and father, he saw no contradiction between these roles and being a middle man between smugglers and their local customers. In that he was no different from his neighbours. Smuggling was everyone's secret. Everyone bought smuggled goods—aristocrats, gentry, clergy, doctors, lawyers, farmers, fishermen and local magistrates—while many others participated in the trade. During one night of unloading contraband from a smuggler's clipper, farm labourers could make more money than they earned in a week on the land.

The long war with France was a boon to smugglers. To pay for it the government exacted high duties on many goods, thus creating an increased demand for cheaper smuggled ones. This increase in smuggling pleased the French; the loss of duty on goods made it harder for the British to pay for the war and subsidise their allies. Meanwhile, the demands of the navy and army relegated to second place the manpower and shipping requirements to combat smuggling. Even the British government obtained French newspapers and other intelligence about the enemy from smugglers. Some smugglers were not averse to giving information to the French authorities for a price; and Napoleon was said to regularly receive English newspapers from one in Bexhill.

Davenant had long suspected local 'free traders' of using the crypt of the ruined priory on his land. His suspicions were confirmed when one day several yards of exquisite French lace were found hidden inside a plucked goose delivered by a stranger for his dinner. The accompanying unsigned note described the gift as 'a little appreciation.'

His half sister, Georgiana, promptly appropriated the lace to trim her wedding gown.

7

"Slave Trade!"

Uttered with such vehemence and passion, the hoarsely whispered words seemed to vibrate with the potency of the evil they defined. Her eyes ablaze, Sarah Rollins glanced furtively around her before she said them, as if she feared they might prove an incantation strong enough to summon Satan himself.

Davenant's lip twitched in amusement. As a boy he had listened with delight—and fear—to Sarah's imaginative telling of fairy tales. It was no surprise that under her influence her adopted son, Henry, had acquired a flare for the dramatic.

Sarah's dramatic utterance came during a conversation with Davenant as they sat enjoying the late afternoon sun on a bench outside the cottage adjoining the forge. Sarah, Davenant's former nurse, was visiting her nephew, Ned, the blacksmith, and his wife, when Davenant called at the forge. Delighted to see her former charge, Sarah insisted he take a glass of dandelion wine with her while he waited for his horse.

'Lunnon' was just a word to Sarah. She had no idea what went on in the city, nor did she care. Her world was the Downsley estate and the surrounding countryside. She always knew about the latest happenings there. These she would relate these at length with many digressions into the life histories of those involved, their antecedents and her relationship to them. The latter were so complicated that when a boy Davenant believed Sarah was related by blood or marriage to everyone in Sussex.

When Davenant asked Sarah what she knew about the new owner of the Gothic castle he visited earlier, he sat back and leisurely partook of his wine, knowing full well that her reply would be a lengthy, convoluted one,

"*The Beeches* they calls it now," Sarah began, "real fancy soundin' name an' all for such a funny lookin' place. First owner called the place *Beechwood*. Never 'eard the like! No wood there: just a few trees. Still, what could yer expect? He wasn't no real gen'leman, see? Just a grocer wiv money an' fancy ways. No notion of what's expected of a gen'leman livin' in the country. Laughed at us, 'e did."

She sipped her wine.

"House's been empty nigh on four years. Folks scared to go near it. Say 'twas haunted cos 'e shot 'imself there." Sarah snorted. "Such nonsense! Yer knows 'ow folks is."

Davenant nodded. "And the new owner?"

"Well, now, like I sez folks don't go there cos they thinks it haunted...so no one knows much. Outta the way, it is, too."

Sarah's ruddy country face darkened and she lowered her voice. "From wot I 'eard t'other day new owner ain't much better than the old un...an maybe a good deal *worse!* Aye!" she went on as Davenant's eyes widened. "I'm not one ter gossip, as yer lordship knows. Says in the Scriptures it ain't right for to bear false witness, I know. But 'eard somethin, I did...at Lewes market."

Davenant cocked his head.

"Nigh on two weeks ago 'twere. I remember cos I 'ad gone over there with my Abraham for ter buy flannel to line a waistcoat. Feels the cold so, come winter, he does. Nice bit o' cloth it, wuz. Well, who should we meet there but my niece, Mary? In service she is in a parson's house... an' very good to 'er they is. Walks over to the White Hart, we all did, where our Harry–'im bein' a nephew an' all on my Abraham's side–is a waiter. Outside we wuz, chattin' to a servant...from *The Beeches.*" She sniffed. "Had been a servant at *The Beeches*, I should say. Been let go, 'e had... on account of his drinking, I reckon. Drunk as a lord, he wuz."

Her hand went to her mouth when she realised what she had just said. "Beggin' yer pardon, my lord," she said, her face red with embarrassment.

Davenant's lips twitched in amusement. "Merely a figure of speech," he assured her. "Do continue, I beg you."

Sarah folded her plump arms. "In a blue coat wiv brass buttons, 'e was...and *uppity!* Full of airs an' graces cos he's from a big city–Liverpool–wherever that may be. Been drinkin' a lot, 'e had and that's when he let slip that is master at *The Beeches* had been in..."

She looked quickly about her, and then thrust her face so close to that of

Davenant, he could not help but draw back.

"Slave trade!"

After delivering this information Sarah sat back, looking very knowing, and waited for Davenant to respond.

There was a short silence while Davenant wondered what he should say in reply to this announcement. "Er... from Liverpool, you say?" he said at last. "Many different goods are traded from there. Perhaps you misunderstood what the fellow said."

Sarah hugged her folded arms even closer.

"I don't tell no lies, yer lordship, as you well knows. Slave trade is what I 'eard and slave trade is what I said. Maybe them folks in Afrikie *is* heathens an' not read the Scriptures, nor knows nuthin' about Christian ways, an' such. But ain't no reason ter take 'em from their kin across the sea to be slaves. 'Tain't right! 'Tain't fittin! 'Tain't Christian!" she declared with a forceful nod. "Vengeance is mine sayeth the Lord! An' didn't He bring 'is vengeance down 'pon the Gyptians, plagues an' all? Made 'em let the Israelites go! Mark my words! Lord'll 'ave is vengeance on them in slave trade...see if he don't.'"

"Well if the man was a slave trader, it must have been several years ago. Parliament abolished the Slave Trade four years ago." Davenant said.

"Not soon enough, if yer asks me. I reckons the Lord 'as already taken is vengeance on 'im at *The Beeches*. Aye," she said in response to Davenant's raised eyebrow. "Just like the Gyptians. Death 'as come to that house. The grandson died in an accident... a few days ago. Buried at St. Richards, 'e is, not far from *The Beeches*. My niece Hattie's daughter, little Rosemary–nigh on eight years, she is–was one of the little girls wot lowered the coffin into the grave. Pretty as a picture she was in her white dress. The old grandfather took ill right after the funeral. A judgment on 'im, if yer asks me."

Davenant allowed himself the passing thought that the precarious state of health of *The Beeches*' tenant could mean he would soon be able to reacquire the house and land it stood on.

Her sermon over, Sarah spent the rest of Davenant's visit deluging him with loving enquiries about the 'apple of her eye': her adopted son, Henry Rollins.

8

If Sarah Rollins could have seen what the 'apple of her eye' was doing at that moment, she would have fallen to her knees and prayed for his salvation, just as she and Abraham did when, shortly after Henry went to live with them, he stole food from the kitchen at Downsley Priory. Instead of beating him, as Henry expected, the couple knelt and begged God to return him to the Path of Righteousness. They then sent him to bed without any supper.

That night there was a heavy storm with lightening that demolished a tree outside Henry's bedroom window. For Henry this was not a coincidence: God had heard his adopted parents' prayers and was warning him to mend his ways.

He never stole again.

Had Sarah been in the stables of Davenant House that afternoon and seen what Henry was reading, she would have regretted she taught him to read. This she had done with the only books she possessed: the Bible, the *Book of Common Prayer* and Bunyan's *Pilgrims Progress*. Henry proved an apt pupil–too apt a pupil.

Reading opened up a world of knowledge for him, not all of which was as spiritually uplifting as that contained in his ma's small library. The tax on newspapers made them too costly for ordinary folk like Henry to buy, but for a halfpenny, or even a farthing, he could buy a broadside on the street. Not for Henry were those epistles urging Englishmen to patriotic deeds, those railing against injustices, or demanding Parliamentary reform. His choice was the sensational, the fantastic, the horrific and the bawdy, particularly when illustrated with garish woodcuts of naked women or blood-drenched mutilated bodies.

Oblivious to everything else around him, Henry lay stretched on some bales of hay reading the confession of a murderer he had bought from the parson of Newgate Prison, to whom the felon had dictated it. The worthy cleric then hawked copies of this missive to the crowd of spectators gathered to watch the murderer's hanging. Among them was Henry, whose fascination with these events would have made his parents offer up even more prayers for his salvation had they known.

Ordinarily Henry had no time in the day to read, but with Davenant away in Sussex, the stable staff's duties were lighter than when he was in town. This was just as well as London was in the middle of a heat wave. With not so much as a whiff of a breeze to relieve it, the sultry air hung dense and unyielding over the stables. Sapped of their energy, men and horses were left lethargic and irritable. Even the flies were incapable of exertion and clung motionless to a pile of horse dung on which they had settled.

Henry, having satisfied himself the horses had been properly cared for and exercised, decreed the stable staff should have some respite from the heat. He took out the small box that contained his library and settled down to read his latest acquisition while the rest of the stable hands began a card game on an upturned barrel.

"Please Mr. Henry," said a small voice, "what is a w…w…waree?"

Engrossed in the bloody details of a decapitation, Henry heard with only half an ear. "It's when somethin' bothers yer in yer head…an' it won't go away," he murmured.

His elbows resting on a bale of hay, Addy knelt before it, frowning at the sheet of paper resting on it.

"No, Mr. Henry that is a worry…W-O-R-R-Y," he said. "This is about a lady. A lady cannot be a worry."

"That's what you think! Wait till yer older, son," quipped one of the card players. The others laughed.

Addy persisted. "Its spelled W-H-O-R-E."

Slowly, very slowly, the individual letters penetrated Henry's brain and formed themselves into…

"Here! You can't read that!"

He jumped up and snatched a broadsheet from Addy's hands.

He was just about to thrust *Memoirs of a Lady of Pleasure* back into his library, when a sudden thought stopped him. He stared at Addy.

"You can read this." It was a statement not a question.

"But Mr. Henry you just said that I *cannot* read it," Addy wailed.

"No. Wot I mean is…yer know how to read, don't yer?"

A JACKETING CONCERN

Addy's face dimpled into a wide smile. "Of course, I can!"

Henry's jaw dropped.

"Newgate seize me! A climbin' boy who can read!'

A thinking man needs both a time and a place in which to do his serious thinking. For Henry this was the quiet smoke he had every night in the alley behind the stables just before he went to bed, a nightly ritual that was a welcome end to long days spent overseeing men and horses.

After the surprise he had experienced that afternoon, Henry was in particular need of some quiet contemplation in the alley that night. The air was cooler than it had been in the daytime and no longer humid, but it was still warm enough for Henry to discard his coat in favour of shirtsleeves. Puffing hard on a short pipe, he leaned against the stable yard wall, staring up at the stars as if he expected to find an explanation of the day's events in them.

"Negate seize me!" he blurted after several fierce puffs of tobacco. "A climbin' boy wot can read! An' write, too! There's more to that boy than meets the eye, I'm a-thinking."

After he took away the broadside from Addy, Henry tested the boy's claim that he could read by having him read from his Bible. Addy obliged with the story of Jonah and the whale--his favourite, he said–and the Twenty-third psalm. Eager to display his learning, Addy also copied out the Lord's Prayer in a good hand and for good measure correctly recited a multiplication table.

Addy's skills only added to Henrys bewilderment about the boy, which had been steadily growing ever since he had come to know him. Addy had been at Davenant House for a week. For the first few days he remained in bed in the servants' attics while he recovered from his fall. Natural youthful resilience coupled with rest and good food soon had him up and about. He was clothed in Perry Davenant's boyish castoffs and well fed. The servants were friendly enough toward him, but in such a busy household they had little time to spare for him. For Venables, however, the presence of a climbing boy in the hallowed halls of Davenant House was not just an irritant but also an outrage, and he wondered about his lordship's state of mind in bringing the boy home. Convinced all climbing boys were thieves, Venables would not permit Addy above stairs for fear of what he might steal. So as Mr. Dingley, who had been charged with his future welfare, was temporarily away on his lordship's business, Addy was left to his own devices below stairs

Rescued from a hard life too, Henry sympathised with Addy's plight and took him under his wing. To keep him out of trouble below stairs, Henry often took him to the stables to see the horses and carriages. The two were soon friends. Addy, who was shy with the rest of the servants, chatted freely to Henry. Because he spent so much time with him, Henry noticed things about Addy that the other servants did not—things that contradicted what he knew about climbing boys. Henry had seen these poor wretches when he was with the circus. Ill-treated as he had been, their lives were even worse. Most climbing boys were half-starved, uneducated, foul-mouthed, bad-mannered and often suffered physical deformities caused by their work.

Addy was not like that. True, he was naturally small, but he was not starved, nor had he any deformities. Then there were his manners and behaviour. "They isn't like wot a climbin' boy's should be," Henry said to the stars. Addy spoke like a young gentleman and he was always polite and courteous. Always called him Mr. Henry, didn't he? Could anyone be more polite than that? And he always remembered to say 'please' and 'thank you.' At meals he used a knife and fork correctly, never put his knife in his mouth, didn't eat with his mouth open, didn't talk with his mouth full and always neatly folded his napkin at the end of a meal. The servants paid no attention, but Henry did. Climbing boys didn't have table manners because they rarely sat at tables, let alone used napkins and cutlery.

Henry blew several smoke rings and watched them waft up into the night sky. This view of the heavens reminded him of something else about Addy. Strange, indeed, for a climbing boy, Addy had had a religious upbringing. Before he went to sleep Addy first looked under his bed, then he knelt and said the Lord's Prayer, after which he asked God to take care of his grandpapa, his mamma and papa in Heaven, and several others whose names Henry did not recognise.

Henry shook his head.

As if all that was not enough to make him wonder about the boy, just two days ago Addy told him that he lived 'in a castle with his grandfather.'

Addy had wandered into the butler's pantry where a footman sat polishing silver cutlery.

"My grandpapa has spoons like these in his castle!" Addy announced, seizing a couple and waving them in the air.

It was at that moment Venables came through the door.

A climbing boy playing with the Davenant family silver!

To Venables that meant only one thing: the boy intended to steal it.

"It is common knowledge the criminal fraternity plant accomplices in great houses to let them in while the household sleeps," Venables informed Henry in a sonorous voice. "Just last week such an incident occurred in Hanover Square. Well, there will be none of that at Davenant House. *I* know my duty! The boy sleeps above the stables in future—not in this house."

"His lordship isn't going ter like that," Henry shot back. "Right kick up, there'll be, when 'e knows about it. Boy was ter be looked after in the house."

"Damn your impertinence" said Venables, incensed at having his actions questioned by one he thought beneath him.

At the recollection of the incident, Henry chuckled, for Venables had sworn at him in the same pompous tone with which he announced, "Dinner is served."

A continual state of war existed between the two servants. The snobbish Venables disapproved of a former circus performer being Davenant's personal groom, particularly because as butler he had no authority over stable staff. For centuries, generations of Venables' had served the Davenants to the extent that the butler's family, at least, viewed themselves as hereditary guardians of Davenant family well-being; its pride, Venables' pride; its dignity, Venables' dignity.

What most irked Venables about Henry was the high esteem in which the other servants held him; that, and the deference they showed him solely because he had actually seen Napoleon in the flesh. This occurred in 1802 when he accompanied Lord Davenant to France during the short-lived Peace of Amiens, during which the English flocked to France to enjoy the delights of Paris. Whenever the subject of the war was raised in the servants' hall, invariably someone would say, "And what's your opinion, Mr. Rollins, you having been to France and seen Napoleon." Or, "Tell us how you and 'Is Nibs escaped the French at the end of the peace." Such awe and admiration from inferiors Venables considered his and his alone.

What neither Venables nor the other servants knew was that Henry's meeting with Napoleon was but a glimpse of him from the other side of a rain-swept French parade ground. Nor did Henry ever voice his disappointment of what he had seen. He had expected an ogre; what he saw was a man not much bigger than himself in a grey overcoat.

Henry exhaled smoke.

"Silly buggar Venables," he muttered. "Full o' hot air…like one of them flyin' balloons. 'E must 'ave apartments to let upstairs, if he thinks Addy is a thief."

He knocked his pipe against the wall to empty out the ashes and took one last look up at the stars.

"There's goings on 'ere 'Is Nibs should know about," he told his celestial audience. "The sooner 'e gets 'ome, the better."

9

Only a day back in town and Davenant was already in one of his blue-devilled moods that not even the satisfaction he should have derived from driving his new team of greys—for which he had outbid a very disgruntled Prince Regent at Tattersalls—was able to dispel.

The cause of his vexation was twofold. First, that morning during his weekly sparring match with Gentleman John Jackson at his gymnasium in Bond Street, the former champion had broken through his guard and given him 'a facer.' This surprised the former champion as much as it did Davenant, his lordship being his star pupil. Jackson, gentleman that he was, tactfully blamed it on the heat. Davenant feared it might be a symptom of the mood that had overtaken him no sooner had he arrived back in town. Either that, or he was getting old.

The other source of his irritation was the weather.

He returned from Sussex to find London still labouring under the heat wave that had descended on it during his absence. On the best of days, the smoke and soot from sea coal fires created a perpetual grey haze above the city rooftops. And even though it was still summer and people lit fewer fires in their homes, there was no lack of smoke from kitchen ovens, factories, breweries and workshops. For days without a breeze to move it, this smoky cloud kept the air stagnant, intensifying the city smells, even in fashionable and spacious Mayfair. A week of high temperatures, sooty specks and humidity had left Londoners lethargic and short-tempered. No one was immune from this torpor as Davenant discovered. Within a short while after his return to town, the feeling of well being engendered by his stay in Sussex vanished.

Henry, recognising Davenant's dark mood, wisely decided to keep his suspicions about Addy to himself until a more suitable time: no easy feat for the talkative Henry. In his present frame of mind 'Is Nibs would have told him to 'shut his rattle.' The heat wave that enveloped the world's most populous city peaked that morning, its hot, heavy air about to be dispersed by the storm that now threatened. An eerie quiet seemed to have fallen over Mayfair as Davenant drove his curricle down Grosvenor Street. There was, too, a palpable air of expectation among those hurrying to get their business done and be home before the storm broke. It was but a matter of time before that happened; the sky was already a vicious grey and thunder grumbled in the distance.

The curricle had just swept into Grosvenor Square when, without looking where he was going, a man stepped from the pavement in front of it, causing the horses to shy and whinny.

"Mutton-headed noddy!" yelled Henry from his perch at the vehicle's rear. "Askin' for a mitt in your mummer…you lily-livered son of…" but he was too busy trying to maintain his precarious position to finish the insult.

Davenant quickly brought the horses under control. "Watch that mouth of yours, Henry, or I'll wash it out with soap."

"Sorry guv, but that noddy warn't lookin' where he was going. Coulda killed us all, he could."

"You exaggerate–*as usual*."

A few passers-by stopped to look at the cause of the row: a squat knock-kneed man in a dirty, ragged frock coat too big for him and a battered hat. But it was his companions that attracted most attention as he limped across the street: three white geese on leashes waddled behind him, the soles of their feet covered with pitch to protect them from harsh ground. Agitated by their encounter with Davenant's horses, they honked and cackled in frenzy. Davenant ignored both man and geese, but Henry could not resist raising a fist to them as they drove by.

Davenant was surprised to see three vehicles already parked outside his home: a travelling carriage drawn by six matching horses, and two chaises. From the latter, servants in the burgundy and silver livery of his brother-in-law, Earl Hesston, were unloading luggage. Davenant's face darkened; his day was going badly enough and needed no further complications. He guarded his privacy and hated to have it invaded by unexpected guests, even family members. Neither his brother-in-law nor his sister, Georgiana, had written to tell him they proposed a visit

Davenant's disposition was not improved by the welcome he received on entering

Davenant House. Instead of a servant to take his hat and cane, he was treated to the long shrill whistle of a bosun's pipe.

"Look lively lads! Admiral comin' aboard," a voice squawked.

Davenant stared at the scene before him.

Beneath the impassive gaze of the Nine Muses was piled a pyramid of trunks, dressing-cases, bandboxes and hatboxes–the impedimenta of a fashionable lady intent on a lengthy stay. And up each side of the horseshoe-shaped staircase toiled a procession of maids and footmen in ones and twos carrying items from this mound. Atop the luggage pyramid rested the herald of Davenant's arrival: a parrot in a gilded gage. Guarding all this paraphernalia was a short grey-haired wisp of a woman with an armful of parasols whom Davenant recognised as his sister's maid. She constantly countermanded commands given by Venables, who appeared to have marshalled every one of the servants to deal with the baggage. In the midst of all this bustle and getting in everyone's way ran a small, longhaired white dog with what looked like the remains of a dead bird in its mouth.

"Move your arse, you pox-ridden misbegotten son of Beelzebub and a one-legged whore," the parrot squawked. "Ain't got all day. Admiral comin' aboard! Admiral comin' aboard! Admiral…"

Davenant's expression froze.

Venables caught sight of him out the corner of his eye and hurried toward him in dignified haste, his usually impassive face for once red with embarrassment at having failed to notice his master's arrival.

"I beg your pardon, my lord. I had not observed your arrival. The Countess Hesston…"

"And the earl, too, judging from all that luggage."

"No my lord, just her ladyship."

Davenant was not only surprised but also suspicious. However, before he could say anything, the parrot launched into its version of *Rule Britannia,* punctuated by the frequent whistle of a bosun's pipe.

Davenant gave the bird a withering look.

"Her ladyship's parrot, my lord," Venables said.

"Where is she?"

"Her ladyship requested she wait for you in the Egyptian Salon, my lord."

Davenant marched toward the staircase. What was his capricious half sister doing here?

By the statues of the Muses he stopped. Was that a child's face looking at him? He shook his head. There was no face. Good Lord! Damn this heat! It was making him see things.

He was half way up the staircase when the parrot again began exhorting admirals, whores and sons of Beelzebub to rule the waves.

"Someone silence that blasted bird!" he ordered, "and I don't care *how* they do it."

Afraid Lord Davenant had seen him, Addy jumped back behind the marble pillar and held his breath. Mr. Venables had told him he must not go upstairs into main house. Addy did not understand why: at grandpapa's house he went wherever he wanted to go. On the few occasions he did go upstairs, Mr. Venables was very angry. Mr. Venables was so angry when he caught him playing with some silver spoons in the butler's pantry, he sent him to sleep in the rooms above the stables. This pleased Addy because he liked horses, and besides Mr. Henry and the stable hands were his friends.

Several minutes went by but no one came and yanked him from behind the column. Addy sighed with relief. Since the lady arrived in her grand carriage all the servants were too busy to take any notice of him, and he was left alone in the servants' hall. There being no one to stop him, he crept upstairs, slipped through the baize-covered door into the hall and hid behind a column. Because of all the activity in the hall, no one noticed him.

Addy peered around the column. The lady, who was very pretty, had gone upstairs. With her was another lady carrying a little white dog. How he laughed when the dog jumped from her arms and chased a footman around the hall. He laughed even more when another footman dropped the hatbox he carried, and the dog grabbed the hat that fell out of it by the feathers and shook it until most of them fell off.

When Lord Davenant arrived, Addy recognised him immediately, for Mr.

A JACKETING CONCERN

Henry had pointed him out that morning in the mews. It was Lord Davenant who had saved him and taken him into his house, Mr. Henry said. Quite forgetting no one must see him in the hall, Addy peered around the column and gazed in awe and admiration at his saviour. Lord Davenant was tall and he wore a dark blue coat with silver buttons that was even nicer than grandpapa's coats. He was a fine horseman, Mr. Henry said, and a boxer, a fencer, a marksman, and could handle a four-in-hand as good as any stagecoach driver. Addy sighed. If his papa were alive, he would do those things, teach him to do them, and take him for rides in a curricle.

How he wished he had a papa–a papa just like Lord Davenant.

So enthralled was at the sight of his hero striding across the hall, that without realising it he strayed from the behind the pillar. Only when Davenant glanced his way as he passed did Addy remember how angry Mr. Venables would be if he were seen there. Quickly he hid behind the pillar again.

10

Georgiana, Countess Hesston, surveyed her reflection in a mirror on the wall of the Egyptian Salon and pouted. Ever since she was a child, she had been accustomed to hearing herself described as handsome, a beauty, 'a diamond of the first water', and other equally complimentary remarks–but not today. Today she looked every day of her one and twenty years–or so she thought.

She stared woefully at her likeness: an elegant figure–but for how long? –in a moss-green travelling gown of light silk, trimmed with gold. From beneath an outrageous hat decorated with osprey feathers dyed to match her gown shone lustrous chestnut curls–but her face! Unlike that of Helen, it might not have launched a thousand ships; nevertheless, it had enchanted dozens and dozens of admirers. Now it looked strained and tired, while those lustrous eyes of hers, whose glances had so devastated her former *beaux,* were red with dark circles beneath them.

Georgiana winced. Such a fright!

It was all the fault of those turkeys. During her journey, hundreds, no, thousands of great gobbling birds on their way to market in London had spilled over onto the highway from the drovers' roads. They obstructed traffic, often slowing it to a standstill, their persistent gobbles straining her already strained nerves. At night the horrid creatures roosted in the fields close by the inn at which stayed, only to wake her at crack of dawn with even more gobbles. After such a journey, who would not look a disaster? And then to arrive in London in the middle of a heat wave. Had it not been for the cool glass of lemonade Venables brought her, she was sure she would have expired on the spot. As it was she feared that in her present state the heat was making her delusional. She could have sworn she glimpsed a child in the hall when she arrived, but then next second it was gone. She was mistaken, she knew; there were no children at Davenant House.

Despite her fit of the dismals, she took some comfort from what else the mirror showed: that the red, orange and yellow décor of the Egyptian Salon was still the flattering backdrop it had always been for her dark beauty. It was here before she was married, under the eagle eye of a chaperone, that she used to receive her admirers. The room was an idiosyncrasy of her half brother Roderick: the only room in the house not in the classical mode

She looked around at the familiar décor: a huge black marble fireplace flanked by carved Nubian warriors; ceilings decorated with moldings shaped like palm leaves; silk wallpaper painted with lotus flowers and the strange picture writing of the Egyptians; vases covered with exotic motifs, statuettes of gods and men, and paintings of pyramids and sphinxes; prints and books about Egypt; chairs and tables with arms and legs like those of crocodiles and other wild beasts. Only one item looked out of place: the glass cabinet that contained Davenant's collection of snuffboxes, one for each week of the year, none of which looked the least bit Egyptian.

Napoleons Egyptian campaign in 1798 had created a vogue for Egyptian style and curiosities in France; but how Roderick had been able to acquire so many of them from what was now enemy territory was as big a mystery as the ancient Egyptians themselves. The mysterious attracted Roderick precisely because he believed that by use of rational enquiry and common sense it could be explained, or would be at some future date. Small wonder then that he had created a memorial to this ancient civilisation. What could be more mysterious than Ancient Egypt–except, perhaps, Roderick himself?

Roderick had always been an enigmatic figure to Georgiana and Perry– almost a stranger. Fourteen years older and their legal guardian, he had held himself distant from them. Governesses and tutors raised them at Downsley while he was away in London trying to redeem the family fortunes. When he did visit, they saw little of him, he being occupied with estate matters or his collection of historical artifacts and natural history specimens. Most of what they knew about him–as a sportsman, gamester and a leader of fashion–they learned from newspaper reports of his escapades, or the overheard whispered gossip of disapproving relatives and teachers, who considered such matters unfit for innocent ears.

A young Georgiana found this raffish aspect of her Roderick's character as romantic and exciting as those of the heroes in Gothic novels she read in secret.

She much preferred this image of him from a distance than the reality of their relationship. He was very strict with her and Perry–particularly her. Whenever Roderick received a report of her misdeeds from a governess, he would stare at her coldly and rebuke her in such a scathing voice it made her tremble, so that in contrast, any punishment that followed was easy to bear. Punishment was never violent, although Perry, being a boy, received an occasional whipping, she would be confined to her room for a day or so on bread and water. But this failed to end Georgianas hoydenish pranks, in which Perry encouraged her. "She's too much a Davenant," elderly relatives moaned.

Once, emboldened by the knowledge that her marriage would end his guardianship, Georgiana asked Roderick, "You were always so strict with Perry and me when we were young. Why? When you yourself…"

Roderick's cold stare stopped her in mid-sentence, but after a moments pause he said quietly, "Our family does not enjoy the best of reputations, me in particular. You know what they call us? The Devil's Brood. Why was I strict? I was your guardian, an association many would consider an obstacle to your success in society. For Perry, being a man, it did not matter so much, but, for you? A young woman. Your behaviour had to be such as would not be detrimental to your future…and I wanted you to make a good marriage. I might add that in spite of my efforts, on many occasions your actions left much to be desired."

Georgiana folded her arms and paced back and forth across the room. Well, she had made a good marriage, one that was a love match, too. She was a married woman now with freedom to come and go as she chose. Then why was she so anxious at the thought of seeing Roderick? She was not a little girl. Roderick was no longer her guardian; he was her brother, and this was her home, a place where she was sure of a welcome and refuge. Or was she? How would Roderick react when he learned why she was here? She stopped her pacing, her face full of woe. It wasn't the turkeys and the heat that ravaged her looks; it was the thought of meeting her brother. She might not be a little girl, but she felt like one–the little girl who had trembled before the cold eyes of her guardian.

She started.

A pair of eyes stared at her now–eyes that seemed to bore right through her, searching out every last one of her secrets. They were those of the black figure, half lion and half human surmounting the clock on the mantelshelf before her. She sighed with relief and smiled at her own foolishness. She was her own mistress with no reason to be afraid of anyone or anything–and certainly not a grotesque clock. She relaxed. She had come to London to enjoy herself, and who was there to say her nay, except her husband? She was going to show him he could not order his wife about in such a manner.

As if to bolster her defiance, she marched up to the fireplace, raised her chin, stared straight into those sinister eyes on the clock and said, "If you are not the ugliest, ugliest, *ugliest* creature I have ever seen."

"Come now, is that any way to welcome a brother?"

Davenant closed the door behind him and advanced into the room.

"Roderick, *mon chèr!*" Georgiana declared with a smile. She ran to him and clutched the lapels of his coat.

Such a lavish display of affection between them was unusual. Davenant frowned and his eyes narrowed. What did it mean?

Georgiana held up her face to be kissed. Gingerly he put his arms around her and dutifully bent and kissed first one proffered cheek and then the other.

"Really Georgiana, did you come all the way to London just to ruin my coat?" he asked, removing her hands from his lapels.

"Dreadful, dreadful, *dreadful* creature!" She pointed to the clock. "And so is that."

Davenant let go of her and languidly raised his quizzing glass to the clock. "Quaint? Perhaps. Dreadful? No. French…*Sèvres* and ormolu. Bes. An Egyptian deity. God of the family." He looked at Georgiana. "If any family needs a guardian deity, it's this one."

Georgiana swallowed–a little nervously, he thought—but quickly brightened.

"Are you not pleased to see me?" she said as she removed her gloves.

"No."

Taken aback, she mouthed a silent 'oh' of disappointment.

"Surprised would be a more accurate description," he drawled. "You've only been married six months. You're still on your honeymoon. Why forsake the rapture of connubial bliss to visit your old bachelor brother?"

Georgiana tripped to a sofa adorned with a sphinx head and lions' feet and gracefully draped herself among its cushions. Davenant took a chair near her.

"At only four and thirty, Roderick, you are not old. And as for being a bachelor? You cannot remain so forever. Your duty to the family is to provide yourself with an heir."

"Perry is my heir."

"Poor Perry!" Georgiana sighed. "Why did he join the navy? He could be killed."

"I assure you he is well able to take care of himself. But surely you have not come all the way to London just to discuss the family inheritance."

Davenant stared at her, tapping his eyeglass against his chin. Without realising what she was doing, Georgiana nervously twisted a glove in her hand.

"By the by, where is your ecstatic bridegroom...my new brother-in-law? Seeing to the bestowal of your carriage and horses, no doubt?" he drawled, well knowing the answer.

Georgiana clenched tight the glove.

"Why...why...he's still in Norfolk," she said quickly and brightly: too quickly and too brightly.

"When, pray, will I have the pleasure of seeing him? When will he be joining you?"

Georgiana made an unsuccessful attempt at a lighthearted laugh.

"Why...I...I... *Je ne sais pas!* He...er...he is...he was visiting a neighbour. Yes, yes, I recall, now it was something to do with...er...er...rotating turnips. Or was it crops? Yes, yes...that's it! Turnips."

Davenant recalled the baggage in the hall, an amount worthy of Wellington's army—or a lady of fashion intent on a long visit. A thought occurred to him and he stared at Georgiana.

"Damn the turnips! Does Hesston know you are here?"

An even worse thought followed.

"Have you left him?" he said quietly in a voice like ice.

From beneath the brim of her hat, Georgiana stole a glance her brother. He had never been this angry with her before, not even for the worst of her former scrapes. Should she try tears? Hers devastated her husband just as they had done her admirers. No. They would not move Roderick. He was a definite disadvantage as a brother: he had had so much experience of women. Besides she had done nothing wrong. *She* was the injured party.

"Well, yes…yes, I have left Edgar," she said determinedly, "but only for a while," adding in an uncertain voice, "until he sees reason."

Davenant leaned back in his chair.

"It won't do, Georgie," he said sternly, using the nickname of her nursery days. "You can't just up and leave your husband on the slightest whim. It's not done. Hesston's your husband…not one of your former addle-headed *beaux,* like that fellow who jumped off Westminster Bridge and fell into a coal barge because you cut him. Suppose Hesston decides to divorce you for desertion? Society tolerates many scandals, but divorce? You would no longer be received in polite society. As head of this family, I order you to return to Norfolk. Davenant House is not a refuge for recalcitrant wives! A day or two to rest your horses…and back you go. In the meantime, you will write a note to Hesston and tell him you are here. He must be out of his mind with worry. To be sure the letter goes out with the evening mail, I'll have a servant take it directly to the General Post Office."

Incensed by his words, Georgiana jumped to her feet and stood before him, her hands clenched by her sides, her cheeks flushed. "You have no right to speak to me in that way!" she cried, "and as for scandal! There have been worse scandals in this family than a wife leaving her husband for a little while. Why you yourself…"

Davenant's cold stare made her hesitate—but only for a moment.

"You were saying?" Davenant drawled.

Georgiana raised her chin. "You yourself have been involved in many scandals. That boy who blew his brains out, for instance…*le pauvre*…after you won a fortune from him at cards!" She shook her head. "For two days and two nights you kept him at play!"

She did not see the look of pain that crossed her brother's face; it was but fleeting.

"He was not a boy. He was five-and-twenty…at an age to know better. It was he who persisted in raising the stakes and continuing the game," Davenant drawled. "I could not…in all honor, refuse…and I could not afford to lose. And he did not blow his brains out. He was shot in a duel two days later."

"A duel in which he deliberately sought death because he was ruined. You gained a fortune and lost the woman you loved because you destroyed her cousin!" Georgiana blurted.

She bit her lip. Oh how she wished she had not said that.

For a moment, Davenant stared at her without seeing, his lips a tight line, but then his usual bored expression returned. He said in a matter-of-fact voice, "That money, together with my other gambling successes, restored the family fortunes, which our father left in such a dismal state. It also provided you with a sizeable fortune when you married.

"Edgar would have married me even if I hadn't a penny!"

"That's because he was fool enough to fall in love you."

Georgiana sighed and her face softened. "*Et je l'adore.*"

"Good. Then the sooner you return home, the sooner the two of you can continue in mutual adoration of each other."

Georgiana pouted. "Edgar has been quite, *quite* odious."

Davenant lips twitched. "That's his privilege. He is your husband."

Georgiana could not help but smile.

There was short silence before Davenant said quietly, "When I spoke of scandal, I was thinking of Hesston. Leaving him like this…so soon after your marriage… will embarrass him and make him look a fool in the eyes of society. If he's half the man I think he is, he won't take your departure quietly."

Quite forgetting she was a lady of fashion. Georgiana flopped down on the sofa—in an inelegant heap of green silk

"I never thought!" she wailed.

"You never do."

She shook her head sadly. "Edgar says I am spoilt and willful."

"You are. I spoilt you."

"You! Why you hardly saw Perry and me."

"That's how I spoilt you: not being there to keep you in hand."

She looked despairingly at Davenant. "Do you think Edgar will be very angry?"

"I would be."

"Oh dear," she groaned.

In a lighter tone he said, "You haven't yet told me what Edgar did that was–how did you describe it?'–odious?"

"Well...he...that is to say, he...he will not open Hesston House for the autumn season," Georgiana replied in a small voice, "and...and he doesn't like my dog Puff sleeping on my bed when we...when we...we...you know."

His lips twitched. "The Hesstons have never been great town dwellers, and besides the autumn season is very short. No doubt Edgar will feel differently next spring...when the season proper begins."

"Oh, but I...I could be *enceinte,* by then...and unable to dance," came Georgiana's strangled voice.

"Quite possibly. Anyone as successful at breeding livestock as Hesston is should be equally proficient on his own account."

"Roderick!"

The brim of the outrageous hat shot up to reveal Georgiana's shocked face.

Davenant drew out his snuffbox. "Don't be missish, Georgie. It ill becomes *you*...a young woman who attempted to elope to Gretna Green with a fortune-hunter."

"I was young...and very foolish."

"You still are," Davenant said, as with studied grace he helped himself to a pinch of snuff.

"'Twas but a romp!" she countered. "Perry was having *such* adventures in the navy. *I* wanted some, too. Why, I had no intention of marrying a...a...oh, I forget what he was. "

"A dancing master–and not a very good one at that! And as for having no intention of marrying him. If you had spent just one night alone in his company, you would have had no choice but to marry him...or be ruined!"

"Well, we did not get far. You caught me climbing out of the window."

"Yes, climbing in and out of windows was a favourite past time of you and Perry. He still climbs in through them if gets locked out while home on leave."

"Edgar does not know about the elopement," Georgiana said with a worried face.

"I took damned good care that nobody knew—and at no small cost!" Davenant replied. "Your adoring dancing master demanded a small fortune to keep his mouth shut and leave Eng…"

A dog's high-pitched barking from somewhere in the house interrupted him.

"Darling Puff!" gasped Georgiana.

In a rustle of silk skirts she ran across room and opened the door to a din of shouts, screams, honks, barks and curses.

In the hall the servants were still busy with Georgiana's luggage. None of them noticed Addy, who had been enticed from his hiding place behind the column by the antics of Georgiana's lapdog."

"You little bastard! So this is where you've been hiding!"

Peeper Malloy, the sweep, and his geese stood at the open front door.

The sight of the geese set Puff barking.

Addy screamed. Malloy lunged toward him as he ran but was prevented from reaching him by Henry Rollins, who hurtled through the open door and leaped on the sweep's back. Terrified, Addy did not see where he was going and ran headlong into Georgiana just as she reached the bottom of the stairs.

Puff barked and barked; the geese honked and honked.

11

Once when Davenant was a boy, an uncle took him to Bedlam for what he thought would be a treat for his nephew: watching the crazed antics of the insane people locked there. Standing at the head of the staircase, Davenant experienced the same shock and disgust at the pandemonium in the hall below him as he had felt then–but for a different reason.

This was his home–not a madhouse!

The marble hall of Davenant House was no longer the place of classical tranquility it was supposed to be, but a scene of chaos from which rose the cacophony he had heard in the Egyptian Salon.

The centre of the tumult was a man doubled over under the weight of Henry Rollins, who clung to his neck with one arm while pounding him with the other.

"Got no business ere, you 'aven't, yer little sod," Henry yelled.

Despite his burden, the man limped as fast as he was able after the sobbing Addy, who Georgiana held by the hand as they ran here and there to avoid him. Whenever he came too close, she brandished a furled parasol at him. Meanwhile the geese, which had broken free of their master, continually beat their wings in an effort to rid themselves of the dog pestering them. Georgiana's maid chased after the dog, trying to catch it.

The normally unflappable Venables was beside himself, unable to control the servants, whose yells and shouts added to the commotion as they sought to snare Puff and the geese, while trying not trip over either of them as they ran among their feet. What remained of Georgiana's baggage lay scattered about the hall: hats and gowns, some spattered with geese urine and feces, lay tumbled from the trunks and boxes, while from his cage the parrot continually assured everyone that "Britons never, never would be slaves."

"Silence!"

Davenant's command reverberated against the marble of the hall.

The voices ceased. Everyone stood where he or she was and uneasily eyed

Davenant.

His coat and waistcoat smudged with soot, Henry slithered from his perch on the stranger's back. Puff, recognising the voice of authority, went silent. Georgiana's maid picked him up and held tight his snout to prevent further barking. A footman covered the parrot cage with a cloth, and even the geese cackles subsided.

"What is the meaning of this?" Davenant demanded.

Everyone began talking at once.

Davenant folded his arms and stared down at those in the hall with a look of frigid hauteur that would have quailed even Wellington.

The voices died away.

Davenant looked at Henry. "Well?" he said.

Delighted to be the centre of attention, Henry paused only long enough to adjust his cuffs and cravat before beginning his narrative.

"I tried to stop 'im, my lord," he said while the stranger rounded up the geese. "No wonder he didn't see us in the square this morning. He's only got one eye!"

Davenant raised his glass to the interloper and saw this was true. Peeper Malloy stared back insolently with his good eye, his other being a jelly-like blob of white in his grubby face.

"I saw him hangin' around outside after you went indoors, milord." Henry went on. He glared at the butler. "Next thing I knows he was up the steps and in the door, cos Mister Venables weren't to there to stop him like 'e shoulda been."

Venables attempted to speak, but Henry had not finished. "So afore you could say Jack Robinson, down I jumps from the curricle, gives the ribbons to one of her ladyship's grooms and after 'im I goes to stop im, but, too late!" Henry said with a dramatic flourish of an arm. "He was already in the ouse."

The butler cleared his throat and pulled his majestic figure up to its full height. "I must apologise, my lord," he began, "for what has just taken place in the hall, but that person," he said, pointing to sweep, "gained access to the house while my back was turned and the front door open. This is not the first time he has sought entry to this house."

"Really?"

"Yes, my lord. He tried to gain entry at the tradesmen's entrance several times this week during your absence. On each occasion he demanded to speak to your lordship. He was informed that your lordship did not have dealings with chimney sweeps, the cleaning of chimneys being the province of the housekeeper or the under butler."

All this time, the sweep had stood slightly hunched over, his one eye scrutinising the hall's splendour: the statues of the Nine Muses, the painted roundels on the ceiling, the mirrors, and crystal chandeliers. The man's insolence surprised Davenant. He must feel very sure of himself and his cause to have so brazenly entered such a mansion.

The sweep stepped forward.

"Keep your distance, fellow," Davenant warned as the odour of soot and spirits emanating from the sweep met his nostrils.

Henry stepped between the two of them to make sure that he did so.

"You Lord Davenant?" Malloy grunted.

"What business is that of yours?" replied Davenant in his most aloof tone.

Malloy glanced around the hall again, paying particular attention onto the scantilly clad figures of the Muses and those depicted in the roundels on the ceiling. The sweep's only eye fascinated Davenant; so powerfully did it convey the man's many reactions, it was as if it had incorporated the latent power of its defunct twin.

"Real swell cove, aren't we? Got a real mort ken. Real warm in the pockets, I'd say we are. Yes. Very high in the stirrups," Malloy mocked.

"He says you got a fancy 'ouse and 'e reckons as 'ow you must be very rich," Henry said in response to Davenant's questioning look.

At the sweep's mention of his wealth, Davenant guessed it was money the man was after. The interview was likely to become an unpleasant war of words, something he did not wish Georgiana to witness.

"No doubt her ladyship and her maid wish to retire," he said, turning to Georgiana, who stood by a marble pillar, Addy peeping from behind her skirts. She opened her mouth to say she did not wish to do anything of the kind, but her brother's unyielding look made her close it again. She took the boy's hand

and led him to the library, followed by her maid with Puff.

"'Ere!" yelled Malloy. He tried to go after them as they disappeared through the door, but Henry and a footman stopped him.

Davenant waved his servants out of earshot.

"Your name?"

The sweep scowled. "Peeper…Peeper Malloy, that's me."

"Why did you break into my house?"

"The door wuz open!"

"The door of my house is often open, but that does not constitute an invitation to every ruffian in London to come calling. I dare say that a case of housebreaking could be made against you, particularly as on previous occasions you were forbidden entry. May I remind you that the penalty for housebreaking is death."

Malloy pointed to the library door. "I want's my boy!"

Davenant frowned.

"Ah yes," he drawled, "the boy. Could someone be so good as to enlighten me as to his identity? Is he employed here?"

"He's me boy, my apprentice, and.. ." Malloy began.

"He's that climbin' boy wot you found, my lord," Henry interrupted. "Cleaned up real well, 'e has… so as you'd hardly recognise him. And he shouldn't a-been goin' up chimneys cos he's two months shy of his eighth birthday, he is, and ain't s'posed ter climb 'em till then." He would have added what he had learned about Addy, but decided this was neither the time nor the place to do so. In silence Davenant tapped his chin with his quizzing glass, trying to recall to whom Henry referred to. Having entrusted Dingley to arrange the climbing boy's future, he had forgotten the child, never expecting to see him again. However, Dingley had been away from Davenant House on business, which explained why the boy was still in the house. Whether or not the boy was the sweep's apprentice did not concern Davenant, but he had too great a sense of his own consequence to permit someone to demand the boy from him.

"Ah, yes," he said at last, "I recollect, now. *That* boy."

"The one as 'ow you kidnapped from me!" Malloy retorted.

"I did not kidnap him," Davenant retorted, his voice suddenly hard. "*You* left him for dead. And no, you may not have him."

Malloy did not reply at once. Instead he looked thoughtfully at the paintings of scantily clad figures from Greek mythology that decorated the walls and ceilings. Then, his one eye gleaming with cunning, he moved closer to Davenant,

"I thought so! A madge cull, eh? The nancy lark wiv the little boys? Specially ones wot is dirty an smelly. Swell cove you may be, but it won't do yer *no* good wiv the judge. Doin' it wiv little boys? Against the law, that is. They hangs yer for that, *too*."

He gave a sly grin. "But no one as to know…if you know what I mean…"

"Aaaaaagh!"

Malloy's strangled yell set the geese honking again.

With one hand Davenant had grasped the ends of the filthy kerchief around Malloy's neck, twisting them tight as he lifted the sweep to the very tip of his toes. His eyes bulging, Malloy tried to pull the kerchief way from his throat as he fought for breath.

"Dear me, your thoughts are every bit as revolting as the rest of you," Davenant drawled. Then his look hardened and he shook Malloy's head as if it were that of a doll. "You foul-mouthed swine! Blackmail won't work with me. I have many vices, 'tis true…but the world is well enough acquainted with them to know that pederasty is not one of them."

Abruptly he let go his hold. Malloy tottered and gasped for air.

Davenant calmly took out a handkerchief and wiped the soot from his hands. "You were saying?" he said politely.

Malloy stepped well back from Davenant's reach and yanked his geese to him. Warily he eyed Davenant while he considered his next move.

He gave an obsequious smile. "Very 'umble apologies, my lord, if I gave offence," he whined. "I'm a poor man, my lord…an' tryin hard to make a living. The boy… he's my 'prentice. How can I earn a livin' without im?"

Although seemingly intent on the study of his fingernails, Davenant watched Malloy out the corner of his eye. To deprive a master of an apprentice was illegal, he knew; but if the boy was under age Malloy would not want to face a magistrate for fear of having to pay a fine. Besides, how could he have any real interest in the boy when he was more intent on obtaining money from Davenant, first by blackmail and now charity? Davenant decided to call his bluff.

"Far be it from me to deprive a man of his livelihood," he said. Your plight… ahem…er…moves me…to change my mind. You may have the boy!"

"My lord!" Henry began.

Davenant's raised hand stopped him. Malloy started in surprise, but in no time he recovered his wits, becoming more obsequious than before.

"Er…well now…er…Peeper Malloy's never been 'ard to get on wiv," he said with what passed for a smile. "If yer lordship…er…wants ter….r…keep the boy…why yer can." He paused, his one eye suddenly imploring. "But it's like this…yer see? Did a lot for 'im, I did. Treated 'im like one of my own, I did."

"Such Christian charity!" Davenant sighed in mock admiration. "To do all that…and without expectation of an earthly reward?"

At the word 'reward,' Malloy's one eye gleamed bright with greed. "Warn't nothing," he said eagerly, too eagerly. "I didn't mind the three…no…four…. no, I tells a lie…the six guineas I paid for 'im."

"You bought him?" Davenant's lip curled with distaste. "So Parliament abolished the slave trade everywhere–except in England?" He stared at Malloy. "I thought it the practice for parents and guardians to pay the master a premium for taking a child as an apprentice–not the other way about."

"Well…er…" Malloy began.

"It is not my custom to buy children," Davenant continued, "let me be quite clear about that. The six guineas I'm going to give you are first: to rid my home of your presence once and for all; and second, for the loss of the boy's services to you and any expenses you may have incurred on his behalf."

Davenant took the money from his pocket and tossed it at Malloy. "One thing more: if you ever come within so much as a mile of this house again, I'll have you charged with housebreaking, trespass and attempted blackmail–and my *chef* will roast those blasted geese of yours on a spit!"

With that he tossed the coins into the air. They fell to the floor among the geese and he walked away, leaving Malloy on his knees scrabbling for the coins among his cackling birds.

In the library Georgiana put her arm around Addy's trembling shoulders and gently pulled him closer to her chair. Wide-eyed with fear, he kept glancing at the closed door. Malloy, the sweep, was out there in the hall. The door was all that stood between them—and Malloy wanted him!

Georgiana smiled down at him and stroked his hair. She felt warm and she smelled of flowers. Gradually Addy's trembles subsided and his breathing slowed. He snuggled closer to her.

"There, there," she soothed. "Don't be frightened, *mon pauvre petit garçon.*"

Addy smiled in sudden recognition. It was not what he said in reply that surprised Georgiana, but the way in which he expressed himself. When Davenant entered the room a short while later, it caused her to exclaim, "Oh Roderick! This darling, darling, *darling* little angel speaks *such* beautiful French."

12

With his quizzing glass held to his eye Davenant peered down at Addy in much the same detached way he studied botanical specimens under a microscope.

All children were an enigma to him. Horses, dogs, even trilobites–those he knew about. But children? They had no place in his world; he had no interest in them and what was more, he did not like them. Although their legal guardian, Georgiana and Perry had been entrusted to the care of tutors and governesses when they were young, Davenant rarely seeing them. True, he had stood godfather to a number of squawking, lace-trimmed bundles, the progeny of family and friends, but that was the extent of his involvement with them. As he could hardly remember the names of these bundles–let alone their dates of birth–his secretary dutifully sent them gifts on his behalf at Christmas and for birthdays.

"Mmm. Yes…'tis true, he has cleaned up nicely," Davenant murmured for want of anything else to say.

Georgiana hid a smile. Faced with a harmless little boy, her sophisticated and worldly brother was so at a loss, he could only repeat his groom's observation.

In silence Davenant continued his inspection of Addy, behaviour motivated by his bafflement about what to do or say in his present situation, rather than genuine curiosity about the boy. Addy looked at his scrutiniser with a child's disconcerting directness, his eyes full of admiration for this giant who had saved him yet again from the chimney sweep's clutches.

The entrance of a footman rescued Davenant from his awkward predicament.

"Pray do forgive me for keeping you waiting, sir, but I…"

Davenant's voice trailed away and he stared in astonishment at the blue-grey eyes that met his.

"I beg your pardon, ma'am, I was expecting…"

"A man?" finished the representative of the League for the Betterment of Climbing Boys with a twinkle in her eyes.

She was a tall young woman, about four and twenty, and despite the heat she managed to look both cool and fresh in a walking gown of dove grey silk trimmed with white that complimented ash blonde curls peeping from beneath a chip-straw bonnet. Her face was not beautiful in the accepted manner; the mouth was too wide, and there was a hint of freckles, like a sprinkle of pepper, he thought, on her upturned nose, the presence of which would have horrified Georgiana. But there was no denying the lure of those eyes: dark one second light the next, like the changing waters of the sea; eyes that shone with intelligence and humour.

"Yes, I confess that is true. My secretary informed me he had been in correspondence with a Mr. Barclay. But this is a most pleasant surprise, nevertheless," Davenant said, recalling the other suprises of the day that had not been so pleasant.

"I should explain," the woman said, "that my uncle, Mr. Victor Barclay, is the secretary of the League for the Betterment of Climbing Boys. He is at present recuperating from an illness in Brighton. 'Tis I who have been answering his correspondence."

"You forged his signature?"

"Indeed, no! That would be both illegal and unethical. My initials are the same as his."

"And whom do I have the honour of addressing?"

"Miss Barclay…Miss Verity Barclay."

"Much as I regret your uncle's illness, Miss Barclay, it does, however, afford me the pleasure of making your acquaintance," Davenant said.

"May I also present my friend and companion, Miss Rebecca Philmore? "

A middle-aged woman with apple cheeks, dressed in black with touches of white, whom Davenant had not noticed before, came forward and smiled.

He bowed to both women. Their behavior in response to this courtesy surprised him: they did not curtsey in return. He held a chair for each of them and then took the one behind his desk. Miss Philmore handed Miss Barclay a portfolio from which the latter removed some papers.

"Thy secretary said thee wished to know about the lives of climbing boys in this city," Miss Barclay began in a quiet but business-like manner. I know my uncle would have called upon thee in person had he been in town. He is always anxious to promote the society's efforts on behalf of these unfortunates. I am here as his representative."

Davenant gave one of his rare smiles. "A most charming one."

Miss Barclay obviously did not notice his flirtatious implication, for she continued thumbing through papers without looking up. When at last she did so, she said, "The League for the Betterment of Climbing Boys is heartened by the interest thou art taking in its work. We hope that thee can be prevailed upon to speak in Parliament on behalf of the society's work."

This was said with such earnestness that Davenant experienced a twinge of guilt—an unusual reaction for him. His attendance in the House of Lords was, to say the least, sporadic.

But it was not just what Miss Barclay said that baffled him; he was puzzled by her manner toward him since he entered the room. She appeared oblivious to both his rank and sex! Apart from their lack of curtsies, neither of the two women addressed him by rank. And as if to emphasise this disregard for his station, Miss Barclay used the now outmoded second person singular—a familiar form of address—when she addressed him. The subject of his rank did not trouble him as much as the other. For the first time in his life here was a woman who showed no interest in him as man. He was not vain, but he was well aware that women found him attractive for a variety of reasons—and not just because of his wealth. Depending upon their age, marital status and the circumstances of their meeting, women were either coy and shy, or bold and flirtatious toward him.

Miss Barclay, on the other hand, was neither coy and shy, nor bold and flirtatious. Quite the opposite, she was straightforward and businesslike: more like a man than a woman.

"The League comprises concerned persons of different professions and beliefs, including those like my uncle and myself, who are members of The Society of Friends," she continued.

"Quakers?"

That explained everything: her disregard for his rank, her manner of speaking and her subdued dress. Quakers believed everyone was equal before God and therefore to each other; they also scorned such worldly vanities as fashion. Davenant lips twitched in amusement. Subdued though Miss Barclay's clothes might be in hue, they were very modish; and he had paid the dressmaking bills of enough former *amours* to recognise Bond Street quality when he saw it.

"That is what some to choose to call us," Miss Barclay said quickly before returning to her main subject. "No doubt thou hast read the observations of the surgeon at Guy's Hospital regarding climbing boys that I enclosed in my reply to thy secretary's letter."

"Quite, so," was his vague reply, instead of the truth, for he had not read the report. To cover his unease, he glanced down at the desk and was relieved to find that the very efficient Dingley had placed the report there. "Permit me to reacquaint myself with its contents," he said.

The surgeon's report proved a harrowing litany of health problems common to climbing boys: cancer of the scrotum, stunted growth, deformities of spine and limbs from carrying overweight sacks of soot; burns, coughs, colds and asthma; death by suffocation while trapped in chimneys; poor diet and early deaths from near-starvation. And if that was not all, they had no proper clothing, and they were sent out to work all hours of the night.

"I must confess I was unaware children so young…" he began.

"It's their small size, you see!" Her voice full of emotion, Miss Barclay interrupted him. "Chimney sweeps want small boys because only they can clean narrow flues. The law says that sweep's apprentices must be between eight and fourteen." She shook her head. "Masters blatantly disregard this. They use boys from four to six years, because they are small."

When Davenant first saw her, he had been struck by the palpable serenity of Miss Barclay's presence to such an extent that he found that the earlier aggravations of his day receded. But now? Overcome by ardour for her cause, Miss Barclay was no longer tranquil; her eyes were afire, her cheeks pink and her breathing rapid. If she could feel so deeply and passionately for unfortunate strangers for whom she cared, how might she express them for a man she cared about? Perhaps he might see her again.

"They steal…of course they do… food, or money to buy food," she went on.

"Their masters half starve them so that they remain thin enough to climb narrow flues. And they are cut off from society because of their bad habits–they know no better–their stealing, their despised occupation, their early work hours and, of course, their dirty appearance. They go months…*years* without a wash! We need people to speak out on behalf of these poor children…persons of consequence… like you. We need new laws. Laws that will be *enforced!*

The two of them looked at each other in silence.

"The climbing boys of London are fortunate, indeed, to have in you an advocate of such convincing eloquence and passion," Davenant said at last. "I would like to help in…"

"Oh, then you will help us! Thou wilt support our efforts?" Miss Barclay sprang from her chair, her blue-grey eyes sparkling. "Thou wilt speak for us in the House of Lords? I felt sure thee would."

Charitable appeals for money, Davenant expected; requests for his time and active participation were a different matter.

"Well…I…" he began. He looked down at his desk as if seeking an answer there. He found one: a bank draft made out to the League for the Betterment of Climbing Boys. Dingley had come to his aid yet again. The draft needed only the addition of an amount and his signature. Quickly he filled in the blank spaces and handed the draft to Miss Barclay.

She looked at it and smiled. "Thou art most generous! *Most generous.* And thou wilt come and visit our school for climbing boys rescued from cruel masters? Oh do say thou wilt!" she said, looking up at him, those blue-grey filled with gratitude and admiration. It was a look any man would find hard to resist. He hoped she did not know about his reputation; she would not be so full of admiration if she did.

"I look forward to visiting you," he began, "… ahem…I look forward to visiting *your* school."

Only when he re-entered the house after escorting the women to their carriage, did he remember that during his conversation with Miss Barclay about climbing boys, he had not mentioned the one lodged in his house. Had the distraction of those blue-grey eyes caused the omission, he wondered?

13

"That boy you found ain't no climbin' boy, guv! Newgate seize me, he ain't! Henry Rollins declared as he faced Davenant across the desk in the lattter's study. When he saw 'Is Nibs handing the two women into their carriage, Henry deemed it a suitable time to tell him of his suspicions about Addy. Nothing like a fair face to put a fellow in a good mood, he told himself. So when Davenant re-entered the house, he found Henry in his path.

"There's goings-on 'ere I thinks you should know about, my lord."

Davenant was about to say, "Not now, Henry," but the earnestness of Henry's expression stopped him. That earnestness was even stronger when, shortly after, Henry made his startling declaration.

Davenant sighed. *That* boy again.

"What, pray, gives you reason to think he isn't a climbing boy?"

"Says 'is prayers every night, 'e does."

"Is that *all?*" said Davenant, annoyed by this inconsequential explanation. Was this going to be another of Henrys stories? "Many people say their prayers before they go to bed. I hope you do."

"Yes, I do say me prayers…and no… that ain't all, my lord."

With great relish, and with particular reference to his own acute observations, Henry told Davenant about Addy's behaviour: his politeness, courtesy and table manners.

"I suppose it is not inconceivable that climbing boys are taught these things by their elders," was the reply.

Henry shook his head. "Not the ones I knows of. But that ain't all." And he went on to relate the incident in the butler's pantry involving Addy and the silver spoons. "Mister Venables said as how boys like him were introduced into houses so as to help gangs steal stuff from 'em."

Davenant frowned. "I introduced the boy into my house. I will speak to Venables."

Henry smiled with malicious glee; his arch-adversary would be reprimanded.

Davenant saw the smile and said sharply, "The contents of this house are Venables' responsibility. Other than that he sweeps chimneys, we know nothing about this boy—hardly a character reference. Venables was right to be suspicious."

Henry was undeterred. "Ain't just 'im saying his grandpa has silver spoons. There's other things he told me," Henry said. "Cos 'e stayed in the stables, I got to know him well. 'E don't talk much wiv others, cos I fink as 'ow he's still scared. But chatters like a magpie to me, he does. Says as 'ow he and his grandpapa live in a castle full of fine pictures an' furniture an' such. Says as 'ow the castles is next to a sleepin' giant…"

"Sleeping giant?" Davenant's eyes narrowed. "What nonsense! This is fast turning into one of your Canterbury Tales, Henry," he warned.

"'Sgod's truth I'm a-tellin, guv. I'm only saying wot I 'eard…and wot I saw. Looks under the bed every night afore 'e goes to bed, 'e does. And 'e as bad dreams because he wakes up sometimes in the middle of the night a-crying the sweep's gonna take him."

Henry saved what he thought was the best part of his story till last. "Sometimes 'e sits a-rockin' imself and singin' songs like ones I 'eard when I was in France wiv yer lordship. Whistled one, I did… to Monsewer Séraphin, your valet. He said it was called, *"Eel ate a buggar."*

In response to his employer's astonished stare, Henry obligingly whistled a few bars of a tune Davenant recognised as *Il était une bergère*.

"Now 'ow comes a climbin' boy knows French songs, Henry Rollins, sez I? Either he's a Frenchie, or has been educated to speak the lingo."

"My sister informs me the boy used three or four French words when speaking to her," Davenant drawled, ignoring Henry's 'I-told-you-so look.' "However, so do a great many people, and I can think of several ways in which even a chimney sweep might have picked up a few words or learned a song. London is crawling with French émigrés."

"Well, he ain't French. Stake my life on that, I would, cos when 'e does talk, he talks English."

Davenant sighed, his annoyance obvious. "So does everyone born in this country. To the point, Henry! To the point!"

"The point is my lord that when 'e does talk English, it ain't like I do…"

"*Thank God!*"

"…or Mr. Venables, that is. No. Talks like you, 'e does, my lord–like a gentleman. Not only does 'e speak English but reads and writes it, too, 'e does. And climbin' boys don't usually read and write. If you wants my opinion…"

"I do not," Davenant interrupted, "but you will pester me until you do give it to me. So?"

"Well, I been a-thinkin' about this real hard, like. Kept me awake at night, it has. And I reckons as how it has to be 'a jacketing' concern."

"Enough of that gutter slang, Henry! What, pray, in the King's English, is 'a jacketing concern?' Explain!"

Henry thought for a moment. Then he said, "Well, it's like when say a person like yourself, my lord, havin' fine houses, estates, money, an' such, is taken off by someone, so that they can take your place and have your fine houses, your estates, your money an everthin' else wots yours, and keep it for themselves."

"You think the boy the scion of a noble house?" said Davenant, unconvinced.

"A scone?"

"Never mind," Davenant sighed. "You surpass yourself Henry. Based on what you have seen and heard, you weave a fanciful tale worthy of the *Arabian Nights*. Whereas I am certain there are much more mundane reasons for the child's behaviour that have nothing–*absolutely nothing*–to do with him being a long lost heir."

Henry remained unrepentant and determined. "With respect, my lord, he ain't no climbin' boy. Newgate seize me if I'm wrong! A proper *little English gen'lman*, 'e is, an no mistake."

14

Davenant stared out at St. James Street through the rain-spattered glass of the bow window of White's Club. Alone for once in what was London's most exclusive spot, the jealously guarded haunt of Beau Brummell and his friends, he experienced that same freedom from care that he did during his solitary rides across the South Downs. It was a feeling at odds with his surroundings, because he was in a room full of people, but no one would dare intrude on him unless he asked them to join him–and he had no intention of doing that.

What a hubble-bubble of a day! And *so* fatiguing! The indignity of a 'facer' from a boxing champion; his curricle almost overturned; the arrival of a recalcitrant sister, not to mention her dog; his home invaded by an insolent Cyclops and his geese; the metamorphosis of a filthy climbing boy into an angelic child and then Henry's ridiculous assertion that that same boy was a young gentleman of breeding and fortune. After all these assaults on his equanimity, he had been in need of respite. So he did what any English gentleman would do when faced with such wearisome domestic circumstances: he went to his club.

He had not expected to find the bow window empty. Brummell and a couple of the windows regular *habitués*, he knew, were out of town. But the others? Those still in London must have stayed home for fear of the damage rain might have done to the cut of their coats or the set of their cravats. Whatever the reason, an empty bow window was a rarity, for no sooner was it constructed than Beau Brummell claimed it as his own. There, surrounded by a chosen few, including Davenant, he held court daily. Like the larger, fashionable society to which they also belonged, the members of the Bow Window Set were aloof and indolent, regarding the rest of humanity as fit only to make sport of and look down on. At their ease in the window, these fashionable men observed and commented–

usually unfavourably—on the clothes and bearing of passers-by on foot or on horseback. For their part, the *beaux* felt that in displaying themselves in the window, they showed great condescension toward those same passers-by. Other club members grumbled and criticised the set for their posturing, but such was

A JACKETING CONCERN

Brummell's reputation in society, they nevertheless considered it a distinction if invited to sit with him in the window. And woe betide anyone who ventured uninvited into the window's hallowed ground so jealously guarded by Brummell and his friends. Indeed, it was often said that it was easier to obtain a seat in the House of Lords than one in White's Bow Window.

Davenant's lips twitched in amusement. In the morning room behind him he heard the voice of the most vociferous critic of the Bow Window Set and himself: a retired general. "Damned popinjay! Just like the rest of that dissipated Bow Window Set!" the old man shouted, his blue-veined jowls and flaccid chins aquiver.

No one in the room could fail to hear him, because the general bellowed everything he said, no matter how slanderous it might be. A lifetime of artillery barrages had robbed him of his hearing, so he used an ear trumpet to hear others speak to him. And because everyone shouted into the trumpet, he shouted back.

The general disliked Davenant as an individual as much as for his membership of the window set. That afternoon he was particularly incensed with him because of the stinging rebuke Davenant gave him earlier. Unaware Davenant was passing behind his chair at the time, the general observed, "Arrogant devil that Davenant! Bad lot the entire family. Don't call 'em the Devil's Brood for nothing! Dozens of scapegraces hanging from the branches of that family tree: men and women! Davenant's sister, for instance, a real hoyden…"

A shadow fell across him and he stopped speaking.

Davenant raised his glass and peered down at the general, a pathetic figure in a snuff-stained waistcoat and unfashionable powdered wig. If anyone other than the old general had made those remarks about his family, Davenant would have called him out.

"Permit me to remind you, general, that no gentleman gossips about a lady at his club," Davenant reminded him. "I, for one, take exception to such conduct, particularly when the lady referred to is *my* sister. Do I make myself clear?"

He had walked on before the general finished his muttered apology.

Just as Davenant arrived at White's, the storm which had threatened all morning broke with a salvo of thunder and lightning that terrified horses and even frightened a few people into thinking the French might have landed. The clouds opened and down had come a dense curtain of rain that beat unmercifully against the bow window, obliterating Davenant's view. Within minutes St James Street was a fast-flowing river of mud and horse dung. Water from overflowing roof gutters turned buildings into temporary cataracts as it swept over cornices, ledges and gargoyles to swell the swirling torrent below. The street quickly emptied of carriages and men, the latter taking refuge in their clubs and shops. There were no ladies about: there never were. No woman who considered herself a lady would risk her reputation by walking or driving along the all male enclave of St. James Street, where she would be subject to the stares and taunts of men. The only thing to be seen on the street was an occasional hackney carriage splashing through the water, its jarvey hoping to find a fare.

In no time the heat and humidity of the past week were gone, the rain cooling the air and washing clean the streets. Only the smoke-darkened buildings that gave London its perpetual grey hue remained unchanged. Not even Noah's Flood could wash away centuries of accumulated smoke stains from sea coal.

The change of atmosphere brought about by the storm affected Davenant, too; his mood lifted, the day's irritations disappearing as fast as the mire that eddied down St. James Street. After all, he reminded himself, Georgiana and her entourage would leave in a day or so; the sweep and his geese were gone forever; and now that Dingley was back, the climbing boy would go, too, just as soon as he made arrangements. And Henry and his tall story about the boy? Davenant actually smiled. Although often cheeky and disrespectful, no servant was more devoted to his employer and discreet than Henry Rollins. Knowing Henry, he would be sure to soon find another tall story to replace the one about the boy. As for the 'facer' that morning at Gentleman Jim's: an extra sparring session a week would no doubt prevent that happening again.

His thoughts turned to Miss Barclay. She had not upset his day, but without realising it, she had challenged him. How could an attractive woman who showed no interest in him, not challenge any man? He would see her again and take up that challenge.

He raised his glass to better observe the street. The rain had stopped by now and St. James Street, its buildings dripping, was returning to life. A weak sun struggled through the clouds in a sky that was beginning to change from grey to pale blue; passing carriages splashed through puddles, the water from which kept pedestrians nimbly hopping to avoid it; and the crossing sweeper at the corner with Piccadilly had returned to sweep a damp path across the street for pedestrians.

His equanimity now restored, Davenant took up a copy of the *Morning Advertiser* that lay on a nearby table and began to peruse it. Later, perhaps, he would seek out his friend Willoughby for a game or two of cards before he returned home.

The general eyed his neighbours either side of him. His outburst had failed to do what he hoped it would do: get their attention. One was engrossed in the *Quarterly Review*. The other sprawled in his chair, his face hidden by an open copy of *The Times* that pulsated in time to his loud snores

Undeterred, the old soldier grabbed the arm of the reader of the *Quarterly Review*, a thin elderly man in a bishop's sombre garb. "Since they put in that window, those nincompoops have made it their own. You need Brummell's permission to sit there! What right have they, sir? What right? They're not the only members of this club. Some of us have been members, sir, *for years.*"

"Er, you were saying, sir?" said the bishop.

The general scowled. The habits of a lifetime never die. In the army everyone had listened when he spoke, and he saw no reason why absent-minded clerics should not do so, too. He pointed to the bow window.

"Him, sir! Like Brummell and the rest of those dandies. Fit for only one thing, sir: the company of their tailors! And do yer know why Brummell and his crowd sit in that window, sir?" He thrust his wobbling chins into the bishop's face. "So that passers-by *will admire their clothes!*"

The bishop sighed and resigned himself to yet another of the general's harangues about the Bow Window Set, tirades he suspected were the outward expression of the old man's envy of other men's youth and vigour. These rants were daily occurrences in the morning room because, having little else with which to occupy him, the general spent his days there. Once he was sure of an audience, the scolds would continue until, exhausted, he nodded off to sleep.

"Bad blood, sir. Bad blood! Rakes and scoundrels those Davenants, sir! And damned if he ain't the worst of all. Should be in the Peninsular fighting for King and Country instead of lolling about in that window!" the general persisted. "Look at me, sir! A soldier all my life." He thumped the fist of his remaining arm on the arm of his chair. "Made a man of me it did, sir. Battle scars from head to toe! Sabre cuts! Sword thrusts! Indian arrows! Lost an arm, I did. Keep it in my study pickled in rum. Yankee musket ball in the arse, sir, at Yorktown…just missed my privates. Only thing that didn't get me was the clap!" He winked. "Not from…any lack…of circumstances, though," he said between guffaws that deteriorated into a fit of coughing that wracked his body.

Embarrassed by this confession, the bishop quickly turned the subject of the conversation back to Davenant. He felt that in light of his calling it was incumbent on him as a Christian to say something charitable about the man.

"Davenant has, I hear, a scholarly interest in many subjects both scientific and artistic," was all he could think to say. He looked quickly about him, then leaned forward and said in a low voice, "Although, I've heard him say on more than one occasion that if he had a son, he would send him to one of those academies run by Dissenters–Quakers, Presbyterians, Methodists_and the like–rather than to Eton and Oxford."

Aghast at even the remote possibility of such perfidy by one of his own class, the general's mouth fell open, his eyes bulged, and his jowls and chins wobbled in horror.

The bishop nodded. "He said he thought those establishments provided an education more suited to the 19th century."

The general crashed his remaining fist on the arm of his chair.

"A Jacobin! A Revolutionary!" he thundered. "No wonder we have riots and strikes. It's the likes of him, with their revolutionary ideas, that sow discontent among the rabble. Makes 'em dissatisfied with their lot! Have us murdered in our beds by the Great Unwashed, he will! Curse him!"

This loud rant woke the general's other neighbour.

Lionel Willoughby's bleary, red eyes peeped around the high back of his leather chair. His faced had a greenish tinge; his cravat was askew.

"'Scuse me," he yawned. "Late night, last night. Damned if I ain't still foxed! Couldn't help but overhear what you said about Davenant." He shook his head. "He's too clever and too much his own man to get tangled up with Jacobins and revolutionaries. And as for raising a rabble? He chuckled. "It would bore him to…"

He stopped in mid-sentence. No one was listening to him.

Every eye in the room was on the bow window, where a young man who was not one of the members of the Bow Window Set had walked in uninvited and joined Davenant there.

15

Davenant recognised the intruder at once: Sir Thomas Hurley, the young man who had spilled champagne on him at Amy Wilson's *soirée*.

The young man smiled sheepishly. "I was hoping we would meet again soon, sir, so that I could apologise for my behaviour toward you at Miss Wilson's. Pray forgive me."

Davenant countered with his most withering look.

Unsure what to say next, Hurley stared up at Davenant in obvious awe of his appearance. Suddenly his eyes widened. It was *too* much. He could not help himself. "Sir," he blurted, "*Your* cravat. A DAVENANT DRAPE! A masterpiece! Why, I doubt Lord Davenant himself could create one better than that."

"I assure you Lord Davenant can do no better than this," Davenant drawled.

He quizzed the young man through his glass. The unlicked cub. Had he no notion of the *faux pas* he had committed. He must be a member for Davenant had not seen him before at White's. What a set down Brummell would give him if he were there. Well, he would give the upstart one instead: not for invading the bow window but for disturbing the peace of his afternoon.

Davenant examined the young man's attire. He winced. It was obviously the work of a provincial tailor. He had seen young squires like this 'johnny raw' before. No sooner they obtained their majority and their fortunes, they raced up to town, determined to cut a dash in society and at the gaming tables. Sadder, but not always wiser, they eventually returned to their estates, that was if they had not recklessly gambled them away. Or if they had lost their fortune at play, they went into voluntary exile abroad or, in rare cases, committed suicide. It was just a matter of time before this young devil took one of those paths.

The young man raised his chin. "Permit me to introduce myself, sir: Sir Thomas Hurley of Framfield Hall, Framfield, Gloucestershire. At your service."

Hurley bowed. Davenant merely inclined his head.

"You have heard of Framfield, sir, and the Hurleys?"

Davenant slowly shook his head.

Hurley smiled. "Well, I'm determined that London shall hear of me."

"It will, indeed, sir, and in a hurry if you continue to make a practice of going where you do not belong", Davenant said, indicating the bow window with his hand.

Hurley's hand went to his mouth and his eyes widened: he suddenly realised his blunder. Others had warned him about the exclusive bow window when he joined White's, but in his impetuous haste to apologise to Davenant, he had forgotten about it. Hurley flushed and swallowed hard. Davenant guessed what must have been going through his mind while he sought a way out of his predicament. He had made a cake of himself. His *faux pas* would be the talk of the town. What should he do? Admit his mistake and walk off with his tail between his legs, or stay and tough it out?

Hurley decided on the latter, for he drew himself up, looked Davenant in the eye and said, "Sir, I'm a member of this club. I have every right to be here. Why, his Royal Highness, the Prince Regent proposed me for admission."

Davenant stared at him coldly. Who did the impudent little devil think he was?

"A member of White's you may be, sir," he drawled, "but that does not permit your *entrée* into this bow window. Only George Brummell himself grants that privilege. And I assure you that his standards of admission are high indeed. You have had the temerity not only to enter this window but to enter it dressed *comme ça?* The cut of your coat, sir? An abomination! Your waistcoat? A disaster!" He glanced down at Hurley's pantaloons. "Your unmentionables are just that, sir: unworthy of mention. And your cravat?" He sighed and shook his head in mock despair. "Your tailor should be hung for sending you abroad in such disarray. As for *entrée* into this window, sir? Brummell abhors anything rural. Your rustic garb would cause him an apoplectic fit!"

Indignant, Hurley began, "Sir, the best tailor in Gloucester…"

"Aha!" Davenant interrupted, "*That* explains much, sir! That explains much. Gloucester is famed for its cheese, sir, not its tailors."

A burst of laughter came from behind them in the morning room. A number of members had come forward and stood watching the two in the window.

Hurley's face reddened.

"I'll gladly give you the address of my tailor, sir," Davenant condescended.

"That's dammed generous of you Davenant!" someone remarked.

There was more laughter.

Hurley stared at Davenant, his face a mixture of astonishment and fury. "Davenant? *The* Lord Davenant?"

"I am aware of no other." Davenant bowed and turned to walk away.

Hurley's eyes hardened and his lips tightened. "A moment, *sir!*" Davenant slowly turned back and stared at him with a bored expression. "Were you addressing me, sir?"

Hurley stared at him, his eyes narrowed, fists clenched at his sides, in a display of combativeness that Davenant thought out of all proportion to the dressing down he had given him. Did the fellow intend to challenge him to a duel just for criticism of his clothes?

"Sir, your fame has gone before," Hurley sneered. "You consider me lacking in matters of dress, but I am not wanting in others. It is well known, sir, that you are always ready for a wager, no matter whether it concern two flies crawling up a wall, or the outcome of a battle; and that you care not how high the stakes–as *some* have learned to their cost."

Outwardly Davenant appeared nonchalant but inwardly he was puzzled. What did Hurley mean by that last remark? Was the young devil playing some deep game?

Bristling at Davenant's insouciance, Hurley cried, "A wager, sir!"

"Hear, hear," the onlookers shouted.

"And the object of this wager?" Davenant drawled, apparently intent on the inspection of his fingernails, "for I am unaware of any impending battles, and I do not perceive any flies on the wall."

"I-I…" Hurley faltered. So impetuous had been his challenge, he had given no thought to what the wager should be.

Ever ready to wager on something or other, club members watched in eager anticipation.

Hurley hastily glanced about him, his gaze coming to rest on the window.

A JACKETING CONCERN

Outside the rain had stopped, but drops of it clung to the horizontal pieces of wood that separated each mullioned pane from the one beneath it. Every so often these drops fell on to the glass pane beneath and slithered down it.

"A race! A race between raindrops!" Hurley announced. "I wager that a raindrop of my choosing will reach the bottom of a glass pane before one selected by you. You accept, my lord?

Davenant, who was now engaged on minute investigation of a thumbnail, shrugged. "As you wish."

"The betting book! The betting book!" came cries from around the morning room. In answer to this summons, a footman appeared with pen, ink and the betting book.

Davenant looked at Hurley. Determined to teach him a lesson he said, "There remains the terms of this wager. Shall we say a hundred guineas each?"

"Four hundred!" Hurley declared in a fever of excitement.

There was an audible collective gasp from members. High stakes for card games and wagers were the norm at White's, but this brash young man's recklessly high stake for a couple of raindrops astounded even these regular gamblers.

If Davenant was surprised, he did not show it. "Agreed," he said, still contemplating his thumbnail.

The wager was entered in the betting book, together with those of members who bet each other on the outcome of the race.

Davenant and Hurley went to the mullioned bow window, and a crowd of club members moved in around them to better see the race.

"I give you choice of raindrops," Davenant said.

"That's more like choice of weapons with you, Davenant," shouted someone in the crowd. Hurley indicated one of the glass panes. "This pane...and this raindrop," he said, pointing to one suspended from the wooden frame above it.

"As there are few other drops ready to fall but the one to the left of yours, I choose that," Davenant said. "Do you approve my choice? Consider, now. Do you think it might give me an advantage over you?"

"Oh, get on with it!" snapped Hurley, impatient to begin.

In silence everyone waited for the first raindrop to fall–everyone that is, except

Davenant. He leaned against the wall to one side of the window, still more intent on the study of the nails of his other hand rather than the raindrops. Hurley, on the other hand, stood rigid at the window, his eyes riveted on his raindrop, his fists clenched tight at his sides.

The crowd of watchers was growing steadily larger as word of the bet and Davenant's participation in it spread through the club.

"Ah!" the crowd sighed as one.

Hurley relaxed and smiled; his raindrop had fallen on to the glass.

Davenant smothered a yawn. No one spoke. All eyes, except those of Davenant, were on the window where the first drop was trickling slowly, very slowly, down the glass. Sometimes it would stop for a few seconds; sometimes it would deviate left or right before moving on again.

"He's off!" a voice shouted, and there were cheers as Davenant's raindrop slipped on to the glass. Davenant languidly raised his glass to watch as his drop trickled slowly down the glass pane. Hurley's drop was well ahead; there seemed little chance Davenant's would catch up with it, let alone passes it.

Sure of victory, Hurley gave a laugh of triumph. "Come on! Come on. Faster, faster," he urged, as if the raindrop were a horse he had backed at the races. He glanced with glee at his rival. His jaw dropped. With a graceful movement of his hand, Davenant was calmly taking a pinch of snuff from a jade snuffbox.

Another collective "Ah!" from the crowd made Hurley turn back to the window. His drop had met an obstacle. A circular ridge in the glass had sent his drop sideways. Davenant's drop, however, barely touched the left side of the ridge and continued its downward path to eventual victory, leaving Hurley's drop still in the middle of the glass pane. Hurley closed his eyes, unable to watch. With a slight bow, Davenant accepted the congratulations and cheers of the crowd. In vain Hurley tried to match his opponent's nonchalance, but his flushed, perspiring face belied his efforts.

"You will have my note of hand before the end of the day," he said with as much dignity as he could muster.

Davenant bowed to him then walked away, swinging his quizzing glass by its black silk cord as he went. The crowd dwindled. The wager would be the sole topic of conversation among club members for hours.

Angry and dejected, Hurley was left alone. He felt a hand on his shoulder.

"Lionel Willoughby at your service," said the stranger. "I'm a friend of Davenant. For all they say about him, he's not really a bad sort, you know. But take my advice; don't try to get the better of him. Better men than you have tried…and suffered the consequences. A sharp mind, one that thinks ahead." He pointed to the ridge in the glass that had been Hurley's undoing.

"'Twas not entirely a question of chance. He knew that could affect the outcome in his favour. But in all fairness, when asked if you thought he might have an unfair advantage, you ignored it."

Willoughby moved away.

Hurley remained where he was, glaring in cold fury at Davenant's retreating figure.

16

Georgiana looked white and tired, a condition Davenant attributed to the rigours of her journey, but she greeted him with a bright smile when he entered her boudoir.

In deference to her unexpected presence in his house, instead of remaining at White's to dine, Davenant had returned home. However, he ate alone; her ladyship, Venables informed him, having retired early, had requested a tray be sent up to her room.

Davenant decided that for once he, too, would have an early night. As he passed Georgiana's door on the way to his bedroom, out came his sister's maid with a request: would he step in and see her ladyship before she retired for the night? He found his sister *deshabillée* in a lace-trimmed, dark blue velvet wrapper with Puff curled up at her feet. Though it was late summer, there was a small fire in the fireplace by which she reclined on a *chaise lounge*.

When he saw Davenant, Puff leaped to his feet and wagged his tail.

"There you are at last!" Georgiana exclaimed. "It's the little boy! I'm in an absolute, absolute, *absolute* fever of excitement about him and cannot wait until tomorrow. There is some mystery about him, I am sure. Tell me everything!"

Davenant was unable to reply immediately, engaged as he was in evading Puff's sudden dash at the swinging tassels of his Hessian boots, which had taken the dog's fancy. Finally he managed to reach an armchair unscathed.

"Sit!" Davenant commanded.

Puff did as he was told. Davenant then pushed a foot under Puff's stomach, gently lifted him up and set him down as far from his chair as his long leg would allow. Unused to such undignified treatment, Puff slunk off to the safety of the *chaise lounge,* lay down with his head on his paws and glared at his tormentor through the thick fringe of hair over his eyes.

Davenant frowned at the white hairs that now marred the otherwise polished perfection of his boot. "Savage beast! How did you come by him?"

"Your secretary Dingley sent him to me for my birthday."

A JACKETING CONCERN

"Dingley? Why on earth would he send you a birthday present?"

"Because *he* has standing instructions from you to do so every year," she said tartly.

Davenant ignored this. "That dog is fat," he said. "Too many sweetmeats, I'll be bound. Needs exercise. Buy your husband some Hessian boots; that'll get the little devil moving."

"Never mind about, Puff," she said. "The boy, Roderick. Henry Rollins told me—oh, it's just like a novel! He is sure the boy was stolen from a good family. How did he put it? Something about a jacket. 'A jacketing concern.' That's it!"

"He used that gutter slang of his to you? I'll have his ears, the foul-mouthed..."

"Don't be angry. I asked him about the boy while you were at your club. He didn't know what else to call it. Besides the Flash tongue is *très drôle, n'est-ce-pas?*"

"*Not* when used by my sister," he said firmly.

"Never mind about Henry! What about the boy, poor thing? Climbing chimneys for a living? *Quelle horreur!* And who was that dreadful, dreadful, *dreadful* man with one eye who was chasing him?"

Davenant gave her a deliberately vague account of finding the climbing boy after he had had a fall. It was not a lie: only part of the truth. Georgiana was curious about the details of the matter, but she knew better than to attempt to interrogate her brother; he was not one who thought it necessary to explain himself to others. He had given his word to Harriette Wilson that he would not mention her involvement with the climbing boy, and he would keep that word. In any case, he would never speak of such a woman as Harriette Wilson to his sister.

"That one-eyed Cyclops who came today wanted money, not the boy. The foul-minded devil attempted to blackmail me in the belief that..." He paused for a moment. "Never mind. It is of no importance. He would not have taken me to court for stealing his apprentice because the child is not old enough to be one—and besides, he left the child for dead."

Georgiana's eyes softened.

"How noble of you to rescue such a poor unfortunate," she said with an appreciative sigh, "a stranger, someone who…"

Struck by a sudden thought, she hesitated. "He isn't…I mean, is he your…oh, dear! Your…"

"Bastard?"

She gasped and her hand went to her mouth.

"You're being missish, again, Georgie, and ridiculous into the bargain," he snapped. "No. He is no by-blow of mine."

He rose and went to the fireplace. Leaning his arm on the marble mantelshelf, he stared down at the fire.

"My reputation is far from spotless, I know," he said, "but no one can accuse me of any lack of propriety when it comes to my family. If I did have a bar… a love child, I would not, as others in society do, introduce it into my home–and certainly not to my sister. But I would provide sufficiently for its continued welfare so that it did not have to sweep chimneys for a living.

"No, of course not," Georgiana said, quietly. "Forgive me. I should know better. You can be very kind, I know. Why, when I think of all you have done for that little fellow Henry Rollins, I am filled…"

Davenant stifled a yawn. "*Such* a fatiguing day."

Georgiana hid a smile. Her brother was averse to expressions of sentiment, particularly when they concerned him. For a moment she reflected fondly on this gentler aspect of her distant brother's character. Then she said, "The boy cannot stay here forever."

"'Gad, no!"

"So what is to be done about him?"

"The answer is obvious," he replied. "If, as you and Henry seem to think, he is from a good family, which I very much doubt, then why not ask him his name and where he lives. *Et voilà!* We return him home."

"I have already done that," Georgiana said.

"Excellent! And?"

"He is called Addy, but his real name is Adolphus." She clasped her hands. "And oh Roderick he wrote it out for me in such a beautiful hand and…"

"His family name?"

Georgiana sighed. "He says he is called 'Addy Dear' and 'Addy Love.' But I think that 'dear' and 'love' are just terms of endearments, and he does not know his family name, or cannot remember it. Perhaps there is some mystery about it. He is still a little confused and frightened, although I did tell him that you had scared away the sweep, and that he would never have to sweep chimneys again."

"Did you ask him where he lives?"

"He said that once he lived in a big house with his grandfather where there were many other houses and ships, but then they moved. Now he says they live in a castle…" Georgiana's voice faltered.

"Yes?"

She took a deep breath and said quickly, "In a castle 'near where a giant sleeps.'"

"So Henry has already informed me," Davenant said dryly.

Georgiana smiled to herself. "Do you remember when Perry and I were children? We thought the South Downs looked like a giant lying asleep?

"I do not."

In a small voice Georgiana said, "Addy says his favourite story is *Gulliver's Travels*—his grandpapa reads it to him —"so he could be mixing fact with fantasy or…"

"He's a liar!"

"Oh, Roderick, no! He is an angel." Georgiana said with a pained expression.

"So was Lucifer until he fell from heaven."

Her eyes filled with tears. "He would not lie! He has been gently raised, no doubt of it! He cannot remain in the care of servants, and he cannot sleep in the stables. Henry Rollins is devoted to you, I know, but you said yourself, he uses gutter slang. Who knows what Addy might learn from him and the others, poor, poor, *darling* little orphan?"

Davenant said nothing, but as he continued to watch her, his eyes narrowed. She was twisting between her fingers the handkerchief with which she had dabbed her eyes: a sure sign she was agitated about something. What game was she up to now?

"I ordered that the boy sleep in the servants' quarters, not the stables," he said. "I have taken Venables to task about that. Since it is long past the child's bedtime,

I take it the servants' quarters are where he is now."

Georgiana stopped playing with her handkerchief. She took a deep breath. "Well, no. Not exactly."

Davenant's brows shot up.

"*Where* is the boy?" he demanded in an ominous voice.

Slowly she raised a hand and pointed to her bedroom door.

Davenant's glass fell from his hand. "He's sleeping in *your* bedroom?"

"No, not there. In my dressing room." Before he could say more, she rushed on, "That boy is gently nurtured and needs a woman's care. I will keep him by me. I've instructed Venables to open the schoolroom for him. At night he will sleep in my dressing room.

Davenant's tone was like ice. "Have you taken leave of your senses? We know nothing about this child." His eyes narrowed. "And if you think to use him as an excuse to stay in town?"

Georgiana's eyes widened in surprise." Of course not," she said, but not too convincingly.

"Like the boy, you, too, mix fact with fantasy. You claim he is well mannered, well educated, well spoken and speaks French, so he must be from a family of some consequence. I have yet to determine those things for myself. He is more likely the son of a family that, having fallen on hard times, has sent him out to work. But, as I have already told Henry, there could well be much more sinister explanations for his behaviour than illustrious parentage. More likely the child was trained in such fancy ways, the better to prey on the rich for criminal purposes."

"Now, who is imagining things?" Georgiana retorted.

"I know of what I speak. I will not go into unpleasant details; suffice to say in London there are thousands of children bred up in crime from the cradle by criminal gangs. They teach them to break into houses, steal, and pick pockets…" He paused to consider his words. "…and other acts…ahem…unfit for a lady's ears. They could just as easily teach manners, grammar and etiquette for illegal purposes. It's all the same to them. As for speaking a few words of French?" He shrugged. "What with the revolution in France and the war, London is crawling with French *émigrés,* so French teachers are ten a penny."

"But it was you who brought him into the house, Roderick, not a gang," Georgiana pointed out.

He sat silent, tapping his chin with his eyeglass, considering what she said.

Had someone deliberately dropped the boy down Harriette Wilson's chimney in hopes of obtaining information with which to blackmail her and her clients? Might someone have known of his tryst with her and arranged matters in anticipation he would take the boy home; thereby providing themselves with future access to his house? Fanciful ideas, perhaps, but from what he knew of the criminal word not impossible

"It may be that some nefarious character or other arranged that I find the boy, so that if I took him home with me, he could later help thieves rob this house. After all," he reminded her, "Venables caught him playing with the family silver. Yet you treat him like a loveable lap dog and are quite happy to have him sleep in the room next to you."

"Well its too late now to send the boy to the servants' quarters," Georgiana said defiantly. "He is fast asleep. You cannot wake him at this hour. And if you expect to find me tomorrow in bed either strangled, or with my throat cut, then you are very much mistaken, of that, I am *sure.*"

Nestled contentedly in a bed in Georgiana's dressing room, Addy could not sleep, although it was late and he was tired. So much had happened to him today.

The sweep Malloy had come to take him, but Lord Davenant had scared him away–forever. *That* bad dream was over: no more dirty chimneys to climb, no more kicks and curses, no more feeling cold and hungry. And now he was to sleep in Lady Georgiana's dressing room instead of the stables. Sorry though he was to leave his friends and the horses in the stables, he felt very much at home in his new bedroom with its silk wallpaper, velvet curtains, thick carpet and the fireplace in which a warm fire now burned. It was just like being back home– only grander.

The thought of grandpapa brought tears to eyes. As he had never known his mother and father, grandpapa was all he had. Grandpapa was love, warmth and safety. He must get home to grandpapa soon, because the old man would be very worried about him. Grandpapa was old and had white hair. Why grandpapa was as old as… His mind struggled for the right word. Grandpapa was as old as a…a…a mountain. Yes. That was it. Someone that old would find it difficult to come and look for him, so he must go and find grandpapa.

He folded his arms behind his head. He was a little boy; he could not find grandpapa by himself; he needed the help of a grown-up. Lord Davenant had saved him from the sweep the first time; and that morning had sent the sweep away when he came to the house for him, hadn't he? Lord Davenant was strong and brave. A Nonesuch, Mr. Henry called him, which meant there was no one quite like him. Would he help him again? Addy considered Lord Davenant's qualifications. He was not as old as grandpapa. He was only as old as a…

After several minutes thought, he decided that if grandpapa was as old as mountain then Lord Davenant must be as old as a tree. That was not too old for him to help a little boy.

And Lord Davenant was able to do all sorts of things that could help a little boy looking for his grandfather. What else was it Mr. Henry called him? A Corinthian. What a big word! Addy mouthed it silently. Mr. Henry said a Corinthian was someone with 'lots of bottom', which meant he was brave. A Corinthian also hunted, shooted, fished, boxed, and fenced–just the sort of person he, Addy, needed to help him.

There was one problem: Lord Davenant didn't like children. "'Is Nibs don't like nippers," Mr. Henry said, "so don't you go getting under his feet."

Addy frowned in the darkness. He might be small for his age, but he had 'bottom', too, he reminded himself. He had fought his kidnappers, climbed a chimney although it hurt him, and fallen down one, which hurt even more! If he showed Lord Davenant that he, too, had bottom, wouldn't he want to help such a brave boy like him to find his grandpapa? He could rescue Bodger from the sweep, too. So he decided he would show Lord Davenant just how brave and fearless, he was, too.

And having decided all this, Addy snuggled down into his pillow and fell asleep to dream of himself and Bodger playing beneath the branches of a very tall tree.

A JACKETING CONCERN

When Georgiana had not appeared by noon the next day, Davenant experienced a mild twinge of apprehension when he recalled his conversation with her the previous evening about the climbing boy sleeping in her dressing room. Venables set his mind at rest. Her ladyship, the butler informed him, was having breakfast—toast and hot chocolate—in bed.

Davenant was surprised. Before her marriage, Georgiana, unlike other fashionable ladies, used to enjoy a morning ride in the park followed by a hearty breakfast. Like her tiredness the night before, he attributed this present state of affairs to the effects of her journey.

It was while he was in the Egyptian Saloon selecting a snuffbox from his collection that he discovered Georgiana's domestic activities had extended beyond just the welfare of the climbing boy. A vase of flowers now ocupied the spot on the mantle shelf where the clock with Bes, the god of family, on the mantelshelf.

Asked for an explanation, Venables said Georgiana had ordered it.

"Put the clock back where it was," Davenant said.

"Ahem...her ladyship *also*..."

"Put *everything* back where it was."

It took a small army of footmen and housemaids all that afternoon to return to their original positions all the items of furniture they had previously rearranged on Georgiana's instructions.

"This house needs a woman's touch!" she said when taxed with the matter.

Davenant was firm. "It won't do, Georgiana," he said. "You are going home. This house has no need of your touch. Lord knows it managed well enough without it when you *did* live here, and your mind was occupied with balls and assemblies."

17

Davenant handed his hat and cane to Venables when the butler met him at the front door. Although no one would have guessed it from the customary bored expression he wore, he was feeling very pleased with himself. He had just returned from an early morning prizefight at which his boxing protégé, the Battling Blackbird, defeated his opponent in a bare knuckles bout of twenty-five rounds. He had also won a considerable sum of money from wagers he placed on the fight.

"Wheeeeeeeeeee!"

Startled by this high-pitched squeal, he turned to see Addy, seated on a large silver salver come sliding down one side of the marble staircase at unstoppable speed. Behind him came Puff, carried forward on his little legs by his own momentum. In seconds the tray reached the hall, where it skidded across the marble floor and came to rest near Davenant's feet. Addy fell backwards and burst into giggles. Puff, having also reached the hall, made straight way for the tassels of Davenant's Hessians; only Davenant's sharp "Stay!" prevented their destruction.

Georgiana, who had given Addy's tray its initial push from the top of the stairs, came running down them, looking demure in green-sprigged muslin with matching sash.

"Oh Roderick, I never realised until now how so, so, *so* delightful it is to have child in the house. Doesn't this remind you of when Perry and I were children? We used to love sliding downstairs on trays. I thought Addy would like it, too, so I borrowed the salver from the dining room."

His giggles exhausted, Addy scrambled to his feet and looked up expectantly at Davenant, after this, his latest attempt to show his lordship he had 'bottom'. Venables, whose Adam's apple had been set aquiver by this abuse of the family silver, hastily retrieved the tray.

Davenant said nothing to Georgiana and Addy. He did not need to do so; his look of haughty *froideur* left neither of them in any doubt as to his feelings about the incident. Without a word, he ignored Georgiana and Addy and walked off to the refuge of his study.

More puzzled than upset by Davenant's reaction, Addy stared after his hero. Didn't Lord Davenant realise that sliding downstairs on a tray took lots of 'bottom'? Why was he annoyed? Addy shook his head. Trying to get his lordship to notice how brave he was had turned out to be much more difficult than he imagined. And he had tried so very hard. He frightened footmen and maids by jumping out at them from behind pillars, so that they often dropped whatever they were carrying. He chased Puff around the house, bumping into people or knocking things over as he went. He slid backwards down banisters, splitting his trousers, shocking more than one housemaid with the sight of his bare bottom. And then he had built a steeplechase out of some of Lord Davenant's books in the library for him and Puff to race over.

What more could he do?

Davenant sat down, put his feet up on his desk and picked up a book. Half-heartedly he flipped through it pages before he put it down again. His study was a masculine sanctuary of leather-covered chairs, its walls decorated with a collection of pistols, paintings of his racehorses and prints of hunting scenes. It was *his* sanctuary, his *only* sanctuary in the house at present. No one dare intrude upon his sanctum. At least here he was sure of some peace.

That a gentleman should govern his behavior with reason and restraint, no matter how trying the circumstances, was Davenant's guiding maxim. He viewed with disgust the fashion among some for sensibility with its displays of affected sensitivity and emotion. But, in the three days since Georgiana's arrival, his customary self-possession had been sorely tested. And he had been brought close to displays of emotion himself–anger, irritation and frustration–by the many disruptions caused by her and Addy. However, he smugly reminded himself, his willpower was such that on these occasions his rational mind had triumphed over feelings.

The raindrops wager between him and Hurley was the root of some of his aggravations. Reports of it in several newspapers reminded him–and the public–

of an episode in his life he preferred to forget: the manner in which he had acquired his present fortune. Although to avoid possible libel action initials not names were used, the public was left in no doubt of the participants' identity.

> *Surely Sir T-- H-- is aware of the fate of a late relative at the hands of Lord D--? The young man would be well-advised to seek the advice of a more experienced gentleman, such as his patron, the P of W, who well knows the perils that can befall a gamester.*

"Odious, odious press!" Georgiana said when she read it. "Why mention that? They imply you deliberately intend to ruin him like... " She stopped then said, "You must prosecute.

Apparently absorbed in what was going on beyond the drawing room window, Davenant did not reply.

"This...Hurley...Sir Thomas Hurley," Georgiana ventured, "is a relation, then...of the Sloane boy...the young man whose fortune you...you won from him? Oh, then he must be related to Arabella, too?"

"He is also a godson of the Regent's late sister, Princess Amelia, so the prince has taken him under his wing," Davenant said, turning at last to face her. "Not that I was aware of that...or his family relationships at the time. 'Twould have made no difference to me, if I had known. I do not recall him. He must have still been in the schoolroom when Arabella and I were engaged."

He took the newspaper and scanned the offending paragraph. "It's a jibe at the prince and his gambling debts—not me," he said dismissively, reassuring himself as much as her. "No doubt one of his detractors paid for it. Whigs and Tories pay to insult each other in print."

Georgiana's continued presence at Davenant House was another result of the wager. Much to Davenant's chagrin, she did not return home as he ordered, thanks to the unwitting aid of the Prince Regent, who invited both her and Davenant to dinner at Carlton House on the morrow. The invitation came as no surprise to Davenant. Forty-nine years old, fat and gouty, the prince still saw himself as the fashionable buck he had been in his youth. To maintain that illusion, he liked to associate with well-known high-flyers. A first-hand account of the wager on raindrops from the participants, plus a little imagination on the prince's part, was all he needed to make him feel a participant. And when the prince learned that Georgiana was staying with Davenant, he invited her to dinner, too, eager not only for her company but to curry favour with her husband, an important Tory magnate. Davenant had no choice but to resign himself to his sister's extended stay. An invitation to Carlton House, no matter how graciously worded, was a royal command and could not be refused. Georgiana's husband might disapprove of the Regent and his set, but died-in-the wool Tory that he was, the earl would not have his wife commit *lesé majesté* for any reason.

Delighted by this turn of events, Georgiana spent much time with her maid combing through her wardrobe for a suitable gown for this event, all the while claiming she had 'absolutely nothing to wear.' But Georgiana's other behaviour puzzled Davenant. She was often listless and lost in thought, so unlike the usually vivacious Georgiana to whom introspection was a stranger. He attributed it to remorse over her rash behaviour in leaving her husband. She continued to breakfast in bed late, and on several occasions, pleading a headache, took dinner on a tray in her room. And when one evening, feeling a trifle guilty for his stern reaction to her visit, he sought to make amends by offering to escort her to a concert, the usually outgoing Georgiana said she much preferred a quiet evening at home.

"Because of the circumstances of my visit, I don't think I should be seen gallivanting about town—even if only for a concert. I've told Venables that I am not 'at home' to callers. Do not concern yourself on my account but continue on in your own way while I am here."

Her request was unnecessary. Davenant always did what he chose, no matter what the circumstances. However, because of his sense of propriety where his sister was concerned, he cancelled a bachelor party that would have filled the dining room of Davenant House with drunken, swearing bucks, jockeys and prizefighters during her visit. Otherwise he continued to go to his usual haunts: his clubs, Gentleman Jackson's Bond Street Academy, a gaming hell or two and Tom Cribbs' parlour. He went not to seek amusement but to escape the disruption Georgiana's presence had wrought in his house. Her decision not to gallivant did not exclude daily shopping trips. The hall of Davenant House was designed like the interior of a Greek temple, but Davenant often returned home to find it looking more like an *agora*–a Greek marketplace–filled with milliners, dressmakers, shoe makers, perfumers, fan makers, jewelers, glove makers, china sellers, cutlers and furniture makers, either there to deliver goods, or to receive orders from Georgiana.

Although he welcomed Georgiana's submissiveness, Davenant was wary of it. Her husband's reply to her note informing him she was in town had been a terse command to return home at once. Her subsequent letter informing him she must remain for the prince's dinner went unanswered. Georgiana was strong willed and, like all Davenants, she was adept at getting her own way. Was this new found docility merely a change of tactics on her part designed, in some devious way, to persuade him to let her stay longer? If so, she was mistaken. He would make sure she left for home after the prince's dinner.

Then there was that damned climbing boy!

The boy evinced none of the humility towards his benefactor that one would have expected from someone of his station. On the contrary, he showed a total disregard for the luxury of Davenant House and its staff, almost as if he thought he belonged there. Although polite and courteous, he treated the house as his playground. Softhearted Georgiana rarely rebuked him for his boisterous acts. Unaware these were Addy's way of showing him he had 'bottom', Davenant complained to Georgiana, "He runs tame in this household as if it were his own!"

He had interviewed Addy in French and found him fluent in that tongue. That he spoke the French of the drawing room, not the slang of the Paris slums, only served to strengthen Davenant's view the boy was either the son of poor French *émigrés,* or had been taught by one of them at the behest of those who sought to pass him off in society for their own purposes.

When asked where he lived, Addy repeated what he told Georgiana and Henry. "My grandpapa lives in a castle near where a big giant sleeps." He did not know his family name. All that he could remember before he woke in the chimney sweep's yard was that French soldiers threw a blanket over his head and he fell asleep.

French soldiers kidnapping an unimportant little boy. Davenant had closed his eyes and sighed in disbelief at mere childish make-believe.

One day Davenant was taken aback to find the boy looking at him with obvious hero worship. "Your house is very nice, and I like it here. But I can't stay very long because I must go home to grandpapa. He'll be very worried about me," Addy said.

Convinced Addy was the kidnapped child of a good family, Georgiana was adamant he should no longer remain below stairs, but in the main house itself; and she insisted the servants address him as "Master Addy." Naturally, the servants complied; to them it mattered little. Georgiana's interest in the boy they saw as just a whim of hers. Only Venables showed his disapproval of Addy's elevated status, referring to him as 'the young person' not "Master Addy." Over Davenant's strong objections, Addy continued to sleep in Georgiana's dressing room. With great enthusiasm Georgiana also took on the role of governess, arguing that such an obviously well-educated boy must continue his lessons. Davenant reluctantly let her have her way; after all she would be going home in a few days, he reminded himself. Meanwhile Dingley was making arrangements for a family on the Downsley estate to care for the boy.

"The sooner the boy leaves the better," Davenant told Georgiana. "It's cruel to show him a better life than he can expect in the future. He will be well taken care of at Downsley. His rowdiness proves to me he is a climbing boy. Why, even Venables is wary of the little devil—and *no wonder!*"

"Send him to Downsley! To be raised by country bumpkins! Oh Roderick, no!"

"Well, what else is to be done with him?"

"Well I know what I intend to do with him. Buy him some new clothes," Georgiana said. "*Le pauvre!* He has nothing but Perry's childhood cast-offs. They smell of mothballs…and they are much too tight. No wonder he split his trousers as he slid down the banisters."

There was a knock at the study door. It was Davenant's secretary Dingley.

"I beg your pardon, my lord, but her ladyship asked me to look out some of your brother's early school primers," he said, politely.

"What the devil for?"

"For Master Addy. I found an atlas and a history text with many pictures in the library, but I noticed an introductory Latin grammar in here the other day."

"Latin?"

"Yes, my lord. During a conversation with the boy, quite by accident I discovered he has the beginnings of that language. From what he says, I believe he is being prepared for public school."

For some time after Dingley left, Davenant sat tapping his chin with his eyeglass. Then he rang for a footman and gave orders that his phaeton be readied to go to Bow Street Police Office.

18

His glum face resting atop the pile of boxes he carried, Henry Rollins weaved his way through the shoppers along Bond Street. Just ahead of him walked Georgiana, her maid and Addy. Instead of accompanying Davenant to Bow Street, Henry had been instructed to drive Georgiana to Bond Street in place of her own coachman, who was unused to city driving. It was not so much that Henry minded driving her; he was flattered she valued his driving skills above those of her own man. But traipsing behind her while she flitted from shop to shop in search of feminine fallfalls? That was an affront to his dignity. He was, he reminded himself, a man's man: Lord Davenant's groom and coachman–not her ladyship's footman. Even the knowledge that this excursion was for Addy's benefit was no balm to Henry's hurt pride.

Georgiana's shopping trips were lengthy affairs and today's was no exception. True to her word that she would buy Addy new clothes, Georgiana dedicated this afternoon to that purpose–and to buying several items for herself, too. One footman had already taken a pile of parcels to the barouche, leaving Georgiana, her maid and Addy among the jostling crowds. Concerned for Georgiana's safety, Henry handed the reins to another footman and went after her, only to be enlisted to carry more packages.

After what seemed like an eternity to Henry, Georgiana finally said, "I think that is everything."

"I have lots of new things, Mr. Henry!" Addy told Henry when he lifted him into the open barouche. "I have suits, some new coats, shoes…and three caps with tassels on them!"

"You'll be all the kick then in that rigout. As fine as five pence! "

Henry did not hear Georgiana's reprimand to him for using slang because his attention was drawn to four *beaux* walking abreast toward them along the pavement. His eyes narrowed. It was almost noon: the time when Bond Street loungers–idle, fashionable young bucks–began their afternoon promenade along the street, tripping up people with their canes, snagging women's petticoats with their spurs and elbowing pedestrians into the gutter–all for fun.

The presence of these loungers immediately restored Henry's flagging self-esteem. He was once again his master's personal groom, and, in the absence of 'Is Nibs, the protector of his sister and her party. Let these swells turn their odious attentions toward Lady Georgiana if they dared. Henry Rollins would deal with 'em.

"Why, I do declare! Mr. Willoughby," Georgiana said as that gentleman detached himself from the quartet and come forward. "And since when did you become a Bond Street lounger?"

Henry relaxed. Lady Georgiana had nothing to fear from him his lordship's friend.

"Dear Lady Hesston. Georgiana. As lovely as ever!" Willoughby replied. "Davenant told me you were in town. And no, I am not here to lounge but merely to show some friends the town. Permit me to introduce them."

The other three men's obvious admiration of Georgiana amused Henry. The sallow-faced one, in particular, seemed most smitten. Men couldn't help admire her. 'A diamond of the first water', she was, and no mistake.

"Captain Allen, lately returned from Wellington's Army in the Peninsular," said Willoughby.

The young man in smart regimentals bowed.

"Mr. Rupert Basingthwaite, who has spent some time abroad," Willoughby said of the dark-faced gentleman beside him. "And Sir Thomas Hurley, who…"

"Has already caused quite a stir in society," Georgiana finished. "You know my brother, I think, sir?"

Enraptured by Georgiana's dazzling smile, Hurley stammered, "It was chance… favoured your brother when we met…at White's…but today fortune has truly smiled on me…in granting me…a meeting…with his lovely sister."

Delighted that she had made a conquest, Georgiana nonetheless modestly lowered her eyes at this mumbled gallantry.

Addy, who was standing in the barouche, had not noticed the four men. His attention was on the continuing scene that was Bond Street: elegant carriages, phaetons, curricles, hackney cabs and carts in the street; fashionably dressed ladies and gentlemen with their servants, thronging the pavements; mercury men and women blowing their horns and shouting the contents of the broad sheets they sold; street sellers selling everything from ribbons to muffins, and everywhere soldiers on leave in red uniforms.

Addy felt a hand on his arm.

"Addy, dear," Georgiana said, "these gentlemen wish to make your acquaintance. Make your bow."

19

Davenant lounged in his chair, idly watching the play of light on the crystal goblet and the ruby red of the port it contained as he twirled the glass stem between his fingers. The dinner, though lengthy, had been excellent, the wines exceptional, so that even Davenant with his dislike of the Gothic, was prepared to forgive the Prince Regent his choice of venue for the meal: the prince had had the tables set in the Gothic conservatory at Carlton House, his London home.

Modelled on the florid gothic of Westminster Abbey's Henry VII chapel, the cast iron and plaster conservatory soared to a fan-vaulted ceiling inset with glazed panels. The arms of English kings, Brunswick princes and Princes of Wales decorated the windows, and statues of ancient kings, bishops and pilgrims stood in niches. By day the light streamed through the roof and windows; at night the brass lamps of ten seven-foot high, black marble candelabra lit the room as they did this evening. The Gothic style of the conservatory was but one of several styles, including French, classical and Chinese, with which the prince had decorated this palace that was claimed to rival Versailles in splendour, if not in size. Despite the enormous cost, especially in a time of war, the house was continually being renovated because the prince constantly changed his mind– and his architects.

The sound of fellow guests relieving themselves nearby roused Davenant from his reverie. Two gentlemen had staggered behind a nearby screen to avail themselves of the chamber pots kept in a sideboard for the convenience of male guests who had drunk too much.

Davenant turned his attention from his glass to the male diners around the table. Led by the prince's current mistress, Lady Hertford, who acted as hostess, the ladies had departed earlier for the drawing room. They were graciously escorted to the door by the Regent himself, who, whatever his other faults, was renowned for his hospitality and social address. There remained twenty or so men chatting and laughing around the table about matters deemed unfit for ladies ears: their horses, racing, boxing, their mistresses and the *demi-monde*. Among them was Sir

A JACKETING CONCERN

Thomas Hurley, who had challenged Davenant to the wager on raindrops. To Davenant's polite enquiry about his friend, Basingthwaite, Hurley curtly replied, "Out of town." Another absentee was George Brummell, whose friendship with the prince was on the wane.

By Carlton House standards, the forty guests constituted a small dinner party. But each of the two courses included at least thirty dishes, most of which the pleasure-loving prince sampled. Davenant, as always, ate sparingly. Georgiana, he noted, hardly touched her food.

Georgiana had kept her promise not to gallivant and, apart from shopping trips, had remained quietly at Davenant House, caring for Addy. She seemed genuinely fond of the boy. Great had been her agitation when, on a visit to the stables to see the horses, Addy narrowly escaped injury from a hay bale thrown from a loft. After this, her behaviour toward Addy became even more maternal than before. This surprised Davenant. Until then he had thought her interest in the boy just another whim of hers—and in the past Georgiana's whims never lasted very long.

Tonight Georgiana was definitely not retiring. Resplendent in white and gold satin, she was her usual vivacious and charming self and, Davenant noted, decked out in the Hesston family diamonds. Annoyed though she was with her husband, it had not stopped her from bringing his family's jewels with her to London. "A goddess returned from exile to the joy of her loyal devotees," was how the prince greeted her; and he insisted she sit next to him at dinner.

Whenever Davenant glanced in her direction, she was invariably engaged in a *tête-a-tête* with the host. As she was due to return to Norfolk the next day, Davenant suspected she was trying to enlist the prince's help to enable her to remain in London. Her husband had still not replied to the letter she sent him, an indication of the earl's continued ire over her absence. This, Davenant guessed, only added to Georgiana's desire to remain in town. She always sincerely regretted her often-impulsive actions but balked at facing the consequences of them.

At the head of the table, the plump Prince Regent lolled in his chair. In a jovial mood he had earlier quizzed both Davenant and Hurley about their wager, the latter being by now very drunk. Between frequent sips of port the prince was telling the story of a rich, miserly aristocrat they all knew, who drank himself senseless one evening in a gaming hell.

"He never tipped the servants there, so in revenge they put the drunken sot in the wrong carriage and sent him to the wrong house," the Prince said. "Well, it's late and dark when the carriage arrives at its destination. A half-blind family retainer helps the fellow upstairs. Puts him in a room already occupied. Next morning the fellow wakes up in bed with a spinster lady, old enough to be his mother! 'Madame, quoth the poor fella, how can I make amends?'"

"Thats obvious!" she cried. Overcome with laughter, tears rolling down his red cheeks, the prince spluttered, "Poor devil! Now…he…he has…a…a Devil's daughter for a wife!"

As the laughter subsided, the prince stared over the rim of his glass at Davenant.

"A little bird tells me," he began, "a dear little bird named Georgiana. Ah, dear, dear Lady Georgiana. She says you, too, have welcomed an unknown into your house. A climbing boy."

Everyone looked at Davenant.

He inwardly cursed Georgiana for being a chatterbox. Outwardly nonchalant, he said, "Indeed, Your Highness, what my sister says is true. The boy was left for dead. I…ahem…happened along…and took him under my wing…so to speak."

The prince's bulging blue eyes twinkled. "Aha!" he said, "but the same little bird tells me there is more to him than meets the eye."

"It would appear so. Although on first appearance a wretched climbing boy, the child exhibits every sign that he has been raised a gentleman."

There was an audible gasp from his listeners.

"I confess I was dubious about him at first. His education to date appears to have been excellent. He reads and writes well, speaks fluent French, and–and this is what caused me to change my mind about him–I recently learned he has a little Latin. Certainly his customary speech is equal to that of anyone in this room, while his manners and habits appear those of a child being raised to eventually take his place in society."

The prince rubbed his hands with glee. "Oho! A foundling! A fairy child!"

A JACKETING CONCERN

Davenant's lips twitched in amusement.

"Far from it, sir. There is nothing ethereal about him. Quite the contrary, in fact. He has drawing room manners, 'tis, true; but he also teases my servants, chases my sister's lapdog all over the furniture, comes downstairs on tea trays and slides down banisters, the latter to the detriment of his trousers. I assure you, sir, that I shall weep no tears when the little devil departs."

There was laughter when a guest remarked, "Sounds like a real gentleman to me."

"Wasso odd bout a blashted climbing boy shpeakin' French?" Hurley demanded. "In France they all do!"

There was more laughter.

"But Davenant if, as you say, the boy gives every appearance of being of good family, surely he should be returned to it as soon as possible," Lord Alvanley said. "Not only for his own well being, but to allay the profound distress his family must be suffering because of his disappearance."

"On that score—indeed, about everything concerning the boy—I confess to being prodigiously disconcerted," Davenant replied. The admission was as much an acknowledgement of his perplexity to himself as it was to his listeners. The more he learned about Addy, the more baffled he became—and the more intrigued. He no longer believed the boy was a criminal. On the other hand, what had an educated child who spoke French and Latin been doing up a chimney? And the boy, his head full of childish fantasies and probably suffering from the affects of his fall, had no real explanation.

"Disconcerted! You, Davenant?" the prince guffawed. "I thought nothing ever upset your equilibrium—not even raindrops. The answer to your quandary is simple. Ask the little beggar his name…and where he lives. And when he tells you, send him home!"

"The boy appears ignorant of his family name," Davenant said. "Perhaps there is some mystery about it. As to where he lives? What he told my sister in that regard may be no more than just a childish fantasy. He says he lives in 'a castle near where a giant sleeps.' Who knows? Perhaps his mind is affected."

"But surely somebody somewhere must know who he is…and where he lives," Alvenley said.

"One would think so." Davenant shrugged. "But whom?"

"Surely, the authoritie… ." Alvanley began.

"Yes. Bow Shtreet Runners!" Hurley interrupted. "Magishtrates! Justishes o' the peace! Horse patrol! River patrol! Penty of 'em to return home a lost child."

"Hear, hear," came cries from around the table.

Davenant looked at Hurley. "These groups cited by you with such pride and vigour are nothing more than a disparate, uncoordinated hodgepodge of law enforcers," he drawled. "Each is confined to its own jurisdiction and sector of society. The militia: riots and civil unrest. The highway patrol: the outskirts of London. The River Patrol: thievery in the docks."

"You seem appear to be very knowledgeable about the apprehension of criminals," someone remarked.

"Far from it. What I have just said I learned but yesterday during a visit to Bow Street Police office."

Aggravation and perplexity had sent him there. The boy's presence and his unruly behaviour had disrupted Davenant House and his life long enough. He wanted to be rid of him. But the boy's knowledge of Latin mystified him; it indicated a middle or upper class education. To teach someone French so that he might move among society to steal was one thing; but one had no need to learn Latin to do that. This educational attainment confirmed what Georgiana and Henry believed; that the boy's learning and fine manners proved he was taken from a family of consequence. If that were the case, such a family must be searching for him; and they would surely seek the help of the Bow Street Runners.

"I had hoped to learn something about the boy at Bow Street—but they knew nothing. The clerk told me the eight Runners willingly apply their time to London—when they are not called away to attend offences committed elsewhere. The afternoon I was there two of them were with Your Highness, three pursuing criminals in the various parts of the country, another witness at a provincial assizes, one poor devil recovering from a criminal attack and the eighth somewhere else."

Davenant sipped his port. "In London…and in the rest of the country, as you know, each parish is responsible for its own law enforcement and protection in the guise of The Watch–'the Charlies.'"

Laughter greeted this reference to parish night watchmen. Their nickname 'Charlies' was a byword for incompetence and ineffectiveness.

"At Bow Street, I learned there is no central authority, no co-ordination of information about crimes in London itself, or in the country as a whole so that if this boy…"

"Devil take you, sir!"

A red-faced man struggled from his chair and teetered before it. "You imply England should be like…like France, Russia, Austria? Have a…a…a central… secret… police force! The tool of tyrants, sir! The tool of tyrants."

Overcome by a mixture of outrage and the alcohol he had drunk, the man flopped down in his chair. Another equally irate, drunken guest took up protest.

"In France Napoleon's police are everywhere. They spy on their own people. Create dossiers on each one. Remove 'em from their homes in the middle of the night! They've so many damned spies they spy on each other. And you want that, sir…*in England*? Why it's contrary to the very notion of English liberty!"

For several seconds no one spoke. Finally the Regent struggled into an upright position and said with great dignity, "The liberty enjoyed by my father's subjects is the envy of those in many lands. I, for one, would strenuously resist to the utmost of my power what you suggest, Davenant."

A loud snore broke the tense silence that followed this speech: one of the outraged defenders of English liberty lay slumped in a drunken snooze.

"I had no idea the defence of liberty was so fatiguing," Davenant observed dryly.

Everyone laughed.

"With respect, Your Highness," Davenant went on, "I plead not guilty to the accusations made against me by…ahem…our friend there. There is no stouter defender of English liberty than myself, fatiguing though it may be. I do not advocate a large and ubiquitous force of police spying on each and every one of us. I merely remarked that law enforcement–such as it is–is fragmented and lacks co-ordination, certainly in London and in the country as a whole."

Davenant shrugged. "With regard to the boy in my care, I do not know if a crime has been committed or not. I admit that from his address and education it appears he may have been separated from his family, a family of some standing. But if this is so, by what means, and for what reason? I do not know. No one has claimed him but then to whom would they report his disappearance? Locally? To the parish constable or a Justice of the Peace? But what can they do? Particularly if the boy has been taken some distance from his home?"

"They could advertise…in the Press… the Hue and Cry Gazette," someone suggested. "The mails are efficient. London papers are read everywhere."

"Have you seen such a notice in the press these last weeks?" Davenant asked. "I have no… . .and I read several daily journals."

"P'raps no one wants him back." Hurley sneered.

"Possibly," Davenant said. "I own I find the situation a mystery."

"D'ya know, Tom," the Regent said to Hurley, "Davenant is a one for the puzzling and mysterious. Dab hand, he is, at it. Searches for pieces of ancient pots, he does, so that he can stick 'em together to see how the darn thing originally looked in ancient times."

"Indeed, sir, your implied analogy that solving a mystery involving people is the same as piecing together an ancient vase is apt," Davenant said. "With an antiquity such as an ancient vessel, one first spends time gathering together as many of the pieces of the original that one can find. One then studies them to see how they may relate to each other. That done, one is able to reconstruct most of the original, even though a piece or two may be missing. *Et voilà!* The mystery of that particular pot is solved."

He shrugged. "Surely solving a mystery that involves people is no different. One need only seek out and gather together all the relevant evidence from different sources to resolve the matter."

"You think, Davenant that our system of law enforcement," Hurley slurred, "is of little use in sholving the mystery of…of the climbing boy…now under your roof? No doubt you think you could do better. Personally, I think the reconstruction o' Roman piss pots is a demn sight easier. Why, I'd wager a pound to a penny you couldn't sholve the mystery about that blasted climbin' boy if you tried, because there is no mystery! He's nothing more than a demned street urchin you want to introduce into society."

"Done!"

"Huh?" gasped Hurley.

"You just wagered me one pound of your money that I cannot solve the mystery that surrounds the identity of the climbing boy in my care. One penny of my money says I can."

There was an audible collective gasp from the diners.

It was a ridiculous wager, Davenant knew. Hurley had used the terms of it merely as a figure of speech. Unusual for Davenant, he had accepted it as a genuine wager almost without thinking, challenged as he was by notion of discovering Addy's true identity. His lips twitched; that devilish streak of the Davenants, which had lain dormant in him for some time, had come to the fore.

"Well I know Tom's been howling for revenge since losing to you at White's the other day," the prince said, "but a pound to a penny?" Used to gambling for very high stakes himself, he could only shake his head in wonder.

What the prince said about Hurley was true. Since he lost the wager about the raindrops, Hurley had publicly stated several times that he had a score to settle with Davenant. Everyone knew it was not the raindrops wager Hurley really referred to; he believed his family honour was at stake. Hurley was a cousin of the young man who got himself killed after Davenant won a fortune from him.

"A pound to a penny! Come, come, Davenant, 'twas but a figure of speech," the prince argued.

"If Hurley is refusing…"

"'Course not!" retorted Hurley, bristling at Davenant's implication.

The prince slapped his thigh. "Capital! Capital!" he declared, adding slyly, "and I would like to have a little wager of my own with you Davenant. I wager you three hundred guineas to that new pair of grays of yours–the pair for which you outbid me–that you will be unable to prove your climbing boy is from a family of consequence."

Everyone stared at Davenant. He was renowned for his judge of horseflesh, his stables the envy of them all. Money was no object to him–but the loss of any of his fine cattle?"

Davenant saw the quick look that passed between Hurley and the prince. The two must have planned beforehand to entice him into a wager that would give the prince a chance to acquire the greys. Davenant's acceptance of a figure of speech as a wager and Georgiana's revelations to the prince about the climbing boy at dinner proved a blessing in disguise to the prince and Hurley. Would Davenant accept the prince's challenge?

A tense silence followed: everyone eager for his answer. He was in no hurry. He sipped his port with deliberation. He could refuse to wager his horses, but that would appear as a lack of 'bottom' on his part. He would let no one think that of him.

"Agreed," he said at last.

Uproar broke out in the conservatory. There was a frenzy of cheers, shouts, laughter, and fist pounding on the table that only ended when the prince finally raised his hands.

Lord Alvanley leaned across to Davenant. "The terms of this wager? And how long will it take?"

Davenant looked enquiringly at Hurley. "I'm sure Sir Thomas already has the answers to those questions."

Hurley had obviously given no thought to this, for his face contorted in a puzzled frown as his drunken brain sought a reply. "Er…er…er…a month!" he blurted.

"Tom, be reasonable," said the Prince. "He'll need longer than that. There may be travel involved. Who knows where his search may lead him?"

"Oh, well then, three mo…"

"Weeks!" Davenant finished. "Three weeks."

Cheers greeted this declaration.

"Damn it, Davenant! You're mad, quite mad!" said the prince, slapping his thigh.

"Three weeks is more than enough," Davenant drawled. "Why it might only take three days, once I learn from the sweep for whom the boy worked where he acquired the boy."

A JACKETING CONCERN

The look on Hurley's face clearly showed that he had not considered such a possibility.

"Why, I will be finished well in time for the start of the shooting season," Davenant added.

His nonchalance stunned Hurley, who could only nod when the prince said, "You agree, Tom?"

"In that case," the prince said, "three weeks from today we shall all dine here together at Carlton House." He took out his watch. "It's now fifteen minutes to midnight. Davenant you have until midnight three weeks from tonight–and not one minute later–in which to solve the mystery, if mystery there be, surrounding your climbing boy."

The guests broke into an excited babble as they bet each other on the outcome of the wager. Footmen were ordered to bring pen and paper, and all the bets were duly recorded.

"And now, gentlemen," said the prince, "let us rejoin the ladies."

20

So symbiotic was the relationship between Davenant and his servants that any change in his regular habits created a domino effect in the functioning of the household. At the age of four and thirty, 'Is Nibs was quite set in his ways; therefore, such alterations were so rare as to create great consternation among the staff when they did occur.

Such was the case the morning following the Carleton House dinner when Davenant's servants were suddenly made aware of an abrupt change in their master's conduct. Rightly, they attributed this change to Davenant's wager to discover Addy's true identity. They knew about it because servants gossiped. Within an hour of the wager being made, Carlton House footmen told the coachmen waiting outside with the guests' vehicles. From then on, news of it flew among the servants of fashionable London faster than the speed of a Royal Mail coach. Long before the newspapers with reports of the wager were delivered the following morning, ladies' maids told their mistresses while they did their hair; valets informed their masters while they shaved them.

The first servant at Davenant House to experience 'Is Nibs transformation was a lowly housemaid. Fourteen years old, this timid country girl from the Downsley estate was awed by London and overwhelmed by the magnificence of Davenant Houses. As she, along with the other servants, rose at dawn to clean the hall long before Davenant came down, she had never come face to face with him, nor did she want to meet him. Indeed, the very thought that she might one day encounter the master of the house terrified her.

That thought was made manifest that morning while she was in the hall washing the staircase marble steps. She heard footsteps coming down to her from above. She looked up. To her horror, she saw a tall man, impeccably clad, hurrying down the staircase towards her: it was none other than 'Is Nibs! Paralysed with fright, she stared as if mesmerised when he gave her a slight nod. Oblivious to the agitation he had caused, Davenant continued on his way and disappeared into his study.

A JACKETING CONCERN

Overcome by the momentousness of the occasion, the housemaid keeled over on to the floor in a faint, knocking over a pail of water. Revived with burning feathers and smelling salts in the housekeeper's room, her first words when she came round were, "Like Moses 'e were…comin' down the mountain with them tablets." The very thought of which sent her into a fit of hysterics.

The incident did not escape the sharp eyes of Venables, the butler, who was also in the hall. The shock of seeing his lordship up at so unseemly hour–an unseemly one at least for his lordship–set his Adam's apple wobbling in indignation. But that was nothing to what he felt at seeing his master hastily trotting downstairs while humming a bawdy ditty like a common errand boy. And then for him to condescend to acknowledge a servant–and a junior one at that. True, it was an almost imperceptible nod, but a nod, nevertheless. What was the world coming to?

Venables and the housemaid were not the only ones to notice the change that had come over Davenant. Below stairs in the kitchen Charles-Henri, the French *chef,* raged at the sudden change in his lordship's eating habits. Instead of his usual leisurely and varied breakfast served late in the morning, his lordship desired only toast and coffee–immediately–in his study, a trembling footman told him.

A morose-looking cadaver of a man, Charles-Henri did, however, have a temper when roused.

"How dare anyone ask me–Charles-Henri–to make *le toast*?" he demanded, pounding a chopping block with a meat cleaver. "*Ah bas!* What is *le toast*? Dried bread. And what is dried bread? The food of the *canaille*–the rabble! *Scaré Dieu!* 'Ave I not made a dinner invitation to Davenant House the most sought after in London? Is not my *poulet au Davenant suprême avec legumes rôtis* a masterpiece of the cooking art? Did not *le Prince de Gaulles* want me for his kitchens at Carlton House? But no, Charles-Henri, 'e is loyal. 'E stay with *milor.* And now that same *milor,* insult me. 'E wants *le toast!* Had not that accursed revolution sent my late master–*monsieur le comte*–to the guillotine, never would I 'ave left France. *Le Comte*–God rest his soul! –was a swine to his family, his servants and his peasants, but *jamais*–never!–swine that he was, did 'e ask me, the great Charles-Henri, to make *le toast!*"

Obediently the sous chefs, *patissiers,* bakers, butchers, scullery maids and the boy who turned the roasting spit listened to this, the latest of the *chef's* many fits of pique. They never understood any of them because they were all English, their French limited to a few words and phrases of French *cuisine,* and Charles-Henri, when angry, lapsed into the dialect of the Marseilles waterfront of his youth.

Unlike his compatriot in the kitchen, Séraphin, Davenant's French valet was philosophical about his master's sudden change of habits. They were easily explained, he reminded himself as he went about his duties in Davenant's dressing room: *milor* was English, therefore he was mad.

A dapper little man, Séraphin had fled France in a hurry following the Peace of Amiens, when his relationship with a certain young footman came to the attention of the French authorities. Within a week of his arrival in Dover, Séraphin had reached the conclusion that *les Anglais* were all mad. How could they not be mad? They lived on an island which, when it wasn't covered in rain was covered in fog–and more often than not both together. In such weather how could anyone retain his or her sanity? And *les Anglais* also ate too much of *le rostbif*, which only increased their madness. He hoped *this* present madness of *milor*–rising early–would be of short duration, for it meant that he had to rise even earlier to prepare for *milor*. He consoled himself with the knowledge that, although in a hurry today, his lordship still devoted a couple of hours to his *toilette* and the all-important business of tying his cravat. It was the latter that gave Séraphin reason to rejoice. That morning, at his very first attempt, *milor* achieved a perfect Davenant Drape.

When Séraphin descended to the hall with the silver tray on which lay a pile of unused cravat bands, he encountered Lionel Willoughby, who had just arrived.

"*Pas d'erreurs*, monsieur," Séraphin sighed in bliss. "*Pas d'erreurs.*"

Willoughby smiled. Davenant's attainment of sartorial perfection, and so early in the morning, augured well for the quest his friend had undertaken.

Willoughby had returned late the night before from one of his several visits a year to the deathbed of his grandfather to whom he was heir. Hearing from his valet of Davenant's wager, he set off early to see his friend. He expected to find himself waiting on his friend in his dressing room during Davenant's lengthy *toilette* but, much to his astonishment, Davenant was already downstairs when he arrived: a major departure from his usual habits. A footman ushered him to the study just as an animated Henry Rollins was leaving it.

Henry, dressed in his Sunday best, turned back and said through the open door, "Just like old times, eh guv? Consider it done. I'll be back afore yer can say Jack Robinson."

He had just been entrusted with a task crucial to discovering Addy's identity: discovering the whereabouts of the one-eyed sweep Peeper Malloy. Malloy must know the name and, possibly, the location of the person from whom he bought the boy. With that knowledge, Davenant would be halfway to solving the mystery. Then all that remained would be to chase down that individual and find out from where he acquired the boy.

The first thing Davenant did that morning was to search the London street directory for anyone named Malloy. As he expected, there were hundreds of addresses listed; finding one known only by the nickname 'Peeper' was hopeless. With a population of a million, London was the largest city in Europe, and continually growing. Relentlessly the city crept outward, overtaking and swallowing up neighbouring villages as its numbers swelled with migrants from all over Britain, and Ireland, in particular. Among the Irish were plenty of sweeps named Malloy, but, as Davenant did not know the Christian name of the one he sought, this was no help to him. And he had no time to call at hundred addresses.

Davenant reasoned that as Malloy's employees had been sweeping chimneys in Somers Town, Malloy must live within walking distance of the area. But where? The quickest way to locate Malloy would be to ask for his address at the Somers Town house where the chimney was swept. Someone there must know about the sweep. In light of his promise to Harriette, Davenant did not want to attract attention to her by going to Somers Town himself. He would send Henry Rollins, whose discretion was assured.

Somers Town, with its French *émigré* community, was enemy territory to Henry, and that appealed to his sense of adventure. "You can rely on me, my lord," Henry said, delighted Davenant now believed Addy was the young gentleman he had claimed all along. "Yer need someone wot knows his way about that hotbed of Froggie spies," he said, "and I'm your man."

For Henry, the wager was as much his as it was Davenant's. The terms of 'a pound to penny' he thought a huge joke. But Davenant's stakes with the prince– his team of greys–Henry viewed a disaster.

"Newgate seize me! Yer greys?" he said, eyeing Davenant with reproach. He shook his head and tut-tutted. "Picked 'em out meself, I did. Bad this is, very bad. Lose them?" He shook his head again. "Never live it down, I won't, if that happens. Sooner I gets ter Somers Town, the better."

"I say, Davenant," Willoughby said as a footman ushered him into the study, "this wager between you and Hurley about the boy! Is it…"

He stopped.

Davenant was not where he was usually to be found: sitting with his feet up on the desk.

"I wasn't aware that you listened to servants' tittle-tattle…but, yes, its true," Davenant said from the window, where he stood peering through a telescope at Grosvenor Square.

"I say, that's a damn fine coat!" Willoughby said, the sight of the superbly-cut dark blue cloth that covered Davenant's back making him temporarily forget why he had come.

"Your taste is faultless, Willow," Davenant said, continuing to peer through the telescope. "I presume your grandfather has yet again been restored to health and has left his…er…deathbed."

"Damned skinflint! The sight of me at his bedside injects new life in him. He doesn't mind me inheriting his title, but his fortune and his estates? Just the thought of it, and he's up and about, riding to hounds and chasing housemaids. Just my luck he'll live as long as Methuselah. Damn him!"

"Enough of coats and grandfathers. Come here…to the window."

There was a new enthusiasm in Davenant's voice, something Willoughby had not heard for a long time; it was such a change from his friend's usual bored tone.

No one was more surprised at the sudden change in himself than Davenant.

He had woken early, eager to start the day, for there was much he had to do, much that he must do with just three weeks in which to do it. When had he last felt like this? He couldn't remember. It was Addy's doing, he told himself, for the first time thinking of the child by name; Addy and that fool Hurley with his ridiculous wager. But that was only the half of it. There was that devilish streak in the Davenant blood; the desire for excitement, intellectual and physical; the exhilaration of a challenge, however risky; the mental sharpness created by uncertainty instead of the blandness of boredom. The monetary aspect of the wager did not matter to him, though he did not wish to lose his greys. It was the task that was irresistible. And that was what he told Georgiana when, on the ride home from Carlton House, she chided him for making Addy the subject of the bet.

"He is not a raindrop on a windowpane! It is wrong to treat him *comme ça,*" she said.

"The boy will neither understand nor care about a wager. He wants to go home to his grandpapa. *Voilà!* Think, how happy he'll be when he knows I'm about to help him do that. If I succeed, at least he will return from whence he came, however lowly that place may be."

"And if you don't succeed?"

He shrugged. "Have I not already promised that ample provision will be made for his future? I was going to lodge him with a family on the estate. However, because of his gentlemanly attributes, I will have Dingley arrange future for him more in keeping with those, if I fail in my efforts."

Georgiana cheered up at this.

Even before the wager, he said, he had taken steps to learn more about the boy. He asked at Bow Street if anyone had sought the Runners help in finding Addy, only to learn that no one had enquired there about a lost boy fitting his description.

"I could take Addy home to Norfolk and care for him there until you find his family," Georgiana suggested. "He's such a darling, darling, *darling* little boy."

"And how would your already irate husband react to his errant wife returning with a darling, *darling* foundling?"

She sighed at the truth in his sarcasm. Then, with her usual enthusiasm, she promised to make all arrangements necessary for Addy's care at Davenant House after she left.

Willoughby took the telescope from Davenant and peered through it. At so early an hour hardly any of the square's fashionable residents were abroad, but there were still plenty of people about: liveried footmen walking family dogs, housemaids sweeping the front steps of houses and polishing brass door knobs, grooms holding horses in readiness for their owner's early morning rides, and two milkmaids and a costermonger going door-to-door with their wares. And across from the window, against the railings of the garden in the square's centre, was a peddler, his face partly concealed by his hat.

"Morning in Grosvenor Square," Willoughby said, lowering the telescope. He looked enquiringly at Davenant, now seated at his desk.

"You've known me since we were at Eton," Davenant said. "You would not say I am given to wild imaginings."

"*You?* Lord no!"

"Then believe me when I tell you that I think this house is being watched… by that peddler almost across from this house by the garden railings."

"*That* poor devil! Not much custom in this part of town for his cheap gewgaws. I doubt even a scullery maid would want 'em. Bit early in the day, too, to be selling those sorts of things."

"*Exactly!* 'Tis my custom to often stand at this window and observe the passing scene," Davenant went on, "but I had not seen that fellow until three days ago, the day after I visited Bow Street. Since then I have observed him for hours at a time. He makes no effort to attract customers. Other than that, I can only conclude from his position in the square that the fellow is interested in the comings and goings at this house."

"Good Lord!" said Willoughby. "Are you sure it's this house he watches and not another."

Davenant nodded.

"A burglar perhaps, planning to rob the place? Or maybe he is in the pay of…"

Willoughby's voice died away in embarrassment. He had been about to say "an irate husband." The wager, he knew, was not the only matter concerning Davenant about which people were gossiping. There were rumours about a suspected *affaire* between him and Letitia, Marchioness of Hanchurch.

As they had agreed to go their separate ways, Davenant had never expected to find himself alone with Letitia again, nor did he have any desire to. So last night he was taken by surprise when, during the flurry of activity as the gentlemen rejoined the ladies, she sought him out.

In a great flood of tears, Letitia had ended their *affaire* a few weeks ago, just before her husband's return from a diplomatic mission in Portugal. Davenant did not expect to cross paths with her again, except for public events such as last night's dinner to which her father had accompanied her. They observed the usual polite courtesies on seeing each other. And that was that, or so he thought until, as he was on his way into the drawing room, he felt an urgent hand on his arm.

"Roderick, I must speak with you!" she said, a troubled expression on her face.

"At your service, as always. Letitia."

Unseen by the others, they moved into the shadows behind the statues of two Chinese mandarins.

"How cold you are," she moaned. "You always called me Letty." Before he could say anything, she went on. "It's Charles. He knows about us!"

He heard the hysteria in her voice and prayed she would not make a scene.

"But Letitia...Letty...there is nothing for him to know," he drawled. "We... er...parted before he returned to England. It was as much your decision as mine."

"Yes, yes, I know! I know! I've told him, dozens of times, that there is no *affaire*, that there was no *affaire*, that I scarcely know you. After all, we were *so* discreet, few people could have even guessed, let alone known."

"Perhaps your maid?"

"Oh no! Never before has she..."

She stopped suddenly.

His lips twitched in amusement at her inadvertent admission he was not her first lover.

How Letitia's husband came to suspect an *affaire* was a mystery—and he did not care. Willoughby had guessed their relationship, but he would not have gossiped about his friend. Neither would Henry Rollins have talked about his late night drives with her to secluded spots.

"He is *so* suspicious," Letitia said, "so jealous, *so* stubborn. He threatens to have us both watched for evidence of…oh, what did he call it? Crim…crim…"

"Crim con," he finished in a matter-of-fact tone. "Criminal conversation. Proof of physical intimacy between a man and a woman. It is the basis for a civil suit against an adulterous wife's former lover—and the first stage of a possible divorce action."

She gasped and put a hand on the wall to steady herself. "Divorce! Surely not! I did not know that's what it meant. He…he…he…d…did not say divorce. He couldn't mean *that!* He's angry, I know. But divorce? I would rather die!"

He sensed the rising hysteria in her voice.

"I would be a social outcast, no longer accepted by polite society—a pariah."

"Calm yourself Letitia…Letty," he said gently but firmly. "There is really nothing to fear. For all I care your fool of a husband can have us both followed to kingdom come. Much good it will do him. As we have both agreed to go our separate ways, he will find no evidence of a current liaison. Nor do I think he will find evidence of our former one."

They were silent while Letitia fought to recover her composure.

He looked down at her. He could not see her face in the shadows, just her elegant figure, but he could hear her panic-stricken gasps for breath and the rustle of her satin gown. She was a passionate woman, surrendering quickly to whatever emotion she felt until overwhelmed by it. At one point she had even wanted them to run away together, an action that would have brought almost as much social censure as divorce. She seemed to have no idea how the game was played, for he had had no intention of conducting a long *affaire* with her. For him she had been but a passing fancy, an object of desire only. He suspected that for her their liaison was but an antidote to sexual frustration caused by loneliness. When she learned her husband was on his way home, desire quickly vanished to be replaced by anxiety; it was then she wanted them to part. He was only too happy to oblige. Almost as soon as the *affaire* began, he had tired of her emotional outbursts and demands. However, he felt it incumbent on him to gallantly offer a few half-hearted protestations of regret at their parting.

His lips twitched. Letitia's overriding passion was not fear of a husband she did not love, but horror of the social exclusion divorce would force on her. Status was all. She was no different from Harriette Wilson: each feared the loss of her own particular social standing.

His words appeared to have the desired effect of calming Letitia, for her breathing became more even and she relaxed.

" And now let us both continue to go our own way as before," he said. "As your husband now seeks to find a connection between us, it was ill-advised of you to meet with me like this."

She sighed. "Oh, I had to see you. To warn you. I could not bear the thought that Charles might harm you." She sighed again. "If only our situation could have been different…"

"I say, Davenant, where the devil are you?" the prince demanded.

Grateful for this reprieve, Davenant stepped into the prince's view, leaving Letitia hidden in the shadows.

"Here, sir," he said, studying this statue of a mandarin. "I must say Your Highness has such a discerning eye for oriental sculptures."

"You think the peddler in the pay of an irate husband of a recent association of mine."

"Well…I…er…" Willoughby stammered. "Dash it all Davenant! No offence meant. Damned bad form to mention a friend's personal affairs."

"No offence taken," Davenant assured him. "Indeed, it is possible you are correct in your assumption. But if the fellow down in the square has been set to spy on me, he is wasting his time. Whoever follows me for the next little while will be led a merry dance because of what I undertook to do last night. "

Willoughby grinned. "Ah yes! Your wager…about a boy whom I have yet to meet. What a lark! You'll let me help? I'll do whatever you want. Can't let you have all the fun. Can't let the prince have those greys of yours, either."

"But of course," said Davenant, who went on to tell him of Henry's errand.

As he did not know how long Henry might be, or whether or not he would be successful that day, Davenant suggested they go for a ride in his curricle.

Before they left, he glanced out the window once more.

He shook his head. "You know there is something oddly familiar about our peddler friend. But where could I have met such a fellow?"

Willoughby laughed.

"*You*, have dealings with the seller of such shoddy gewgaws? You must be mistaken."

"Perhaps but…"

Again Davenant shook his head. Then with renewed enthusiasm, he said, "Enough of peddlers! Now for a run with my greys. I may not have them very long. Let's enjoy them while I do."

21

'I am not sure if there is a Heaven," Davenant shouted to Willoughby above the babble of voices surrounding them, "but I now know there is a Hell: *a street full of old clothes!*"

In a clamour of Cockney, Yiddish, Irish, Gaelic and English rural dialects, the inhabitants of Monmouth Street, London's oldest used clothing market, voiced their astonishment at the two strangers who walked among them. In a street devoted to the sale of cast-off clothing, their like had never been seen before: two gentlemen dressed in the subdued elegance of superbly tailored garments.

Had it not been for the success of Henry's mission to Somers Town, Davenant and Willoughby would never ever have had cause to visit such a place. However, early in the afternoon a triumphant Henry had returned from Somers Town and presented Davenant with a grimy trade card for one '*Patrick Malloy, Chimney Sweep, Figg Alley, Monmouth Street,*' obtained by him during a flirtatious interlude with a housemaid in the house next door to that of Harriette Wilson.

Monmouth Street, just behind St. Giles-in-the-Fields Church–the fields now long gone–was a half mile of narrow curved road lined on each side with three-storey buildings, their ground floors used as shops. Crowded with stalls, open cellars and pedestrians, the street was no place to drive a curricle, let alone a carriage. On Henry's advice Davenant left his vehicle and horses in the comparative safety of his coachbuilder's yard in Long Acre.

"Even if yer could drive down there in a vehicle, folks there would 'ave everyfink off it wot weren't nailed down. More than likely eat the horses for supper, too," Henry said.

As usual Henry exaggerated, but there was truth in what he said. St. Giles parish was home to an odd mixture of rich and poor, the latter a cosmopolitan mix from many parts of the world and the British Isles. The wealthy lived in the northern part, in the squares around the British Museum. The poor, as if seeking succour from the patron saint of lepers, beggars, and outcasts, were huddled in dwellings near the church, the site of a former medieval leper colony. Across the wide High Street from the church was one of London's most famous 'rookeries,' a base and a refuge for thieves, murderers, muggers, footpads, coiners and forgers. The poor Irish immigrants who lived there because they could afford no better, were perceived by the rest of society as being guilty by association with the criminals. St. Giles' polyglot multitude also included Lascars, Asian sailors of the East India Company, forced to survive on the streets until rehired for an outward bound company vessel; black men and women, former slaves and servants, known locally as 'St Giles' Blackbirds,' and many from the English counties, drawn to London in search of work.

In Monmouth Street, Jewish used-clothes dealers plied their trade, while from theadjoining streets of Seven Dials, sellers of songbirds, knife-grinders, street entertainers, crossing-sweepers, hawkers, ballad and print sellers, shoemakers and dog breakers spilled out into the surrounding area. East of the church were the Drury Lane and Covent Garden theatres, frequented by rich and poor alike. These were surrounded by a maze of alleys and courts where the lowest of London's prostitutes offered men 'a threepenny stand-up.'

Though they knew the name Monmouth Street was a synonym for tawdry attire, Davenant and Willoughby were as astonished by the street as its residents were by them. To newcomers like themselves the buildings that lined each side of the street appeared to be brightly festooned as if for a public celebration. Closer inspection, however, revealed that these decorations were not garlands and banners but second, third and fourth-hand dresses, coats, breeches and pantaloons that were for sale. And the roadway itself was crowded with stalls and carts displaying used silk handkerchiefs, parasols, umbrellas, shoes and boots.

Monmouth Street and London's other old clothes markets existed because clothes were more than just a covering to keep a person warm in the cold, dry in the rain, or cool in the heat. In a society in which all clothes were laboriously made by hand, they were also a personal asset that could be resold many times. For the poor and those who suddenly found themselves in reduced circumstances, clothes were currency, trade goods, often the only personal asset of value they possessed to use as security at a pawn shop, or to trade for another item. Clothes found their way into the markets in two ways: their owners rid themselves of them to old clothes dealers who tramped the streets, or they were stolen and fenced there.

To Davenant, who thought nothing of paying three hundred pounds for a coat and changing his shirt several times a day, the notion of wearing another's cast-off attire was repugnant. Even when deeply in debt, he had still bought his clothes from his tailor, running up large bills for which the unfortunate man had waited years for payment.

There was something incongruous, certainly absurd, and even impertinent, about the sartorial elegance of Davenant and Willoughby amid the shabby wardrobe that was Monmouth Street. Because of his height, Davenant was the more noticeable in a dark green coat of superfine cloth, yellow pantaloons, snowy white linen, his cravat tied in a perfect Davenant Drape, his beaver hat worn at a jaunty angle. In response to this showy intrusion, a procession of ragged, unruly boys and girls tagged along behind the interlopers. Dirty, their runny noses in the air, these urchins preened and postured, imitated the men's walk and mimicked the voices of the two 'swells' to the delight of the crowd.

Such disrespect was too much for Henry Rollins, who was behind Davenant and Willoughby. He shook a fist at the boy leading the impromptu parade.

"Be off with yer!" he shouted, "unless yer wants a muzzler from me."

"This will prove more effective than threats, Henry," Davenant said.

He took a handful of small coins from his pocket and flung them high in the air. Before the money even clinked on the filthy cobblestones, the urchins fell upon it in a tangle of flailing arms and legs, yelling and screaming as they fought for it.

"Newgate seize me! Must 'ave all been on the watch wiv telescopes," said Henry, amazed by what happened next.

As if alerted by some sixth sense that there was money to be had, dozens of screaming, yelling children poured out of Monmouth Street's doors, cellars and alleys to join the fray.

Intent on finding Peeper Malloy, Davenant ignored these antics. He and Willoughby elbowed their way ahead through the jostling crowd, and Henry had to run to catch up with them.

Malloy's trade card gave an address in the immediate neighbourhood, but finding it was proving no easy task. In their search for Figg Alley, Davenant and Willoughby had already gone up one side of the street and down the other, jumping over sprawling beggars and skirting open cellars as they went.

"Don't reckon 'as 'ow they bothers with numbers and addresses around 'ere, my lord," Henry said as Davenant sidestepped two small children playing in a puddle. "Maybe we should ask for 'im by name."

"Such perspicacity, Henry!" Davenant drawled. "You surpass yourself."

Although he did not know the meaning of perspicacity, Henry beamed at what he assumed was praise.

"Wot can Hannah Cohen do for such a fine gen'leman?"

A fat woman in a greasy muslin cap and grey gown stepped out from a building hung with women's dresses, whose frills and flounces fluttered gently in the breeze.

Smiling, the woman clawed at Davenant's coat sleeve with dirty, broken fingernails. "Lovely coat, that. Give yer a guinea for it, I will."

Davenant's voice was ice. "Touch this coat at your peril, madam."

Unruffled, Hannah grinned. "A dress is it, then? For a bit o' muslin? Or fer yerself, eh?" She winked. "I hears as 'ow some fine gen'lemen likes wearin' ladies' clothes more than they likes the ladies wots in em."

"I have nothing to *sell* you," Davenant drawled. "I want to buy from you. Not a dress but information, providing you have what I want. *I* will give you a guinea if you can tell me where I can find the one-eyed chimney sweep called Peeper Malloy."

"Why didn't you say so afore?" she said, her eyes on the coin in his hand. "Knows Malloy by sight, I does, but not to speak to. Come to think of it, haven't seen him for a few days. Probably drunk. Strange, ain't seen his wife neither, nor his 'prentices. Figg Alley? Five houses down. Dunno how you missed it."

22

Georgiana, with Addy and her maid, was travelling slowly east along The Strand in her carriage. Georgiana had persuaded her brother to let her stay one more day so she could give Addy a farewell treat before she left: a visit to the Exeter Exchange to see the wild animals there. She wanted Henry to drive them because The Strand was a busy and often congested route to the City's financial district, and her own coachman was unused to such traffic. But Davenant refused her request, saying he needed Henry himself that afternoon, although he did not tell her where he was going,

With his nose pressed to the carriage window, Addy gazed at the goings-on in the street. The carriage had slowed down because of the traffic, so he had more time to enjoy the sights. Not only was Addy excited about the trip, but because Georgiana had told him that Lord Davenant was going to find his grandpapa for him.

Georgiana was of two minds about telling him at first. The short time factor of the wager was cause enough alone for failure. She feared raising the child's hopes, only for him to have them dashed within a few weeks. On the other hand, with everyone in London talking about it, particularly the servants, he was bound to hear about it, so she thought it best that he hear it from her.

"Now dear, dear Addy," she told him, "Lord Davenant will do his very, very, *very best*, but even if he does not find your grandpapa, you will be well taken care of."

Steadfast in his childish belief of his hero's omnipotence Addy cried, "He will! He will!" when she told him. "After all he saved me from the sweep, didn't he?"

Addy liked Georgiana, but he was not sorry she was leaving. He knew it was wrong to think that, but he couldn't help it. She was very kind and made a great fuss of him, it was true, but she treated him like a baby instead of the big boy with 'bottom' that he was. She called him 'dear, dear, *dear* little Addy' and 'my sweet little pet.' It was true he was small for his age—but he did not like to be reminded of it. Then too, she had odd moods. Often when he played or did lessons with her, she would become quiet and stare for a long time at nothing in particular. Sometimes she would burst into tears and sob that she would miss him as much as he would miss her when she left. That was not true for him; he would not be lonely. He would live in the big house with his hero, Lord Davenant, and Mr. Henry would be his friend. Perhaps, if he showed he had even more 'bottom' than before, his lordship would take him for a ride in his curricle.

Georgiana did not like Addy visiting the stables, afraid that he would be kicked by a horse, or learn bad language from the hostlers. However, as a treat she relented sufficiently the morning of their visit to the Exchange to let him go visit the stables to see the horses harnessed to her carriage for their ride.

Just as Addy and Henry stepped out to walk to the stables, a smart carriage, drawn by four of what Henry described as 'real fine cattle' drew up just ahead of them. A distinguished-looking gentleman with silver hair leaned out of carriage window. "You there!" he shouted to Henry. "You're Davenant's man, aren't you? Come here!"

Henry, who acknowledged no man but Davenant as his master, took his time walking to the carriage. He drew himself up to his full height, puffed out his chest and taking great pains not to drop his aitches—even adding a few in places—in the mistaken belief it made him sound dignified, said, "I have that honour, sir, yes. Hand who—hif I may make so bold has to hask—ham I a-speakin to?"

"The Duke of Ryedale."

At this, Henry removed his hat and gave a curt nod of recognition, then stood with his nose in the air and waited for the duke to say more. But the duke was not looking at Henry: his gaze was on Addy.

Henry cleared his throat to attract the duke's attention.

Flustered, the duke said, "Ahem...yes...er...er... are you happy in his lordship's service?"

Henry's reply was emphatic. "Indeed, I ham, sir."

"And...er...er...you would not consider a similar position elsewhere...er... say, with myself?" the duke murmured, his gaze going back to Addy, who peeped up at him.

"Thankee, kindly, sir, but no."

"The boy, there…er…er…one of your stable boys, is he?'

"That he hain't!" Henry said, indignant. "A little gen'lman, he his. His lordship's pro-toe-jay. Lives wiv him, he does, at Davenant House."

"Ah, yes. The boy…in the wager," the duke muttered to himself. He looked again at Henry. "Well…er… if you should…er…change your mind about my offer…"

The duke handed his card to Henry and told his coachman to drive on.

"Such fine horses, Mr. Henry!" Addy said as they watched the carriage drive away. "Will you leave his lordship to work for that gentleman?"

"Newgate seize me! Course not! Lost without me, 'Is Nibs would be," said Henry, relieved that now the duke had gone he could drop his aitches once more.

Georgiana let down one of the carriage windows, letting in the sound of the traffic's roar, the many smells of the street and the ever-present, ubiquitous specks of London soot. She leaned out the window. About a hundred yards ahead, covered in paintings of animals and signs proclaiming its attractions, the three storeys of the Exeter Exchange jutted out unevenly into The Strand. Addy's eyes, however, were on a much more interesting advertisment for the menagerie; across the street from the carriage a grumpy looking camel was being lead up and down the pavement by an attendant.

"We're nearly there," Georgiana said, but the roars of the lions and tigers inside the Exchange that made Addy shiver drowned out her voice

Addy was not the only one frightened by these sounds. Prompted by instinct, the carriage horses, sensing danger, reared and squealed. The vehicle lurched, flinging Georgiana and Addy back against their seats. One of the footmen perched behind the carriage lost his balance and was thrown to the ground. The roars of the big cats prompted growls and screeches from the menagerie's other animals. Again and again, the terrified horses reared and squealed, causing the vehicle to jerk and rock wildly, while the coachman, almost as scared as his charges, struggled to bring them under control.

Frightened though she was, Georgiana was not a woman for faints and hysterics. With a sharp slap to the face she silenced her maid's hysterical outburst, and then set about trying to open the carriage door so that they could all get out. Rolling from side to side on his seat, Addy wished it was Mr. Henry driving and not Lady Georgiana's coachman; Mr. Henry would know what to do! But determined to demonstrate the 'bottom' expected of a future colonel of the British Army, he did his best to be brave.

Passing horses being frightened by animal noises from the Exchange were a regular occurrence. Other than giving the frightened horses a wide berth, pedestrians paid little heed unless they became as violent a spectacle as Georgiana's thrashing horses were fast becoming. Then they would stand and watch the performance from a safe distance but make no attempt to go to the aid of a vehicle's passengers. So it was in this case that a mob of men, women and children quickly gathered to watch the drama. None of them made any attempt to go to the assistance of the carriage's occupants until three gentlemen elbowed their way from the back of the crowd and ran toward the carriage.

23

"Hallo, there! Anyone about? "

Davenant's voice echoed hollowly across Peeper Malloy's yard.

There was no answer.

Davenant looked about him. A high brick wall topped with iron spikes separated the yard from the dilapidated three-storey buildings surrounding it, their windows either boarded up or stuffed with rags. Bags of soot were stacked in every available spot, the acrid smell of their contents hung heavy in the air. Against one wall leaned a tumbledown building with broken windows and missing roof tiles. The only other building was a small wooden shed against which was propped a wooden handcart.

Figg Alley, Peeper Malloy's address, turned out be but another of the thousands of alleys secreted away in that shadowy other London beyond both the sight and comprehension of those who lived in the fashionable West End. Small wonder Davenant and Willoughby had passed it by without noticing it; all that remained of the street sign was the grey silhouette it had left on the blackened wall at its entrance. Flanked on either side by tall, dirty, windowless walls, the narrow dark alley ended at a rickety wooden fence on which a sign advertised Malloy's business. The palings of the gate and fence were so loose, it took only a prod from Davenant's cane for the unlocked gate to creak part way open on rusty hinges and reveal the empty yard.

After calling several times and receiving no response, Davenant sent Henry to search the hut while he and Willoughby investigated the brick hovel. There was no reply to his knock, and finding the door unlocked, Davenant and Willoughby entered.

"Good Lord!"

Davenant had anticipated dirt and squalor, but not destruction.

There were white ashes in the grate and what little furniture there was had been smashed. A toppled dresser lay on the floor, its metal dishes scattered, and its few china plates smashed. A small wooden table lay on its side, its legs broken;

the remains of a meal that must have been on it–cheese covered in thick green mould and meat swarming with maggots–lay strewn across the dirt floor among broken wooden chairs and stools.

"Someone obviously left in a hurry," Davenant remarked. He shuddered. The room was cold; its stone walls, bare except for a faded print of St. Paul's Cathedral, exuded damp. Unlike in the yard, there was only the faintest whiff of soot, but there was a much stronger odour: one that made both men quickly take out handkerchiefs and cover their noses with them. Recognition of it chilled Davenant. He had known it often enough while with the army during General Moore's retreat to Corunna–the smell of death.

It came from the curtained doorway of an adjoining room. Davenant raised the ragged fabric with his cane. In the room beyond was a bed covered with a tattered quilt.

"At least one person was in no hurry to leave," Davenant said quietly. "No hurry at all."

Willoughby peered around his friend. He was unable to prevent a shudder. On the floor, lay the body of the chimney sweep Peeper Malloy, his one good eye staring up at the ceiling,

24

Outside in the yard once more, Davenant took several deep breaths to rid his nostrils of the hovel's stench.

"Damn!" he said, his voice echoing back to him from the walls of the surrounding buildings.

Only a few hours after his search began and his hopes of discovering Addy's true identity in just a few days had been shattered; the person who was the key to the matter lay dead. Inwardly he cursed himself; he should have reckoned on something like this happening. Violence and death were commonplace enough in St. Giles; but full of confidence, he had not considered that might happen to Peeper Malloy.

But his disappointment was momentary; it vanished with the realisation that Malloy's death represented an even greater challenge to his ingenuity than when he began his quest earlier that day. To have found Malloy alive and able to tell him from whom he acquired Addy would have been too easy, the matter solved within a few days, or even that afternoon, his undertaking shorn of the stimulation it offered and the urgency its completion in three weeks demanded. Someone must know from whom Malloy bought the boy: a wife, children and other climbing boys. But they were not in the yard.

Sickened by the stench in the hovel, the queasy Willoughby had headed for the door first, leaving Davenant to investigate the murder scene, for murder it had been. When he knelt to inspect the body, he noticed faint ligature marks around the sweep's neck. Robbery had been the motive—that was evident. Close by was an open tin box with a lock that had been forced and in it were a few small coins. A couple of bricks had been yanked from the wall to reveal a cavity just large enough to hold the box. Judging from the destruction in both rooms, either Malloy had put up quite a fight, or his killer ransacked them in search of valuables. But the murderer must have been either in a hurry or clumsy, for he had missed something of value. Closer inspection of the body revealed Malloy's fingers clutched a few links of chain from which hung a fob seal. With some difficulty Davenant managed to pull the chain from between Malloy's by then rigid fingers.

Outside in the daylight, Davenant studied the fob. Made of gold, it was dirty and needed a polish; but he could make out the intertwined Roman letters 'ABC' on the seal's face and what appeared to be–of all things–an elephant's head superimposed on them. It was not an item a sweep would use or could afford to buy. There were only two ways Malloy could have acquired it: either he found it, or he stole it. Knowing the reputation of chimney sweeps, Davenant was sure it was the latter.

Henry, his green and gold-striped waistcoat smudged with soot, emerged from the yard's only other building.

"Them geese is gone," he said, pointing to a small enclosure surrounded by wooden bars that was empty but for some straw and an overturned plate. "From wot I can see I reckons as 'ow the climbing boys slept in the shed, guv. Nuffink left there now, 'cept this," he said, holding up a bundle knotted in a grimy blue silk handkerchief. He undid it and spread its contents on top of some bags of soot: two silver buttons, an ivory one, an inexpensive snuff box with the picture on its lid of a man and woman having sex, two dirty silk handkerchiefs of indeterminate colour, a few halfpennies and farthings and, sparkling among this dross, a small gold ring on a chain.

Davenant held it up to the light. "Not what one expects to find in a hole like this," he remarked to the still white-faced Willoughby.

His friend was about to reply, but Davenant's frown stopped him.

Over Willoughby's shoulder, Davenant had spotted a sudden movement behind a row of bags of soot piled a few feet high in the middle of the yard. Motioning Henry to stand by the gate, he went to one end of the row and with a nod indicated that Willoughby go to the other. When everyone was in place, Davenant leaped forward and made a grab behind the bags. His objective–a small and very dirty boy–yelled in fright. Seeing his route blocked by Davenant one way and Willoughby the other, the boy scrambled up over the bags of soot to escape. He slipped and fell into the mud but quickly picked himself up and scooted, head down, toward the gate–and straight into Henry's waiting arms.

A JACKETING CONCERN

The boy struggled to escape, but Henry held firm. He gripped hold of the boy by an ear and holding his writhing prisoner at arm's length to prevent being covered in soot, marched him back to Davenant.

"Newgate seize me!" Henry said with disgust. "His face is dirty enough to grow mustard and cress on it!"

Willoughby groaned and buried his face in his handkerchief.

Both hands resting atop his cane, Davenant eyed the squirming boy.

"Your powers of description, Henry, are as graphic as they are dyspeptic," he drawled.

The boy was so small, his age was hard to guess. Except for two white circles around his eyes, his entire face, neck, arms and legs were as black as ebony, covered by an accumulation of ingrained soot that hid any distinguishing features. His body was so thin, his filthy shirt and coat hung limp from it like washing on a line, and his too short, tattered trousers exposed skinny legs, bony ankles and bare feet.

"Your name?" Davenant demanded.

The boy stood silent and sullen.

Davenant's eyes narrowed. A menacing tone replaced his drawl. "Perhaps you did not hear me the first time…*your name?*"

"Bodger," muttered the boy, recognising an implied threat when he heard it.

"Bodger what?"

"*Bodger!* Nuffink else!"

"A succinct appellation," said Davenant. "Baptism must have taken all of two seconds. Why were you hiding?"

" I weren't hidin.' I work 'ere–leastways I did work 'ere."

"Then perhaps you can explain how the dead body of your employer came to be lying in there," Davenant said, turning as if to lead the way back to the hovel.

"No! No! Not in there! I wont! No! No!" Bodger yelled as he fought unsuccessfully to free himself from Henry.

"Did you kill him?"

Henry held Bodger's arms behind his back. Breathless from his exertions, Bodger shouted, "No! No! I didnt do nuffink! Honest! Honest! Mick did it.

Killed Malloy, he did."

"Let him go, Henry," Davenant said quietly.

Henry let go his hold. As Bodger staggered back something fell to the ground from inside his clothing. He bent quickly to retrieve it. Before he could thrust it back inside his ragged shirt, Davenant took it from him: a half-eaten crust of bread so dry it crumbled under the light press of fingers.

Davenant stared at the crumbs on his gloved hand. The price of bread had soared because of the war with Napoleon. A loaf now cost the same as twenty pounds of potatoes. For someone as poor and half-starved as Bodger, dry breadcrumbs were preferable to no bread at all.

"When did you last eat, Bodger?" The gentleness in Davenant's voice surprised Willoughby and Henry.

Bodger hung his head in silence.

"I think food, rather than threats and force, will prove more effective in loosening your tongue," Davenant said.

25

Addy rubbed his face against the lion cub's tawny fur, feeling the animal's warm body vibrate with the purrs of its owner dozing contentedly in his arms. Just a few months old, the cub was nevertheless heavy, and Addy had sat on a bench so that he could maintain his hold in comfort. The air in the Exeter Exchange was warm and heavy, redolent with the smells of straw and the humid sweetness of animal dung; these and the cub's rhythmic purrs made Addy feel sleepy and his arms slackened as he relaxed.

"Careful, Addy, or you will drop him!" warned Georgiana, who sat beside him.

Addy raised his head and tightened his grip. Being allowed to cuddle the lion cub was his reward for being brave earlier when the frightened horses of Lady Georgiana's carriage nearly bolted. Sir Thomas Hurley, Mr. Rupert Basingthwaite and Captain Allen, who were strolling nearby, had seen the plight of the carriage and its occupants and rushed to the rescue. Cheered on by the crowd, Captain Allen scrambled on to the box of the lurching coach to aid the struggling coachman. Meanwhile, his companions, despite the danger from the rearing horses, managed to grasp the bridles of the lead animals. It was only after they had brought the vehicle and its horses under control that the three men discovered the identity of its passengers.

"Thank Heaven, Lady Hesston, that we were here," Mr. Basingthwaite said as he helped her from the carriage.

Although a little unnerved by the incident, the intrepid Georgiana, soon sufficiently recovered her composure enough to take pleasure in Basingthwaite's admiring glances. She fluttered her eyelashes and leaned on his arm, murmuring, "Brave, brave, *brave* Mr. Basingthwaite. What dreadful fate might we have suffered if you–and these other gentlemen, of course –had not been here? I hardly dare think of it," she added with a particular sigh that made her appear fragile, a sigh she had used to good effect with past admirers

Her performance was cut short by the appearance of Hurley and Addy, who joined them while Captain Allen saw to the carriage's removal from the immediate area of the Exchange.

"I was brave, too, wasn't I, Lady Georgiana?" Addy said eagerly. "I didn't cry or scream, did I—not like your maid," he added with some scorn.

"Yes, oh yes, you were very, very brave!" Georgiana said, clasping him to her in a suffocating embrace. This being no way to treat a young man with 'bottom' in front of gentlemen, an embarrassed Addy struggled to free himself. But his discomfiture was of short duration for the gentlemen were quick to laud his bravery, too.

Captain Allen rejoined them and begged to be allowed to escort Georgiana and her party safely back to Grosvenor Square in the carriage. Georgiana would have none of it. She had brought Addy to the Exchange to see the animals, she said, and would not deny him the promised treat. There was no arguing with her, so the three men insisted they escort her and Addy on their tour. Georgiana, however, had other ideas. Flattered by Basingthwaite's attentions, she decided to enjoy one last flirtation before she returned to Norfolk. There would be no harm in it, she told herself: after all, she would be leaving tomorrow.

"I declare that after all that has happened, I am too fatigued to climb several flights of stairs," she said as they entered the building. "May I presume on your kindness still further, Mr. Basingthwaite?" she said with another of her special sighs. "Although I must confess I find the noises of the animals alarming; nevertheless, I will remain here on the ground floor and rest. Would you be so good as to procure a chair and a glass of water for me?" She smiled at Hurley and Allen. "And would you gentlemen be so kind as to show Addy and my maid the animals?"

Basingthwaite was only too eager to allay her fears and remain with her. "No gentleman would permit a lady to stay unescorted in such a public place," he assured her. "It will be not only an honour but a pleasure to stay here with you."

Much taken with Georgiana, the captain wanted to stay, too, but he had to content himself with complying with her request to escort Addy. So for over an hour Addy and Georgiana's maid, accompanied by Hurley and Allen, toured the brightly painted rooms, looking at the lions, tigers, monkeys, bears and wolves caged in them.

A JACKETING CONCERN

They returned to the ground floor to find Georgiana and Basingthwaite deep in conversation. This intimate *tête-a-tête* annoyed the jealous Allen, who was anxious to get into Georgiana's good graces. For a shilling patrons could hold a lion cub for a short while. Allen offered this treat for Addy.

It had the desired effect on Georgiana. "*Quelle bonne idée!* A reward for being a brave boy," she said, giving the captain a devastating smile.

"Her name's Dora," the attendant said when he gave the cub to Addy. "Her ma's dead."

"Oh, and so is my mama," said Addy. Tenderly, he nuzzled Dora's head with his chin. Dora yawned and licked one of his hands. He giggled. "It tickles…" he began, but shouts and yells from the top of the staircase stopped him.

"Give way! Give way! Animal escaped!" a voice yelled.

Immediately alert, Dora leaped from Addy's arms to the floor and stood, her tail swishing, her bright golden eyes fixed on the staircase. Down it on all fours came a monkey, weaving in and out among the frightened patrons on the stairs. Behind the animal came an attendant brandishing a whip. No sooner it reached the bottom of the stairs, the monkey saw Dora. It screeched in fright. One look at each other was enough for both animals: blind instinct took over. No matter that Dora was not full-grown; to the monkey she was a predator. There were no trees for it to climb to safety, but there was an open door. In a sudden dash on all fours, the monkey was out in the street.

Born in captivity, Dora had not yet learned to hunt; but she responded from her innate instinct for the chase. She sprang after the monkey and disappeared through the open door.

"Dora! Dora! Come back, Dora!" Addy yelled, running on impulse after the cub.

"Addy! Come back?" Georgiana called as she ran after him. But two of the Exchange's attendants who had gone after the cub got in her way and she was unable to reach him.

Drawn by the excitement below, the customers on the upper floors rushed downstairs, swelling the number of those on the ground floor as they pushed forward through the front door, eager to see what was happening outside. Thrust along by this crowd, Georgiana was shoved through the open door, Basingthwaite, Allen and Hurley trying to push their way from behind to reach her. Bruised and scratched, her dress torn, Georgiana was pushed and pulled this way and that when shouts of "Lion escaped!" and "Man-eating lion loose!" sent the throng into a frenzied panic. Her head swam and she felt faint. Someone trod on her foot: she screamed. Unable to maintain her balance, she felt herself slithering to the ground. She screamed again, this time not in pain but at the realisation she was about to be trampled underfoot.

On top of a lamppost a short way from the Exeter Exchange, the monkey sat alternately barring its teeth and screeching at the lion cub circling the post. A noisy crowd, titillated by fear and anticipation, gathered a safe distance away clamouring for blood like an audience at a Roman arena. But after several unsuccessful attempts to scale the post, the cub lost interest and padded away. Wanting a spectacle, the bystanders would have none of it; they hooted and shouted at her. Scared and confused, the cub went on the defensive. Like an alley cat she barred her teeth at the onlookers, hissed and swished her tail from side to side

Addy pushed his way to the front of the crowd. "Dora," he called. Don't be afraid."

And before anyone could stop him, he ran to her.

This swift action alarmed the cub even more. She turned and raced across the road, sending the frightened crowd scattering before her. Just then a brewery wagon loaded with beer barrels and pulled by four Clydesdales turned from a side road in front of her. The cub was across the street before the horses were aware of her, but Addy, running behind, found him almost under the hooves of the vehicle's lead horses.

A hand suddenly grabbed his shoulder from behind.

"Thank God, we reached you in time!" said Basingthwaite pulling him back to the pavement just as Willoughby reached them.

26

Unable to breathe, Bodger writhed in Davenant's unremitting grip, his arms wildly flailing the air, his eyes bulging as if about to pop out of his black face. Contrary to his earlier stated intention not to use force on the boy, it appeared Davenant had changed his mind. With the thumb and forefinger of one gloved hand he tightly pinched closed Bodger's nostrils, while his other held shut the boy's mouth

Across the table from them, Willoughby looked up from studying his pocket watch. "One minute, exactly," he announced.

Davenant let go his hold.

"Yer…nearly…killed me," Bodger panted, gasping for air

With a rueful glance at the soot stains on his York tan gloves, Davenant said, "Nonsense! Merely my old nurse's tried-and-true remedy for the hiccups."

The three of them were in a cook shop that Henry had found for them in Great White Lion Street, a turning off Monmouth Street, and one of the seven streets that formed the points of the star-shaped Seven Dials. It was here the locals with no ovens or kitchens brought the dishes they prepared at home to be cooked, or bought already cooked food.

"Smells like someone farted, it does," was Henry's description of the gaseous reek of boiled cabbage that assailed their nostrils as they walked in.

Willoughby turned white and reached for his handkerchief.

Henry shrugged. "This grubbery is about the only eatin' place you'll find about here."

The cabbage smell was borne on vapour from the kitchen that misted the shop's windows, making it difficult for some ragged bystanders in the street to see the two 'swells' inside. They pushed and shoved for a better view, their noses flattened against the dirty windowpane like pig's snouts snuffling in a trough. The few customers at the counter were mostly women in tawdry finery, their faces powdered and heavily rouged. One glance at them was enough to tell Davenant the cook shop was where local prostitutes ate–if they could afford it–before beginning their evening's work in Covent Garden's dingy streets and alleys.

"I think she is giving me the eye," Willoughby remarked when one of the younger women winked at him.

Bodger, who was fast stuffing the remnants of his dinner in his mouth, cocked an eye in the woman's direction and grinned. Between mouthfuls, he said, "That ain't… all she'll… give yer. That's…Sweaty Betty. She's got…the clap."

Willoughby winced and looked away.

Despite the shortcomings of his dirty establishment, the shop's owner at first balked at admitting such 'a filthy little devil' as Bodger. But at the sight of Davenant's gold, he obligingly cleaned off the crumbs from the shop's only table, dusted off the benches and laid out some iron spoons.

Given his rapid consumption of a large meal, Bodger's violent attack of hiccups was inevitable. Kept half starved by Malloy and never knowing when he would get his next meal, Bodger had learned to eat whatever food he could get as soon as he got it. The meal Davenant ordered for him was the sort of food he could only dream about before. Hardly stopping for breath, he put away a mountain of boiled mutton, baked potatoes, soggy cabbage and a pint of porter from a nearby tavern. Now he ogled what was to be the climax of this feast: a slab of suet pudding studded with lumps of fat the size of walnuts on the plate before him. He closed his eyes and inhaled the pudding's aroma. He opened them to see Davenant push the plate out of his reach.

"Starvin' I am!" he said, indignant.

"Poor devil!" murmured a haggard but lavishly rouged prostitute as she passed the table. There was a chorus of sympathetic murmurs from her sisters at the counter.

An icy stare from Davenant silenced them.

"You may have it," he told Bodger, "*after* you have taken time to digest what you have already eaten, and *after* you have told me what I wish to know."

Bodger sighed, then, recalling Henry's whispered admonitions to be respectful to his benefactor, he added a reluctant "Yes…sir."

"Why did you run away in the yard?"

"I thought you wuz the constable, didnt I? Or the beadle. The constable would fink I killed Malloy cos I wuz the only one in the yard–but I didn't, *honest!* It wuz Mick wot done it. But whose gonna believe me? A climbin' boy?"

"I believe you," Davenant said quietly, "but why did you go back to the yard?"

"To get me fings, that's why."

"You mean these?" From his coat pocket Davenant took the handkerchief containing the trinkets Henry found in the hut. Bodger stuffed it inside his torn shirt.

"And this?" Davenant held up the gold chain and ring. Bodger made a grab for it, but Davenant was too quick for him, and he put it back in his pocket.

"The theft of these alone could get you hung or sent to Botany Bay?"

'Botany Bay? Where's that then? Other side o' the river?"

"The other side of *the world.*"

"Cor!" Bodger said, impressed.

"From whom did you steal them?"

"I didn't. Well…not really," Bodger said. "The ring an' that Malloy took from the new boy."

Davenant eyed him with suspicion.

Bodger responded with righteous indignation. "Took it back, I did. Lookin' after it for him, I wuz."

"The boy named Addy?"

Bodger's reaction surprised Davenant.

His eyes suddenly filled with tears that ran down his cheeks, leaving lighter streaks on his sooty face so that it resembled the hide of a zebra.

"He wuz my best mate," Bodger sobbed. "An' he's dead now cos of that bastard, Mick." His teary eyes looked forlornly at Davenant. "He wuz a baby, he wuz.'E didn't know nuffink about anyfink. Looked after 'im, I did…'cept I didn't look after 'im good enough cos now he's dead," and he covered his face with his hands and continued to bawl.

Davenant sat silent until Bodger's sobs gradually died away. Then he said quietly, "I have the honor to inform you that Addy is not dead, but very much alive. He has recovered from his fall and is now being well cared for at my home."

Bodger looked up, a huge grin on his tear-stained face. "*Honest?* Mick and Malloy said Addy wuz dead—or as good as, any rate."

"You have my word as a gentleman."

Since their encounter in the sweep's yard Bodger had been by turns hostile, suspicious and guarded. Now he knew Addy was alive, any lingering resentment he felt toward Davenant evaporated in a burst of cordiality.

"A gen'leman an' a scholar, you are, an' no mistake," he said. He held out his hand to Davenant. "Here, tip us your daddle! Any mate of Addy's is a mate o' mine, too!"

Davenant tried not to notice the damage Bodger's sooty paw inflicted on his yellow glove as they shook hands. "You too, guv!" Bodger said, holding out his hand to Willoughby.

By now the three at the table were the only ones beside the owner remaining in the shop. Only a few gawkers remained outside the steamed up window, watching them as they might a Punch and Judy show in the street.

Satisfied there was no one in immediate earshot, Davenant said to Bodger, "Do you know how Malloy came by Addy?"

Bodger shook his head. "Nah. Master just brung 'im to the yard one day cos t'other boy died in the hospital. Addy wuz fast asleep, an 'e slept a long time. Reckons as 'ow they musta give 'im somefink to knock 'im out."

Bodger's gaze strayed to the suet pudding. Davenant pushed it further away.

Bodger sighed.

His life of hardship might have toughened him, but it had not deprived Bodger of feeling, for with some emotion he went on, "Master and the Missus laid 'im down on some sacks of soot and left. Sat and watched 'im for a bit, I did. Looked like a baby, 'e did. So white! I knew as 'ow we would be mates. He opened is eyes and looks around the shed where we slept real puzzled. It's dark in there, an' yer cant see well…but we seed each other."

He grinned. "Well right away I sees he ain't daft like t'other one. 'Tip us yer daddle, sez I. Lets you an' me be mates, cos there's only really the two of us. The young un—the master's boy—he's daft and lives in the 'ouse. The others ain't too bright, either."

Bodger leaned toward Davenant as if to tell him a secret. "Leastways, master finks the boy is his. I reckons he's Mick's. See him and Nell at it, I have… through the window. When her's on the Blue Ruin her don't know who she's doin' it wiv."

"Blue ruin?"

"Yer don' t know much, do yer? Just like Addy. I 'ad to tell 'im, too. Blue Ruin's gin!'"

Davenant's lips twitched in amusement at the condescension in Bodger's tone. He guessed the boy to be about ten years old, although his knowledge of the world and cocky manner made him appear older. Bodger had not known childhood, only hardship and violence. Yet it had not crushed his spirit, or left him devoid of feeling. From the way he spoke, it was obvious he had revelled in the role of Addy's mentor and protector; it made him feel important.

"Do you 'ave a grandpapa?" Bodger asked suddenly. Davenant's lip's twitched again. "I did," he said. "He is now dead."

"Addy said he had one. Wanted to find him," he did. "Not me," Bodger went on. "From the workhouse, I am. Ain't goin' back there." He clenched his fists and pointed the index and middle fingers of each hand at Davenant in imitation of two pistols. "Get me a pair of muzzlers, I will, and go on the high toby."

"A highwayman, eh? They usually end their days kicking the clouds from the hangman's noose outside Newgate Prison?" Davenant said.

"Gotta catch me first, they 'ave," said the cocky Bodger. "An' *I* knows a thing or two, I does," he added with a wink.

"Enough of your future ambitions! It's Addy that interests me—not you."

"All right, all right, keep yer shirt on! I said I'd tell yer, an' I will," Bodger said. "Well, he wuz scared bout goin' up a chimney. I told him wot would 'appen so he wouldn't be scared." He gave an impish grin. "Sometimes I did scare him… just jokin' though. Like when I told 'im about this 'orrible, 'orrible, pain that a climbin' boys often gets about the jockum."

"Jockum?"

"Yer jokey. Yer know," Bodger grabbed the crotch of his ragged trousers.

"I take it you mean one's privates."

"Privates? Is that what yer calls it?" Bodger snickered. He leaned forward and whispered, "When it gets real bad, they takes yer to the 'ospital and they cuts it out—*wiv a knife!*"

"What a delightful sense of humour," Davenant remarked to Willoughby. "I think he refers to cancer of the scrotum, a disease common among climbing boys."

Willoughby shuddered.

"Don't do no good, though. The operation?" Bodger said. "Most dies. That's wot 'appened ter Dan. He didn't wanna go ter horspital. Master didn't wanna take 'im either cos 'e wouldn't be able to work. Nell made 'im though." His eyes narrowed and he said in a deep voice, "And 'e never comes back—*not never!* An' I hopes as how Mick'll have ter go to hospital and have 'is cut off, too. An' I hope's as 'ow it hurts 'im like hell!"

"Ah, yes, Mick. He killed, Malloy, you say?"

"Well I seed 'im, didn't I? Malloy locked us boys in the shed at night, but I worked some boards loose, I did, so I could go outside for a piddle. Don't like doin' it in a bucket cos it smells. Sees him and Nell through the window, I did. She'd been at the gin shop, she 'ad. Reckon she met Mick there cos Master 'ad turned him off days afore. Standin' over the body, Mick wuz. They took off… all of em: Mick, Nell and the boy."

"Why would Mick want to kill Malloy?"

"Reckons Malloy found out about him and Nell and they got into a fight. Malloy wuz really angry with Mick for losing Addy. Mick's been in trouble with the law before. Killed someone so I 'eard, up west. Wuz scared they'd fink 'e let Addy die. Mick dragged me back to the yard, he did, and Malloy sacked him on the spot fer losing Addy. Only just bought 'im, he had cos he'd lost Dan. Didn't like losing his money."

Bodger gazed upon the suet pudding as a lover gazes on his beloved. Davenant shook his head, so Bodger went on with his story.

Malloy spent several days trying to find out what had happened to Addy, Bodger said, because he, too, feared trouble with law. About a week ago, a few days afore he died, Malloy came home one day with more money than he made in a week. Davenant guessed this was the money he paid Malloy to be rid of him.

"Malloy and Nell went out drinking with it. Didn't come home all night. That's when this 'swell' called," Bodger said. "Upset he was cos Malloy weren't there. Queer one, he wuz. Reckons as 'ow he wanted people to think he was someone else."

"Why do you say that?"

"He pretended to talk like old McLeod wot sells birds up at the corner here." And rolling his Rs with relish, Bodger mimicked a Scots accent. "Couldn't keep it up, though, this geezer, so I knew 'e wuz just pretending. Asked questions 'bout Addy, he did."

"Did you know him? Would you know him again if you saw him?"

"Didn't see his face cos it wuz late at night and dark…but know his voice, I would, anywhere."

"And then a few days later Mick returned, killed Malloy and took off with Nell and the child, and Malloy's money?"

" 'Sright."

"I must find Nell. She must know from whom Malloy bought Addy. Do you know where Mick and Nell are now?"

Bodger grinned. "Wiv Malloy's money first thing they'd do 'ud be a tavern crawl till the money ran out. An' knowin' the way they drink, that wouldn't be long."

"And after that?"

"Dunno for certain…but I'd guess the Holy Land…round Charles St."

"The rookery?"

Bodger nodded. "Best place for Malloy to hide from the law. No one finds yer there even if someone rats on yer, cos constables too scared to go there to get yer."

Satisfied Bodger had told him all that he knew, Davenant suggested he accompany him to a magistrate to report Malloy's murder.

Bodger shook his head. "They won't believe me, guv. They'll fink it wuz me wot done it."

Davenant had no chance to reply, for just then Henry, who had been dispatched to the watch house to report finding Malloy's body, arrived with a constable.

Violent deaths being a regular occurrence in St. Giles, the constable was indifferent about his task. If he thought it unusual for two gentlemen to visit a sweep's yard, he did not say so. He asked a few questions, and then requested Davenant and Willoughby accompany him to the watch house to give statements.

When Davenant turned to speak to Bodger again, the boy had gone—and so too had the much-coveted slab of suet pudding.

27

With a pained expression Davenant looked down at Georgiana, who lay against his chest sobbing as if her heart would break.

"Georgiana, I beg of you," he entreated, "do have a care for this waistcoat. It is new and my tailor assures me that there is none quite like it in town."

Georgiana drew back and stared up at him, her eyes brimming with tears. "Odious, odious, *odious* brother!" she wailed. "My life is quite ruined and all you can think of is…is…your waistcoat!"

Davenant laid her gently back against the pillows and moved from his seat on the bed to a chair next to it. He took a handkerchief from his coat pocket and dabbed at his waistcoat.

"And what is so ruinous about having a child?" he drawled. "After all, it is not as if you are unwed."

With a shriek, Georgiana turned and buried her head in the pillows.

"Did you know about the child before you left Norfolk?"

"Yes. No. Oh… I wasn't sure," came Georgiana's muffled voice from the pillows. "I didn't think it would happen so soon. I didn't want anything to change." She turned back and looked at him. "Having a child seemed so…so… *so* irrevocable."

He raised his quizzing glass and studied her face with some amusement. Her pregnancy explained her uncharacteristic behaviour since she arrived in London; he should have guessed. She would not go home to Norfolk tomorrow as planned; the doctor had ordered her to remain at Davenant House for some time to come.

He had returned home from St. Giles to find his house in uproar yet again: a doctor attending Georgiana in her bedroom; her hysterical maid unable to speak coherently; Puff sitting outside his mistress' closed door wailing like a banshee to be let in; and Mr. Basingthwaite and Captain Allen anxiously pacing the drawing room after escorting Georgiana and Addy home. Sir Thomas Hurley, because of his dislike of Davenant, had declined to accompany them.

From the two gentlemen Davenant learned what happened at the Exeter Change. While they deprecated their own efforts in rescuing Georgiana from the mob and Addy from being run over, they were full of praise for the courage the two of them had shown in such dangerous circumstances. They promised to call again soon to learn how Georgiana fared. After they left, Davenant questioned the doctor and learned his sister was pregnant. She had suffered a twisted ankle, and that would soon mend; but the doctor was adamant she rest and undertake no long journeys for several weeks, until he was sure all was well with her and the child.

Tapping his chin with his glass Davenant studied Georgiana. Among the plump silk pillows she looked small and lost. "Why, if you suspected you were going to have a child, did you leave Norfolk for London in such haste?" he said.

"I didn't want anything to change. I wanted everything to stay the same. I didn't want old harpies counting to nine on their fingers when they saw me."

'I doubt most of them could count to two, let alone nine."

'And I didn't want…I didn't want…" Her voice trailed away.

"You didn't want to grow up and take responsibility for someone else."

Tears rolled down her cheeks again and she nodded. "But then I began taking care of Addy, and oh, Roderick, I found that I really would like being a mama! That it didn't matter so much if I could not go dancing all the time…or go to London every time I wanted."

"You'll be in London for a while, now, whether you like it or not. The doctor insists you remain here and rest."

"The doctor is a fool!" Georgiana wailed. "I must go home–at once! I received a note from Edgar, today. He is very angry I went away. He demands that I return home."

Davenant shook his head. "Out of the question. If I let you travel and something happened to you and the child, I would not forgive myself."

She sat up. "But I *must* go home!"

"Really Georgie you are the most contrary creature. First you do everything you possibly can to remain in London…and now that you are unable to leave, you want to go."

"Dont you see? The baby? Edgar doesn't know!" Her eyes softened. "I must be the one to tell him," she sighed. "I want to see the look in his eyes when I do. To share with him the delight, the pleasure of that precious moment in our lives."

"Write to him."

"*Roderick!*" she said in dismay as she fell back against the pillows. "How would you like to receive a letter telling you that you were going to become a father?"

"In my present bachelor state, I would find such intelligence...er...how should I put it? Disconcerting?"

She saw his lips twitch and she could not help but smile, too.

He patted her hand. "Now, do not worry," he went on. "I will write to Edgar today. I will not mention the child: merely tell him you are under doctor's orders to remain in London. And I'll suggest he join you here so that he can escort you home when the doctor thinks you are well enough to travel. You would like that wouldn't you?"

She smiled and nodded eagerly.

"Meanwhile, you can continue to supervise Addy's care from your bed, although he cannot remain sleeping in your dressing room. Your maid should sleep there instead, in case, in your present state, you have need of her at night."

"But where will Addy sleep? Not in the nursery! It's dusty and full of cobwebs."

"He can have Perry's room. It's next to your dressing room, so he will be close by."

"So everything is settled. And if it makes you feel better, I'll even suffer you to change the furniture about again–well, occasionally that is," he said.

Georgiana dabbed her eyes with a handkerchief

"That's right. Dry your tears. Edgar will come around. Forget what happened this afternoon. With rest, you will recover, and your child will be well, for it appears you did not suffer any great harm."

"And all because of those brave men: Mr. Basingthwaite, Captain Allen and Sir Thomas Hurley. You will thank them won't you?"

"I have thanked two of them, though I fear Hurley is in no hurry to receive my thanks."

Georgiana's eyelids began to droop as she nestled down under the bedclothes.

He sat with her for a little longer until she began to drift off to sleep. As he opened the bedroom door to leave, she murmured drowsily that he was "truly the dearest, dearest, *dearest* of brothers."

Davenant closed the bedroom door behind him and leaned against it with a sigh of resignation. Georgiana would be staying with him for some time, and now he, who was not given to rash gestures, had made one: he had promised to invite her stuffy husband to stay, too. Climbing boys, sisters and brothers-in-law: his tranquil bachelor establishment was fast becoming a hotel.

After the day's events he needed the calm of his study. He was about to descend the staircase when he became aware of muffled sobs nearby. He looked both ways along the corridor; there was no one in sight. He frowned. Who was crying? Where were they?

At the end of the corridor, a Chinese vase, as wide as it was tall, stood by the wall, partly obscuring a sofa from his view. On impulse he went and walked around it. There, on the red brocade sofa Addy sat hugging Puff while he sobbed his heart out.

In the commotion surrounding Georgiana's return home, everyone had forgotten Addy.

"Oh, Puff," he moaned, "it's my fault Lady Georgiana is hurt. Per…per…perhaps she will die! The…the…then…Lord Davenant would be very cro…cro…cross with me…and…and he will not find grandpapa." His shoulders shook and he buried his face in Puff's fur.

"Maybe…he'll send me back to…to…to the sweep man!"

Davenant raised his quizzing glass and peered at Addy. It was the first time he had been alone with the child who was the object of his wager, for until now that was how he thought of him: an object. But now he was face to face with this sentient human being, he was not sure what to do. He had always thought of children–on the rare occasions he did think of them–as nuisances, like wasps buzzing too close on a summer's day. Children were alien to him, and sobbing children were even more so.

Puff noticed Davenant first. He wriggled free of Addy and jumped to the floor, preparatory to an assault on the tassels of Davenant's Hessians.

"Sit!" Davenant said, his automatic response whenever Puff came close.

Puff obeyed.

Addy looked up in anguish at the sound of Davenant's voice. Unaccountably touched by this sight, the usually self-assured Davenant did not know what to say, or do. He continued to stare at the boy through his glass for some time. Addy stared back, tearful and anxious. Feeling foolish just standing there, Davenant sat down next to him.

In silence the two eyed each other uneasily.

Finally, after clearing his throat several times, Davenant said quietly, "You must not blame yourself for what happened. It was not your fault the lion escaped. Lady Georgiana, Mr. Basingthwaite and Captain Allen have explained all. Lady Georgiana told me you were very brave when the carriage horses nearly bolted. Lady Georgiana is not going to die, although she will have to remain in bed and rest for a while.

Addy sniffed. "Really?"

Davenant nodded.

Addy brightened. "And…and did she really say I was brave?" he asked, eagerly.

"You have my word as a gentleman."

Addys tears stopped and the smile he gave Davenant was like sunshine after rain. Again they faced each other in silence. Then Davenant remembered the ring in his pocket.

"This afternoon, I met your friend Bodger."

"Bodger!" Addy exclaimed. "You saw him? Mick didn't kill him?"

Addy's smile widened when Davenant assured him that Bodger had escaped Mick and the sweep.

"He gave me this," Davenant said, dangling the ring and chain. "He was… ahem…looking after it for you."

Addy took them and gently fingered the hair entwined in the gold band. "That is my mama's hair," he said softly. "I don't remember her. Her hair is all I have of her." Sighing with satisfaction, he put the chain around his neck and tucked the ring inside his shirt.

"Thank you! Thank you!" he said, looking up at Davenant with adoration.

Although taken aback by this, Davenant was surprised to find himself gratified by it, too–perhaps more gratified than he cared to admit. "Ahem…do not mention it. And pray, have no fears about my search for your grandfather. I have no intention of discontinuing it."

"And I'll help you," Addy promised. "I'll draw a picture of grandpapa's castle. Then you will know it when you see it."

"Er…yes…most helpful, I'm sure," Davenant humoured him. "And you must promise to behave yourself: not frighten my servants, slide down banisters or bother Lady Georgiana while she is indisposed."

Addy nodded solemnly. Mention of Georgiana's indisposition reminded him of something that was bothering him. "If I'm very, very, good, can I please, please, *please* go to the stables again and see my friends and the horses? Lady Georgiana said I must not go there cos it was not safe." He peeped from under his lashes. "I like her very much but sometimes she…" He stopped. It was wrong to be disrespectful of one's elders or to criticise others.

"Makes a fuss?" Davenant finished for him. "So true. Yes, you may go to the stables. Oh, and instead of Lady Georgiana s dressing room, you will sleep in my brother's room, next door. "

Addy's eyes shone. "Your brother! Who is in the navy? Who was at Trafalgar?"

"Yes, that one. He has several models of ships in his room."

Without Davenant realising it, one of his hands had somehow come to rest on Addy's curls. Embarrassed by this mark of affection, Davenant quickly drew his hand away

Happy at the outcome of this conversation, Addy threw himself against Davenant and hugged him.

Grimacing at this second assault on his waistcoat, Davenant murmured, "Quite ruined, quite ruined."

28

Davenant raised his quizzing glass the better to observe the painting on the wall before him of an amorous encounter between the Greek god Zeus and a nymph. His lips twitched. Such contortions! Well within the purview of the gods, no doubt—but the limited physical capabilities of mere mortals? Still one might try—sometime.

With the grace and dignity of a dowager duchess, his hostess, Mrs. Dewberry, a middle-aged lady in a dark blue morning gown and lace cap, poured coffee from a silver pot into a delicate china cup. She glanced at Davenant several times out the corner of her eye as he examined the picture.

"Some gentlemen, particularly those of advanced years, need a little—How shall I put this? —encouragement?" she said of the painting. This was accompanied by an ingratiating smile that crumpled the thick layer of cosmetics on her face into a network of cracks that resembled an old oil painting.

The other paintings in the room were in similar vein: erotic scenes from classical mythology by journeymen artists. Aside from these, the room was furnished with the taste and elegance of a Mayfair drawing room. Such taste and manners were only to be expected of someone who did what Mrs. Dewberry did: daily entertain in her brothel the richest and most powerful men in society. Her house was one of the five high-class bordellos in King's Place, a narrow street between King Street and Pall Mall, establishments whose prices were so high as to exclude all but the wealthiest men. Their close proximity to St James' Palace and their royal patronage had earned them the designation 'King's Brothels.' That put them conveniently beyond the reach of the law as well as adding to their standing. To further enhance her establishment's prestige in a society that regarded all things French as *à la mode,* Mrs. Dewberry often pronounced and wrote her name as Du Barry, the name of a libidinous French king's mistress.

"Jupiter!"

At Mrs. Dewberry's summons, a black boy about twelve years old, who was leaning against a high-backed chair in a corner of the room, ran forward. He represented Mrs. Dewberry's latest attempt to outdo her rivals in King's Place: an African pageboy in exotic garb to wait on her and her clients. To this end he wore a blue silk turban decorated with a white feather pinned with a crystal pin, a long blue brocade tunic and curly-toed, red leather slippers.

"Yes, ma'am," he said in an accent that revealed the closest he had ever come to Africa, or the exotic East, was London's East End.

He took the cup of coffee from his mistress and, grinning broadly, carried it to Davenant, who now sat in an armchair.

If she thought Davenant's call too early in the day, Mrs. Dewberry gave no indication of it. Not for nothing had she been a successful procuress for several decades. Business was business; and her business was to cater to the sexual whims and fancies of wealthy, idle men. If this meant taking her 'nuns' to Brighton in the summer, to Newmarket for the races, or receiving early morning callers, then so be it. These continuing efforts to satisfy her exclusive clientele were making her rich.

Again she smiled at Davenant, the smile of a merchant anticipating a quick, profitable sale. Her surprise at seeing him, and her delight that she might once more count him a client, quickly rid her of the previous ill will she nursed toward him because of his long absence from her establishment. In his younger years he had patronised her house occasionally and been very popular with her girls. 'The Rod,' they called him among themselves, a *soubriquet* that was more a compliment to a particular part of his anatomy than an abbreviation of his Christian name. In recent years his need for female physical company had been met by his *affaires* with fashionable society women, most of whom were married. Mrs. Dewberry had nothing but contempt for women who had sex with men other than their husbands. This was not due to any moral scruples on her part: she had none. No. It was because such women were bad for her business; they took customers from her and gave for free what she offered for a price. How could a poor old woman like her make a living in the face of such competition?

Certain Davenant was there to spend money on one of her high-priced whores, the paint on Mrs. Dewberry's face split into an even finer network of cracks as her smile broadened. But in that belief she was mistaken. 'Peeper' Malloy's death was a setback to Davenant's quest but, far from discouraging him, it had spurred him on. Mick had murdered Malloy for his money, and now Mick, Nell and her son were hiding somewhere in St. Giles' rookery. He must find Nell, for she would know from whom Malloy bought Addy. Yet not even the possibility of arresting a murderer could budge the St. Giles' parish constables to agree to Davenant's suggestion that they search the rookery for the couple. They rarely ventured there, they said. What was the point? In that shadowy warren of passages and alleys, protected by other thieves and cutthroats, a criminal could evade the law forever. Disgusted by the constables' *laissez-faire* attitude, Davenant took action. Honour among St. Giles' criminal population there might be, but the cynic in him was certain there would be at least one person willing for a reward to lead him to the couple's hiding place. He immediately had one posted in the parish. Nevertheless, with only three weeks to accomplish his task, he could not afford to wait idly by for someone to come forward from the rookery, for no one might. In the meantime he must pursue other avenues of enquiry to find someone who knew from whom the boy was bought. There existed an underground market for the buying and selling of children. Many were sold into prostitution; a fate that might have befallen Addy had not the sweep bought him. A drugged Addy could have been passed along a chain of child sellers before reaching the sweep; such a circumstance would make Davenant's job more difficult, but not impossible.

That was why, the morning after his visit to St. Giles, Davenant called on his first alternative line of enquiry: Mrs. Dewberry. Not only did she know about society's sexual predilections, she also knew where and by what means these could be satisfied. In addition, Mrs. Dewberry was a rarity in her profession, a bawd who was honest in money matters and discreet in dealing with her clients. Again, such qualities were not due to moral scruples on her part; it was simply because they worked well for her in business.

"And how might I be of service to your lordship?" she asked, her smile, if anything, even more ingratiating than before.

"Tell me where and from whom one can buy a boy in London?"

Mrs. Dewberry started, causing the coffee to spill from her cup onto the carpet. She was shocked–an unusual state of affairs for someone in her profession.

Little boys? Lord Davenant! Who would have believed it? Was that why he had taken in that climbing boy? And now he wanted another boy–or boys! Why else visit a brothel? Was he bored sexually–or was he finally showing his true colours?

Broad-minded though she was, she disapproved of sodomites and pederasts for the same reason that she did married women who had *affaires;* such behaviours robbed her and other self-respecting bawds of business. Why did they do that? Why couldn't they be like other men and visit her house?

Some of her previous ill will toward Davenant returned. Her eyes narrowed; he'd get no little boys at her house. On the other hand, business was business, and she hated to turn away a customer of Davenant's standing. Maybe he was bored with all those society women and needed a change. She could arrange that.

Davenant's lip twitched at Mrs. Dewberry's reactions. He could guess what was going through her mind. But he cared little what people thought about him, and nothing at all for the opinions of one of Mrs. Dewberry's calling.

Mrs. Dewberry quickly regained her composure. She smiled condescendingly at him. "Providing gentlemen of the highest standing–the highest in the land, she said with a nod in the direction of St. James' Palace–"with introductions to young ladies of beauty, charm and manners is the business of this house. These charmers possess a variety of–How shall I put it? –accomplishments? Whatever a gentleman might desire. Perhaps your lordship is in search of something–How should I put it? –Different? I know of a young lady, one with a slim boyish figure, who–How should I put it? –could be persuaded…for a sum…to dress in boyish attire and –How should put it? –perform like one."

"It appears that you have –How shall I put it? –Mistaken my meaning," Davenant drawled sarcastically. "I asked if you knew where boys can be bought in London–that is all–information for which I'm prepared to pay handsomely."

Mrs. Dewberry put down her coffee cup and was silent while she considered this. At last she gave a sigh of resignation. After all, not only business was business; money was money, whichever way she earned it. She had heard of places, she said: certain public houses in The Strand, certain child wholesalers in St Giles. She mentioned names and places.

"My information is second-hand, naturally, as I have no personal dealings of that sort," she said with a cloying smile.

The glacial reception Miss Barclay, the Quaker philanthropist, gave Davenant when he called on her after leaving Mrs. Dewberry was in harsh contrast to the fawning cordiality of the one he received from the bawd.

Her lips compressed, her cheeks flushed and her blue-grey eyes dark, Miss Barclay received him in the library of her uncle's home in Gracechurch Street. The irony of such a greeting from a professed Christian was not lost on Davenant: his lips twitched in amusement. Undaunted by this display of anger in a woman usually so serene and composed, he was fascinated by it and even–unusually for him–excited by it. He found himself thinking how much better suited a blue gown would match those flashing eyes than the dove grey one she wore.

"I only agreed to see thee," she said, coldly, "because thy note requested my help for a climbing boy...and because of thy interest...thy generous interest...in our cause." She bit her lip. But...but...I would be less than honest," she rushed on, "if I did not tell thee that I was dismayed and...and...yes, angered to read in the public press that you... and your associates...had made that poor climbing boy the subject of a...a...a wager! And more... I learn that his poor innocent boy now resides in your house...the home of a...a..."

Davenant sighed. So she had learned of his reputation.

"A rake? A scrapegrace?" he finished for her.

Her cheeks flamed and she covered them with her hands and turned away. Anger gave way to embarrassment. "Oh! Oh...I did not mean...Oh, I should not think such things, nor say them. It was unpardonable of me."

Davenant's lips twitched again. "You did not say them. I did. And why not say them? Everyone else does." In a quieter vein he went on, "Let me set your mind at rest about the boy. Despite my less than spotless reputation, I give you my word he has not witnessed so much as a single orgy since he came to stay in my home. In fact, no matter what my detractors claim to the contrary, no orgy has ever taken place there."

She turned to him, her expression pained. "You mock me! "

"Indeed, no. Your concern for his welfare… for the welfare of all climbing boys…does you great credit. You will, therefore, be pleased to learn that this particular boy is under the care of my sister, the Countess Hesston, who is staying with me. He sleeps in my brother's bedroom, enjoys three excellent meals a day prepared by my French *chef,* wears Bond Street clothes, drives out in my carriage and is tutored in Latin and other subjects by my secretary, an Oxford scholar."

Miss Barclay stared at him in astonishment.

"And you need have no fear of my…corrupting…influence on the boy," he continued. "I rarely see him. To be honest with you, for the most part I shall be glad to see the back of him. His presence has disrupted what was a tranquil bachelor establishment. As for the wager?" He shrugged. "I stand to gain nothing from it. Indeed the odds are stacked against me. But it does have a positive side. The short amount of time span it gives me to find the boy's family is proving a definite stimulus to my efforts–efforts I had begun prior to the wager."

She considered his words in silence.

Davenant picked up the book she was reading when he arrived. His eyes widened at the title: *A Vindication of the Rights of Women* by Mary Wollstonecraft. Intrigued, he skimmed through it, unaware that Miss Barclay had come to his side.

"Pray forgive…" she began.

He looked at her. Eyes downcast, she looked very contrite.

"Please forgive my previous impertinence," she said. "I am very ashamed of my behaviour. It was wrong of me to condemn thee. The Light exists in everyone, I know, no matter whom. Although I confess that the injustices of the world often anger me so much that I forget that."

Davenant gave a wry smile. What would his secretary say to that? Dingley hoped to take Holy Orders and obtain one of the livings he held. As such, he was intolerant of all Nonconformists and their beliefs. "Why, they believe that the Light shines through all, no matter how lowly," Dingley said, "so they have no regard for rank and status—a situation that would lead to the destruction of society. They also consider dancing, music, elaborate dress, gambling, racing and other diversions as worldly vanities. And they are pacifists: they will not fight!

Davenant's lips twitched. Miss Barclay's greeting had shown no evidence of Quaker pacifism. It was a pity about the dancing, though; he would have enjoyed dancing with her.

"I promise you that you will find it difficult...nay, impossible...to find the... ahem...Light...in me," he said.

She smiled, her eyes shining like sapphires.

"But I do believe I have discerned it in you. Why, your great kindness to one climbing boy in particular...your generosity toward many others...proves it. As for your wager? Perhaps 'tis but an instance of the Lord 'moving in mysterious ways, his wonders to perform.' For the sake of the climbing boy, let us be friends."

He took her outstretched hand and raised it to his lips. "By all means let us be friends—but not just because of the boy."

She blushed, turned away and went and sat in an armchair. Obviously she was not as indifferent toward him as a man as she had appeared when first they met. He took a seat next to her.

"Thou showest great generosity of spirit in thy attitude toward the boy," she said. "'Tis true that all are equal before the Lord, but many in thy position, while showing him charity, would not have treated him as thou hast done...like one of thine own."

He made a self-deprecatory gesture with his hand. "Hardly," he said. "I have not adopted him. That brings me to my second reason for this visit."

"Second?"

"My first was a desire to renew my acquaintance with *you*," he said quietly. "The second reason is the boy, Addy."

Miss Barclay turned pink again and hurriedly said, "The boy is being tutored *in Latin* by your secretary? An Oxford scholar? How can that be? These boys are always ignorant and illiterate. Masters entirely neglect their education. They are supposed to send them to Sunday school...but few, if any, do. Do you know there are more than five hundred climbing boys in London...but only twenty can write their names?"

He told her about Addy's conduct since his arrival at Davenant House.

"A strange tale, indeed," she said. "Certainly his behaviour is not that of the poor wretches who clean chimneys. It must be as thee and thy sister suspect: that he was removed from a genteel family against his will. Does he remember how this happened?"

"No. I suspect it is too painful for him. Nor does he know his family name; I suspect some mystery there. He knows he is an orphan. His grandfather, he says, lives 'in a castle near where a giant sleeps.' No doubt that is a childish fantasy."

She smiled and nodded. "Surely the sweep that bought him can be persuaded to tell you who the seller was."

"That was what I had hoped, but unfortunately when I called upon him, I found him dead."

"Oh!" she gasped. "May his soul rest in peace." She paused a moment then said, "Thou thinkest the League for the Betterment of Climbing Boys can help you? That is the *real* reason for thy visit?"

"Yes," he said, adding with meaning, "although as I have already said, it was not the *only* reason for it."

Miss Barclay was immediately all practicality. "Many climbing boys are illegitimate or parish children, sold by disreputable beadles or workhouse overseers. But most come from, or were enticed, from the poorest of homes. It is quite common…" Tears welled up in her eyes. "Oh, 'tis terrible to relate! Often parents *sell* their children to sweeps for a few guineas or so."

Davenant leaned forward and covered one of her hands with one of his. "And are children sometimes stolen–even from the better sort of homes–and sold to sweeps?"

"Yes. Several years ago…in Yorkshire… there was a case that would appear to parallel that of your climbing boy."

When asked if she or the committee knew the names and locations of those who sold boys to sweeps, she was unable to help. "We know only what the boys whom we care for tell us," she said. "That is not much as they are ignorant, and by the time they come to us, they have forgotten where they come from.

Naturally, those persons who buy and sell children hide their activities from the attention of the authorities."

Charmed by the serenity of her face with its freckled nose and her ever-mysterious blue-grey eyes, Davenant was reluctant to leave. They spoke a little more about climbing boys and her work with them, and then their conversation turned to other subjects. Miss Barclay's education, he learned, had been extensive: a Quaker academy, at which there was no distinction made between the education of girls and boys. And she proved knowledgeable and well read about many subjects, so that more than hour past before either of them realised the time.

That was not the case with Henry Rollins, who sat glumly waiting outside the house in Davenant's curricle. With his coat collar turned up and his hat pulled down over his eyes, Henry hoped none of his pals who happened along would recognise him. His reputation and self-esteem would suffer mightily—or so he thought—if he were seen waiting outside the home of a Cit banker. Waiting for 'Is Nibs outside Mrs. Dewberry's house was a different matter. There was an air of distinction about that. Only rich and fashionable men went there. But Gracechurch Street? People in trade lived and worked there! What did 'Is Nibs want with the likes of them? And why had he stayed so long?

When the front door finally opened, Henry saw Davenant taking leave of Miss Barclay. So that was it! A bit o' muslin! He should have guessed. But a Cit? Henry shook his head.

Davenant climbed into the vehicle and took the ribbons. Noticing Henry's turned up collar, he said, "Have you taken a chill, Henry?"

"No, guv. Don't want anyone to see me *here,* waitin' outside a house full o' Cits!"

"Alas, Henry, you are a snob. You fail to see the Light in them."

But he was thinking of the blue-grey eyes of one Cit in particular, not Cits in general when he said it.

29

The Prince of Wales squeezed Addy close.

Addy winced and fought hard not to cry out when the jeweled star on the prince's blue coat scratched his cheek. As it was, he was uncomfortable enough in his present position without this added hurt, there being hardly any room for him on the prince's lap because the stout royal thighs were almost entirely taken up by the overhanging royal belly.

The prince was among the steady stream of visitors who descended on Davenant House to leave cards or pay calls in hopes of seeing the boy whose metamorphosis from climbing boy to young gentleman was the talk of society.

Davenant encouraged this interest, believing such public attention might yield more leads than the few he was now pursuing in search of Addy's family. In this he was unintentionally aided by his friend, Beau Brummell. Regarded as the sole arbiter of what was and what was not *de rigueur* in society, the Beau's pronouncements were considered indisputable. After encountering Addy and Georgiana as they drove in Hyde Park, Brummell was heard to state publicly on several occasions, "Only a fool would deny Davenant's protégé is a young gentleman." This pronouncement sufficed to make Addy all the rage in society. However, as Davenant had no intention of putting the boy on show, callers at his London home were told the child was either at his lessons, or not at home, and that he might be seen—from a distance—when driving with her ladyship in Hyde Park.

Addy, who was unaware of the interest in him, thought the ladies and gentlemen who smiled and waved handkerchiefs at him when he was out for a drive were just being friendly, and he waved back with enthusiasm. His days were spent in lessons with Mr. Dingley, playing, visits to the stables with Henry Rollins, carriage outings, and impromptu cricket games in the Grosvenor Square garden with Willoughby and Basingthwaite. The latter two, Georgiana often coerced into being subjects for the watercolours and drawings with which she often occupied her convalescence.

A JACKETING CONCERN

When it came to society's latest fashion—even when only a small boy—the Prince Regent liked to think he was in the vanguard, and even more so in Addy's case, because he was party to the wager that created it. So it was no surprise to Davenant when, within days of the wager, the prince told him he wished to meet Addy.

"My mamma and sisters are in a fever of concern about the boy," the prince said by way of an excuse, "and will not rest until they have a firsthand account of him."

What did surprise Davenant was the prince's decision to call at Davenant House rather than summon Addy to Carlton House. His extravagant debts and his treatment of his estranged wife, Princess Caroline, had made the prince unpopular with his father's subjects, and his public appearances were often greeted hostility and ridicule of his fatness. But the prince, ever the courteous First Gentleman in matters of civility, insisted on paying his respects to the recovering Georgiana, too. Of course, the fact that her husband was a rich and influential Tory was not lost on the prince, either.

Accompanied by his usual entourage of cronies, the Regent arrived at Davenant House in a flurry of carriages and outriders that seemed to fill Grosvenor Square. To spare his royal guest the embarrassment of heaving his obese body upstairs, Davenant escorted him to a ground floor salon where Georgiana, reclining on a sofa, and Addy, awaited him. Georgiana made a weak attempt to rise, but the prince was at once all concern; he begged she not undertake the slightest movement on his account for fear it might delay her recovery. He took a chair next to her, patted her hand with his pudgy one and commiserated with her on the indisposition caused by her fall. Unaware of her pregnancy, the prince advised her, "Frequent blood letting is what you need, madam. I highly recommend it. Have them several times a week, myself. Definitely beneficial to my health and wellbeing. "

Georgiana's face turned white, and she was hard put to manage a weak smile of thanks. Davenant, fearing she might faint from nausea, immediately led Addy forward to prevent more of the prince's queasy medical advice.

The prince grinned with delight like an eager child with a new toy when

Addy made the bow he had practised all morning. He grabbed hold of him and, huffing and puffing, heaved him up to sit on what little room there was on his lap. One of his equerries placed a small lacquered box on the table beside them. The prince picked it up and opened it.

"These are for you," he said to Addy with that false jollity adults often use when speaking to children. "Sugarplums! I know how much little boys like them. I did when I was your age, and I still do," he added, helping himself to one before offering the box to Addy.

"Do you…know…who I am?" the prince said, his cheeks bulging with sugarplum.

Addy stopped nibbling his sugarplum and said, "You are the Prince Regent," then, remembering Georgiana's earlier admonitions, added, "Your Highness."

The Prince held out a hand to one of the gentlemen attending him. "A guinea, McMahon!"

It took the prince's pimply-faced secretary a few minutes of fumbling in his coat pockets before he was finally able to hand one to the prince.

The prince held up the coin to show its head. "And who is this?"

"That is, your papa, King George the Third. God Save the King!" Addy piped.

"Hear! Hear!" cried everyone in the room.

The prince beamed. Addy wriggled around to face him.

"My *grandpapa* lives in a castle—just like your papa."

The prince roared with laughter, so everyone else did, too.

"Would Your Highness care to see the picture Addy drew of his grandpapa's castle? It is very good," Georgiana said like a proud mamma. She handed the prince a small sheet of paper. "He is quite the artist."

Davenant, who stood leaning against a high-backed chair, groaned inwardly and rolled his eyes. As he promised, Addy had already presented Davenant with a couple of fanciful, childish chalk drawings of what he claimed was his grandfather's home. Now he was pestering the prince with them. Damn Georgiana for encouraging him.

The prince barely glanced at the picture. "Oh capital, capital!" he said with false enthusiasm. He winked at Davenant. "Shouldn't have much trouble finding the place from this, eh?" He looked down at Addy. "For this fine work of art you may keep the guinea."

Addy smiled shyly. "Thank you...Your Highness."

"Tell me, young man, what do you intend to become when you grow up? An artist perhaps, eh?"

"Oh, no! I am going to be a colonel...in a red coat and...and... ride a white horse!" Addy said in a breathless rush.

"Oho! Come to ask me for a commission, have you?" the prince laughed, and again everyone else did. Addy, being a polite little boy, did so, too, although he did not understand the joke.

"Now, let us see what you know," said the prince with more huffs and puffs as he set Addy on his feet. He set spinning the terrestrial globe on the table next to him. "Can you find England for me?"

Relieved to be free of his awkward perch, Addy took one of the two remaining sugarplums the prince offered him: the prince had by then eaten the rest.

Addy smiled and nodded. With both hands he stopped the globe and scanned its Northern Hemisphere.

Davenant stifled a yawn.

The prince's visit was proving a bore, taking up precious time that he could have much better spent on his search. He was weary, too. Fit as he was, several days of unproductive nighttime visits by him and Willoughby to workhouses and seedy establishments mentioned by Mrs. Dewberry had left him drained. These pursuits caused him to be conspicuously absent from his usual haunts and society's social events. On the rare occasion the public saw him in the street, or driving his curricle, he appeared preoccupied, his thoughts elsewhere. It would have amused him to know that the ladies, particularly those who read novels, were sure he must be in love; their men folk scoffed at such a notion.

Though members of fashionable society saw little of its owner, Davenant House saw plenty of them. Georgiana claimed many of the callers had ulterior motives for their visits. "They care little about Addy," she said of the mamas who called with their unmarried daughters. "They seek only to introduce them to you…in hopes you will offer for one of them. *Ma foi!* To think that not so long ago those same mamas would have nothing to do with you."

"Once in possession of a large fortune, even a disreputable fellow like me is considered eligible. Do you know now some shortsighted ladies describe me as handsome?" he said, which made Georgiana laugh. "Thank you for receiving them for me, but don't let them tire you."

"Oh, they don't, said Georgiana. "*Cest très amusant*–like a Punch and Judy show. Her eyes twinkled and she smiled mischievously. "Besides 'tis not just fond mamas who call."

Davenant frowned.

Several of her former admirers used society's interest in Addy as an excuse to call on Georgiana. These foppish, idle men-about-town did not concern him, nor did Willoughby and Basingthwaite. Disgusted by what he viewed as Hurley's lack of sportsmanship in using his wager with Davenant as a personal vendetta, Basingthwaite had severed all connection with him. He had accepted Willoughby's invitation to share his chambers, and the two were often to seen about town together, particularly at Davenant House. An old friend, Willoughby was always welcome there, and Basingthwaite's unassuming ways and his rescue of Georgiana and Addy at the Exeter Exchange made him a favoured guest. But Davenant did object to the visits of Captain Allen and the Duke of Ryedale, which appeared to be of a much more serious intent than the others.

Quite besotted with Georgiana, the captain deluged her with bouquets and poems he had written in her praise. If admitted to her presence, he spent the time gazing at her in mute adoration, a situation that even the vain Georgiana found tiresome. The duke was a rich, middle-aged widower, who a year ago had sought Davenant's permission to pay his addresses to Georgiana. Davenant refused him: Ryedale was too old for her, and he was certain the duke's only interest in finding a new wife was solely to provide himself with an heir.

Reluctantly, for he was not one to confess to any shortcomings, Davenant acknowledged to himself that he was wrong about Ryedale. The duke must be in love with his sister. What other reason could he have for calling so often now? After all, the duke was far too staid an individual to let himself be caught up in society's rage for a climbing boy-turned-gentleman.

"I'll tolerate no *ciscebos* in this house," Davenant had warned Georgiana. "Don't encourage either of them."

At this Georgiana burst into tears. "I don't want anyone else but Edgar...and he is so, so angry with me," she wailed. "When I wrote and told him the doctor had ordered me to stay in town, he didn't believe me. He wrote such a horrid, horrid, *horrid* reply," she sniffed. "He said if I didn't return home as he ordered, he would drag me back...b...b...by...my...my nose!"

"What an ungracious fellow!" her brother said.

To cheer her up, he had recounted some of the fanciful tales then circulating about Addy. "One dowager told me she believes him to be a French spy sent across the Channel in a hot air balloon," he said. "Another fellow in a phaeton in Bond Street–it almost locked wheels with my curricle–told me in no uncertain terms that he is sure he is the former Dauphin, and that he managed to escape the clutches of the French Revolutionary Government." His lips twitched. "He persisted in this view even when I reminded him that the dauphin, if alive, would now be a young man not a boy. Oh yes, and at least one broadside now being shouted in the streets claims a supernatural connection between Addy and the comet now visible at night sky."

Davenant was glad the general public was talking about the boy. Even if some of what was said was ridiculous, it might jog someone into remembering something they had heard or seen that might help him. Without mentioning Addy by name, he had also placed advertisements for information about a missing boy in several of the London papers that circulated in the provinces. To date there had been no replies.

Davenant took stock of the usual friends and sycophants surrounding the prince. Like the Regent, they were there more to keep up with society's latest craze than because of any real concern about Addy. The one exception was the Duke of Ryedale. Spending most of his time at his northern estates, the duke was not a member of the raffish Carlton House Set. Davenant's lips twitched in amusement. He was sure Ryedale was using the prince's visit as but another excuse for him to again see Georgiana. All eyes were on the three around the globe: Addy, Georgiana and the prince. Ryedale was no exception: he was unable to take his eyes off Georgiana. Davenant felt a twinge of pity for him. He, too, had known the pain of a lost love, but, unlike the duke, he had recovered.

"There!"

Addy's stubby forefinger swooped down onto the map of England.

"And there is London," he said, moving his finger to the dot that was the city. Slowly he moved his finger east toward the sea. "The-ships-go-down-the-river-to-the-sea," he recited mechanically as if he had learned it by rote. "Then-they-turn-the-corner," he said as his finger swung around into English Channel, "and-go-down-the-sea… around-the-corner-of-France."

Addy stopped and looked at the prince. "'Boney' lives in France. He eats snails and little English boys."

The prince feigned horror. "Oho, can't have that now, can we?"

At the Bay of Biscay the finger stopped while Addy considered its next move. At last he said, "Then-they-go-across-this-big-sea-first. It is called the At-lan-tic," he explained as his finger crossed to the Caribbean and Brazil. "Then-they-go-to-Africa." Abruptly the finger shot east to the African coast, and began making its way south. "Then-they-go-around-this-pointy-bit," he noted as the finger rounded the Cape of Good Hope, "then-across-this-other-big-sea." The finger sped across the Indian Ocean, to the sub-continent. "Around-another-pointy-bit and up-here-to…"

Addy stopped and frowned again as he strove to remember its name. "Cal… Cal…Cal… Cal-cut-ta!" he proclaimed with a grin. "Calcutta is in India."

"Bravo!" said Prince, leading the applause.

Flushed with pleasure, Addy looked up at him. "That's the way ships go to India. There are elephants and tigers there! I have a tiger from India."

"You've taught him well, madam," the prince said to Georgiana. "Knows his way about the world a sight better than some admirals, what?"

In expectation of laughter, he glanced about him; he was not disappointed.

"A most successful visit!" Georgiana declared after the prince left. "Even that old bore Ryedale was quite charming. He seemed quite taken with Addy."

"To please you, no doubt," Davenant drawled. "By the by, is this some new fantasy of the boy? Tigers? India? The sea route there? Or did he learn that from you or Dingley?"

"No," said Georgiana. "With Dingley he is studying European geography. And if I had taught him, I would naturally have shown him that the quickest route to India is not by way of Brazil, but past Spain and down the east coast of Africa."

"On a map that appears the quickest route," Davenant said, speaking more to himself than to her, "but a ship would find itself becalmed in the Doldrums for days and unable to travel. Those who have travelled to India know the quickest way is west across the Atlantic before turning east to be carried to The Cape by the trade winds."

"Bette, told me what mama said about the way papa went to India on a big ship," Addy said, when questioned, "and I remembered it."

A father travelling by ship to India? Was this a childish fancy like grandpapa's castle and sleeping giants? Of course, if Addy was from a well-off family, as he appeared to be, then it could be true. Either way, it only deepened the mystery surrounding the boy, a mystery that in spite of his concerted efforts to date, Davenant was no nearer to solving than when he had begun a week ago.

30

"Newgate seize me!" Henry gasped when he realised what the occupants of the darkened room were doing.

There was no attempt to conceal squirming bodies and thrashing limbs; no effort to hush groans and shuddering cries. And if more were needed to prove the Black Horse, Tottenham Court Road, was more than just a public house, there was a strong smell of stale sweat and another even more intimate one. But what shocked not only Henry but the usually *blasé* Davenant was that many of the boys and girls having sex together in the low beds lining the walls had not long reached puberty.

The landlord was a short thickset man with straggling, greasy hair, in shirtsleeves and breeches, whose strong smell revealed an aversion to soap and water. He took out his watch and looked at it. He grinned at Davenant, revealing several missing teeth and shreds of food trapped between the remaining rotten ones. " 'Bout time some of 'em were outta there. Been at it long enough, they have," he said, banging loudly against the open door with his fist. "If they ain't got wot they want by now, ain't my fault. You can speak to 'em. Not too long mind! Time's money."

Initially the landlord was suspicious of Davenant and Henry, fearing they could be a threat to his lucrative livelihood. The Black Horse was one of the most notorious of London's many 'flash houses', gathering places for murderers, burglars, muggers, coiners, footpads, shoplifters and pickpockets of both sexes and all ages to meet, sleep, eat, drink, hide from the law, have sex and fence stolen property. With such an assembly of vice under its roof, the Black Horse was an excellent academy of crime, where the young were tutored in all manner of wrongdoing by skilled professionals. With all this at stake, the landlord could ill afford to take chances with strangers.

Although roughly dressed, these two strangers were still better turned out than his other patrons; and even though the little chap, who at first did all the talking, spoke the underworld's Flash tongue as if he had learned it at his mother's knee, the landlord was certain the two were not what they seemed. The tall man's air of command, his obvious physical strength, the way he carried himself and the deference his companion showed toward him indicated someone in authority. A gang leader intent on muscling in on the landlord's business? Or was he the Law in disguise?

If the two were the Law, they weren't the constables or Bow Street Runners he had paid off with money and tidbits of information about criminal activities, so he could remain in business. If they were gang members, they were new to the area, for he had never seen them before; he knew most of the local ones, they being his regular customers. In his line of work you could never be too careful, and he had been on the verge of telling his bullyboys to throw them out. Davenant assured him that though he sought information about a boy—for which he was willing to pay—he and his companion were neither the Law nor gang members, but the landlord was still leery of someone who spoke so posh despite his rough disguise. However, where money was concerned, the landlord was always willing to take risks. Davenant's liberal hand with his money eventually persuaded him to let this tall stranger question his staff and customers. Davenant must be a rich pederast searching for a hapless boy who had escaped him, the landlord decided. But to be certain the strangers did not steal any of the stolen property stored on the premises, sneak off with one of the girls, or pick a fight with a patron, the landlord insisted on accompanying them when they made their rounds of the flash house's occupants.

Immediately following the Prince Regent's visit, Davenant had set off with Henry for the Black Horse, yet another of the many underworld locations he had gone to in search of information about Addy. To be sure of leaving no stone unturned, he had drawn up a list of all the London locations given him by Mrs. Dewberry and the Bow Street Runners where a boy might be bought for labour or sexual purposes. Each armed with one of Georgiana's sketches of Addy, he and Willoughby then divided the list between them to save time, each undertaking to call at half the addresses.

When visiting the London underworld's most dangerous spots like the Black

Horse, Davenant and Willoughby went in the rough disguises Henry bought for them in Monmouth Street's old clothes market. Disguise or no disguise, most of the people they spoke to were quite willing to co-operate —for money, of course—once they were sure their questioners were not the Law. Too worldly to be easily shocked, even Davenant was astonished at how easy it was to buy a child in London if one knew where to go.

"Why bother looking for a lost boy? We've got just the sorta kid you're looking for, right here—at the right price," he was told, even by parish beadles, elected public officials, many of whom were not averse to selling an orphaned child from among those in workhouses under their jurisdiction.

His calls at the secret 'molly houses' proved a waste of time; they were invariably the haunts of adult male homosexuals—not pederasts—who were there to meet their own kind. The 'mollies' were delighted with the attention of such a tall, attractive man as Davenant. Occasionally one made careless by drink would address him by name. "I had no idea, Davenant, darling, that you were one of us." However, the women's attire and cosmetics they wore prevented him from identifying them. Others turned away when they saw him, for fear he might make public their sexual proclivity, homosexuality being a hanging offence.

For Henry Rollins waiting outside such establishments was even worse than being forced to linger outside a Cit's house. "Newgate seize me! What's me mates gonna think if they sees me ere?" he complained.

"That you and I like wearing dresses?" Davenant suggested, with a just a slight twitch of his lips.

Henry stared in horror; it was several seconds before he realised that Is Nibs was teasing him.

Davenant was about to enter the room to question its occupants when a door along the corridor opened and a girl of no more than fourteen, with a pretty face and golden curls came out followed by a man buttoning up his breeches. The man nodded to the landlord and winked at the others as he passed them.

The girl stopped before Davenant and Henry and appraised them.

"Lor, pa!" she said when the landlord gave her an affectionate pinch on the cheek, "two of em! Theyll have to wait. The last one? A right bull 'e was. A girl needs time to catch her breath."

"Newgate seize me!" Henry gasped. "His daughter! She's one of his pros…"

"Pray excuse my companion, miss," Davenant interrupted. "It's your help I want…and that of your friends…not your body."

The girl peeped up at him and smiled. "A pity cos you looks like yer knows how to treat a girl."

Davenant had just shown her the sketch of Addy when there came a loud shriek. Running along the landing came a girl followed by a boy, both naked and both laughing. From their size and the immaturity of their bodies, Davenant guessed the girl to be about twelve and the boy a little older. They pushed passed the group on the landing and disappeared into one of the rooms.

"At that age, even I still had both my innocence and my virginity," Davenant murmured, more to himself than anyone in particular.

After two dreary, unsuccessful hours spent questioning the inmates, Davenant was relieved when he was finally able to leave the depravity of the Black Horse for the comparative fresh air of Tottenham Court Road outside. No one recognised Addy from the sketch they were shown, nor had anyone been able to give him any helpful information. Stymied though he was by his lack of progress, Davenant was more determined than ever to find Addy's grandfather, no matter what it took to do so.

They changed their disguises at Willoughby's rooms in Piccadilly. On their way home Davenant called at Hatchards, the Piccadilly booksellers, leaving Henry outside with the curricle. On the stone seat in front of the shop where footmen waited for their employers sat a burly, middle-aged man with a florid face and red nose reading a newspaper. In a serge coat, flannel waistcoat, striped trousers, and shoes with steel buckles, he was the embodiment of John Bull, a solid, law-abiding Englishman. But it wasn't the man's *toilette* that interested Henry; on several occasion that afternoon he had noticed the man following behind the curricle in a hackney carriage

Carrying a small brown paper parcel, Davenant emerged from Hatchards and climbed into the vehicle.

"Hopes as how yer don't think I has windmills in my head," Henry said, handing him the ribbons, "but I thinks we're bein' followed."

"I know," Davenant drawled. "I've suspected that for two days."

"Newgate seize me! Some cove a-plannin' to rob yer–or worse."

"I don't think so. If that were the case, he could have done so last night… when I walked home in the dark."

His suspicions were first aroused, he said, when a man resembling the one on the bench trailed him to a child wholesaler, in a dingy St. Giles alley. When Davenant left, he became aware he was being followed by a hackney cab, although he could not see the passenger. "Last night, you remember, I went to a gaming hell in St. James. With the intention of testing my suspicions, I told you Willoughby would drive me back and sent you home. Then I stayed at the tables till early morning. If someone was following me, he would still be on the trail no matter how late, so I walked back to Grosvenor Square to see if anyone followed me."

Though he knew Davenant was well able to defend himself with fists and a swordstick, Henry was alarmed he had not been asked to accompany him. London's dark streets were dangerous and no place to walk alone at night. True, there were always plenty of people about, but many of them were thieves, muggers and prostitutes.

"I woulda helped yer catch him," he said.

"I did not wish to…er…catch him," Davenant replied. "I just wanted to ascertain that I really was being followed. Last night the fellow had several opportunities to attack and rob me in unlit areas between Piccadilly and Grosvenor Square–but he did not. Obviously that was not the reason he was following me."

To get a good look at his pursuer, Davenant enlisted the aid of two of the many whores plying their trade in Piccadilly. Making a living as a prostitute in London was not easy because there were so many of them, the sheer volume of their number shocking foreign visitors to the city. The two were only too happy to obtain the equivalent of a week's earnings for doing nothing more exacting than stopping Davenant's pursuer under a street lamp. From a nearby dark alley, Davenant watched with amusement as the two prostitutes grabbed the man, a common enough occurrence in nighttime London.

"Hi, hi, now, leave me be! Stop that," the man spluttered when one made a playful grab at his crotch. "You should be ashamed of yourselves. I'm a respectable married man!"

"That's what they all say, dearie, just afore they lifts me skirt," one of the woman laughed. "Means they aren't gettin' enough at home. That's why they comes a-lookin for the likes of us."

"Respectable are yer?" the other woman jeered, "so 'ow come you're out this time o' night in Piccadilly?"

"Beneath the oil lamp the man s face was clearly visible to Davenant: he was the man now sitting outside the bookshop.

Davenant's lips twitched as he recalled the incident. It was not the first time he had been followed: duns, creditors, those in the pay of irate husbands and fathers– even a jealous mistress had shadowed him. He was certain his present stalker was intent on obtaining evidence of an illicit liaison between him and Letty Hanchurch for her husband. Unlike the peddler watching Davenant House, this agent of the marquess appeared to work in tandem with another younger man, a redheaded individual.

Henry was all for relieving 'Is Nibs of this stranger. "Me and some of me mates from The Running Footman, we'd scare im off," he promised, referring to the tavern patronised by Mayfair's stable staffs, where his reputation for fisticuffs was renowned. He had often given 'a bunch of fives' to a taproom patron who offended him.

Davenant would have none of it.

"I have become quite attached to my latest shadow, as I am to the others who keep watch on me," he said. "However, if my new shadow is to follow so close, I wish he would find himself a better tailor. And his shoes? Buckles! So unfashionable…at least for the fashionable. I shall permit him to keep company with me until such time as I think fit, for I find him quite amusing. For want of a better appellation, I shall call him Buckles."

"But why would he be a-followin' you, my lord?"

"What an inquisitive fellow you are, Henry. Suffice to say, I believe him to be in the pay of…ahem…a husband of a former friend of mine."

Without taking his eyes off the road ahead, Davenant snapped, "Wipe that grin off your face, you impudent devil!"

And for the umpteenth time in his life, Henry wondered how it was that his employer always knew what he was thinking and doing even when 'Is Nibs had his back to him.

31

After another futile visit that evening with Henry to yet another flash house, it was nearly two o'clock in the morning before Davenant retired to bed. Weary as he was, sleep would not come, his mind overactive with images of what he had seen in London's underworld since he began his enquiries.

Such mental agitation was new to one usually in command of himself. But now his quest had an increased urgency, ten days having gone by since he began, leaving just over two weeks to complete it. In spite of his diligence and Willoughby's help, he knew no more now than the day he made the wager. Lack of progress and days and nights amid the depravity of London's underworld had taken its toll even of one so worldly as himself. In an effort to relax, he sought respite in the work he bought at Hatchards: Mary Wollstonecraft's *A Vindication of the Rights of Women,* which he had discovered Miss Barclay reading. He had got no further than the first page, before his mind filled with visions of her blue-grey eyes and the serenity of her face. Ignoring Miss Wollstonecraft and her arguments on behalf of women, he leaned back against the pillows, the better to savour such delightful thoughts. His eyelids drooped, the book slipped from his hand to the floor and in no time at all he was fast asleep.

Down in Grosvenor Square all was in darkness: its surrounding mansions just looming masses, their white stucco and ornamental stonework invisible. What little light there was came from a waning moon that peeped occasionally from behind the clouds and the flickering glow of the squares oil lamps that still remained lit. But although dark, the square was neither empty nor silent. In the infrequent moonlight, shadows of human figures glided occasionally across walls before disappearing into the waiting darkness. A prostitute on the prowl? A drunken gentleman unable to find his own front door? A burglar? A mugger? There were whispers, too. A cat screeched and hissed to mark its territory. Its harnesses jingling, a carriage carrying late night revellers rattled over the cobbles. And in the garden in the square's centre, a sharp breeze sent the first of the fallen leaves scuttling before it like frightened rabbits.

These were not the only sights and sounds in the square. A faint bobbing light and the thumpity-thump, thumpity-thump of a stout wooden staff announced the arrival of The Law in the hefty shape of one Jem Biggs, a watchman on his rounds. Popularly and derisively known as Charlies, parish watchmen were famed for their general ineptitude, and Jem was no exception. For the sixteen pounds a year the parish paid him, he did as little work as possible, moving only as fast as the belly overhanging his belt and his asthmatic cough allowed. Not that Jem ever shirked his duty when called upon to perform it. He was always quick to shake his rattle to summon help when he saw a crime in progress. As this sound also warned the criminals, giving them a chance to flee, it saved Jem the unnecessary exertion of arresting them.

Jem was a helpful soul, too. For a little of the 'ready' passed under a tavern table, he would promise burglars to look the other way when they operated on his beat. After all, he shared a kinship with them: like many Charlies he had been a burglar himself once. And when not dozing in it, he rented out his watch box to prostitutes to entertain or rob their clients. In return these ladies paid him either in money or kind, although all he could manage now was a quick fumble of the breasts or a grope under a skirt. Still it was better than nothing; and he was always one to make the most of any opportunity that presented itself no matter however meagre.

If the darkness was not playing tricks with his eyes, he saw such an opportunity outside Davenant House. Just visible by the light of a nearby oil lamp stood a man grasping the ankles of another standing on his shoulders as he attempted to scale a column of the portico to the balcony above. Burglars! Two of them! And he had caught them red-handed!

There was a forty-pound reward for anyone who caught and brought a burglar to justice. This had to be shared with witnesses, of course. Not being one of superior understanding, it took Jem a minute or two to realise that *he* was the *only* witness. It was also usual for the owner of the property to reward the person who caught the burglar. Jem grinned. Lord Davenant was rich; likely he would match the law's reward, if not more. Eighty pounds, or may be more. A man like him could do a lot with that; set himself up in a little business, perhaps. No more walking the beat on cold winter nights, no more suffering the indignity of having his watch box knocked over by drunken young men-about-town while he was in it.

In the still of the night air, voices carried across the square

"Careful, Manvers! You nearly dropped me!" one of the men said in alarm.

"I-I-I can't hold you mu-mu-much longer."

Jem snorted. Such a lack of professionalism! Why, the entire square could hear them. Now in *his* day as a cracksman…

Jem Biggs was not the only person who heard the voices.

Georgiana's bedroom was on the third floor, immediately above the portico. Asleep on Georgiana's bed, Puff woke with a start when his sharp ears picked up the sound of the voices. His bark woke Georgiana.

"What's the matter Puff," she whispered as she peered drowsily into the darkness.

Puff barked again just as Addy, rubbing the sleep from his eyes, ran in from Perry's room just along the corridor where he now slept.

"I-I-I heard…voices…outside," he whispered. "I think…"

The sharp retort of a pistol outside made them jump and set Puff barking.

Georgiana scrambled from the bed, grabbed Addy's hand and the two of them ran from the room, Puff at their heels.

Startled by the shot, Jem Biggs dropped staff and lantern and dived for cover behind the pilaster of the nearest house. There, this representative of The Law huddled, sweating profusely, his breath short, his heart thumping and his teeth chattering.

Although used to a life of luxury and ease, Davenant's reactions had been sharpened while attached to Sir John Moore's army during its retreat to Corunna. The shot had him out of bed and on his feet in a trice. In the darkness he fumbled for the pistol he kept in the drawer of a bedside table. He found it just as Georgiana,

Addy and Puff rushed into the room.

"Burglars, Roderick! Burglars. Oh my jewels!" Georgiana gasped, hugging close a frightened Addy, while Puff barked at their heels.

Ignoring them Davenant dashed to a window and threw it open just as a second shot sounded.

Down in Grosvenor Square all was quiet once more. Despite the shots, no lights appeared, no windows opened. Any residents who had been woken by the commotion were not evident, no doubt hiding behind curtains, thankful in the knowledge that this night their homes had escaped the attention of London's criminals.

It took some minutes after a second shot for Jem Biggs to summon up enough courage to leave his hiding place and resume his duties. Only when satisfied he was in no danger did he step from his shelter. On the pavement in front of Davenant House lay the sprawled figure of one burglar, beside him knelt the other repeatedly wailing, "Oh my God! Oh my God!"

Above, framed at an open third-floor window by the sudden brief light from the moon, the shadowy figure of a man stood holding a pistol.

Just before dawn a tall gentleman entered the parish roundhouse, his elegant attire at odds with the greasy greatcoats and battered hats of the watchmen. A constable led him to the lock-up where the night's haul of malefactors languished on a stone bench: two young men in naval uniform. One lay curled up asleep in fetal position, his head on his rolled up greatcoat, his cheek resting on his hand, his face as tranquil as that of any sleeping baby. The other sat next to him, his head in his hands, moaning, "Never again! Never again!" when he was not vomiting into a bucket placed at his feet for that purpose.

The constable pointed through the bars at the sleeping man. "What we'd like to know, my lord, is if he's really your brother like what he sez he is…or is he just a mad man whose gone and got himself dressed up in the king's uniform?"

The gentleman did not hesitate.

"He is both," he said.

32

Like generations of his family's second sons before him, Perry Davenant was expected to enter the church. This was not due to any family pretentions to piety that was hardly to be expected in one, which had had over the centuries more than its share of black sheep. Like most aristocratic families, the Davenants held the livings of churches on their estates. To boost their influence in these parishes, they tried, whenever possible, to grant those livings to family members and supporters who had taken holy orders with the Church of England.

But with little liking for academic studies, Perry, by fair means and foul–mostly foul–had persisted in his efforts to have a naval career. He had himself expelled from Eton by the simple expedient of attaching an explosive device to the headmaster's carriage. Having long been accustomed to schoolboy pranks, the coachman was quick to spot the device–just as Perry intended. A triumphant Perry was sent home together with the headmaster's ponderous letter of explanation.

> *As the Young Gentleman appears to have a predilection for Fulminating Devices,* the headmaster wrote, *he might better be engaged in applying this Bellicose Faculty of his to the destruction of His Majesty's Enemies on the present Field of Mars rather than in the Grove of Academe.*

So Perry joined the navy.

At twenty-one, he had been tested in battle and not found wanting; he had earned some prize money and had just been promoted to lieutenant. Such an enterprising individual was, therefore, undaunted at finding the front door of his home locked and barred. As he had done on many previous occasions, he sought alternative entry through a window. He thought it a lark when he and his friend, Lieutenant Manvers, were imprisoned by The Watch for attempted burglary of his own home.

Sporting one very black eye–a consequence of his nighttime adventure–Perry had risen after only a few hours sleep to see Manvers off by stagecoach on the last leg of his journey home. Returning to Davenant House, he was surprised to find that his usually indolent brother, his *toilette* immaculate, already up and just finishing a frugal meal. Much to the delight of the *chef*, Henri-Charles, Perry ordered a hearty breakfast and, between mouthfuls of chops and kidneys, explained to Davenant the reason for his unusual arrival.

He and Manvers, having been granted leave, had posted up from Portsmouth. As Manvers time in town was limited to the next day, no sooner they arrived in London, they went out on the town. After a visit to Vauxhall Gardens, a tavern crawl well into the early hours of the morning had left them both drunk. As Manvers had nowhere to stay, Perry invited him to Davenant House.

"A parson's son. Never been…on the town," Perry said with his mouth full. "He lost…some money…at cards…lost his virginity, too. Sorry…'bout…the hullabaloo."

A thought struck him. He stared at his half-brother.

"You're a crack shot. No wonder Manvers dropped me. Scared the devil out of us. How come you didn't kill us–or least wound us?"

"I did not kill you because I did not fire," Davenant drawled. "You had already fallen when I reached the window after the first shot."

"Well, if you didn't fire, who did then?"

Davenant tapped his chin with his quizzing glass and considered this question.

"I don't know," he said at last, "but I have my suspicions. This house is being watched, and I am being followed by those in the pay of…er, ahem…an irate husband."

Perry burst out laughing. "Must be very irate to be shooting at you."

Davenant's eyes narrowed and Perry's laughter trailed away.

"I hope you did not injure yourself," Davenant said, changing the subject.

"Just this eye. No matter! Fit as a fiddle, me. Used to rough and tumble aboard ship. Manvers broke my fall. Couldn't try a ground floor window because of the railings in front of the house." He grinned. "We were both too foxed to know any better."

"Let us hope you show better agility when climbing to the crow's nest than when you scale the lofty heights of Davenant House."

Perry chuckled. The bright brown eyes and chestnut curls that heightened the beauty of his twin, Georgiana, gave him a boyishness at odds with the weather-beaten face of one battle hardened by six years of naval life.

He was unsurprised to hear of Georgiana's visit. Willoughby and his friend Basingthwaite had told him when he and Manvers met them at Vauxhall the previous evening.

"Got married, didn't she?" he said, intent on the ham.

"*You* were at the wedding," Davenant said. "As a consequence of those nuptials she is now with child."

"Blister it! Georgie a mother? Now she'll have to behave," was the best Perry could manage by way of brotherly concern.

"You will not bruit it abroad. Her husband has yet to be told."

"That farmer fellow? Bit of sobersides…but damn fine rider to hounds!"

"You refer, of course, to our brother-in-law, Earl Hesston, a leader in new farming methods."

"Damn Hesston. What about your wager? A climbing boy! In all the papers…talk of the wardrooms. Admiral, himself, deigned to ask *me* about it."

"Surely the officers of His Majesty's navy have better things to do than discuss my affairs."

Perry gave a rueful grin. "No, we don't. Blockading is a damned bore. Need a battle or two, we do. It's my guess we'll be at it with the Yankees again, soon," he said rubbing his hands in anticipation. "They don't like us searching their ships and impressing their sailors."

"Well, then," Davenant said, "if only to curb your display of belligerence, I'll tell you.

"Buckets of blood!" Perry declared when Davenant had finished. "Wondered what was different about you. Now I know. You're…well, enthused…invigorated…less dissip…"

He shrivelled beneath his brother's stare.

"As impudent as ever, I see."

Perry saw his brother's lips twitch and he relaxed and smiled. "Do tell! How fare your efforts to solve the mystery? Three weeks! Why, with your cool head and your luck, I'm surprised you..."

Perry stopped, realising this sounded like censure of his brother.

"Haven't solved it already," Davenant finished. "That's what I had expected, too.

"However, the sweep that bought the boy was murdered before I could speak to him."

"Murdered?"

"Yes. A common occurrence in his neighborhood. Let us hope your arrival, unseemly though it was, proves a harbinger of better luck for me, otherwise I will lose my new pair of greys, which will sorely grieve me."

"A pair of greys!" Perry said, rubbing his hands again. "Can I take 'em for a run?"

"No. While you are here, and as long as you stay out of trouble, you may have the use of any horse in the stables, the use of my boxes at Covent Garden and Drury Lane, and you may draw on my bank for whatever funds you need. But my greys? *Definitely* not. Henry is correct in his assertion that you drive as if 'every bat in hell were after you.' I may not have my greys for long, but I will not have them run into the ground by you while I do."

33

"I won! I won! I've captured your ship!" Addy yelled, pointing his weapon down at Perry.

The latter, in a gesture of mock submission, fell backwards onto the staircase, where the two of them had been thrusting and parrying at each other with wooden rulers in a mock sword fight. As he fell Perry threw wide his arms, accidentally flinging his ruler out over the banister. Davenant, who had just arrived home, saw the ruler hurtling towards him as he handed his hat and cane to Venables. He ducked, and it flew over his head and clattered to the floor behind him.

In silence Davenant rose slowly from his enforced crouch and stared coldly at the scene before him. Georgiana, who was at the head of the stairs watching the battle, saw him first. She ran down and helped Perry to his feet, and the two of them, shame-faced at being caught in such a childish escapade, stared at their brother while Addy grinned in triumph.

Perry ran his hands through his ruffled hair and straightened his clothes. "Sorry 'bout that," he said. "I was just showing Addy how a naval boarding party goes about boarding an enemy vessel with cutlasses. The ruler just slipped from my hand."

"Oh, it was such fun!" Georgiana said eagerly. "Perry was the enemy and Addy," she smiled down at him, "was the valiant navy lieu…"

Her voice trailed away, and she was left open-mouthed as Davenant, his face wearing the coldest of cold looks, stalked off without a word.

Alone in his study Davenant sat down at his desk and put his feet up on it. With a sigh he leaned back in his chair and closed his eyes.

Why had he been so angry with Perry? He and the boy were just playing. After all, he had had far worse things than a ruler thrown at him.

After the boredom of blockade duty, it was natural that the high-spirited Perry would want a carefree leave. Since his arrival, Perry had spent most nights on the town with friends, returning to Davenant House in the early morning hours–

more than once by climbing through a window—and staying abed until well after noon next day. But in spite of his nightly high jinks, Perry still had plenty of leftover energy for fun and games with Addy.

It had been love at first sight for Addy when Georgiana introduced him to her twin. He stared in awe at the smiling young man in a blue naval uniform with shiny brass buttons. He had a new hero! One who was young enough in age that he could have been a brother, but old enough to be fighting the French. The two were immediately friends and Perry, being very much a boy at heart, spent a great deal of time with Addy, when the latter was not at his lessons. Perry taught him nautical terms, showed him how to tie various knots—using cords from the curtains when string was unavailable—let him wear his lieutenant's hat, explained the workings of sextant and telescope, took him to see the Admiralty semaphore station at Chelsea and the ships moored below London Bridge. In return Addy gave Perry a love and an awe that bordered on veneration, hanging on his every word as if it were gospel. One day Davenant overheard Addy tell Henry Rollins, "I've changed my mind. I won't be a colonel when I grow up after all. I'm going to join the navy like Mr. Perry instead and be an admiral like Lord Nelson."

Davenant was not the only one piqued by Addy's adoration of Perry. Georgiana was frequently put out of countenance because Addy would go off somewhere with her twin when she wanted to be with the boy. Even Puff moped because his playmate did not spend as much time with him as before.

Was his anger that afternoon because the mock battle between Perry and Addy was a tacit reminder of the closeness they shared? Could it be, like the others, that he unconsciously resented their relationship? Indifferent though he was to toward children, Davenant had to admit he had become accustomed to Addy's presence and his playfulness. Was he jealous because the boy's former wide-eyed adoration for him now belonged to Perry? Jealous? With a snort Davenant dismissed this notion. Such nonsense was beneath *him!* Besides, he had other more serious things to think about.

His enquiries were almost at a standstill, and despite his efforts there seemed no prospect of improvement during the remaining period of the wager. For days now Georgiana and Perry had rarely seen him. He rose at what his servants considered an unseemly hour, and, after a frugal breakfast, left in his curricle with Henry, returning just before dinner. After this he would be off again, not returning until the early hours of the morning. The only things that did not change, despite this hectic increase in his activities, was the length of time he took to create a Davenant Drape, and his weekly visits to Gentleman Jackson's Bond Street gymnasium.

The many forays he and Willoughby made into the underworld in search of clues to Addy's real identity proved fruitless. He was fast running out of options: only one or two locations remained to be visited, and there had been no response to the reward posted in St. Giles. This surprised Davenant, so sure was he that money would prove a sufficient lure for inhabitants of the crime-infested rookery."

He sighed. He was tired; the zest and energy with which he had begun his quest had flagged, as had the public's interest in Addy. Visitors no longer called at Davenant House to see the boy who had transformed into a young gentleman. In the clubs of St. James the wager was forgotten and so was Davenant, because he was rarely there. Society, including the fickle prince, had other interests: the newest rage, the latest gossip and the most recent scandals. The only person beside himself and Willoughby in whose mind the wager remained uppermost was Thomas Hurley. When they met in Vauxhall Gardens, a drunken Hurley often taunted Perry about it.

Davenant opened his eyes. With time so short what more could he do? Where else should he look? He stared up at the ceiling; there was no answer there. He sighed. Hurley and the prince were well on their way to winning their bets. To Hurley would also go the glory and prestige of beating him, not to mention making him look foolish, while he would lose one penny and a pair of very fine horses.

"Damn it!" he said, opening his eyes.

He took his feet from the desk and was about to get up from his chair when he noticed three drawings Georgiana had left on the desk. Two were sketches by her of Addy to replace ones tattered and torn from continued used by him and

Willoughby in their enquiries. The other was a chalk drawing by Addy of his grandfather's castle, a childlike fancy of towers with pointed roofs and crenellated walls, which the boy thought would help him find it.

As Davenant studied the drawing, without him realising it, his lips slowly relaxed into a smile. If only the picture could help him. But it was just the imaginings of a boy with big brown eyes who more than once asked him, "Did you find my grandpapa today, my lord?"

It was then that Davenant realised the exigencies of the wager were of no great account. The orphaned Addy's only relative was his grandfather. What mattered was that he, Davenant, find the old man and return the boy to him, no matter how long it took, no matter what he had to do to achieve that, no matter if he lost the wager. It would not be the first wager he had lost, nor would it be the last. And although Henry might not think so, much as he would hate to lose his greys, he could always buy another pair, the equal of or even better than the ones he would lose.

It was just then that the study door opened and a footman entered bearing a letter for him.

34

"You have only to call if you need me, Miss Barclay. I shall be outside."

There was no mistaking the inference in the voice, or the look on the face of the soberly-clad Joseph Pratt as he ushered Davenant into the presence of Miss Barclay.

Davenant's lips twitched in amusement. Since his arrival at the home run by the League for the Betterment of Climbing Boys, the Quaker Joseph Pratt had treated him with unspoken hostility very much at odds with the pacifist tenets of his faith.

The home was in a row of run-down attached houses not far from Monmouth Street. Davenant had no difficulty finding it from the directions given in Miss Barclay's note. In sharp contrast to its dilapidated neighbours, the narrow, two-storey white-washed house boasted bright blue curtains at the windows, and a green door with a shiny brass knocker, flanked by tubs of geraniums. As Miss Barclay was teaching several of the former climbing boys when he arrived, Davenant requested Pratt give him a tour while he waited.

With little ceremony, Pratt hurried him through the rooms: a combined dining room and parlour, a small classroom and a kitchen on the ground floor, and two bedrooms, each with five beds upstairs.

"Volunteers from the league assist the matron, and there is also a cook," Pratt said. "The school houses, clothes and feeds ten boys. We teach them reading, writing and arithmetic in hopes of fitting them for healthier occupations than chimney sweeping. All of them were abandoned by their masters because of illness or injuries incurred through their work, or were no longer small enough to climb chimneys."

But if Pratt's explanation was scant on details about the boys, the physical state of the ones Davenant saw told him more about them and their needs. Like plants deprived of rain and light, they were bent and shrivelled, with legs made bandy from carrying heavy bags of soot; and their young faces, at last cleansed of years of ingrained soot, made them look older than their years. Some had arms and legs in fixed positions, the result, one of them told Davenant, of broken bones not properly reset, and a couple of them could only walk with the aid of crutches.

The reason for Pratt's quiet antagonism toward Davenant became clear when they met Miss Barclay: as he left the room, Pratt cast a fond but proprietary look at her.

"From what your…er…friend…said, he appears to think I may represent some danger to your person," Davenant said after the door closed.

Miss Barclay smiled. "Joseph…Mr. Pratt…is an old friend…of my family…and a business associate of my uncle. Since my father's death, he has been a great help to me. He cares much for my welfare. He escorts me here from my home and back again every day because he fears for my safety in this neighbourhood."

"Well, I'm glad to hear that. This district is a dangerous area for a gently-reared female to be alone in. But Mr. Pratt seems to regard himself as more than just a friend. An admirer, perhaps? You have many, I am sure. Few men could fail to admire you."

Her chin went up. "Thou mockest me again," she admonished.

His usually bored expression actually melted into a wide smile that made him look almost boyish. He laid his hat and cane on a table. "*Au contraire*," he protested, "I pay you a compliment—a very sincere one."

Chastened as he was by the unremitting failure of his efforts to date on Addy's behalf, her letter had raised his hopes. It indicated Fortune, which had so often smiled upon him at the gaming tables, was about to do so on his current venture. Strangely for him, he felt light-hearted—even flirtatious.

"Is that what you think women desire? To be paid compliments all the while?" she said.

Most of the women he knew did desire that, but it would have been ungallant to say so. Her quiet indignation amused him. But beneath it he detected an undercurrent of agitation. He was not a vain man, but he was experienced enough to recognise that even though she might feign indifference, she was more interested in him than she was consciously aware.

"We are capable of much more than primping and…and wearing fashionable clothes. We women have minds. We are not dolls. Our last conversation," she went on, "led me to believe that you were different from other gentlemen in that regard…that you…"

"Yes?"

"…that you found a woman's thoughts…her opinions…as interesting as her appearance."

"I certainly think that of you," he said quietly. "There are many things I admire about you. And surely I may be allowed to express that admiration. Or do you consider compliments, like dancing, a worldly vanity that offends your Quaker sensibilities?"

She lowered her head so he could not see her face. He moved closer to her.

"Or perhaps your life is so sheltered you are unaware of the admiration men feel for you."

Her chin shot up, her eyes dark with indignation. "*I* do not lack for…" Shocked by the sudden realisation what she had been about to say did imply vanity on her part, she covered her mouth with her hand.

His lips twitched. "Admirers?" he finished for her. "I did mean that. Indeed, I count myself among them. But perhaps you prefer to be worshipped from afar… to keep them at a safe distance…like your…ahem…friend… Pratt?"

With a twitch of the lips and a twinkle in his eye he said, "However, my own case seems much more hopeful. You wrote and 'begged me' to call 'at my earliest convenience!' *Et voilà!* Here I am! Further, your letter promised me that I would '*not* be disappointed by my visit,' that 'someone here was eager to see *me,*'" he teased, using phrases from her letter out of context.

Her blue-grey eyes turned even darker. "Thou…thou…thou art the most… the most…" Overwhelmed by indignation, she struggled for the right word.

He shook his head in mock despair. "So very true."

She could not prevent a smile.

"You have a beautiful smile," he said.

She smiled again.

"We progress! I paid you a compliment—without incurring your displeasure."

She regained her composure, her face resuming once more its serene expression.

"As I informed thee in my letter," she said, changing the subject, "there is someone here whom I think thee would wish to meet…someone who can help thee with thy search."

She excused herself and left the room.

Not long after she returned, her arm around the thin shoulders of small bandy-legged boy in a sailor suit. Although small, from the tightness of his clothes across his body, the boy appeared to be gaining weight. His face was wan as if it had been deprived of sun, its skin dry and peeling, but his cheeks were pink.

Mystified, Davenant raised his glass and stared at the newcomer. The child must be one of the schools climbing boys. He frowned. He knew only two climbing boys: Addy and…

The boy grinned. There was no mistaking the mischievous glint in his dark eyes. He held out a hand.

"Tip us yer daddle, guv!"

It was Bodger.

He had been living on the streets in St. Giles, stealing and picking pockets in order to survive, when he heard about the reward offered for information about Mick and Nell.

" I can't read but Ma Cohen read the poster to me," he said to Davenant. Learned it off by heart, I did. '*A gentleman offers a reward of twenty-five pounds for anyone with information about the whereabouts of a woman known as Nell Malloy, her son Eddie, and the journeyman sweep known as Mick.*' "

"And who, pray, is Ma Cohen?" Davenant said.

"Me and the other boys sell the 'andkerchiefs we steals to her, an' she sells 'em on her cart in Monmouth Street," said Bodger. "I knew it must be you wot put up the money ter find Nell, Mick and the boy cos you wuz looking for 'em before."

Certain the trio must be hiding in the rookery, Bodger went in search of them. Dirty and ragged, he looked no different from the rookery's occupants, so he was able to wander at will among the labyrinth of courts and alleys without arousing suspicions. One night, after a lucrative day of stealing, he was able to afford a bed in one of the rookery's doss houses. It was there that he saw Nell and her son, Eddie.

"After Nick and Nell spent all Malloy's money, that bastard Mick dumped Nell and Eddie. Had to go on the streets, she did, to support 'er and the boy–an' buy her gin. I wanted to help her cos she'd been good to me. Knew'd you'd do right by her, I did, cos you done right by Addy. As for Mick, I'd be glad to see 'im hang, I would.'

"The poster also stated those who had information should inform the parish constables, who would, in turn, tell me," said Davenant. "Surely there must be others beside you who knew where Nell was."

Bodger's reply explained why there had been no previous response to the posters.

"No one ever tells the constables anyfink!" Bodger said, aghast at the idea. "Keep the reward for themselves, they would. Anyways, they're scared to go in the rookery. Didn't know 'ow I could find you on my own," he continued, "but then Ma Cohen told me about this place. Said there wuz good, honest people here who'd write to you for me. So 'ere I is. Wanted to help yer, I did, cos you're a mate. Always ready to help a mate, I am."

"You cared nothing for the reward?"

Bodger gave a sly grin. "Ah well, gotta 'ave somethin' for me trouble, I have–even for a mate."

"When Bodger told me his story," Miss Barclay said, "I realised here was someone who could help you and so I wrote to you." She patted the boy's head and smiled at him. "Because all the beds here are occupied, I took him home to stay with me. As you can see, with creams and soap and water, I have been able to remove a great deal of soot from him. That is why you did not recognise him at first. Some soot remains embedded in his skin. But apart from a bad cough, for which he is being treated by my uncle's doctor, he is in good health–and he has a very hearty appetite."

"If you can take me to Nell, you will get the reward," Davenant promised Bodger. "Furthermore, I shall make arrangements for your future, so that you never have to sweep chimneys again."

"Thou art truly kind," Miss Barclay said with a grateful smile.

So intent was Davenant on this smile that Bodger had to tug at his coat to get his attention again.

"A gen'leman and a scholar, you are guv. Tip us your daddle on it! Good as done it is."

Struck by a sudden thought, Miss Barclay exclaimed, "The St. Giles rookery? That dreadful place! But the danger!"

"The boy will safe with me," Davenant assured her. "Besides has he not already demonstrated he is capable of surviving out there?"

"I was thinking of…thee," she said quietly.

He took her hand and raised it to his lips. "I am honoured by your cocern for me, but I am no stranger to danger."

"She your moll, then?' Bodger said after she had left the room.

"No. She is not—as you call it—my moll. And you will at all times refer to her as *Miss* Barclay," Davenant said, giving one of Bodger's ears a sharp tweak.

"Reckons as though she likes you—anyone can see that," Bodger dared, but only after he made sure his ears were beyond Davenant's reach.

35

Deftly sidestepping the urine and feces flung from a chamber pot out of a window above him, Davenant then found his way blocked by a pig—the skinniest he had ever seen—as it trotted across his path. Fast on the animal's heels came two bedraggled women; the first brandishing a meat cleaver, the second yelling, "Kill yer, I will, Bridie O'Toole, if yer harms me pig."

To cheers from the crowd in the street, pig and pursuers disappeared into a nearby dark alley. The screams and yells from that spot lasted several minutes before they ended in a long, strangled screech that sent shivers down Henry Rollins' spine. Then, after a long pause, the pig ambled back into the street: the only one of the three to do so.

"Streuth! Call this the Holy Land? More like the Slough of Despond," said Henry, always eager to exhibit his learning whatever the circumstances.

"It has never happened before—and I will be at pains to see it does not occur again—but I agree with you," Davenant said of this latest example of life in St. Giles rookery they had witnessed that evening.

St Giles' rookery was not the only rookery in London, nor was it the largest—but it was by far the most notorious. Located at the eastern end of Oxford Street, and bounded by Bainbridge Street, Charlotte Street, Broad Street and High Street, it was a warren of miserable streets, courtyards and alleys crowded with ramshackle and derelict houses and hastily-built shacks. Within minutes of his arrival within these squalid boundaries, Davenant realised the reputation of St Giles' rookery was well deserved. Compared to its brutalised humanity, the poor working people he had seen in Monmouth Street and Seven Dials seemed almost genteel by comparison.

Day or night, there was no best time to view the rookery. Like most of east London, it was overshadowed by the permanent pall of smoke and grime from factory chimneys, particularly that of the Horshoe Brewery in Bainbridge Street. Though the darkness of the night obscured the rookery's most squalid features, the darkness and bizarre shadows made for a palpable sense of menace that had

Davenant and his companions continually on the alert. Hardly a building was whole. Those still standing had countless loose bricks, holes stuffed with rags and timber supports to keep them from falling. The rest were tumbled down, what remained of their brickwork jutting up like rotting teeth. Here and there, between houses either side of the streets, stretched washing lines hung with clothes so ragged, there seemed no need to have washed them. Through holes and rents in these clothes, the moon shone, creating strange silhouettes in the night sky. Below, people were everywhere. Gaunt ragged men and women loitered, jostled, brawled and lay among the refuse. Although it was late evening, barefoot scrawny children played in the dirt and pools of stagnant water, many of them with potbellies and deformed limbs, the telltale signs of starvation and rickets.

Large numbers of Irish Catholic immigrants, too poor to live elsewhere, were among the inhabitants, their presence and their religion, giving rise to the rookery's derogatory nicknames 'Holy Land' and 'Little Dublin.' The Irish were looked on as no better than the criminals they were forced to live among: forgers, footpads, coiners, robbers and murderers, pimps, prostitutes and muggers, for whom the rookery was a refuge and hiding place. With so many people, most of whom spent so much of their lives outdoors, noise was constant. Shouts, screams, yells, curses and laughter punctuated their *lingua franca*: St. Giles Greek, a mixture of slang and underworld cant. Almost as plentiful as people were the animals: mangy curs, feral cats, rats–and pigs.

Rookery society was a hierarchy based on greed and need. Half a dozen landlords leased out whole streets of houses to others, who in turn rented out individual houses. These householders in turn let individual rooms. As few of these room renters could actually afford the fee on their own, they let spaces in their rooms to those who wanted a night's lodgings. Many times that night Davenant witnessed twenty or more people crammed into small, airless rooms. Strangers to each other, men, women and children lay five or six to a bed, or on the floor. Packed in with them were the vegetables, birds and rabbits in cages, old clothes, pots, pans and oysters they sold on the streets. These, coupled with the odour of unwashed bodies, created such a stench that at times Davenant and his companions found it hard to breathe, and they were sent scurrying outside for the comparatively fresher air of the street.

In addition, life in the rookery was pitted with hazards. Davenant and the others quickly became adept at dodging the contents of chamber pots thrown from windows, snarling dogs, hissing cats, scurrying rats, unconscious drunks and the occasional pig that had escaped the cellar in which it was usually kept.

Henry nodded in the direction of Bodger, who was walking ahead leading the way.

"Sure 'e ain't leadin' us astray, guv? Wouldn't want ter get lost 'ere."

Bodger turned, put up his fists and took a threatening step toward Henry. "Shut your mummer! Me and 'Is Nibs, 'ere…" He looked up at Davenant. "… we're mates, see. Always on the square with a mate, I am."

When, after returning from his meeting with Bodger, Davenant announced he was going to search the rookery for Nell the next night, Henry was horrified to learn Bodger was to be his guide. "Don't trust that little perisher, I don't. I'd better come wiv yer," he told an amused Davenant.

"I have no intention of going there with just a ten-year-old boy for company. There may well be trouble there. Mr. Willoughby and Blackbird are going with me," Davenant assured him.

Relieved, Henry nodded approval. Blackbird, the boxer, whose real name was Elijah Hawkes, was Davenant's pugilist protégé and Henry's friend. A black man from Nova Scotia, Blackbird boasted a powerful physique acquired while working aboard whaling ships. After seeing a display of his fisticuffs in a tavern brawl, Davenant had become his patron. Blackbird could go more than twenty-five rounds barefisted without getting a mark on him. He had acquired his nickname while living in St. Giles; black people who lived there were called St. Giles' Blackbirds.

Willoughby, however, was unavoidably forced to forgo his participation in the venture when a courier brought him yet another summons to his grandfather's deathbed.

"Trust him to spoil my fun," he moaned.

Basingthwaite, who now lodged with Willoughby, was quick to offer his services. Davenant gladly accepted the offer, knowing Basingthwaite could hold his own if they found themselves in a fight; he had witnessed the man's boxing prowess at Gentleman John's Academy.

"Why you and Mr. Basingthwaite could both make a living in the ring, if need be," said Gentleman Jim, impressed.

Always up for a fight, Perry wanted to go, too, but Davenant would not hear of it. A naval officer brawling with the riff raff of the rookery would do his career no good. So, as he did most evenings, Perry took himself off for a night on the town with his friends, leaving Georgiana to lament, "It's so, so, *so unfair* that you men have so much fun while I am left at home."

At Willoughby's lodgings in St. James, Davenant, Basingthwaite and Henry changed into rough disguises and armed themselves with pistols before Blackbird met them with a hackney carriage. After collecting Bodger from Miss Barclay's home, they drove to St. Giles-in-the Fields Church, on the opposite side of the High Street from the rookery; the closest the driver would go near it. It was at the church's Resurrection Gate that processions accompanying criminals to be hanged at Tyburn used to pause for the condemned to enjoy a drink of ale, a charitable act presumed to fortify the condemned against the fires of Hell. It was ironic, thought Davenant, that there was an even earthlier hell just across the street.

Rookery folk did not poke their noses into a neighbour's business, the business almost always being illegal, so no one accosted the three roughly- dressed men and a boy as they roamed the rookery. They appeared just another St Giles' gang on their way to do mischief in the world beyond the rookery.

The search began badly. Nell and Edie were not where Bodger had first found them. "Kicked out o' 'er room her wuz cos 'er ain't got no blunt for the rent," Bodger said after speaking with the landlord there. "Knowing her, she boozed it away in diddle shops. She'll be dossing the darkeys at a dossing ken…or doing a starry."

"Spent all 'er money in the gin shops an' now she's sleepin' in cheap lodgings… or out in the open," Henry explained. "Though if yer wants my opinion…"

Davenant ignored him. Nell had to be somewhere in the rookery; she was too poor to live anywhere else.

They began a methodical search of doss houses, the cheap, temporary nighttime lodgings of the itinerant poor. With Bodger leading, they made their way through a never-ending warren of fetid alleys and courts, stopping at every house that advertised a bed for the night. The stench inside these buildings was overwhelming. At times they found themselves up to their ankles in rotting garbage, human excrement from overflowing privies, and mud. Some of the houses they visited were connected by trapdoors and holes in the walls, all created so that criminals could make fast getaways on the rare occasions the law entered the rookery. More than once, by traversing these holes and trapdoors, they made their way along a row of houses overflowing with temporary lodgers without stepping outside until well up the street from where they began.

"Like a Stilton cheese full of maggots, they are," Henry observed after one such journey. "Good job Mr. Willoughby ain't 'ere. Be sick as a pig, 'e would."

"Henry, I beg of you!" Davenant groaned. "Our senses have suffered enough this evening. Don't you agree, Basingthwaite?"

That gentleman could only nod in reply.

For two hours they trudged on, but with no luck. Except for the occasional bouncer who suspected them of trying to obtain free lodgings, they were unmolested. And anyone who did try to stop them thought the better of it when they saw their pistols and the imposing physiques of Davenant and Blackbird. But the indifference they encountered, though it allowed them to pass undisturbed, made locating Nell a problem: no one knew or cared where she was.

As their search wore on without any sign of Nell, Henry's grumbles about Bodger increased. "He's up to summit, that bast…"

He got no further. His foot slipped in something soft and slimy hidden by the darkness.

"Christ Almighty!"

Henry's appeal to his Saviour was drowned in a sudden outburst of squeaks and rustles on the ground beneath him. He lost his balance, tripped over another unseen obstacle and found himself flat on his stomach face to face with several rats.

"Shit!"

This exclamation served a threefold purpose: it identified the cause of his fall, expressed the shock it had given him, and his horror at encountering the vermin he had disturbed. The rats, despite Henry's invasion of their territory, remained where they were, watching the intruder with bright-eyed curiosity and twitching noses.

"Henry?" Davenant said, concerned.

Henry looked up. "No bones broken, guv. Give us a hand up then, Blackbird, old son."

Blackbird gave a low chuckle. With a swift movement of a well-muscled arm, the boxer reached down, yanked Henry to his feet and sniffed. "Phew! Smell likes a privy you do, little man."

"That's cos 'e didn't look where 'e wuz goin,' said Bodger as he rejoined them. "You stink!" he told Henry.

"Keepin' my eye on you, I wuz," Henry shot back. "Guide us through the rookery, would yer? Pshaw! Yer knows yer way round here 'bout as well as a polar bear knows 'is way cross a desert."

"Enough!" snapped Davenant, who was staring down at what the lamp revealed. Among the rotting vegetation, dirt and animal droppings lay the obstacle that caused Henry's fall: the body of a man with an empty bottle in his hand, sagged against the wall of a house, his feet sticking out into the street.

At first Davenant thought him yet another drunkard in a stupor; they had seen plenty of those that night. He bent and felt for a pulse. "Dead," he said, shaking his head, "and by the looks of him for some time."

He motioned Blackbird to lower the lamp. The worn upper of one boot had parted from its sole to reveal the man's bare toes. From the many bite marks on the shoe leather and the toes, it was obvious Henry had interrupted the rats at their supper. Now they waited ready to resume their feast once the intruders left.

Davenant rose. His action disturbed the body and it slipped sideways with a soft thud that set the rats squealing again. "We will report the death to the parish officials when we leave. Although I doubt they wll be in any hurry to remove a body from this hell hole."

"Newgate seize me!" said Henry. "Them rats is as big as cats."

"Even bigger 'round Monmouth Street, they are, Bodger asserted. "Big as dogs!"

"Sez you!"

"'Struth!"

"Enough!"

There was an underlying weariness to Davenant's sharp remonstrance. By now they had scoured every doss house they could find and still there was no sign of Nell. He had been optimistic when Bodger announced that he knew Nell's whereabouts: too optimistic. He expected immediate results–not a long, fruitless search. He had been thwarted yet again. He was even beginning to think Henry might be right about Bodger, after all.

There was only one thing to do: go home.

"We have been to every lodging in every court and every damned alley in this godforsaken place," he said. "There is no sign of Nell. We will go."

Bodger grabbed his hand. "No, guv! Oh, no! We can't. Not yet. There's another doss house…in the courtyard…up ahead. He pointed to where a faint glow of light showed from between two buildings. "Coming to tell yer, I wuz when that noddy fell over. We gotta look there," he begged. "We gotta!"

36

The only light in the small courtyard came from the flickering wick behind the dirty glass panes of an oil lamp above the open door of a run-down, three-storey house. On the wall beside the door was a crude hand-painted sign that explained the house's purpose: *Beds for sale 3d each.* Inside, the house was similar to all the other doss houses Davenant had visited that night: a dark, narrow hall smelling of stale sweat and tobacco, with a room on one side of it and a staircase to the upper floors on the other.

In the alcove under the stairs, the house's proprietor sprawled in an armchair from which protruded much of its horsehair stuffing. In front of him on a plank supported by a barrel and a chair was a tin full of coppers, halfpennies and farthings, a half-eaten hunk of bread and cheese and two lighted candles that had burned low. The man rose from his chair and leaned across the counter for a better view of the new arrivals.

"Threepence for the night… each of yer…if yer wants a bed," he grunted, displaying a mouthful of rotting teeth interspersed with bits of bread and cheese.

"We don't want beds. We merely wish to search for a friend we believe maybe here," Davenant told him.

The man rested his hands on the counter and thrust his face at Davenant. "Knows that game, I does," he sneered. "And while yer searchin'–as yer calls it–you'll scare off some of me lodgers…and take their place fer free! Off wiv yer, now!"

He reached out an arm behind him. But Davenant was too quick for him, and in an instant he was behind the counter. He grabbed the proprietor's arm, twisting it behind the man's back and jabbed the pistol he held in his other hand under the man's chin. In the alcove beneath the stairs, Henry found the man's pistol and stuck it in his belt.

"My dear fellow, you flatter yourself," Davenant said to the proprietor. "I would rather spend a night in the stables with my horses than one in this hostelry. A quick search of this pigsty is all my five senses can stomach. Now, let us be about our business."

Before the man could reply, Blackbird gagged him with his own neckerchief while Henry tied his hands behind his back with another. Then they threw him back into the chair.

With Davenant leading with the lamp and a pistol at the ready, the four of them made their way up a broken staircase that creaked at every step, with a banister that wobbled at their touch. The rooms on the two upper floors were full of people, several sharing a bed while others slept on the floor. There they met the same sickening smells and the same curses they heard at the other stops that night–but still no Nell.

The only other room was an attic reached by a short set of stairs with an even more rickety banister than the others. The smell of unwashed bodies, decaying vegetables and heavy, cheap tobacco smoke met Davenant when he opened the door. There were no beds. Several men, some puffing clay pipes, sat on the floor in the middle of the room playing cards by the light of a solitary candle. From one dark corner came the moans of a man and a woman having sex, as oblivious to their fellow lodgers as they were to them. The remainder of the twenty or so men, women and children lay on the floor around the room. From the number of people crammed into the room and its place atop such a dangerous flight of stairs, Davenant guessed this was where those who could not afford the full price of a bed were lodged for less money.

What talk there had been stopped when the strangers entered. In the wary silence that followed, all eyes were on them. With pistols at the ready, Davenant and Henry advanced into the room, while Blackbird and Basingthwaite took up position just outside the door.

"Do not be alarmed," Davenant said to the lodgers. "We intend you no harm. My companions and I merely seek a friend."

Carefully scrutinising faces as he went, Bodger made his way among the bodies. As they lay so close together, it was impossible for him to avoid stepping on some. There were mutters from those he disturbed, mutters taken up by others angered by the intrusion. At this, Blackbird and Basingthwaite moved into the room with pistols at the ready. But in spite of their anger, no one tried to stop Bodger, no doubt afraid of the wrath they might incur of what they believed were the pistol-toting members of yet another St. Giles gang.

Bodger gave a sudden shout of triumph. "Its her, guv! Her and the boy!"

Davenant scrambled over bodies to where Bodger was shaking a shadowy figure laying slumped against a wall.

"Remember me, Nell? Bodger? Come to find yer, I ave. Mick won't hurt you no more. This here gent is a mate of mine. He will help yer, but 'e needs your help first."

Davenant knelt down beside Nell and raised the lamp, recoiling at the reek of spirits as she slowly raised her head. In the lamplight he saw a young woman aged beyond her years by liquor and poverty. Bloodshot watery eyes stared unseeing at him from a face coarsened by drink, framed by lifeless locks tinged with grey. Curled up beside her lay her simple-minded son, Eddie.

"Listen, Nell," Davenant said, his voice low and urgent. "My name is Davenant. The boy? Addy? You remember him?"

Nell's head lolled as she tried to focus on him. She nodded slowly.

"He's not dead," he went on. "He is in my care. I want to return him to his family. I need to know where Malloy got him. From whom did he buy him? *Think*, now!"

She stared at him vacantly. He shook her gently. "Who-sold-the-boy-to-Malloy?" he demanded, emphasizing each word.

There was no reply. Nell's head drooped on her breast and her eyes closed. No longer cowed, the lodgers had become louder and more vocal in their mutterings at the sight of one of their own being, as they thought, manhandled by a stranger. Those that had been lying down were either sitting up, or resting on one elbow, and a few got to their feet. Davenant heard their irate shouts behind him.

"Bugger off!"

"Scarper!"

"Leave her be!"

"Sod off!"

With his back to Davenant, Henry faced the room's resentful occupants with a pistol. "Getting' nasty, they are, guv," he said over his shoulder. "Reckons we should go."

Davenant handed the lamp to Bodger and dragged Nell to her feet. "She and the boy go with us," he said.

Bodger took Eddie's hand they began making their way back to the door. Behind them, backing slowly came Davenant and Henry, each with an arm around Nell and a pistol in the other hand pointed at the threatening lodgers. Basingthwaite and Blackbird swept forward to assist them. The sudden draft caused by the movement of Basingthwaite's overcoat snuffed out the card players' candle, leaving the room in darkness, for by then Bodger and the lamp were outside on the landing.

"Charlies, they are! Dont let 'em take her!" a voice with an Irish brogue shouted somewhere in the darkness.

"Get 'em lads!" yelled another.

Bodger was already running downstairs, dragging the frightened Eddie with him, when the others reached the door.

"Downstairs, the rest of you, quick! I'll hold them off, if necessary," Davenant said as he slammed shut the door. He pushed Nell toward Blackbird and Basingthwaite; they grabbed hold of her between them and began their descent.

"I'll stay wiv yer, guv," Henry said.

Without a word Davenant pushed him down the stairs.

With yells and curses the angry lodgers beat and pushed against the closed door. On the other side of it, out on the dark landing, Davenant braced his back against the door, pushing hard to counter the opposing force until he was sure the others had reached the ground floor. Then putting both hands on the bannister, he leaped over it. With a loud crunch it broke under his weight, and he fell down onto the flight of stairs immediately below. He staggered to his feet and jumped again over the banister on to the next landing just as the furious lodgers finally stormed the attic door. Unable to see where they were going in the dark, propelled forward by those behind them, the leaders fell screaming through the broken banister, while the rest rushed headlong down the stairs to the next landing, trampling over the fallen bodies that writhed there.

"Kill the bastards"

"They got Nell!"

"Get 'em!"

The cries and the pounding feet bought lodgers from the other rooms on the lower floors. Caught up in the excitement of the moment, they had no idea what the commotion was about, nor did they care. Spoiling for a fight, they set on those who had disturbed their slumber. Stairs and landings were filled with a mindless mob of brawling and tumbling lodgers that moved forward inexorably down into the hall and spilled out into the courtyard. Too late to evade the screaming horde of fighting men, women and children, some with broken bottles and knives, Davenant and the others were instantly caught up in the fray.

Davenant had anticipated they might encounter trouble in the rookery. For that reason he had taken Henry, Basingthwaite and Blackbird with him, none of them being strangers to the art of pugilism. In addition to sparring each week at Gentleman Jackson's Academy, he had, when younger, fought in many a brawl. He threw himself with gusto into the fight, delivering his punishing right to any members of the mob who dared set upon him. The mindless ferocity of those who did, he found exhilarating. Sparring with Gentleman Jackson was insipid by comparison.

"Chicken-hearted cowards! Take me on, if you dare!"

Davenant heard Blackbird's yell above the noise of the crowd and knew the boxer would deal swiftly with anyone who did dare to do that.

He caught a glimpse of Basingthwaite coolly disposing of an assailant and somewhere among the crush of bodies he knew Henry would be, too. All three could hold more than their own in a fight. What concerned him was the safety of Nell, Eddie and Bodger. The last time he had seen them they were in the comparative safety of a shadowy doorway where Blackbird and Basingthwaite put them. Nell's safety was crucial and not just for compassionate reasons; she had yet to tell him what she knew about Addy. He must get her and the boy away, for the riot was not only growing with people from beyond the courtyard coming to join it: it was also becoming more violent.

There was only one thing to do.

Reluctantly Davenant socked one last jaw. Then with all his might he yelled,

"In the street! In the street! After 'em, lads!"

In a unified roar, the rioters took up the cry, "In the street! In the street! After 'em! After 'em! After 'em!"

As one, the howling mass of humanity, if that was what it could be called, rushed off into Dyott Street. In minutes the courtyard was empty, the roar of the mob growing fainter and fainter until there was silence.

Davenant looked around him. At least two rioters lay dead or unconscious in the dirt, and several others were dragging themselves away on all fours. By the feeble glow of the lamp over the door, he saw Basingthwaite leaning against the wall. On one of his cheeks there was a telltale dark patch.

"You are hurt?"

Basingthwaite shook his head. "Nothing of consequence. Blood from a cut," he laughed. Some of those devils had knives!"

After having made sure the mob had disappeared for good, Henry and Blackbird swaggered back from Dyott Street.

"Bunch o' dromedaries, all of 'em. Couldn't hit a ball with a bat, let alone plant one on the Blackbird," the prizefighter boasted.

"Then none of us is the worse for that little…er…disturbance," Davenant drawled.

"No thanks to that there Bodger," Henry said. "Warned yer about 'im, I did, guv. Said he'd lead us in ter trouble, I did…and look what 'appened. And where is 'e now, I'd like ter know?"

"Right behind yer! "

Henry jumped.

"Come quick, guv!" Bodger implored Davenant. "It's Nell. I think she's dying."

The bloodied bodies of Nell and Eddie lay in the doorway where they hid during the riot. Davenant knelt to examine them; they had been stabbed several times. He took Nell by the shoulders and gently shook her. "Nell!" he demanded. "Nell, can you hear me?"

He felt for a pulse: there was none. It was the same with Eddie.

"Damn!" he cried, angry not for the loss of a life, but because Nell had died before he could question her. Anger quickly gave way to remorse for his lack of feeling. He sighed. At least he could show her respect. He took off his ragged overcoat and fashioned it into a pillow that he slipped under her head.

Overcome by the loss of the one person who had ever shown him kindness in his hard life, Bodger burst into tears and walked off to sob in the shadows.

"Poor wretch. To die like this," Basingthwaite murmured, "and before you were able to speak to her, too."

No sadness on Bodger's part, no matter how deeply felt, could ever cause him to forgo the one thing he loved doing the most: eating. And when he returned to Miss Barclay's home after the visit to St. Giles, he accepted with alacrity the offer of a bun and a cup of milk before he went to bed. His grief over Nell's death had temporarily quieted him, but though forlorn he still tackled his snack with his usual gusto.

It had been late when Davenant, Henry and Bodger arrived at the Gracechurch Street house. The servants were in bed, but Miss Barclay had waited up for them. She let them in and took them to the kitchen, where she sat them down at the table for some welcome refreshments.

Basingthwaite and Blackbird had taken leave of the others in Oxford Street; the former to return by another cab to Willoughby lodgings; the latter to spend in a nearby tavern some of the money Davenant gave him for his night's work. After informing the parish authorities of the deaths of Nell and Eddie and arranging for their funerals, Davenant, Henry and Bodger took a hackney carriage to the Barclay home. The journey was made in silence, in light of Bodger's loss, Henry observing a momentary truce in his ongoing war of words with the boy. Bodger and Davenant felt the loss the most. Davenant's motives for this being more self-serving because of the part Nell was to have played in his enquiries, he again experienced guilt when Miss Barclay expressed her concern.

She noticed their dejection at once. "Thou art injured?" she asked, looking from one to the other.

Davenant shook his head. Quickly he explained all that occurred in St Giles. He ended with an apology for his ragged appearance of himself and his companions. "My tailor is not *au fait* with the fashions of the rookery," he said with a rueful twitch of his lips.

"It is not by the cut of his coat that I judge a man," she said, smiling.

He gazed down at her, the two of them briefly lost to those around them.

Henry's loud, "Ahem!" put an end to their silent exchange of glances. Davenant turned and asked Bodger what he knew about Nell's death.

"Nuffink much," he mumbled, his mouth full of bun. "Him," he said, indicating Henry, "and that other fella what wuz wiv us...they put Nell, Eddie an me in a doorway...afore, they joins the fight." He looked at Miss Barclay. "There wuz so many of 'em about, I was pushed into the crowd an' the fighting. Nell an Eddie's stabbin' musta happened after that? Some had knives." He gulped some milk and wiped his mouth on his sleeve. "That ain't all. He was there! *The cove* what come around Malloy's yard askin' questions the night when Malloy and Nell wuz at the gin shop."

`"But that was at night," Davenant said. "You didn't see his face."

"Told yer afore I recognised his voice, though... recognise it *anywhere*. Heard it tonight, I did, loud and clear in the fight."

"Among that yelling and screaming mob? How could you?" There was incredulity in Davenants drawl.

Indignant, Bodger retorted, "'Twas him, I tells yer! Know that voice anywhere, I would. Pretending again, he wuz, to sound different...like 'e did afore. Maybe he killed Nell."

Henry was scornful. "There wuz a lot of knives about! Anyone coulda killed that little doxy."

Bodger's eyes filled with tears. "Don't speak like that 'bout Nell!" he shouted. "Wuz good ter me, she wuz—well sometimes, anyway."

He took Miss Barclay's proffered handkerchief and wiped his eyes and blew his nose with it. His face crumpled. "She wouldna hurt much, would she, when she died?"

With a smile of reassurance, Miss Barclay gently shook her head. This had the desired effect. Bodger relaxed and he smiled as he began recalling memories of Nell.

"Let him speak," Miss Barclay whispered to Davenant. "It will help ease his grief."

"Always mumbling Nell wuz when she wuz on the Blue Ruin," Bodger said. "All sorts of daft things." He grinned. "Last thing she said afore I got caught up in the fight was somethin' daft. Always remember it, I will."

Davenant tensed.

Had his questions to Nell actually penetrated her drunken stupor? Had she mumbled a belated reply to them to Bodger?

"What?"

The question was like the crack of a whip.

They all looked at Bodger.

Bodger basked in this attention, unaware of the suspense he was creating. He cocked his head on one side, his face creased in concentration. "Um, now, let me fink," he said, taking what seemed to Davenant an eternity to remember.

"Smug!" he said suddenly. "That was it!"

"Smug!" said Davenant, at a loss.

"Hang on. I ain't finished. Still thinkin' I am. Smug…smug…smug… smuggler! That's it! Smuggler! Whatever that means."

Davenant grabbed him by the shoulders. "Yes! And?"

Bodger stared up at the ceiling as if seeking to find writ large there the words he sought. "Er…smuggler…smuggler gone…gone. Got it! 'Smuggler gone away.'" He grinned at Davenant. "Don't make sense, do it? Musta been the gin talking."

Davenant's reaction astonished the other three. For a minute or two he stared uncomprehendingly at Bodger. Then his manner abruptly changed. Those lips of his that rarely smiled did just that. His smile became wider and wider until he actually burst out laughing.

37

With an awe bordering on veneration, Willoughby's valet watched as Davenant's nimble fingers went about the intricacies of turning a muslin band into the sartorial *tour de force* that was a Davenant Drape.

Summoned in haste to attend his grandfather's sickbed yet again, Willoughby had left his manservant behind. However, the valet felt more than compensated for his master's desertion by being called to wait upon Lord Davenant, a gentleman whose *toilettes* were almost as famous as those of Mr. Brummell. That his lordship and the lodgings' other resident, Mr. Basingthwaite, had been on secret business together that evening, only added to valet's pride. Since Davenant's return to change from his disguise back into his own elegant attire, the valet had hovered about him while he bathed and dressed, falling over himself to serve such an arbiter of masculine elegance.

But although his fingers were going through the customary motions of folding and tying a cravat, Davenant's mind was preoccupied with matters much more important than a Davenant Drape. What an evening! What at first appeared a fruitless visit to the rookery had actually been, with the exception of Nell's death, a productive one; and all because that little devil Bodger had recalled Nell's drunken gabble before she died, "Smuggler gone away."

Smuggler reminded Davenant of the Conway brothers, whom he had seen at Ned Ticehurst's smithy. It was then he realised why the peddler watching his house seemed so familiar: he was one of the Conways. Nell was drunk when she mumbled what Bodger thought were the words 'gone away.' But what she could have said was "Smuggler Conway," a belated answer to Davenant's earlier question about who sold Addy to Malloy. When asked, a sleepy Bodger yawned, "Could be. When 'er wuz on the gin, there's no tellin' what she meant."

Since a few days before Davenant's wager, the peddler had appeared daily in Grosvenor Square. He was never seen to sell anything because he had nothing worth buying–but that did not keep him away. Now that it was likely a Conway sold Addy to the sweep, one of the brothers was watching the house because of

Addy's presence there, not because he planned to rob it. But why, after selling the boy, was a Conway still interested in him? Did he fear Addy might identify him as his kidnapper? If so, why stay close to the boy, where he could be identified? Addy, who often viewed the square with Perry's telescope, had not recognised him, but then he had not seen the men who kidnapped him. Was the Conway watching the house in hopes of stealing Addy to ransom him back to his family? But if ransom was his aim, why, instead of selling the boy to a sweep for a few guineas, had he not demanded one after kidnapping him? And why were the Conways involved in this? The coast, not London, was their home, their strong suit smuggling, although the blacksmith said they would do anything for money—even murder. Had someone hired them to kidnap Addy? If so, who? And why?

One person had the answers to these questions: the Conway brother readily available to Davenant in the square. Tomorrow, he would waylay the fellow, obtain those answers and take him before a magistrate. And those answers, Davenant was certain, would tell him where to find Addy's grandfather. Conway would be charged with kidnapping and stealing the boy's clothes he was wearing when he took him, the latter a hanging offence, not to mention any charges of smuggling outstanding against him. Addy would be returned to his grandfather, and he would win his wager in good time.

Davenant stood back from the mirror the better to view his completed cravat. Willoughby's' valet sighed. Until his dying day he would remember being present at the creation of this masterpiece. If only his own master were as attentive in matters of dress as his lordship.

The valet moved to the dressing table on which was an array of perfume bottles. "Attar of Roses?" my lord. "Hungary Water, *eau de Cologne*, or perhaps this?" He unstoppered a small crystal bottle and offered it to Davenant. "A regular favourite of Mr. Basingthwaite. From foreign parts, I believe."

Davenant drew back his head in disgust at the sweet heavy odour. "Gad! No gentleman should wear that!" He waved away the bottle. "As my friend Brummell says: carbolic soap—lots of it—and plenty of fresh linen *daily* is all that is necessary for a gentleman."

The valet acknowledged this sartorial maxim with a bow.

A JACKETING CONCERN

His *toilette* finished, Davenant went in search of Basingthwaite. He found him reading in Willoughby's parlour; he, too, had bathed and changed.

"Once again I am in your debt," Davenant said. "First you come to the aid of my sister, and then you came to my aid this evening with those fists of yours. We must have a friendly bout sometime. I trust you are none the worse for your injury."

"I am glad I could be of service. And my injury? 'Twas nothing."

And Davenant saw this was true.

"My only regret about tonight", Basingthwaite went on, "is that we were unable to obtain any information about the boy from the woman, Nell."

Davenant would have said more but a loud commotion at the apartment's entrance prevented him. Red-faced and fuming, Lionel Willoughby burst into the room.

"I take it your early return augurs well for the health of your grandfather," Davenant drawled. "He is still with us?"

"To hell with him!" Willoughby thundered, "and the sooner the better! He wasn't dying! The message was a trick...a bloody rotten lie! The old fool was alive and kicking when I got there. Hellish row we had! Accused me of going there to wheedle money from him! As if anyone could wheedle money out of that *demned skinflint!*"

"A trick? Who would want to play a trick like that on you?" Basingthwaite asked.

"Demned if I know!" Willoughby thought for a moment then added, "No. I do know who did it: that blasted old moneybags himself! Manipulates his family like chessman on a board, he does, just for the hell of it. What annoys me most is that it prevented me joining your St. Giles caper. How did it go, by the way?"

"I will tell you later," Davenant said.

Confident now that the mystery would be solved once he questioned the peddler Conway, Davenant's spirits lifted. With victory in sight and his energy restored, he felt he could afford a diversion. "The night is still young and Harriette Wilson's sister, Amy, is holding her weekly *soirée*. Why not pay her a visit?"

"Anything to forget grandpapa," Willoughby said when Davenant suggested it.

"And the rookery," Basingthwaite added.

Davenant raised his quizzing glass and surveyed the usual bevy of lovelies who were always present at Amy Wilson's gatherings. Although several of these belles tried vainly to catch his eye, none of them appealed to him. This surprised him because he had gone without the physical aspects of female companionship for several weeks, and Amy's friends were the *crème de la crème* of the *demi-monde*. Yet attractive though they were, he found himself comparing them unfavourably with Miss Barclay, who, though not their equal in looks, possessed a charm all her own.

"Hello Davenant!" a voice hailed him.

Richard Sheridan, the playwright and politician, leaned against a nearby wall, watching the guests.

The tipsy Sheridan indicated the crowd with a shaky hand and chuckled. "All the world *is* a stage, eh? All players in their own little dramas: troubled Hamlets, sensuous Cleopatra's, jealous Othellos, virginal Juliets—not too many of those— shrewish Katherines and arrogant Petruchios. See that fellow coming towards us. Reminds me of a chap I once auditioned for the role of a certain thane in 'The Scottish Play'."

Each with an arm around the waist of a young woman, Basingthwaite and Willoughby pushed their way through the crush of people toward Davenant.

"Davenant," Willoughby said, permit me to introduce Eliza…"

"The love of your life," Davenant finished. "Dick here is indulging in one of his pastimes: casting the assembled company in dramatic roles," he said, introducing Basingthwaite to Sheridan.

"Honoured as I am to meet the author of *The School for Scandal* and *The Rivals*, I must, however, confess I have no interest in the theatre, sir," Basingthwaite said, looking embarrassed by this admission." I've no wish to offend you, sir, but I never go there. Theatre is but an illusion, a spectacle attended by those who go there to be seen by others rather than view the performance."

Sheridan struck a mock dramatic pose. "Don't like the theatre! I despair of you, sir, although you don't look like a Philistine to me. Why, for a moment there, I even thought you were an actor. You remind me of someone who auditioned for me once. He wanted to play a certain Scottish thane."

"The Scottish play? Shakespeare?" Basingthwaite shook his head. "Not I, sir. I have never trod the boards. Perish the thought!" He smiled at his companion. "And now, if you will excuse me, I have a prior engagement with this young lady."

"So have I!" said Willoughby, giving his companion a squeeze.

Davenant and Sheridan watched the four of them go.

"Basingthwaite as Mac…" Davenant began.

"Don't you dare, sir!" Sheridan interrupted. "Unlucky for an actor to say that name."

"I am not an actor."

"Neither was that fellow your friend reminded me of," Sheridan replied with laugh, "but he thought he was."

38

As he stared down at the body's lifeless face, Davenant was unable to prevent a shiver. It was not what he saw that made him do this–at least that was what he told himself. Death was nothing new to him; he had witnessed it before on the battlefield. No, he shivered because it was cold and damp inside the "dead house". The heavy wooden door was closed and little light and none of the sun's warmth penetrated the two narrow windows in the thick stone walls.

The attendant raised his lantern to provide a better view. Despite its blue-tinged pallor and bulging eyes, there was no mistaking that face.

Basingthwaite sighed and nodded. "Yes, that is Sir Thomas Hurley."

With a puzzled frown, Davenant studied the corpse of the young man who had been so eager to become a fashionable *beau*. The disparity between his body and those of the man and woman with whom he now shared the 'dead house' was as obvious in death as it would have been when they were living. So much suffering was etched on the faces of the raggedly-dressed pair; it was hard to tell whether they were young or old. They were just another two of London's many poor, who each year sought relief in suicide from the hopelessness of their days. The river's human detritus, they were fished out of the Thames and taken to one of the "dead house's' for drowned bodies situated along its banks. They would go to their graves unidentified and unmourned, their passing noted as a mere number in the Bills of Mortality, their final resting place a pauper's grave.

In contrast, there was no hint of despair or sadness on Hurley's face. Even in death his body still possessed much of that youthful force and arrogance that characterised him in life. Davenant experienced a twinge of pity. Death had come too early for this young man. Hurley had been full of his own importance, overly sure of himself and with foolish, quixotic notions of avenging family honor by challenging Davenant to a wager. But in that he had been no different from many other young men, who denied their inner doubts with rash acts and impulsive behavior. Irreverent though it was in the circumstances, Davenant could not help a wry twitch of his lips when he noticed that Hurley, despite his dislike of him, had taken to heart his criticism about dress. Damp and reeking of the river though they were, Hurley's coat and breeches were what attracted the attention of the two mudlarks who found him, the attendant said. The boys were scavenging among the debris in the river shallows early that morning when they saw a body in the slime at the water's edge by Westminster Bridge. Used to such sights, they paid little attention at first until one of them noticed the body's elegant clothing, a sure sign the corpse would contain valuables. With some difficulty, for Hurley's coat pockets were full of stones, the boys pulled the body ashore. Two officers of the Horse Guards returning to barracks by way of the bridge saw the mudlarks riffling the dead man's pockets and gave chase. In their haste, one of the mudlarks dropped the man's pocketbook. This contained papers, which, although damaged by water, were still legible enough to identify their owner. Seeing the documents owner had a title and in hopes of a monetary reward for his trouble, the attendant sent word to Hurley's lodgings first: the coroner, second.

As his master rarely returned home after night's carousing until the following morning, Hurley's manservant had been unconcerned when he did not return the night before. When the constable informed him his master had drowned, the valet directed him to Willoughby's lodgings, where Hurley's erstwhile friend Basingthwaite lived. Only Willoughby was at home, and he went at once to Gentleman Jackson's gymnasium, where he knew Basingthwaite would be and found him sparring with Davenant.

The news stunned Basingthwaite. "Suicide? No! No! It can't be. There's some mistake," he said. "It can't be him. Its someone else…someone who attacked him…stole his pocketbook. Yes. That must be it. And Hurley lies injured elsewhere."

He would go immediately to view the body, he said. Only when he had satisfied himself that it was really that of Hurley would he then inform the deceased's family. Davenant at once offered to drive him to the "dead house" in his curricle.

Davenant, too, thought it must be a case of mistaken identity. Hurley's bravado in wagering the notorious Lord Davenant had earned him leadership of a group of St. James' bucks with whom he spent his evenings carousing in low taverns, brothels, gaming hells and at Vauxhall Gardens. Even by the standards of a society that regarded heavy drinking as normal, Hurley's drinking was considered excessive. Basingthwaite was no doubt correct in his assumption that a drunken Hurley had been attacked and robbed by the person on whose body his valuables were found.

That was before he and Davenant went to the "dead house".

"Did it 'isself," the attendant grunted. "Coat pocket's full o' stones. That's what suicides do to make sure they drown proper, like. He musta got caught up by a barge tiller. That's why 'e didn't sink."

Basingthwaite grimaced. "You…you mean he jumped from the bridge?"

"Perhaps he was pushed," Davenant suggested.

The attended shook his head. "Nah. 'E jumped. Lucky he was, though."

"Lucky?" Davenant looked up from the body. "One can be lucky at cards," he drawled, at the races or in love—but death? My good man, death is a decidedly *unlucky* occurrence for all of us. Pray, what makes you say he was…ahem… lucky?"

The attendant was matter-of-fact. "Seen a lot 'as jumped off the bridge, I 'ave. Their heads gets banged against them big stone supports below the bridge somethin' terrible, or they gets whacked by a barge tiller," he said, adding with relish, "covered in marks, they is: bruises, broken bones, faces smashed. But this one? Not a mark on 'im. No one saw him jump, so we'll take the stones out of his pockets and the family will think he fell in cos he was drunk. That way he'll get a Christian burial."

"No one saw him jump, or be pushed? Strange, indeed," Davenant said. "Westminster Bridge is full of traffic day and night. What makes you so certain he jumped?"

The attendant was indignant. "Knows a jumper when I sees one, I do! And seen plenty, I 'ave!"

With that he rested his lamp on a stone ledge and drew the cover over Hurley's face once more. The lamp illuminated some items that lay on the ledge. Davenant picked them up and examined them. They were the usual things a gentleman carried on his person: a pocket book, a ring and a watch. There was also what appeared to be a dirty rag.

"His things," the attendant said in response to Davenant's query. "Mudlarks got nufink cos the soldiers stopped them."

With a sniff of disgust, Davenant held up the rag; it was damp and reeked of river slime.

"Nuffink important. Floatin' near 'im, it wuz. 'Is handkerchief, I reckon–or what's left of it," the attendant said. "Or maybe it was thrown off a boat. All sorts of stuff in the river."

"Definitely someone's handkerchief: its silk," Davenant said, drawing the fabric between the thumb and palm of his hand until they met a large knot tied in a corner of it. With some effort he managed to undo this. A small round object fell on to the stone floor with a faint 'ching.'

Davenant bent and picked it up. It was a coin.

He motioned the attendant to raise his lantern as he pulled back the cover from Hurley's head. Gently, he raised the dead man's chin and examined his neck.

"Not a mark on him?" he murmured, more to himself than the others. "There you are wrong, and I think the coroner will agree."

Leaving Basingthwaite to provide the "dead house" attendant with details about Hurley's next of kin, Davenant stepped outside and went and stood at the top of the stairs leading down to the river. Glad to be free of the "dead house"'s' gloomy damp and all it contained, he breathed deeply of the fresh breeze blowing off the water. All about him, throbbing and vital, stood London with its perpetual roar and one million people. Behind him were Vauxhall Gardens, the pleasure grounds of rich and poor alike. On Westminster Bridge traffic rattled and rumbled; across the river was the imposing vista of Westminster Hall and Westminster Abbey; further along, Whitehall and Horse Guards Parade; and in the distance, dominating the skyline, the dome of St. Paul's Cathedral surrounded by a forest of city church spires. Most of the river traffic was concentrated down river at the huge docks, where ships of many flags loaded and unloaded cargoes that made

London the world's biggest trading centre. But here at Westminster Bridge and up river there was still plenty of traffic: barges hauling sea coal to power inland industries, others going downstream with farm produce, building stones and hay for London's many horses, fishing boats trawling nets, and waterman in their wherries, yelling and cursing at each other.

Amid all the vigour and noise of the city the "dead house" looked out of place, as did the body of the once spirited, rowdy Hurley now lying there.

Davenant tapped his chin with his quizzing glass.

Willoughby had told him he saw Hurley at Vauxhall Gardens the previous evening. "Basingthwaite and I were in a supper booth with our…ahem…lady friends. It was about midnight and we'd just met Perry. Hurley was on his way out. Said Vauxhall was too tame for him. He'd been drinking but he wasn't drunk…well, not as drunk as I've seen him, anyway. When we quizzed him about it, he laughed. Said Ma Dewberry had sent word she had a new young chit that would interest him. Said he wanted to be sure he was 'up to snuff' for a few furlongs with her. Made a few sarcastic remarks to Perry about you and the wager. That hothead brother of yours was all for calling him out, but I managed to calm him."

"Was Hurley alone?"

"He was when I saw him. But after? Who knows? Place was packed. Such a crush!" Willoughby winked. "I was busy with my bit o' muslin, so was Basingthwaite. Went off with her into the bushes, and Hurley disappeared into the crowd." Willoughby shrugged. "All those alleys and grottos there? Plenty o' places to meet someone."

"Oars! Oars!"

Repeated shouts from a group of watermen below the stairs brought Davenant back to the present. Watermen and their wherries were no longer the main transportation along and across the water as they been when London Bridge was the only bridge over the river. The erection of more bridges, particularly toll-free Westminster Bridge, ruined their lucrative trade, sending many of them to work in the docks. But people who enjoyed water travel, particularly to Vauxhall, could always find an eager waterman.

A JACKETING CONCERN

When Basingthwaite emerged from the "dead house", Davenant was nowhere in sight.

A bluff-looking John Bull of a man with steel buckles on his shoes standing nearby the "dead house" noticed his bewilderment. "He's down at the water's edge," he told him.

And that was where Basingthwaite found Davenant deep in conversation with two watermen. They were telling in him in no uncertain terms what they would do if they caught the person who had stolen one of their boats the previous night.

39

The line of vehicles headed for the Westminster side of the bridge was at a standstill. A wagon loaded with turnips and pulled by four ambling oxen had lost some of its load, forcing the traffic behind to wait while the driver retrieved it. It was slow work, and some of the more impatient waiting drivers vented their frustration by shouting and yelling curses at the wagoner. Only fear of Davenant's censure prevented Henry Rollins from joining in the outcry. Unperturbed by the delay, Davenant sat calmly holding the ribbons. His face might wear its habitual bored expression, but he was busy scrutinising the bridge, his mind on Hurley's death.

Westminster Bridge was toll free so there were no toll keepers who might have recalled seeing Hurley arrive or leave the bridge the previous night. A line of the new gas lamps flanked each side of the roadway across the bridge. Every night many of those who could not afford the price of a bed in a doss house slept on the stone seats in the bridge's embrasures. With so much light and so many people always about, anyone who attempted to jump from the bridge at night could not help but be noticed–and even prevented from doing so.

"So tragic! His whole life before him," Basingthwaite said with heavy sigh.

It was the first time he had spoken since they had left the 'dead house'. Believing his silence and ashen face was due to the shock of seeing the body of his former friend, Davenant had not intruded on his anguish.

"I shall go down at once to Gloucestershire and inform the family of his death. It's the least I can do. Pray be so good as to convey my excuses to your sister. Willoughby and I were to accompany her and Addy to Hyde Park this afternoon. We were going to play cricket with the boy."

"Georgiana will understand, but I know Addy will miss you," Davenant said. I know how much he enjoys playing cricket with you, Willoughby and my brother."

"I feel perhaps in some way to blame for Hurley's death," Basingthwaite lamented. "If I had not withdrawn my friendship, I might have prevented him from…" unable to finish, he shook his head.

"You think Hurley committed suicide?"

"You heard yourself! He put stones in his pocket to make sure that he sank!"

His eyes on the road ahead, Davenant asked, "Why would he do that? He had every reason to live: the notoriety of likely besting me in a wager, not to mention the satisfaction of seeing me lose to the Regent the horses I am now driving. He was living life to the hilt: drinking, gambling, carousing and womanizing, and had not, as yet, run through his fortune. He had no reason to kill himself. I await the postmortem results, but I think it just possible he may have been murdered–possibly strangled–by someone and thrown into the river."

"Murdered!" Basingthwaite gasped. "By a mugger? A footpad? Or perhaps, because of the riotous life he led, by someone of whom he had made an enemy. Although not long in town he could have made some."

"Muggers and footpads do not usually bother to dispose of their victim's bodies, and they rob them," Davenant said. "Hurley was not robbed. And, if I am correct in my belief, his body was weighted with stones and dumped in the river to dispose of it. As to the other alternatives you mention, you may well be right, although any enemies he might have made among gentlemen in society would have challenged him to a duel, not murder him."

Basingthwaite said nothing but shook his head in apparent bewilderment.

"Odd, don't you think," Davenant went on, "that three people connected with this wager of mine have died in violent circumstances? First Malloy, then his wife, both of whom could have helped me solve the mystery, and their son. And now Hurley, who instigated the wager."

"Oh coincidences, surely," Basingthwaite said. "Malloy and the woman were killed in St. Giles. Life is cheap there: violent death a daily occurrence. Malloy's journeyman was seen standing over the sweep's body? Obviously he murdered him for money. And his wife and son were killed in a riot. They are common enough in St Giles and in this city. And how can you be so certain Hurley was murdered by anyone: footpad or enemy? There were no marks on him were there?"

"Perhaps initially there were not any, but when I looked, some light ones were beginning to appear on the neck."

"Oh."

"Coincidences or not, these deaths add an intriguing element to this bet of mine," Davenant said. His lips twitched. "One wonders what will happen next. Not another death, I hope".

"So in spite of Hurley's death you intend to carry on with the wager?" Basingthwaite said.

The line of vehicles in front of them began to move forward. Davenant's greys moved off at a walk.

"Of course," Davenant said. "Daily it becomes more of a challenge, all the more so as there is little time left for me to complete it. Besides, if I gave up now, it might be thought I arranged Hurley's death because I had no hope in hell of winning—which seems very much the case so far."

"I confess I had not thought of that," Basingthwaite said quietly.

"And then there are my greys," Davenant added wryly. "Henry will never forgive me if I let them go without effort, will you?" he said over his shoulder to Henry, perched behind them.

Henry groaned.

"I care little for the opinion of others," Davenant continued, "which is just as well as my reputation leaves much to be desired. But a gentleman does not welch on a wager; and I will never give anyone reason to say that about me. If I lose, the debt will be paid to Hurley's estate. By the bye, speaking of my reputation, have you heard what my detractors now whisper about me? That my visits to places where boys are bought and sold indicate…ahem…unnatural practices on my part? I wonder now, who would start such rumours?"

Basingthwaite's eyes widened and he shook his head.

"That will not stop me, either," Davenant went on. "I would not give up, even if I could. Gave my word to that little devil, Addy, that I would do my utmost to return him to his grandfather, no matter how long it takes and no matter if I lose my greys."

Henry groaned again.

"Besides I am making progress," Davenant added.

"Progress? Basingthwaite frowned. "How so? The woman died before she could tell you anything."

"Ah, but I have not told you. She did speak a few mumbled words to Bodger. She named the man who sold the boy to the sweep. A couple more coincidences: he is a smuggler. Comes from near my Sussex estate. Disguised as a peddler, he has been keeping watch on my house. Now I know who he is, I realise that he is there because Addy is at my house. He will not be there for long. He had not arrived when I left this morning, but he should be there when I return, for he is constant in his habits. I intend to confront him—take him before a magistrate and learn from him where he obtained the boy. Then it will be just a matter of days at most before I restore Addy to his grandfather."

Basingthwaite's jaw dropped. "I...I...I had no idea..."

Davenant glanced sideways at him. "Promising, isn't it?"

Basingthwaite did not reply.

By then they had crossed the bridge.

Impatient though he was to return home and confront the smuggler Conway, who was watching his house, Davenant made two stops on the way back to Grosvenor Square. The first was to drop off Basingthwaite at his lodgings; the second was a call at Mrs. Dewberry's bordello in King's Place to ascertain whether or not she had actually sent a message to Hurley at Vauxhall Gardens the previous night.

The bawd was all fawning smiles of welcome until he mentioned Hurley; then her smiles vanished.

"Send a servant to Vauxhall to summon a customer here?"

Mrs. Dewberry face turned so red with indignation that not even the thick coating of rice powder and rouge plastering her skin could hide it.

"Certainly not, my lord! I am shocked you would even suggest such a thing. *This* house does not tout for business like some low Covent Garden brothel. We have no need to. We cater only to gentleman of the very first consequence. Sir Thomas Hurley came only twice, my lord: twice too often as far as I am concerned." She lowered her voice. "His...ahem...interests were such as to

make even me and my…ahem…young ladies blush. Like them young he did–
too young. As a friend of the Prince of Wales he had the best this house has to
offer. But when it came to settling accounts? So belligerent! Gave one of my
footmen a broken nose. I would not have admitted him, again."

"No doubt he had not accustomed himself to fashionable ways," Davenant
drawled, knowing full well that Hurley's behaviour was just as common with her
more illustrious clients.

Mrs. Dewberry failed to notice his sarcasm.

With a chubby, beringed hand she clutched his coat sleeve. "I'm not one to
speak ill of the dead," she said, "but to get himself drowned? No *real* gentleman
would do such a thing. I beg you will not mention abroad that he was on his way
here when he died." Her voice became a whine. "I'm just a poor woman trying
to make a living. My clients! The mere mention of death and my establishment!
So, *so* very bad for business."

With a thumb and forefinger, Davenant removed the hand defiling his tailor's
latest creation. His lips twitched. It was happening again; he seemed to be
making a career out of protecting the reputation and businesses of whores.
With a wry glance at the pornographic paintings on the surrounding walls, he
promised, "You have my word as a gentleman that I will say nothing that would
bring dishonour to this house."

Mrs. Dewberry's smile of thanks turned to a look of horror when, on his way
to the door, he added, "However, I cannot make the same promise for my friends
who were present at Vauxhall when Hurley said he was on his way here."

There was no sign of the peddler in Grosvenor Square when Davenant returned
home.

And although he remained at Davenant House all day frequently checking
the square with the aid of a telescope, the peddler never appeared. Davenant
was more puzzled by the man's absence than disturbed by it. Since his first
appearance in the square, Conway had never missed a day there until now? Why?

Again, just when the answers he sought seemed within reach, they had been
snatched away from him. What should he do next? What would happen next?

He felt sure he had not seen the last of Conway. When he retired to his bedroom that night, he was on edge with anticipation and expectation–but of what he did not know. In the early hours of the morning, unable to sleep, his mind a whirl, he rose, lit a lamp and stretched out on a day bed, hoping to find some respite from his anxious mind in perusal of the *Vindication of the Rights of Women*. But he read only a few pages before he fell asleep while thinking pleasant thoughts about Miss Barclay.

40

Like the occupants of Davenant House, the residents of Grosvenor Square had been long abed when Jem Biggs, the watchman, waddled into the square from upper Brook Street with his staff and his lantern.

This night Jem moved more slowly than he usually did. He had good reason to dawdle: two golden guineas now clinking in the pocket of his greasy overcoat, slipped to him under a tavern table by a stranger. In return for this largesse he had agreed to delay his arrival in the square tonight. He had also promised to ignore the two burglars who would be on the roof of Davenant House.

Jem had been only too delighted to oblige; he had a score to settle with the Davenants. He mistakenly arrested Lord Davenant's brother for burglary when he discovered him and a friend trying climb through a window of the house. A natural mistake to be sure; but to the affronted Jem it resulted in the loss of the forty pounds given for the arrest of a person found in commission of a crime, and continuing ridicule from his fellow watchmen

The sounds of a carriage and horses startled him as they swept by into the square. This was no case of late night revellers returning from a ball, or a gentleman going home after an evening at his club. This was a travelling carriage and, judging from its steaming horses, one that had travelled fast and long that night. Jem peered after it in alarm; it stopped before Davenant House.

A condition of Jem's pact with the burglars was that he be lookout for them and give warning if trouble arose. So, true to his word, Jem hobbled off across the square as fast as he could —which was not very fast.

Curled up in bed in the crook of Addy's arm, Puff woke with a low growl. His sharp ears had caught sounds inaudible to humans. He sat up and stared motionless around Perry's bedroom. There, since Georgiana's accident, Addy had slept instead of in her dressing room. When Perry came home on leave he insisted Addy remain where he was, taking a guest chamber for himself.

There were more noises, louder, but still not loud enough for humans to hear.

A JACKETING CONCERN

Puff nudged Addy's cheek with his damp nose. Addy stirred and opened his eyes. Puff's dark shape and quivering snout were just visible to him in the darkness.

"What is it, Puff?"

Immobile and rigid, his gaze on the window, Puff continued to growl.

"Sssh, Puff," Addy said.

He got out of bed and with Puff under his arm crept to the window and pulled back the velvet curtain a little. All the bedrooms that looked onto the square had tiny balconies surrounded by ornate railings. These were purely to ornament the house's façade, for none of the rooms had doors opening on to the balconies, only windows.

As Addy could neither see nor hear anything on his own darkened balcony, he would have gone back to the bed. But the continued tension in Puff's body and the dog's persistent growls were undeniable: something was going on outside. He pulled the curtain further back to see what he could of the balcony that ran from Georgiana's dressing room next door to her adjoining bedroom. He twisted his neck as far as he could. He could see little of the neighbouring balcony but now he could hear scraping sounds and low voices.

He was not afraid because he was a boy with 'bottom'—everybody said so—and one day he was going to be a Royal Navy admiral. Besides, he knew who was making the noise. Unlike the other times when he was drunk, this time Mr. Perry, with help from his friends, must have managed to climb up to the bedroom balconies. He heard the window of the dressing room being opened. He grinned. He would scare Mr. Perry when he climbed through it; Mr. Perry would not mind for he was a friend.

With Puff under his arm, Addy opened the bedroom the door and went out into the corridor.

As on other nights since the beginning of her enforced stay in London, Georgiana slept very little. She who had once delighted in the noise and bustle of the city now detested it. She who had once slept soundly no matter how late she returned home from ball, now woke at every sound, be it a carriage rattling over the cobblestones, a party of drunken bucks or, worst of all, The Watch's half-hourly shouts.

Anxiety about the strained relationship between she and her husband was the cause of much of her sleeplessness. Since his peremptory note ordering her home, she had heard nothing from him. He had not replied to the letter telling him she was under doctor's orders to remain in London. Perhaps she should have written and told him about the baby. She had resisted this suggestion of her brother because she thought it cold and impersonal; she longed to see the love and pride in Edgar's eyes when she told him herself. Now she wondered when that would be; the doctor was adamant she remain in town several weeks. Dear staid Edgar, always so ready to acquiesce to her wishes, was angry with her, angrier than he had ever been about any of her antics since they were married. If she remained away much longer, anger could turn to rage. And then what? Might he no longer love her? Even want to divorce her?

Hot and feeling sorry for herself after so much tossing and turning, Georgiana sat up in bed, clasped her arms around her legs, rested her chin on her knees and stared morosely into the darkness. No one cared about her! Roderick only waited for the day she returned home. Addy preferred the male companionship of Perry, Willoughby and Basingthwaite to her. Even little Puff did not love her! No longer content with spending most of the day with Addy, Puff now also spent his nights on the boy's bed instead of on hers.

The perspiration on her skin felt cold and damp, which only added to her misery. She reached toward the bottom of the bed to pull back over her the rumpled coverlet she had kicked off. In her wretchedness she did not at first notice a chill in the room until she gave an involuntarily shiver. Had her maid forgotten to check that the bedroom windows were completely closed? She could detect no ripple of movement in the curtains that covered them.

"Admiral comin' aboard! Admiral comin' aboard!" came the scratched voice of her parrot through the open door of her dressing room, where her maid slept. Eliza's snores must have disturbed the bird, whose cage was kept in there.

"Admiral comin' aboard! Admiral comin' aboard!"

The parrot's squawks were not the only sounds coming from the dressing room; someone was moving about in there. There was a whispered curse, and then Georgiana felt a strong current of cold air.

Wakened by the parrot, Eliza must have got up and opened the window. But why do that this time of night? Was she ill? Feverish perhaps? And the cursing? Eliza never swore.

Georgiana smiled, her woes forgotten. Perry was up to his tricks again. This time, no doubt helped by his friends down on the pavement, he had succeeded in climbing up to the bedroom windows. That explained the curse. If anyone knew how to swear, it was Perry. He had gone out that evening with friends as he usually did. Now he was returning home in his usual manner. She had better make sure he did not wake Eliza; her nervous maid would have hysterics if she woke and found a man in her room.

Glad of this unexpected diversion, Georgiana jumped out of bed, determined to take her twin to task for his nocturnal escapade.

"Lawks a mercy on us!"

At Eliza's scream, Georgiana froze.

"'Where's the boy?" demanded a voice she knew was not Perry's.

"I'll not tell! I'll not tell!" Eliza cried.

Possessed of the same audacity as her twin, Georgiana neither fainted nor had hysterics when she realised a man had broken into the house and attacked her maid. She groped her way to the dressing table, where she stored a small travelling pistol. Unable to find the right drawer and with no time to lose, she fumbled hastily for the three-branched silver candelabra that stood atop the dressing table.

"Let go! Let go!" Eliza screamed

Out in the corridor, Addy heard the first scream just as he reached the dressing room door. He couldn't help a mischievous chuckle. Oh dear! Mr. Perry had woken Eliza when he climbed through the window.

He put down Puff, who was by now barking furiously, and opened the door.

Georgiana grabbed the candelabra with both hands and half ran, half stumbled to the dressing room's open door. Unable at first to see anything in the darkness, she hesitated, but she heard the attacker's curses and Eliza's sobs. Then outside the moon suddenly emerged from behind the clouds, sending a pale beam of light through the window; it was then Georgiana saw the two figures struggling on the bed.

But before she could do anything, she felt her nostrils touched by a wisp of something soft, and then another, and another and another until what felt like thousands of remorseless fiends tantalised her nose into an explosion of sneezes that left her helpless, her presence exposed. Unable to see the bed and his victim clearly in the dark, the intruder had stabbed at random, hoping some of his jabs would strike home. This, and her quick defence saved Eliza from all but a few minor cuts from the attacker's knife; but he had slashed the pillows and a padded quilt, releasing clouds of feathers that were being wafted about the room by the air from the open window.

Alerted by Georgiana's sneezes, the attacker spun round.

By the moon's weak light he saw Georgiana and beyond, Addy framed in the open door.

"You're the little sod I want?" the man hissed. He lunged across the small room to Addy, but a growling Puff, his teeth barred, blocked his way.

Addy stared at the man.

"Run…Addy…run!" Georgiana urged him between sneezes.

Addy needed no second bidding.

Yelling, "Come on, Puff!" he hoisted his nightshirt above his knees, turned and ran back along the corridor, the dog hard on his heels.

With a roar the man made to go after him, but Georgiana, her sneezes having temporarily subsided, barred his way. Unable to stop, he ran into her; his upraised knife hit the candelabra she held and fell from his hand. The intruder hesitated for a few seconds just long enough for Georgiana catch her breath—then he grabbed her.

She screamed. The man's face was in darkness, but she could feel his bulk and smell his sweat. He seized the arm with which she wielded the candelabra in a crushing grip, forcing it up and away from him and grabbed her other shoulder. With her empty fist she pummelled him, but her attacker was well built, his body solid muscle; her blows only succeeded in sending a searing pain shooting up her arm.

With Puff in his wake, Addy fled along the shadowy corridor, knocking over ornaments and vases from side tables as he went. Davenant's room was just two doors down from that of Georgiana, but to Addy it seemed to take forever before he reached it.

With both hands he turned the heavy brass door handle. Once inside the darkened room, he ran to the looming shape that was the four-poster bed, clambered up on to it and pounded the covers with his fists in the mistaken belief that Davenant was beneath them.

"Wake up, my lord! Wake up!" he yelled, while Puff ran around the bed barking. It was a few minutes before the excited Addy realised there was no one in the bed.

Davenant's command, "Quiet!" from the shadows silenced Puff. "Entering bedrooms unannounced is a bad habit of yours," he said to Addy.

It was then Addy became aware the room was not in complete darkness. On a table near the fireplace, a lamp burned low. By its light he saw Davenant in his shirtsleeves, standing by an open drawer, loading a pistol.

Addy scrambled down from the bed and ran toward him. "A burglar…in Lady Georgiana's dressing room…he's got a knife!" he gasped.

A scream came from down the corridor, but with lamp and pistol in hand Davenant was already at the door.

"Stay here and keep that damned dog with you!" he said as he went from the room.

Without any light to guide him, Addy stumbled about until he found the day bed. Then he picked up Puff and together the two curled up on it.

Her breath coming in gasps, Georgiana was frantic; her attacker had the upper hand. Depleted by her feeble struggles against such a relentless foe, she was close to fainting. But just when she felt sure all was lost, those remorseless fiends that attacked her nose before actually came to her aid. She exploded again in wave after wave of violent sneezes that startled her attacker into weakening his hold and spattered his face with a mixture of mucous and spittle. Although weakened, Georgiana had sufficient presence of mind to seize the advantage. She was able to muster just enough strength to raise the heavy candelabra. Aided by the force of one last powerful sneeze, she brought it down on her attacker before, exhausted, she collapsed against the wall.

The blow missed the man's head but struck his shoulder so hard, it sent him reeling backwards in the direction of the window.

"Stop or I'll shoot," Davenant shouted from the doorway.

Realising the game was up, the man turned to the open window behind him: his only means of escape.

Davenant fired.

In the confined space of the dressing room, the shot was like a thunderclap.

The intruder had one leg over windowsill and was about to climb out when he was hit. Weak and confused from Georgiana's blow, he was knocked backwards by the shot that hit his shoulder. He fell from the window to the pavement three floors below with a scream that sent shivers down Georgiana's spine

Below in the square the driver of the travelling coach fought to control his horses, sent rearing and squealing by the shot and the burglar's scream as he fell.

The carriage's only passenger, a man, who had just descended, stared in horror at the body slumped on the pavement before him. A fast-growing pool of a dark liquid seeping from beneath it was plainly visible in the light of the carriage lamps. He glanced up at the house in search of the window from whence the body had come. Only one window showed a light.

"My God!" he groaned. "Georgiana!"

He ran up the steps and slammed the front door again and again with both fists while shouting, "Open up! Open up!"

A sleepy porter finally opened the door. The newcomer thrust him aside and disappeared into the cavernous darkness of Davenant House.

Convinced the house was under attack both from within and without, the porter pulled the bell rope. "Burglars! Burglars!" he yelled.

A JACKETING CONCERN

Huffing and puffing, Jem Biggs finally reached Davenant House. He gaped at the body lying on the pavement and saw at once it was the man who had bribed him; he was glad the fellow had paid him in advance. He glanced around him. Some of the square's residents must have been awakened by the uproar, for lights appeared in the windows of a few houses. Without more ado Jem took the rattle from his greatcoat pocket and twirled it to rouse a hue and cry.

Never let it be said by either the residents of Grosvenor Square, or his partners in crime, that Jem Biggs had failed in his duty toward them.

"He's dead, isn't he?" Georgiana said in an agonised whisper.

Davenant stood with his back to her, looking out the open window. Shocked by what had happened, he hardly noticed the travelling coach below.

"Yes," he said. "I only intended to wing him…in the shoulder but…" He shook his head.

He glanced across at her. She looked like an apparition in one of those Gothic novels she liked to read; her face was as white as her nightdress, her hair a tangled mass. But before he could go to her, there was a pounding of feet along the corridor. A breathless Venables in his nightshirt and several similarly clad footmen with candles and blunderbusses crammed into the open dressing room door. Behind, wrapped in shawls, their hair in curl papers, jostled the housekeeper and some of the maids. They stared open mouthed at the scene before them, those at the rear pushing forward for a better view.

"Make way!"

A man in a travel-stained greatcoat and muddy boots elbowed his way through the servants.

Georgiana stared at him, her face bloodless.

"Edgar!" she shrieked.

Then she did something she had never done before: she fainted.

The newcomer leaped forward and caught before she reached the ground.

Perry in nightshirt and dressing gown, his nightcap askew, elbowed his way through the knot of servants.

"Such a hullabaloo?" he yawned. "The one night I go to bed early and it's worse than Trafalgar! How's a fellow supposed to sleep?" He noticed his brother-in-law on the floor with his unconscious twin in his arms. "Oh, hello Hesston!" he hailed him, as if they had just met in the street. "You here, too? Haven't seen you in an age."

The earl was too busy trying to revive his wife to reply. "Georgiana! Georgiana, my darling," he cried, furiously patting her cheek. "Speak to me! Those things I wrote…forgive me! I didn't mean them!"

Davenant's wry gaze surveyed the tableau over which a few remaining feathers still fluttered: Georgiana recumbent in her husband's arms, a yawning Perry, an unconscious lady's maid on the bed, dumbstruck servants and a parrot dead of fright in its cage.

"A delightful if unexpected family gathering," he observed. "We really should have more of them".

But there was no humour in his voice when he said it.

From down in the square came the voice of Jem Biggs, The Watch.

"A half hour after three of the clock. A fine night and all's well."

41

The pile of crumpled linen cravat bands on the dressing table bore mute testimony to the fact that that morning Lord Davenant was not being as attentive as he usually was to the creation of the cravat style that bore his name.

"*Quel dommage!*" Séraphim whispered to Earl Hesston, who sat watching his brother-in-law at his *toilette*. "*Milor,* he think of what happen last night–and not his cravat."

The earl sighed and shook his head. How anyone could expend so much time and effort, even at the best of times, on such an inconsequential act as tying a cravat, was beyond his comprehension. That Davenant should want to do so the morning after his house had been broken into and his sister and her maid attacked astonished him. After all that had happened, what did it matter that his fastidious brother-in-law could not tie his cravat to his liking?

Despite Georgiana's efforts to the contrary, unlike Davenant the earl never made any concessions to fashion in his dress, regarding such fripperies as mere transient caprices of society. But then, as he often self-righteously reminded himself, *he* was a much more responsible person than his pleasure-loving brother-in-law. Conservative in both politics and outlook, he believed that when God–the god of the Church of England–created the world, he appointed each person to a particular station in life; some persons like him to higher ones than others. *His* God-given task was to be the exemplary head of his family, to preserve the honour of its ancient name and to be a good steward of its heritage and estates, duties he took very seriously–too seriously, some said. Any attempt by principal or design to overturn the order of this world, he considered heresy.

At the sight of the earl's censorious face reflected in his looking glass, Davenant's lips twitched. What was it Georgiana found so attractive in this unprepossessing man with the ruddy complexion of a yeoman farmer, whose serious air made him appear much older than his years, although he was younger than Davenant? That the earl disapproved of him and went to no great pains to hide it was a continual source of amusement to Davenant. Even his consent to Georgiana's marriage to him had not altered Hesston's view that his brother-in-law was not only a radical, but an idle ne'er-do-well dandy overly-concerned with clothes, horses, gambling, pugilism and women. That his disapproval might deep down stem more from envy rather than shocked propriety, Hesston would have denied in horror.

Angry at Georgiana's unannounced departure from Norfolk, the earl had at first suspected her desire to remain in London was due to Davenant's influence. When she wrote and told him she was under doctor's orders to stay, he suspected the physician was one of those medical men, who for a fat fee, indulged the unfounded hypochondriacal whims of fashionable ladies. Although he sorely missed Georgiana, injured pride made him ignore her pleas to join her in town. But when she had persisted in her claim to be acting on doctor's orders, he feared she really was ill; his love for her got the better of him, and he raced up to London to ascertain the truth. If she were ill, he would remain to care for her. If she was just feigning sickness…well, Edgar Hesston was not a man to be trifled with.

But last night when he arrived to find Davenant had just saved Georgiana from a murderous attack, anger and suspicions were forgotten. The passionate lovemaking that cemented their reunion, the loving words and explanations and the news that he was to become a father all contrived to put the usually grave Hesston in a mellow mood.

He had not gone to bed until the early hours of the morning, but that did not prevent him from rising before everyone else to take, as he usually did when at home, a morning ride; this time in Hyde Park on one of Davenant's horses. Much to the delight of *chef* Charles Henri, he then ordered and ate a substantial breakfast, without *le toast,* earning from the Frenchman the accolade *un vrai aristo.* After the events of the previous night, Davenant, Georgiana, Perry and Addy remained late abed, so not until well after noon was he able to wait upon his brother-in-law, whom was by then at his *toilette.*

"Pray do not reproach yourself," he said with a wave of his hand when Davenant expressed his regrets for what had happened to Georgiana while under his roof. "But for your timely intervention who knows what might have happened?" He shook his head. "Scandalous! That's what it is when respectable people cannot sleep peacefully in their beds because of such ruffians! Georgiana is my responsibility and, I confess," he continued in an apologetic tone, "of late I have been remiss in that responsibility. There has been some…ahem…slight estrangement…between us. I fear I am to blame."

Davenant's lips twitched; obviously, Georgiana had already worked her wiles on her unsuspecting spouse.

"The sooner I take her home the better, especially now that she is in…er… ahem…" Hesston swallowed hard. "She is…in…er…er…a delicate condition."

"Hesston! You sly dog! Congratulations!" Davenant said in feigned surprise.

As if he had been caught publicly in the actual act of procreation, Hesston turned scarlet.

Davenant stopped fiddling with his current attempt at a Davenant Drape. "I have an idea, he said. "Instead of returning home immediately, why don't you and Georgiana take a holiday? You have had a long, tiring journey, and she needs time to recover from last night's ordeal. I am going down to Downsley tomorrow morning. Why not join me? Perry shall come too…and Addy, of course. We shall be a merry party."

The earl sat silent while he considered this invitation; he was not one for travelling far from home, and he had done enough of that in the last day or so.

Davenant waited until Séraphin left the room. He did not want him, the other servants or Addy to learn the real reason for his invitation. They all believed last night's attack was an unsuccessful burglary attempt. What he was about to say might frighten them.

"I am going to take you into my confidence, Hesston," he said, the jollity gone from his voice. "My invitation is not entirely altruistic. The man who broke into this house last night came to kill Addy, whom I am sure Georgiana has already told you about. He attacked Georgiana's maid in the mistaken belief the boy slept in that bed. From what I learned when I questioned the fellow's accomplice at Newgate early this morning, they were both employed for the task by a mysterious stranger."

He paused. He had been more intrigued than surprised when he discovered the identity of the body lying on the pavement outside his house early that morning.

"When I inspected the body of the man I shot, I recognised him at once," he said. "He is a smuggler from near Downsley. He has been watching this house for a while. It was he who sold Addy to a sweep. Yesterday I had hoped to learn from him where he obtained the boy, but he did not appear in the square until last night, when I shot him. Three others have been murdered in connection with this wager, two of who could have solved the mystery for me. At first, because of their location and circumstances, I thought the deaths a coincidence, but after last night, I think otherwise. Because last night's murder attempt was unsuccessful, there is sure to be another. Someone wants the boy dead. Someone doesn't want me to learn his real identity. I sincerely believe Addy to be in great danger here in London; there are too many criminals willing to do anything for money. He will be safer at Downsley with all of us to guard him. Besides, in Sussex resides my only remaining hope of solving the mystery: the man who has the answers I want–the brother of last night's burglar."

"In that case, Georgiana and I accept your invitation," Hesston said. "You can rely on my help to protect the boy." He gave a faint smile. "I feel obliged to him. He is the reason that demned lapdog no longer sleeps on my wife's bed. I must confess that when I read in the press of your wager involving a climbing boy you had taken under your wing, I thought such an association beneath you. However, Georgiana tells me the boy was being raised a gentleman and was forcibly removed from his true station in life? Shocking! Shocking!" A thought occurred to him. "By the way, where is he? I have yet to meet him."

"Where he spent most of the night–asleep in my bed."

Hesston's eyes widened and his eyebrows shot up.

"Hesston! I am surprised at you! Such impure thoughts!" Davenant said in mock dismay. "Pray do not be alarmed. My vices are many, 'tis true, but they have never been…ahem…unnatural? The boy fell asleep in my room last night after warning me about the burglar."

Davenant actually smiled at the recollection of finding Addy and Puff curled up asleep on the couch in his room where he had left them. He covered them with a quilt and went to his bed. But a few hours later he was woken by Puff's wet nose rubbing his face when the two of them climbed into his bed.

"It's cold on the couch," Addy explained, snuggling beneath the sheets.

Davenant dismissed the earl's mumbled apology and returned to his task.

For a while there was intermittent small talk between the two men; but for Hesston there were limits to even this newfound camaraderie, watching his brother-in-law tie cravats chief among them. Eventually he murmured he had important business to attend to and left.

At last, having completed his *toilette* with a Davenant Drape that was to his satisfaction, Davenant got up and went to the window. As he had expected, a number of sightseers had gathered before the door of Davenant House. Lured by sensationalised accounts of last night's events hastily rushed into print and now being hawked in the streets by broadsheet sellers, they stood in a semi-circle around the bloodstains left by the dead Conway. And coming across the square to join them was Buckles.

Davenant shrugged. Let the public gape and indulge their bloodthirsty tendencies; if they believed what they read–that a burglar had been shot in the act and accidentally fallen–that was all to the good. It was what the servants believed; even more important, it was what Addy believed, for he did not want Addy to learn by chance that someone tried to kill him. The only ones who knew the truth at present were himself, Georgiana, Perry and now Hesston. All could be relied upon to keep quiet for Addy's sake. That left Georgiana's maid, but she was so distraught, she could remember nothing about last night and was now under a doctor's care.

It was clear now why Conway had watched the house. It was no secret the boy slept in the dressing room; Georgiana had often mentioned it in conversation with others, and servants talked. What Conway had not known was that because of Georgiana's indisposition her maid slept in the dressing room instead of Addy. But Conway had not acted on his own initiative, nor had he acted alone, as Davenant discovered.

Immediately following the attack, Davenant went to Newgate Prison, where the smuggler's accomplice had been taken. It turned out to be Mick, the journeyman, formerly employed by the dead sweep Peeper Malloy, who bought Addy. The ill-fated Mick was caught by some of the servants at the back of Davenant House as he hastily descended from the roof.

"When he ain't cussing, he's crying his eyes out," the turnkey said as he unlocked the cell door. "Sez he didn't do it." He snorted. "That's what they all say."

Both hands resting atop his cane, Davenant stared down at Mick. The worse for the drink that he had had bought for him outside prison to ease his woes, Mick sat hunched on the cell's stone floor, his legs manacled to the wall. He looked very sorry for himself.

"Permit me to introduce myself. I'm Lord Davenant, Addy's friend," Davenant drawled. "At last I make your acquaintance: Nell's *beau*–and her husband's murderer. The perpetrator of other crimes, too, I am told."

"I didn't do it!" Mick screamed. "I didn't kill Malloy!"

"The boy Bodger saw you standing over the body."

"Lyin' turd! Malloy was dead when Nell and me found 'im. Took his money, we did, but I didn't kill im. I swear it!"

"Then who did?"

"How the 'ell do I know? Coulda been anybody. He didn't 'ave many friends… if yer knows what I mean."

"You and Nell took his money. Then what?"

"Went up town, we did, 'er, me and Eddie. Lived high fer a while. Spent it on booze and stuff. But I had enough of her whining an' took off."

"You abandoned them?"

Mick's eyes filled with drunken tears. "Loved 'er, I did, but the poxy whore give me the clap!"

"The course of true love never did run smooth," Davenant observed in mock sympathy.

Mick nodded and sniffed. "Said Eddie was my kid, she did. I ask yer now," he implored Davenant. "Do I look like the sort of fella who'd 'ave a barmy little kid like that Eddie?"

"I would need considerable time to consider my answer to that question, time

I cannot spare," Davenant replied. "By the bye, in case you do not know, it is my sad duty to inform you that Nell and Eddie are dead. They were killed in a riot."

"Good riddance!" growled Mick, unconcerned. Then his voice became a whine. "Wots goin' to happen to me, now? That's what I wanna know."

"Let me see," Davenant said, "burgling my house, stealing Malloy's money, suspected murder, not to mention charges of theft and assault elsewhere. Undoubtedly you will hang."

Micks wail outdid that of a whole host of banshees. He burst into sobs.

Davenant watched for a minute or two before he said, "I can make no promises, but it's just possible my attorney might be able to have the sentence changed to transportation." Privately, Davenant thought this doubtful, but he needed Mick's help. "But first I want some information."

"T-t-transportation," Mick whimpered. "Awful, that is. They sends you away and yer never comes back."

Davenant was matter-of-fact. "I doubt you will be missed. But better by far than being hung outside this prison and your body dissected at Surgeons' Hall. Well?"

Reluctantly Mick nodded agreement.

Conway had come looking for him in a tavern frequented by chimney sweeps, he said. Because Mick was used to climbing roofs, the smuggler asked him to help rob a house in Grosvenor Square, for which he promised a fat reward.

"At first I thought it was gonna be a pigeon lay," Mick said.

"Pigeon lay?"

"Stealin' lead from the roofs of houses. But Conway said it was jewelry 'e wanted. All right be me, that wuz."

The two of them reached the roof by way of the buildings and outhouses at the rear of Davenant House, Conway proving as adept at scaling a roof as Mick.

"Sailor fella 'e wuz, used to climbing ships masts," Mick explained. "Tied the rope to a chimney and then let him down from the roof to the balcony." Mick shook his head. "Coulda knocked me down wiv a feather when I heard all the screamin' and shootin.' I didn't know he was goin' to kill someone, honest I didn't," he said with false earnestness. "Done a lot of bad things, I 'ave, guv, but never murder. Very particlar 'e was, about everything," he went on. "On edge the whole time, scared like. Said if the job weren't done right, someone would come down real 'ard on him cos he'd played that person false in the past."

"Did he say whom?"

Mick shook his head.

Davenant turned impatiently from the window. The urgency of his undertaking was greater now than it had ever been when all he had to do was find Addy's family in three weeks. He was caught up now in something far more sinister than a silly bet that would cost him a penny and a pair of greys; Addy was in imminent danger of being murdered.

The victims of three of the four murders to date were of people with information that could have solved the mystery of Addy's identity. The murders happened each time he was just about to question them closely about what they knew. Last night's attempted murder of Addy, who was the heart of the mystery, clearly indicated that whoever committed the murders feared Davenant was closer than ever to a solution. Not only did someone not want Davenant to find out who the boy really was, they wanted to be rid of Addy once and for all—and it was obvious they would stop at nothing to do that. Last night's murder attempt had failed, but he had no doubt there would be another one if the murderer was not caught soon. Whoever hired Conway to commit murder last night had to be responsible for the deaths of Malloy, Nell, Eddie, and Thomas Hurley. A post mortem had revealed the latter did not commit suicide by drowning but was strangled before being thrown in the river.

How close was Davenant to solving the mystery?

Conway came from the Brighton area, where he and his brother led a smuggling gang. Mick said Conway brought Addy to London. The two brothers were in close partnership, so the surviving one must know about Addy's kidnapping and the identity of the person who wanted Addy dead. It was imperative Davenant go to the South Coast at once, find the other brother and extract from him—by whatever means necessary—the identity of the mystery person. He would leave for the coast today and on the morrow Addy would leave with the others for the safety of Downsley Priory.

But before he left town he had an important call to make, for Addy was not the only one in danger—so were Miss Barclay and Bodger.

42

Anxious though he was to call on Miss Barclay before he left town, Davenant was temporarily delayed by some unexpected morning visitors of his own.

To give everyone a time to recover from last night's events and to avoid the prying questions of the curious, he had told his servants the family was not 'at home' to callers. However, such instructions never applied to his friend Willoughby, who arrived accompanied by Basingthwaite, to commiserate with Davenant about the night's happenings.

"When I heard about it, I knew there must be more to it than meets the eye," Willoughby said when Davenant had told the full story.

He readily accepted the invitation to join the house party at Downsley Priory when Davenant explained why Addy and the others were going there. "I was thinking of going down to Brighton for a spell, any way," Willoughby said, "and Downsley's not far away. You can count on me to help keep the boy safe."

"Tut, tut," Basingthwaite said. "What's the world coming to when such things happen? You killed the smuggler fellow who tried to kill the boy? That's a relief! And his accomplice could tell you nothing about the person who hired them?" He shook his head.

"Never fear. The man's brother lives near Downsley," Davenant said. "He is the key to finding that person—and Addy's grandfather. "There is no time to waste. I must find him before the murderer strikes again. I am going south today."

As the Prince of Wales had already invited him to stay at the pavilion, Basingthwaite declined Davenant's invitation to Downsley. "But I shall make a point of calling there often to assist you in protecting the boy," he promised.

The Duke of Ryedale did not enjoy perpetual *entrée* at Davenant House, but as he called just as Davenant escorted Willoughby and Basingthwaite to the front door, Davenant could not avoid him.

"F-f-forgive the intrusion," the duke said with a distracted air no sooner the study door closed. "I learned of what occurred last night while visiting friends in the square. I-I- I felt I must call and express my concern."

Davenant bowed acknowledgement. Polite though it was for the duke to call, it was also odd. They were not friends, and he was no longer Georgiana's suitor.

"It's dreadful! Defenceless women attacked in their own beds? Er...Lady Georgiana? She was not hurt?"

"Neither she nor her maid."

"Pray convey my sympathy to her for what must have been a trying ordeal and...er... my best wishes for her health."

"I will certainly do so."

In the silence that followed the duke continued to look ill at ease.

Then suddenly he blurted, "No one else was harmed? The...the...boy? The subject of your recent wager, for instance? A...a...shot was fired, I hear."

"He was nowhere near when it happened."

Ryedale sighed with relief. "Thank God for that!"

He paused for several seconds then murmured, "A...a...again my sympathy to you...oh... er...and Lady Georgiana." He bowed and quickly left.

Baffled by his behaviour, Davenant could only conclude Rydale was still enamoured of Georgiana and had called out of concern for her.

Hesston returned not long after.

"I'd like your advice...on a personal matter," he ventured.

"Hesston, you amaze me! Are you sure I won't lead you astray?"

He handed Davenant a small velvet jewel box. "I've bought this for Georgiana. It's a...a..."

"A peace offering? A symbol of your enduring love?"

"Um, something...er...like that. You have so much more experience when it comes to... to...er...such matters," he finished lamely.

Davenant opened the box; it contained an emerald and diamond ring. He held up the ring to the light to inspect it. As if mesmerised by the sparkle of the darting green and white rays of the stones, he stared at it.

Hesston's worried voice interrupted his reverie. "Well? What do you think?"

"Forgive me," Davenant said. "I was lost in admiration of your taste. Georgiana will love it! As for myself? *I am quite inspired by it. Quite inspired!*"

Then abruptly he excused himself and quickly left the room.

43

His facial muscles skewed to hold the loupe in his right eye, Phillip Rundell was taking his time studying the hallmark on the inner rim of the gold ring Davenant had given him because was a little annoyed with his lordship.

As senior partner of Rundell, Bridge and Bridge, silversmiths and jewelers, Rundell considered it his duty to wait personally on such an esteemed client as Davenant. In addition to having the care of the Davenant family jewels and plate, his firm had given loans against it when the family's fortunes were low. It also supplied the jewelry his lordship gave to his amours. As it was now whispered Davenant's affair with a certain marchioness had ended, Rundell assumed his lordship's presence in his shop meant he had a new ladylove, which would mean more business for him. So he was more than a little piqued when Davenant merely handed him the ring and asked him to decipher from the hallmark's symbols the name and location of the ring's maker.

At last Rundell removed the loupe from his eye. With a confident smile he announced, "Made eight years ago…at this very establishment. No need of a makers mark to tell one *that*; craftsmanship speaks for itself. A mourning ring. Hair braided through the gold, the deceased's hair being the usual embellishment for such items."

Davenant sighed with satisfaction.

It was not Hesston's ring that caught his eye when his brother-in-law showed it to him, but its hallmark. This included the symbols of the item's maker, the year it was made and the city in which it was assayed. All he needed do was to identify from the hallmark the symbol of the jeweler who made Addy's ring. Information about its buyer–Addy's grandfather–would be in that jeweler's records. Armed with that knowledge, he could easily restore Addy to his family within a matter of days. It was all so simple. Why had he not thought of it before?

Would the grandfather know who it was wanted Addy's death? Surely not him. Addy spoke so lovingly of the old man. But why had he not raised a hue and cry when the boy vanished? Conway's brother must have the answer. And even if the boy was returned home, his mysterious enemy must be prevented from making another attempt on Addy's life.

Addy did not want to part with the ring, not even for an hour or two. It was all he had to remind him of the mama he never knew. It had been stolen from him once, and he might not see it again if he let it go. At first not even the combined efforts of Davenant, Georgiana and Perry could persuade him to temporarily relinquish the ring to Davenant. In vain did they remonstrate with him that Davenant only wanted to borrow it for a little while, because it could help him find his grandpapa.

Eyes downcast, hands clasped behind his back, Addy shook his head.

Even Davenant's intimidating stare was of no avail.

"Impertinent, ungrateful boy! Why, I have a mind to put you on bread and water for a week," Davenant threatened.

It was Perry who saved the day. Drawing Davenant aside he whispered, "He hero worships you for the way you tool a pair. He wants so desperately to ride with you in your curricle. Why not take him with you? It will take his mind off what happened last night. Then he's bound to loan you the ring."

Addy's eyes implored Davenant; the latter glowered. Not averse to using coercion on occasion, Davenant resented its use against himself.

In silence Addy continue to gaze up at Davenant with admiring eyes; such appreciative scrutiny even the hardest heart would find hard to resist.

Davenant broke the silence. "Er...hero worship, you said? Really?"

And that afternoon fashionable Mayfair stared in disbelief at the sight of Davenant, a man who disliked children, driving by in his curricle, accompanied by a grinning boy bouncing up and down in his seat.

"Look at me, Mr. Henry! Look at me!" shouted Addy.

Perched behind him, Henry smiled and grabbed his coat collar.

His eyes on the road ahead, Davenant ignored the stares of the curious, but not his groom's amusement. "Wipe that grin, which I know is there, from your face, Henry or I will remove it for you!" he said over his shoulder.

"I'm just happy to see the boy happy," said Henry, who almost fell from his perch in astonishment when Davenant lifted Addy into the vehicle at the start of their journey.

George Brummell saw them as he was being carried along in his personal sedan chair. Arriving later at Brookes Club he announced, "I've just seen Davenant driving with that boy protégé of his quite *en famille*. I'd wager he has either gone mad or he's in love."

The betting book was called for, the odds being heavily in favour of Davenant being incarcerated in Bedlam within the week.

When they reached Rundells, Addy willingly handed over his ring, and was quite happy to be seen by passers-by in Davenant's curricle with Henry while they waited outside.

"Pray be so kind as to furnish me with the name and address of the person who ordered this ring. I wish to return it," Davenant demanded.

Rundell's smile vanished.

"Impossible, my lord!" the jeweler said, shocked. "Our customers are assured their dealings with us are confidential. If your lordship would care to leave the ring with me, I will trace the item in our records and return it to its rightful owner."

Instead of replying to this directly, Davenant changed the subject to one that Rundell held dear: profit.

"I have been giving a great deal of thought recently to increasing my collection of snuffboxes," he drawled. "Having only a different snuffbox for each week of the year is limiting. One for each day of the year–including Leap Year, of course–would be so vastly diverting, don't you think? Naturally, should I should decide on such a course, I would look to you for the design and manufacture of some… ahem…perhaps *all* of those additions."

He paused, drew a handkerchief from his pocket and began to polish his quizzing glass with it.

"On the other hand," he continued, "it occurs to me that at a time when our countrymen are suffering the hardships of prolonged war, the purchase of expensive jewelry of *any* description could be construed as an unpatriotic extravagance. Perhaps as gesture of patriotism, I and my friend Brummell–He has such influence on fashion, doesn't he?–should urge society to refrain from the purchase of such items until the end of hostilities–whenever that might be."

He raised his glass to his eye and stared at Rundell–and stared and stared and stared.

Davenant's appeal to Rundell's pecuniary instincts had the desired effect. The jeweler left and returned a short while later with a leather-bound ledger, which he smacked down on the counter.

"It may take you some time to find what you're looking for, my lord," he said, his voice curt. Then muttering he had business elsewhere, he departed, leaving Davenant alone with the ledger.

44

Through the open French windows Davenant and Miss Barclay watched Addy and Bodger playing in the garden of her Gracechurch Street home. Overjoyed at meeting each other again at long last, the two boys whooped and hollered as they chased in and out among the bushes, leap-frogging over each other's backs and jumping over flowerbeds.

Miss Barclay smiled. "Bodger is well and makes excellent progress. He can write his name and he shows an aptitude for figures. Oh, and he passed a whole day without stealing a thing!"

"It is no surprise he fares well under your excellent care," Davenant said as they turned back into the room.

"Joseph...Mr. Pratt is trying to persuade Bodger to deposit his twenty-five pounds reward from you in the bank to prevent it being stolen." Miss Barclay sighed. "Life in St Giles has made him suspicious of giving his money to a stranger to lock away. Not even the knowledge that his money would grow with interest moved him to agree. "

Davenant felt a momentary sense of satisfaction. He was not the only one who had had to deal with a stubborn child that afternoon, particularly as that other someone was the pompous Mr. Pratt. He gave Bodger one of his rare smiles as the two boys came racing through the open window.

"Don't trust that there Pratt fella, I don't," Bodger whispered to him when Miss Barclay was out of earshot. "Reckons as 'ow he's after your moll. Miss Barclay, I mean," he added in response to the Davenant's glare. "You look after my money. Trust yer, I do. Done right by me an Addy, yer did. Yer won't steal it. Got no cause to, cos yer rich".

"I will on one condition: you stop stealing." With that, Davenant grabbed hold of Bodger by the arm and extracted a lace handkerchief and a silver thimble from one of the boy's pockets.

"Oh, I thought I had mislaid them," Miss Barclay said when he returned the items to her. "Stealing has been so much a part of Bodger's life—a way of surviving—it will be a while before he stops."

"For one so young, Bodger knows too much of the ways of the world," Davenant observed.

"Indeed, he is too worldly-wise for a child," she replied, "but I do not think he will become a complete cynic."

"Unlike me?"

"I do not believe that is true of you, either. Like Bodger, thou art kind, although, unlike him, thou does thy best to hide it."

"And your kindness clouds *your* view of me," his voice suddenly harsh.

Miss Barclay smiled gently and shook her head.

On the way to Rundell and Bridge, Davenant had called on Miss Barclay in Gracechurch Street, where it had earlier been arranged for Addy to be reunited with Bodger and spend an afternoon there.

When he returned there from the jewelers to take Addy home, he found Miss Barclay in the library reading Popes *Rape of the Lock* aloud to Miss Philmore. After Addy and Bodger went outside to play, and Miss Philmore disappeared to order tea, he asked her opinion of the poem.

"Mr. Pope thought women silly, brainless creatures with no thoughts in their head but adornment! The...the...the audacity of the man! He declares, 'All women are rakes at heart!'"

His lips twitched in amusement.

"Miss Barclay for someone whose beliefs requires her to eschew violence, you exhibit considerable fighting spirit. It is fortunate for Mr. Pope that you and he never met, for if you had I would have feared for his person."

A hand went to her mouth to cover a gasp, and then she smiled. "Thou hast discovered one of the defects in my character: I have a temper."

"On the contrary, I see no defects in your character," he said quietly, "only admirable human traits: your care and concern for all climbing boys, for instance, and Bodger in particular. Both of you are the reasons for my visit; I have news that affects you both."

Quickly he told her about the deaths of Malloy, Nell, her son and Hurley, and last night's attempt on Addy's life.

"Thou thinkest the deaths more than coincidence, dost thou not? That they are connected?"

"Yes, I suspect it. Each occurred just as I appeared to be getting closer to resolving matters. Although just exactly what these connections are, I do not know. I now think that when Hurley and I made this bet, we unwittingly embroiled ourselves in a sinister plot. But I have no idea what that might be. Because he did not succeed last night, whoever tried to kill Addy will try again, I am sure."

"So Addy is in peril?"

"Yes."

"Oh, and you, too," she said, spontaneously stretching out a hand to him, "for you have the care of him."

He took the proffered hand with one of his and covered it with his other.

"Pray do not alarm yourself about Addy," he assured her. "Tomorrow he goes to my Sussex estate. He will be much safer there, surrounded by my family and servants. London is too full of scoundrels willing to commit any crime for the right price."

"That is an excellent notion," she said, content to let her hand remain in his.

"As for myself, I am honoured by your concern. But have no fear on that score. I am well able to take care of myself. And that brings me to the second reason for my call."

"Second reason? There was another?"

"My wish to see you was the first, of course."

A footman entered with a tea tray, and Davenant let go of her hand. When the door closed, he said, "I am concerned for the safety of you and Bodger."

She considered this while she poured tea. "I had not thought of it until now," she said, handing him a cup, "but in light of the three deaths…yes, I take your point. Bodger could have information about the murderer of the sweep, his wife and child; he recognised a voice in St. Giles as someone who questioned him earlier about the sweep. You think whoever killed the others to try and stop you might try and kill Bodger as well as Addy?"

A JACKETING CONCERN

"As always, Miss Barclay, you are very perceptive. However–and I do not wish to alarm you–the danger to Bodger brings into question your safety while he is with you. Although this house appears very secure, and I've no doubt your servants reliable, I venture to suggest it might be better for the two of you to leave London for a while."

She smiled. "I am to join my uncle at Brighton in two weeks time. Joseph… Mr. Pratt is to escort me."

"May I take the liberty of advising you to go earlier, say, within the next day or so?"

"So soon? You think it necessary?"

"So much so that were it not for you religious scruples about weapons, I would suggest you keep a pistol handy."

There was a short silence while she considered this; finally she said, "Bodger and I will do as you suggest. We will go down to Brighton the day after tomorrow. As to the rest? I trust in the Lord."

He rose, and raised her hand to his lips.

"Your decision relieves my mind of a burden. Addy is going down to my home near Brighton at once with my brother-in-law and sister. Being so close, the two boys will have many opportunities to get together." He paused. "Will you permit me the privilege of calling on you and your uncle in Brighton when I come down later?"

"Later?"

"I will not be joining the others immediately."

She stared at him, puzzled.

"Yes," he said. "Information I received this afternoon makes it necessary for me to alter my travelling plans. I have more pressing business to deal with concerning Addy."

45

Thirty seconds.

Forty seconds.

Fifty seconds.

By the light shining from the inn's windows, Davenant watched transfixed the persistent advance of his pocket watch's second hand.

One minute.

One minute ten seconds.

One minute fifteen seconds!

The hostlers jumped back from the coach. The driver cracked his whip and with a jolt the coach shot forward, quickly gathering speed until it was once again averaging between eight to ten miles an hour.

Davenant lay back and closed his eyes. Since the coach left London at eight o'clock that evening, he had feigned slumber most of the way, a tactic designed to keep at bay the intrusive attentions and rant of the vehicle's only other passenger, one Mr. Peter van Leyden, a merchant—and judging by his girth, a prosperous one—of Boston, Massachusetts. That gentleman had spent the entire journey so far grumbling incessantly about the British, King George and the Royal Navy. Most of his anger was reserved for the latter, whose captains stopped and boarded his ships, ostensibly to search for navy deserters, but actually to forcibly press his sailors—American citizens—into its service and to interfere with his trade with Britain's enemy: the French. All this and more failed to elicit Davenant's sympathy. Only when the mail coach stopped to change horses did he open his eyes. A noted whip, he was impressed by the speed—under two minutes—with which the coach's horse relays were changed every ten miles. Fascinated, he timed the changes at each stop and compared them with the previous ones. The change of horses at the last stop was the fastest that night.

Summoned to readiness by the guard's horn while the vehicle was still some way from the stop, each hostler at every halt knew exactly what he had to do. No sooner the coach stopped, a gang of them would swarm into action with four fresh horses. Quickly they would unhitch the relay that had bought the vehicle the last ten miles and harness a fresh team. So accustomed to the procedure were many of the horses, that they would often make their own way unaided to their stalls at an inn's stables. The coach's guard would throw down the bag of mail intended for that location and catch another bag of forward mail tossed up to him

Light and narrow in build and carrying few passengers, Royal Mail coaches were the fastest means of communication between London and other cities, towns and villages, and the fastest land transportation. Because he could not afford to waste time, instead of travelling post or driving himself, Davenant chose the mail for that reason. Travelling at its present speed, the mail would reach his destination in just under twenty-four hours after leaving London.

"Going to Liverpool?"

Earl Hesston reacted with a mixture of surprise and disdain to Davenant's announcement that he would not be going directly to Downsley. "I don't think I know anyone of consequence who went there."

"Well now you will be able to say that you do. Who knows? Perhaps I will bring Liverpool into fashion…and *everyone* of consequence will go there," Davenant replied.

Now that he was on the point of solving the mystery, he could not risk the possibility of his journey being known, for fear the murderer would strike again at Addy, and at himself, Badger and Miss Barclay. Aware that unlike Georgiana, her husband would not bruit the information abroad, Davenant confided to him the reason for his unexpected journey. His inspection of the jeweler's ledger revealed Addy's ring was made for a Liverpool man: Walter Gilden, who must be the boy's grandfather. To the others he said only that he must stay in town a few days longer before going to Sussex.

The Liverpool address intrigued him. The smuggler had taken Addy to London from the South Coast, but there was no telling where the boy had been before that.

One other person was surprised by Davenant's unexpected journey, not because of its destination, but because 'Is Nibs intended to go without him. "Who knows what might happen to yer?" an upset Henry said. "Whoever tried to kill the boy, he'll be after you, too. I should drive yer, or yer should go by post—but *mail coach?*"

"Your concern for my welfare is touching," Davenant replied, but I am quite capable of taking care of myself. Why, I'm not even taking my valet. The mail is the fastest way to go…and with Addy in danger, speed matters more than my comfort."

Henry was somewhat mollified when Davenant added, "Besides, I have work for you. You are to go with the others to Downsley and help Lord Hesston and Perry protect Addy. You are also to find out all you can about the smuggler Conway. Ned Ticehurst should be of help there."

So that neither Addy's would-be murderer nor Buckles would follow Davenant north, or worse, be a fellow passenger, Henry was sent to buy a ticket not only for Davenant but also those for any unsold seats on the Liverpool coach. To further confuse anyone who might try to follow 'Is Nibs, Henry also booked seats on a couple of other mail coaches going to different destinations.

Although the mail was not the most comfortable of equipages, Davenant relished its speed. He would have given much to be handling the ribbons himself; he had done that more than once on stagecoaches along the Brighton Road after having bribed the driver. But neither a Royal Mail coach nor its driver and guard were to be interfered with. On the roof at the vehicle's rear, the guard kept a blunderbuss and sword, and would not hesitate to use them against highwaymen or others who impeded his charge. No matter what the road and weather conditions, no matter who tried to obstruct it, delivery of the mail was paramount. Passengers were secondary and expendable, carried only because they helped pay for the service. In the event the coach broke down, the guard would take one of the horses and ride off to deliver the mail, leaving passengers to fend for themselves.

The merchant's voice interrupted Davenant's thoughts. "I'm surprised to see, sir, that this coach has only two passengers. In America, sir, *we* know how to run a business at a profit. There would be no empty places on a coach like this in America, sir!"

Davenant opened his eyes. In the dim light of the coach's interior he saw that his companion had removed his hat and was in the act of donning the nightcap he had just taken from the carpetbag he had with him.

"However, that being said," van Leyden continued, "we can at least make the most of the situation. Each of us, sir, has an empty place beside us in which to more comfortably repose ourselves for the night."

Davenant's lips twitched. "I beg to differ, sir. This vehicle has been booked to capacity—by me." And leaning against his side of the carriage, he stretched his long body the empty sixteen inches next to him, rested his legs across his bag standing on the floor between the seats and put his feet up on the empty place next to van Leyden.

"I, sir, have more room in which to repose myself because I have paid for all the unoccupied seats. That includes the one next to you: a seat, sir, on which you presume to trespass," he said, nudging the American with the toe of his boot. He yawned and stretched his arms. "I bid you good night, sir. Oh, and a pleasant journey!"

With that he closed his eyes, and the outraged merchant was left to mutter curses directed at Britishers in general and the one sitting opposite him in particular, until he too fell asleep—in an upright position.

The rest of the journey was uneventful. There was no more conversation between the two passengers, Van Leyden having withdrawn into a sulky silence after Davenant commandeered most of the coach's interior space. There were a few short stops at inns for food, and during one of these Davenant employed a servant to quickly shave him. Despite the coach's speed, he still managed to tie a passable Davenant Drape, so that when he arrived in Liverpool late the evening following his departure from London, his appearance was such that no one would have guessed he travelled without a valet. At an inn near the docks he took rooms, dined and engaged one of its servants as a temporary valet. After breakfast the next day, he hired a horse to take him to his destination.

Liverpool owed much of its growth and prominence as a trading centre to a century or more of the Slave Trade, which Parliament had finally abolished five years before. But slaves were not its sole merchandise. In spite of dire forecasts about the effects loss of the trade would have on its economy, Liverpool was as busy as ever, trading with North and South America, the West Indies and Africa. Davenant saw for himself the truth in the saying: 'Everyone in Liverpool is a merchant.' A forest of ships masts rose from the River Mersey and the docks that bordered it. Warehouses stretched for miles in every direction; there were hundreds of cranes on the wharfs, mountains of barrels, bales and boxes, and everywhere sailors, merchants, clerks and brokers shouting, arguing and cursing.

The growing town was fast insinuating itself into the countryside, enveloping villages as it went, so that it was a while before Davenant reached open country. He had no difficulty finding his destination, for he had been told at the inn that Norbury Park was so impressive it was hard to miss. When he entered the estate's main gates, he expected to see a splendid mansion amid well-manicured gardens in an extensive park. Instead, he saw a deserted, rundown house in a jungle of weeds.

He slowed his horse to a walk as he went up the long drive and looked about in dismay at the dereliction; it did not bode well for his visit. Trees once sculpted into the shapes of birds and animals had remained untrimmed so long, they appeared like spectres from a nightmare. What once must have been neat flowerbeds and trim lawns were overgrown with waist-high grass and weeds. No water flowed from a stone fountain depicting Poseidon and attendant dolphins, and leaves and branches filled the surrounding pool. There were no signs of life anywhere: no one on the terrace or lawns, no gardeners, no maids or footmen, no carriages in the drive, no horses in the stables. The only sounds were the harsh cawing of rooks in the trees and the clip-clop of the hooves of Davenant's horse.

Davenant dismounted before the massive double doors of the Jacobean house and tethered his horse. His attempts to ring the front door bell resulted in nothing more than a faint scraping noise. He walked slowly around the house, peering through ground-floor windows. Dark, silent rooms, empty of furniture confirmed his first impressions that the house was uninhabited. Addy's grandfather, Walter Gilden, was not here.

"Damn!"

His curse, like a pistol shot, sent dozens of cawing rooks into the air in fright. Was the address he obtained from the jeweler's ledger the wrong one? Had he taken a wrong turn and ended up at a different house from the one he sought? And if this was indeed Gilden's home, where the hell was he? Was he dead?

There was nothing more he could do here. He would go back to Liverpool and see what he could learn there; someone must know something about Gilden.

He returned to his horse and was just about to mount when a sudden noise stopped him.

In a scene reminiscent of the Gothic novels his sister loved to read, one of the house's double doors gradually creaked open. A stooped grey-haired man with a face resembling a dried gourd peered around it as if he expected to be pounced upon at any minute. His eyes widened in alarm when he saw Davenant, and he began to push shut the heavy door.

"Don't be afraid," Davenant said. "I mean no harm. I seek the home of Mr. Walter Gilden. Is this it?"

Fear vanished from the man's face. He stopped trying to shut the door, but instead of replying, he put his hands over his ears and shook his head.

46

The day after Davenant left for Liverpool, the Hesstons, Perry and Addy drove down to Downsley Priory with an entourage of servants and chaises carrying a quantity of baggage that would have rivalled that of the Queen of Sheba on her visit to King Solomon. Lionel Willoughby accompanied them in his curricle.

"Keep a careful eye on Addy," Davenant warned before he left. "Whoever tried to murder him in London will try again. You can rely on the servants and villagers at Downsley. It's strangers you have to watch for."

At Downsley Priory the house party quickly settled into a round of sightseeing, social calls, walks, picnics, evenings of cards, musical entertainment and trips to Brighton. Addy was given the run of the large house and extensive gardens but warned on pain of severe punishment not to venture beyond them. He was at home in them at once, conceding they were much nicer than grandpapa's castle and garden. Everyone was at pains to keep him entertained. His childish enthusiasm was infectious, and the adults were soon active participants in his fun. With Perry he explored the grounds and the crypt of the ruined priory. And with him and Willoughby he enjoyed many games of cricket. Even Earl Hesston forgot his dignity on more than one occasion and joined Georgiana and Addy in croquet on the lawn.

In Sarah Rollins, who acted as his nurse, he found boundless sympathy for his sufferings as a climbing boy. "Angels come in all shapes and sizes," she said when he told her of Bodger's kindness to him. "The Lord watched over thee."

"So did my mama and papa in Heaven…and Lord Davenant. He is going to find my grandfather," Addy said between mouthfuls of one of Sarah's fresh-baked buns.

On the surface the house party appeared to be like any other enjoying the pleasures of country life. But among the adult members there lurked an undercurrent of anxiety. Aware of the hidden menace to Addy, but not knowing from where it might come, they felt an apprehension that none of their activities could dispel. Wherever Addy went, one or more of them went with him. His bedroom was between that of Georgiana and her husband, and Perry; and both the latter and Hesston kept pistols close at hand. Meanwhile, Henry Rollins went in search of Conway.

Unaware of threatening danger, Addy delighted in his holiday, particularly his visits to Brighton to see Bodger. These began no sooner they reached Downsley, Georgiana being in a fever of curiosity to meet the rich Miss Barclay, a woman said to be indifferent to the feminine pastimes of clothes, jewels and balls. A woman with such notions at first seemed to Georgiana as strange as a mountebank at a fair. But she had never heard Roderick praise the intellect and qualities of any woman as he did those of Miss Barclay. Georgiana, being softhearted, suspected a romantic attachment, desired to meet its cause and intended to encourage it if she found the woman, despite her strange attitudes, to her liking.

Her snobbish husband did not approve of either of them calling on the niece of a Cit banker.

"But I promised Roderick I would take Addy to see his friend Bodger at Miss Barclay's house. He said I was to invite them both to Downsley."

"A climbing boy? Here?" Hesston demanded. "Davenant must be mad! Doubtless the boy will steal everything he can lay his hands on!"

She gave him one of her most engaging smiles. "Miss Barclay and I will mind Bodger. Besides Bodger is to live on the Downsley estate. He must get to know everyone."

Perry guessed her real intention after he, Georgiana, her reluctant spouse and Addy returned from their first call on Miss Barclay. "A delightful creature," she declared. "We dealt famously together–just like sisters."

"*Sisters!*" Perry spluttered. "Oho, so that's your game, is it? Why, if you're not one already, in twenty years time you will be one of those ghastly matchmaking mamas one sees at balls and assemblies. Don't let Roderick learn what you are about or it will go ill with you."

"Perhaps he has a mind for it himself," she retorted.

"Wedding bells? Roderick?" Perry scoffed. "I'd wager a year's pay that's the last thing on his mind. He's known dozens of women and never married any of them! And Miss Barclay ain't the sort to become a man's mistress."

"Perry!" Hesston said, shocked, "a gentleman does not speak in that indelicate manner before a lady–and certainly not before *my wife!*"

Unabashed Perry retorted, "'She may be your wife but she's still my sister!"

Ignoring them, Georgiana said, "True Roderick has had many…ahem…attachments…but that does not mean he is lucky in love. *Au contraire,* it shows he has not yet found true love."

"I dare you to tell him," Perry said.

"I am not trying to make a match," she persisted, " but he has good reason to admire Miss Barclay. She is charming, possessed of excellent understanding and has a decided air of refinement. I own she is no great beauty, but she has a lovely complexion–I wonder what she uses on it. Crushed strawberries? I must ask her. — Her figure is excellent, her deportment graceful, and though her *toilettes* are *un peu sobre,* they are modish withal."

"She's a charming lass, I grant you," Perry said, "but a *Cit's daughter,* Georgie? Come now, Roderick knows his duty to his family."

"A Cit's daughter she may be, but her accomplishments are considerable," Georgiana persisted. "Her education has been quite remarkable. She has studied Euclid–whatever that is. And although some might fault her for being so bookish–I confess I do find it *un peu* tiresome, myself –she has opinions on many subjects. Roderick says she is the first woman he has met who doesn't entirely bore him to tears. What an accomplishment!"

A thought struck her. "Oh dear, that must mean he thinks I'm boring, too!"

"A Cit's daughter and a Blue Stocking to boot!" Perry groaned. "You saw for yourself despite her learning she is not gauche," Georgiana said. "She and Roderick both share the same superior understanding."

He husband snorted.

"Oh! He does, *really*, Edgar, even though you and everyone else think him a dreadful rake. Miss Barclay told me she enjoys their conversations together. Anyway, no matter if she were as ugly as a gargoyle and stupid to boot, too–she *is* an heiress!" she finished in triumph.

Perry was blunt. "Roderick don't need the money."

"Dreadful, dreadful, *dreadful* boy! Such things are of little import if one is in love."

Perry gave a rueful grin. "They are of great import when you are second son like me. Perhaps I should offer for her. And not so much of the boy if you please: I'm your senior by ten minutes."

"You two would not suit. She is much cleverer than you. And she is a Quaker. They do not like fighting. She wouldn't have someone like you, whose career is war, and you would certainly not give up the navy."

"Well I can't see Roderick giving up anything for any woman either, however charming. Quakers do not approve of gambling, boxing, racing, cockfighting and drinking, and Roderick does all of those."

"Mmm. I had not thought of that. Still, it is hearts and minds that matter," Georgiana said. "Roderick and Miss Barclay are as well suited as Edgar and me," and she smiled at her husband.

Perry grinned. "It's something more physical that matters, to Roderick."

"Perry! Sister or not, desist in this manner of conversation at once," Hesston ordered. Perry shrugged and turned away.

"I grant you Miss Barclay is a fine young woman with many excellent qualities, but that does not change the fact that she is a Cit's daughter, with religious beliefs that show an appalling lack of regard for rank and position," Hesston said. "I confess I find much to disapprove of in Roderick, but for once I agree with Perry; Roderick is very conscious of the duty he owes his family."

The earl was not the only one concerned about Georgiana's visits to Miss Barclay: so was Henry Rollins. He thought they signified her approval and encouragement of 'Is Nibs' friendship with Miss Barclay, a circumstance that worried him.

. Despite the demands of his wager, 'Is Nibs had found time for several calls at Miss Barclay's home. 'Is Nibs' interest in the welfare of climbing boys was the supposed reason for these visits. But why so many? And why did these calls take so long? No one could be *that* interested in climbing boys, Henry told himself.

There could be only one answer to these questions and it alarmed Henry: 'Is Nibs was smitten. Even worse, he was smitten with the Quaker niece of a Cit, who lived in unfashionable Gracechurch Street!\ Henry had seen what happened to fellows smitten by females: they married them. After which they became but a shadow of what they had been.

'Is Nibs wed?

That would mean the end of life as Henry knew it–and of 'Is Nibs,' too, of course. No more sharing confidences; no more visits to the races, cockfights, boxing matches, gambling dens, seedy taverns and gaming hells; no more racing stagecoaches down the Brighton Road and no more visits by 'I Nibs to his latest bit o' muslin while Henry waited discreetly for him.

Henry needed no crystal ball to envisage how a Lady Davenant would change *his* life: driving her to morning calls, afternoon calls, family dinners and trips to dressmakers, milliners, perfumers, glove makers and shoemakers, to name but a few of the needs of fashionable ladies. She would want to be driven in style to balls, the opera, court functions and assemblies, for which he, Henry, would have to wear fancy livery and a powdered wig, the latter which made his head itch. He would have to seek out docile mares for her to ride and to accompany her when she rode them. And what if there were children from this union? His lordship would want an heir, wouldn't he? Then he, Henry, would have to contend with pony rides, riding lessons and driving governess carts. Henry shuddered in horror at the thought of it all. And if that was not enough, 'Is Nibs no longer seemed to care about losing his greys. For several nights Henry's slumber had been broken by bad dreams because of these concerns. However, his anxiety was eased a little on hearing the earl and Mr. Perry say 'Is Nibs knew his duty to his family too well to ever marry a Cit!"

Nevertheless, Henry determined to keep a close watch on 'Is Nibs and Miss Barclay to make sure matters did not get out of hand. The sooner his lordship found Addy's grandfather, the sooner life would return to normal. 'Is Nibs would no longer have reason to visit Miss Barclay, and he would return to the enjoyment of women suited to his elevated station: married aristocratic ladies and high class doxies like Harriette Wilson. 'Is Nibs would marry one day, it being his duty to do so and produce an heir, but Henry intended to do whatever he could to ensure that day was a long way off.

47

Under a late afternoon sun Addy paddled slowly along the shoreline peering into the water. The wide, flat arcs of the ebb tides waves flowed lazily up over the sand and rippled over his bare feet. The breeze that played with his curls suffused his cheeks with colour and when he licked his lips, he tasted salt. He called Puff to come and join him in the water, but the little dog stayed where he was on the sand at the water's edge, barking at the squealing seagulls as they wheeled and dived above him.

A little way up the beach Miss Barclay, her companion Miss Philmore, Perry, Bodger and Henry Rollins stood on the sand watching him. They waved at Addy; he grinned and waved back. He was enjoying himself: more than a little at Bodger's expense. Trips to Brighton to see Bodger were his favourite pastime, particularly when they included a visit to the beach, like today. And just as Bodger had often teased and frightened him about things in the world of chimney sweeps, Addy, now back in the world he knew, teased his friend. "There are stars in the sea," he told Bodger. "I'll show you," he promised when they reached the beach. "I'll find one for you today."

When the Downsley party arrived at Miss Barclay's Brighton residence that afternoon, they found the town *en fête* for its favourite visitor and the bevy of friends he bought with him. Church bells were ringing as they always did when the Prince Regent arrived. Disliked though the prince was by the British public in general, in Brighton he was regarded as a benefactor. His continued patronage of the town and the creation of his sumptuous, if opulent pavilion, together with the popularity for sea bathing, had transformed the former fishing village of Brighthelmstone into a fashionable resort. This transformation brought an increase in population, and the village had expanded mainly eastward, with rows of smart houses and villas to own or rent. Brighton, or 'London-by-the-Sea,' as it was often called, now boasted comfortable inns, assembly rooms with a master of ceremonies for balls, theatres, races, hot and cold baths, lending libraries, an elegant promenade overlooking the sea, a military encampment for the prince's regiment and twenty-five coaches a day to and from London. Few complained about these changes. Those that did were fishermen, whose former net-drying grounds, The Steyne, an elongated triangle that divided the town, was now a fashionable promenade for visitors.

Miss Barclay, Perry, Addy, Bodger and Henry had gone down on to the beach. Georgiana, aware of the admiring glances she was receiving in her dress of primrose silk with matching bonnet and parasol, remained on the promenade with her husband. Her excuse being that, unlike Miss Barclay's stout little half boots, her green Moroccan leather sandals were no match for the pebbled beach.

Aware the prince was on his way from the pavilion, a crowd was gathering on the esplanade just east of The Steyne, above the beach where the Downsley party stood. On the shingle families picnicked, while nearby fishermen, sheltered by the hulls of their upturned boats, mended their nets. Between the pebbles and the water's edge the receding tide had left a wide swath of wet sand on which children played and built sandcastles, a Punch and Judy show entertained a knot of people and a man offered donkey rides. Like miniature Noah's Arks on wheels, rickety wooden bathing machines were being dragged by tired nags across the sand and out into deeper water, where 'dippers,' stout, hardy women with arms like the trunks of oak trees, would plunge the occupants in the water.

"I found one! I found one!"

From the shallows at the water's edge Addy waved a red starfish. "See! A star fell from the sky and into the sea!" he shouted to Bodger as he began making his way back up the beach.

Unsure if his friend was teasing, Bodger's eyes narrowed. The sea was a strange force he had never encountered until he arrived in Brighton. Unlike London's river, he could not see the other side; it just seemed to go on forever until it met the sky in the distance. It both frightened and fascinated him: one moment it was calm and gentle like now, another it crashed loudly on the beach in high waves. Perhaps a force so powerful could draw down stars from the sky.

"He's teasing," Perry said. "It's a dead fish."

Addy's search had taken him some way along the beach from the others. Their view of his return was obstructed when the creaking wheels of a bathing machine became stuck in a rock pool and hid him from sight. Shrieks from inside the bathing machine alerted Perry that it might contain young ladies clad in nothing more than flannel bathing shifts. Ostensibly to observe vessels out at sea, but actually in hopes of seeing a well-turned ankle or a shapely bust, he trained his telescope on the immobile vehicle, whose driver was struggling to free it. All Perry saw was a frightened face with wobbling chins peeping from the bathing machine's rear. Disappointed, he was just about to shut his telescope when the bathing machine lurched forward to reveal Addy chatting with a burly middle-aged man—a man with steel buckles on his shoes.

"Newgate seize me!" Henry cried. "That's the cove wots been a-followin' his lordship. "Wots 'e want wiv the boy? No good, I'll be bound."

Buckles heard Henry's shout and at once took off up the beach toward the esplanade in the opposite direction

Perry snapped shut his telescope. "After him Henry! I'll take care of the boys," but Henry was already on his way.

Because the tide was at its lowest ebb, Addy was some distance from the others. Bodger was the first to reach him. "You…all right…young un?" he panted.

Addy stared at him, uncomprehending. "'Course I am." He shook the starfish at Bodger. "Why shouldn't I be? I told you, there's no need to be scared of the sea."

"What did that man want?" Perry demanded on reaching him.

Addy grinned. "Such an odd fellow, Mr. Perry, but very nice. I dropped the starfish in the water and he helped me find it again."

"What did he say to you?" Perry asked, trying to sound calm.

"He asked if I had two toes the same size on one foot, that's all. He ran away before I could tell him that I do." He pulled his right foot out of the wet sand into which it had sunk and wriggled his toes; the little toe and its neighbour were the same size. "Why would a funny old fellow like that want to see my toes?"

Perry had no answer.

For such a thickset man, Buckles proved surprisingly swift on his feet. Despite the difficulty of running up over banks of loose pebbles, he managed to put some distance between himself and Henry before the latter left the sandy area below the shingle.

Several obstructions forced Henry to slow down. First the Punch and Judy show's audience obscured his view; then he had to swerve to avoid some children building a sandcastle and others playing tag. These divergences put him straight in the path of a recalcitrant donkey as it suddenly veered from its appointed path. Too late, Henry found the animal's head only inches from him just as it kicked up its back legs and sent its rider, a small boy, flying forward at Henry. The two fell in a sprawling heap of arms and legs on the sand. The boy howled; his mother shrieked; and the donkey man cursed his fast-retreating animal. Ignoring them, Henry, covered in sand, scrambled to his feet and took off across the pebbles just as Buckles began climbing the steps to the esplanade. By the time Henry had traversed the beach and mounted the stairs to the top, Buckles had disappeared among the crowd gathered around the prince.

"Buggar!"

"Mind your language, Henry," a voice warned. "Leave him be. I know where he is going… and whom he is going to see."

Henry turned and saw a familiar figure standing with Lady Georgiana and her husband.

It was 'Is Nibs.

48

When Georgiana and her husband met Davenant on the esplanade, she thought he appeared distracted, a condition she attributed to travel weariness. But fatigue had nothing to do with his demeanour: unbeknown to her he was still preoccupied by a scene he had just witnessed in the coffee room of The Ship Inn.

When he arrived at Downsley by curricle from London, he learned everyone was at Brighton; so, pausing just long enough to change his clothes, he rode over to join them. At The Ship, where he stabled his horse, he noticed a carriage bearing the arms of the Duke of Ryedale in the yard. This surprised him, for the staid duke rarely sought Brighton's pleasures. What surprised him even more was the sight of the duke and Buckles deep in conversation at a table in the coffee room. What business could Ryedale have with a man employed by a cuckolded husband to follow him? Was he seeking alternative employment because the task of proving a connection between Davenant and the marchioness had proved fruitless? If he had not been in a hurry, he would have tackled Buckles there and then. But after what Henry told him about what happened on the beach, it appeared he had been wrong about Buckles: it was not Davenant but Addy who interested him. But why? Instead of being the marquess' hireling, was he, like the peddler, in the pay of the person who wanted the boy dead? Might that be the Duke of Ryedale? Was that why he called at Davenant House the morning after the murder attempt on Addy?

With all these new questions and the possibilities they raised in his mind, it was small wonder his sister thought him distracted. But then much to her surprise she saw him smile. It occurred to Davenant that the answer to these questions was not far away; after all, Buckles was always close at hand and could be easily caught—and the sooner the better.

Half striding, half slithering over the banks of shingle as they gave way beneath his feet, Davenant made his way down the beach. Watching him from the esplanade, Georgiana remarked to her spouse, "He looks quite *en famille*, does he not?" when Addy and Bodger, with Puff frisking at their heels, ran across the sand to greet him, and Miss Barclay followed on Perry's arm. "It's quite, quite charming," she sighed.

Shaking his head, the earl led her away to join the chattering, laughing crowd of men and women led by the Prince Regent that was coming toward them.

The romantic Georgiana would have been gratified to know the sight of Miss Barclay's blue-grey eyes when the heiress and Davenant met on the beach quickly dispelled any weariness and mental distraction her brother felt. One look at those smiling eyes and Davenant temporarily forgot Addy, the wager, murders, Buckles, Ryedale, smugglers and Liverpool. The *ssssh* of the waves, the squeals of the gulls and the shouts and laughter of people on the beach receded like the tide. He was conscious only of Miss Barclay, her smile and outstretched hand. He heard only her voice and saw only her face, the delicate pink of her cheeks heightened by the breeze, and her eyes as unfathomable as the sea. Unlike many of her contemporaries she did not dampen her dresses so that they clung to her figure; and the breeze playing with the curls escaping her bonnet gently rippled her white muslin skirts about her body in such a way that it made him think of foam-flecked Venus rising naked from the waves on the shores of Cyprus.

Naked and foam-flecked was not, he knew, how a gentleman should think of a woman such as Miss Barclay, but Davenant was loath to banish this delicious image from his thoughts. Besides, he reminded himself, his interest in her was more than just sexual. How often that face and those eyes had come unbidden to his thoughts while he was away. Whether or not this was love was another matter. He had known many women since his fiancée jilted him–and that had been long time ago.

Aware that he was *de trop*, Perry tried unsuccessfully to hide a smirk at the sight of his worldly brother looking, as he later told Georgiana, 'for all the world like a love-sick spoony.'

"Race you!" he yelled to Addy and Bodger, and together they and Puff headed off to the esplanade.

Davenant took Miss Barclay's outstretched hand.

"Welcome," she said. "I hope thee had a safe journey and rewarding one."

'The most rewarding thing about my journey is seeing your smile of welcome on my return," he said.

"Thou shouldst not speak so," she rebuked him.

She took his proffered arm and, with her companion following at a discreet distance behind, they walked up the beach.

"I forgot, I am not supposed to pay you compliments because you consider them meaningless vanities. Well, I assure you Miss Barclay, that they are not," he said quietly. "I missed much about you: your face, your eyes, your voice, your…"

"Please, I beg of you, she interrupted, do not speak so. It is not…I…" She got no further.

"Guv! Guv!" Bodger cried, tugging Davenant's coattails.

Perry and the boys had just reached the top of the steps to the esplanade, when Bodger turned suddenly and ran back down them again to the beach.

"That blokes 'ere! The one wot came around askin' questions at Malloy's yard. The one I 'eard in the fight afore Nell wuz killed. I 'eard im again…up there… wiv them swells," he said, pointing up at the esplanade.

Davenant looked up at the promenade where the Prince Regent held court surrounded by a crush of cronies, sycophants and fashionable gentry drawn like moths to a flame. The people in that gay throng were members of a social world to whom visits to a chimney sweep's yard, or participation in a St. Giles riot, were alien concepts.

Bodger must be mistaken.

49

"You *found* Addy's grandfather!"

"Yes…"

"*C'est mervielleux!*" Georgiana cried before Davenant could finish. "Addy will…"

"… and *no*."

Her smile vanished.

"Restrain your praise, Georgie," Davenant drawled, "'tis precipitate. What I *found* was the home, or rather the former home of the man I am sure is Addy's grandfather. What I was shown were the portraits of two people, one of whom I believe is that of his mother. But my visit to Liverpool raises more questions than it answers. For the moment I forbid you to tell Addy anything I recount to you. I know it is not in your nature to cause trouble Georgie, but your tongue often runs away with you. Addy is a child who has been through a great deal. None of us want to build up his hopes of reuniting with his grandfather with careless words, only to see those hopes dashed if they prove wrong."

"Of course, Roderick," Georgiana promised.

Perry, Willoughby, Hesston and Basingthwaite, nodded agreement. They and Davenant had just rejoined Georgiana in the drawing room after their port.

Davenant's week in Liverpool had been the main topic of conversation at dinner that night after they returned from Brighton. Concerned about Addy's security, Davenant insisted the conversation be in French, so the servants would not overhear and then gossip about it after. When Georgiana left for the drawing room, she begged the gentlemen not to linger too long. "My French is not good," she said. "I need to hear it again in English to be sure I know all."

"So although the outcome of your journey was not the success you had hoped, it was not an entire failure, either?" Willoughby said after the servants departed the drawing room. "You discovered that Addy is the grandson of man of wealth and consequence, a man whose whereabouts, if he is alive, are unknown."

Davenant nodded.

"From the beginning, Roderick." Georgiana demanded as she poured tea. "*Everything.* What is it like to travel by mail coach? To go *so* fast! *Such* an adventure! I would love it."

"Thunder and turf!" Willoughby exclaimed. "Two hundred miles in less than twenty-four hours! Wish I'd been with you! Wish I'd been holding the ribbons."

"There was nothing adventurous about it," Davenant said. "And you, being very fond of comfort, Georgie, would not have liked it. It was one continuous jolt. But no matter. I slept most of the way."

"And Liverpool? she said. "Does it have fine houses? Elegant avenues? Shops? Theatres? Assembly rooms? Balls? Or is it but ships and taverns full of rough sailors and low women?"

"Although I did not go there in search of the civilised aspects of society, what I saw leads me to believe that though commerce is its chief occupation, Liverpool is not an uncivilised backwater. Yes, there were ships aplenty and taverns with sailors, no doubt most of whom are rough. As to low women? I do not know—and neither should *you*, Georgie!

"And the silent, empty mansion! Cawing rooks! Creaking doors! That frightening old man!" Georgiana went on, her eyes shining. So, so, *so* Gothic!"

"*You* would think that," he said. "On the contrary, the caretaker proved an amiable fellow, although deaf as a post. Fortunately, he could read and write, so I wrote down my questions and he his answers. He was glad of a visitor, he said, for he only saw people when he went to the village. He invited me in, provided me with tea and crumpets and gave me a tour of the house. Nothing very Gothic about that. There was little to see. Most of the furniture and paintings had been removed, but some miniatures had been overlooked. The caretaker identified them as the house's owner, Walter Gilden and his adopted daughter, Elise, who died shortly after childbirth almost eight years ago, a date that coincides with Addy's age."

Davenant sipped his tea. "It was Gilden who ordered Addy's mourning ring. I am certain he is Addy's grandfather and the daughter is his mother. All the evidence points to that, although I perceived no resemblance to Addy in the woman's portrait."

"Where's the grandfather?" Perry asked.

"That's a mystery, which brings me back to what I said about not raising Addy's hopes. You see my visit to Liverpool suggests some previously unforeseen difficulties. First, the grandfather may be dead. Second, if alive, he may not want the boy back; he may be glad to be rid of him."

Georgiana stared at him, horrified. "His grandpapa not want him? I don't believe it. Why, the boy thinks the world of him."

"Addy is a child, Georgiana. For children there is little difference between fact and fantasy, and Addy has his share of childish fantasies. A grandpapa who lives in a castle near a sleeping giant? A pony? A tiger? It was a house not a castle I saw in Liverpool. No giants. No ponies. No tigers. The warm loving grandfather Addy wants to return to could just be fantasy, a pretence that spares him from the reality of someone who may not want him. Certainly, none to whom I spoke had a kind word to say about Gilden, by all accounts a hard, ruthless man."

Basingthwaite broke the short silence that followed. "As an outsider in this matter," he ventured, "it is perhaps not for me to comment…"

"Nonsense!" Georgiana stopped him. "You are almost one of the family. You helped Roderick in St. Giles, rescued Addy and me at the Exeter Exchange, and you take such an interest in Addy. He loves your visits and games of cricket with you. Your observations are not just welcome—they are expected."

The others nodded.

"In that case," Basingthwaite said with a shy smile, "if as you say, Davenant, the grandfather is dead, or doesn't want the boy, surely the boy's dead father must have relatives who would welcome the child with open arms."

"Ah yes. The father. Who was he? Where did he come from? That is another mystery," Davenant said.

"You discovered his identity?" said Basingthwaite.

"No."

Basingthwaite sighed and shook his head.

"Your sympathy for the boy does you great credit, Mr. Basingthwaite," Georgiana said with a smile. She turned to Davenant. "Now Roderick, tell us all."

A JACKETING CONCERN

"The caretaker," Davenant said, "knew little about the house's original occupants, he having been engaged shortly before Gilden and his grandson left the area several years ago, when the child was small."

But after questioning the rector at the parish church and enquiries at the Custom House and various coffee houses patronised by merchants, Davenant said he had managed to piece together the Gilden family history.

Like many Liverpool merchants, Gilden acquired his wealth from the Slave Trade's lucrative triangle of commerce. Rum, cotton goods, flintlocks, iron, beads and other trinkets were shipped from Liverpool to the West African coast, where they were traded for slaves. This wretched human cargo was then shipped across the Atlantic in overcrowded ships and sold to plantation owners in the West Indies and America. For these sales the trader received either cash or a draft drawn on a European bank, which he used to buy more goods to trade for more slaves, with ample profits left over for him.

"Gilden began as a labourer in the docks," Davenant said. "His intelligence and drive caught the eye of a merchant, who made him first a clerk and then his factor in Africa, where he rounded up slaves for shipment. A robust constitution and ambition enabled him to survive four years in a climate that kills most Europeans in two. He used his stay in Africa to scheme and deal on his own account–to the detriment and bankruptcy of his employer, whom he eventually bought out."

Afraid that his employees might do to him what he had done to his former employer, Gilden ran his business with an iron hand, often going to Africa and the West Indies to check on them. In the Indies he met and married the young widow of a French planter who died during a slave uprising in Santa Domingo. The woman, who had a distant connection to French aristocracy, had a little daughter, Elise.

"Gilden's enemies–of whom there are still many–claim the marriage was merely one of convenience. Gilden was not a man of sentiment or feeling," Davenant went on. "The wife sought security for herself and child. The revolution had begun in France and because of her family connections, she feared to return there. Gilden apparently saw marriage to an aristocrat–even a minor French one–as a way to achieve respectability and advance his future ambitions to become a member of the landed gentry at home, perhaps even buy a seat in Parliament. Shortly after the marriage, the wife died in a fever epidemic that swept the island. Gilden, a man who scorned close ties, had become, for the first time in his life, deeply attached to another human being: his stepdaughter, Elise. On her he bestowed all the love and affection he could not show—dared not show—in the business world, and she adored him. He adopted her, returned to England and bought a house and estate near Liverpool, the house that I found empty."

Georgiana sighed and dabbed her eyes with her handkerchief, "So, so, *so* touching."

By then there was a strong movement in Britain to end the Slave Trade, which for a century or more was an accepted part of the country's economy. Gilden left that trade and diversified into insurance, banking and manufacturing. He was determined Elise, his heiress, would have her pick of the most eligible suitors in the land. With this in mind, he went to great lengths to distance himself from associates of his slave-trading days. Wealthy and now the owner of a fine country estate, Gilden was at last a member of the gentry.

"But even with Elise, Gilden could be at times as overbearing and ruthless as he had been in business," Davenant said, "and he could not bear to be thwarted. During a visit to Bath, Elise fell in love with an attractive older man she met there. Although everything about the man denoted wealth and breeding, there was some mystery about him. Polite enquiries about his family and life elicited only evasive answers. He claimed estates and business interests in the tropics and had the tanned complexion to prove it. As you know," Davenant went on, "glib-tongued fortune hunters living beyond their means so as to ensnare naive young heiresses are common in Bath. There was no way of ascertaining the man's claim to wealth in the East. His bronzed complexion could have been no more than the application of walnut juice.

"The naturally suspicious Gilden was sure the man's intentions were dishonorable," Davenant said, "perhaps because there was much in this man that reminded him of himself. Gilden wanted Elise to marry a son of one of the best families, not a fortune hunter, or someone in trade. Because Gilden refused permission for them to wed and forbid Elise to see the man again, the couple fled to Gretna Green and married there.

"Those I spoke to knew little about the husband or the details of the marriage. Gilden never spoke of them because he was close to no one except Elise. The couple set up a temporary home in the country near Bath but, after a few months, the husband left to go abroad. Some claim Gilden paid him off, but I think that unlikely. Elise died shortly after giving birth to a child. Overcome with remorse and guilt at her death, Gilden took the child, a boy, into his care. From then on the story is vague. It is thought they moved about quite a great deal: no one knew for certain. It is as if the grandfather did not want anyone to find them."

"I am not surprised the old man did not want to be found. No wonder he has enemies! He sounds quite horrid," Georgiana said. "But I am sure Addy is his grandson even though he shows no resemblance to the daughter's portrait. Addy must take after his father."

"You think the grandfather is dead?" her husband said.

"I think it a possibility," Davenant replied. "Consider! A wealthy man, as determined as Gilden was reputed to be, would leave no stone unturned to find a lost much-loved grandson. He would hire persons to scour the country for the child. Advertise in the Press. Offer large rewards for information. In short, he would create a public uproar of such magnitude that no one could fail to hear about it. *That* has not happened; so yes, I think the grandfather could be dead. He has plenty of enemies. Perhaps Addy's kidnapper killed him; perhaps he died from natural causes. But though death seems the most likely reason for the grandfather's disappearance, as I have already said, it is possible he made no effort to find the boy because he does not want him."

"But why?" Georgiana demanded.

Davenant shrugged.

"Gilden trusted no one, hardly surprising when you consider his character. Even Elise, the one person he did trust, betrayed him. Perhaps, after his initial guilt about her defiance, he

changed his mind about Addy, resenting the thought of his wealth passing to him, the son of a rebellious daughter and a son-in-law he mistrusted."

When Davenant finished, there was silence in the drawing room, until Basingthwaite said, "Your visit to Liverpool having raised more questions than it answered, what do you intend to do now?"

"All is not lost. There remains the other Conway brother, Gil, who like his dead brother did, lives somewhere along the Sussex coast. Henry has been searching for him. The two brothers worked together, so Conway must know from whence Addy was taken and therefore where the grandfather is, if he lives. More important, he knows whom it is wants Addy dead."

50

In a half-hearted attempt to reconstruct a pot made by an ancient Celt, Davenant toyed with the clay pottery shards spread out before him on the desk. His interest had been piqued when he discovered them, near the village of Little Twitten, because they indicated continuous occupation of the area going back beyond the Romans. Tonight there was no sign of his initial enthusiasm for the project. He had only managed to interlock a few of the pieces, the relationship of the many remaining ones to each other eluding him.

After the events of his visit to Liverpool and those in Brighton that afternoon, Davenant sought to clear his mind and consider his next moves by relaxing with his favourite pastime in the quiet of the library. Georgiana had gone to bed early, giving her delicate condition as the reason. Her husband had readily accompanied her, claiming tiredness following a busy day. As he watched them leave the drawing room, Davenant could see that sleep was the last thing on the minds of the newly reunited couple. Willoughby and Perry were playing billiards; and a short while before, Davenant had bid farewell to Basingthwaite, who left for his hotel in Brighton.

Far from helping him relax as he had hoped the pot project would do, the many odd-shaped shards of clay were suggestive of the pieces of information concerning Addy he had acquired to date. Some pieces fit together to give a tantalizing glimpse of what the pot's actual shape might be, but the remainder confounded him. There were pieces missing, pieces that would connect the others; he needed to go back to the village and search for them.

"Damn!" he said. "So many pieces! So much still missing!"

But his mind was not on the pot when he said it. There were more questions for which he must find the answers: questions about Addy's grandfather, the boy's father and the mysterious person or persons who wanted the boy out of the way. And the stakes were much higher now than that reckless wager between him and Hurley: now it was a matter of life and death for a little boy.

Impatiently, he pushed the shards aside. Some of them came to rest on the latest of Addy's drawings of his grandfather's castle that were supposed to help him find it. This picture was even more elaborate than the previous ones, with stick men with bows and arrows lining the ramparts and a cannon with black smoke pouring from it. He sighed. What he needed was information, not the product of a child's vivid imagination.

He leaned back in his chair and put his feet up on the desk. It was too early to go to bed yet, for he was not tired; besides, he was expecting a visitor. Henry had told him Ned Ticehurst would have news for him tonight.

The only light in the darkened library came from the candles of a three-branch candelabrum on the desk. Their flames sputtered, a reminder that he should close the partially opened window before the draft blew out the candles. Just as he reached the window, he heard the call of a seagull from the terrace, followed a few seconds later by another: Ned Ticehurst's way of signaling his presence when delivering contraband to his customers at night.

Ned's solid figure rose up from the garden on to the terrace just as Davenant threw open the window. The sudden rush of air into the room blew out the candles.

"At last!" Davenant said.

"Sorry to be so late, my lord," Ned whispered back, "but I didn't want to risk being seen. Gil Conway would have my hide if knew I'd squealed on 'im."

While Davenant fumbled with the flint to relight the candles, Ned hoisted himself over the low windowsill, then pulled shut the window and drew the curtains.

Davenant raised the lighted candelabra to Ned's nervous face.

"Free traders 'ave a way of a-dealin' with informers," said Ned, glancing over his shoulder at the window. "I've no mind to be left to starve in an empty well or rolled over the cliffs in a barrel. Conway would do that an' worse if he knew I'd been a-talkin' to you. I reckoned if I came at night no one would see me, or if they did, they'd think I was makin' a delivery like I usually does."

Davenant set down the lighted candles and poured a glass of brandy from a decanter he took from a side table. "Here, drink this! You look frightened."

"The devil himself would be afraid of the Conways," Ned replied. He took a swig of brandy and smiled. "Nothing like a drop o' fine brandy to set you to rights—and I only sells the best."

"The less said about that the better. You have news of Conway?"

Ned glanced again at the window before he said, "He's out for your blood, my lord. Says you killed 'is brother, Harry. Says he'll have your hide. Words out among free traders…all along the coast."

"I wounded his brother: I did not kill him. He died in a fall from a window."

"That's as maybe, my lord, but Conways never ones to bother with the truth, specially when they got someone in their sights." He took a gulp of brandy. "Been layin' low, Gil has, since his brother died, hidin' out like, reorganising his gang…but 'e cant stay away from his grog for long. In Brighton 'e is, cos he knows you're here. Ship in Distress—tavern in the old town—is where you'll find him an' his gang when they're not smuggling. Be careful! Sober, he's bad; drunk, he's a bastard!"

"I'll take my chances. I want to talk to him. His brother sold a boy to a sweep, a gently-raised, well-educated child whom I've undertaken to return to his family. To do that I need to know how he came by the child."

"Not surprised Conways kidnapped a boy," Ned said. "Neither of 'em cared for anybody—not even their own kin. Heard tell Harry 'ad a child by a woman and abandoned 'em both."

"Then Harry's departure from life was no great loss to the world?"

"Aye. An' speakin' of departures, it's high time I was making mine," Ned said.

They went to the window. When Davenant drew back the curtain, he was surprised to find the window already open a couple of inches from the bottom; Ned had not shut it completely.

After hurried farewells, Ned hoisted himself over the windowsill onto the terrace, from whence he quickly disappeared down into the darkness of the garden.

The sudden rush of air into the room had gutted the candles again, but instead of going to relight them straightway, Davenant remained at the open window, staring out on the darkened terrace from which wafted the faint scent of the last of the late summer roses. Knowing how anxious Ned was about the reason for his visit, Davenant had not told him he noticed the window had been open during their conversation just enough for anyone who happened to be on the terrace to overhear them. Not that there was much danger of that: at this time of night no one was about. Gil Conway and his gang would be drinking at the Ship in Distress in Brighton. But what of the dogged Buckles? Davenant had seen him in Brighton that afternoon, and Buckles was always close on his heels. If Ned had managed to avoid being seen by the guards posted in the grounds, Buckles might have, too, and then he could have listened at the open window. If so, he could still be in the garden.

Buckles' encounter with Addy on the beach indicated he was more interested in the boy than following Davenant. As it now seemed Buckles was working for the Duke of Ryedale, then obviously the duke must be interested in the boy. Why? Addy did not recognise the duke when he and Henry encountered him in Grosvenor Square and the duke offered Henry a position with him.

That afternoon, after the encounter with Buckles on the beach, Davenant questioned Henry about Ryedale's earlier offer of employment.

"Aw guv, yer don't 'ave to worry none," said Henry, who assumed 'Is Nibs feared he might quit his employ. "Yer know I wouldn't leave you."

"I'm gratified to hear that, but that is not what concerns me. Tell me, when gentlemen offer you employment, as I know they often do, do they usually ask you yourselves, or do they do so through an intermediary?"

"An inter what?"

"Does someone other than the gentleman himself ask you?"

"Of course! A head coachman or a groom. Sometimes a gentleman's secretary."

"Was Addy with you when the duke spoke to you?"

"Why, yes. Goin' to the stables, we wuz. Carriage pulled up right alongside of us, it did, in Grosvenor Square.

"Ryedale saw Addy?"

"Looked right at 'im he did. Stared real hard." Henry's face puckered into a frown. "Come to think of it 'twere odd the likes of 'im speakin to the likes of me…him bein' a duke an' all. Wouldn't normally speak to someone like me, he wouldn't, not even to offer me a position."

A thought struck Henry, the same thought that had struck Davenant, a thought they both found distasteful.

"Newgate seize me!" Henry said, his eyes wide with horror. "Is he? You know! Little boys? But he wuz married weren't 'e?"

Davenant shrugged. "Marriage does not preclude such interests."

"Dirty old buggar! Oughta be hung!"

"Addy did not recognise him as someone he knew?"

"No. He was only interested in his 'orses."

Davenant closed the window and drew the curtains. He relit the candles, poured himself another brandy and stretched out in an armchair. If that was the duke's reason for his interest, why choose Addy? And why go to the lengths of having someone follow the boy? After all, as he, Davenant, had recently discovered, it was very easy to obtain a boy for that purpose in London.

It was high time he confronted Buckles; the fellow was no longer an amusement to him; he had shadowed him long enough. As for Conway? Despite his threats, Davenant doubted he had much to fear from someone Ned said spent most of his time drinking when not practising his calling. Conway had the answers about Addy. Getting him to talk would be difficult—he would not want to help the man he believed his brother's killer—but not impossible; Davenant was prepared to use whatever methods necessary to make that happen. There was also another person who could help him: Harry Conway's woman. Abandoned by Harry, surely she would be eager to get even with him by telling everything she knew about the kidnapping. A mother herself, she would want to see a lost child restored to his family.

Tomorrow he would seek out Conway at the Ship in Distress, but tonight he would enjoy Ned's brandy.

Sudden shots from the garden made him almost drop his glass.

Davenant dashed into the hall just as Perry and Willoughby burst from the billiard room with their cues held at the ready. Down the stairs with Puff at his heels came Earl Hesston, struggling into a dressing gown. Up on the landing Georgiana stood in a nightgown and wrapper, hugging Addy; and from below stairs rushed some of the servants, a couple of the footmen armed with blunderbusses.

"Too close to the house to be a poacher" Perry said. "Must have been one of the men on guard against intruders…"

"Or an actual intruder," Hesston finished.

"Whoever it is, let's get at him!" Perry shouted. His billiard cue held as if it were a pike, he readied himself to charge the front doors just as there came a frantic knocking on them from outside.

At a nod from Davenant, two footmen cautiously opened the double doors.

In the open doorway stood Basingthwaite, leaves and twigs on his coat, mud on his boots. With him were two of the armed men posted in the grounds holding between them a flustered, red-faced middle-aged man.

"Forgive me…if my shot…alarmed you," Basingthwaite panted. "It happened when I was leaving the grounds. A man's shadow…in the bushes. I thought he might be…after Addy. I dismounted and followed him best I could…in the dark…through the garden. He was close to the house, so I fired a warning shot with my pistol. These stout fellows of yours appeared and helped me catch him."

"He were up to no good, all right, milord," added one of men. "We found a ladder…up against a wall of the house. Reckons he wanted to get in and do mischief."

"I am eternally grateful to you for your trouble, Basingthwaite," Davenant said. "My servants will find your horse for you tomorrow. In the meantime, the least I can do is offer you my hospitality for the night."

He stared down at the intruder. "It's too late to talk now," he told him, "so you, too, will partake of my hospitality until tomorrow, when you will explain your actions of these past weeks."

The intruder shook himself free of his captors and, in effort to look dignified, drew himself up to his full height. "I refuse to say anything until I've consulted with my principal in this matter," he said pompously.

"In that case," Davenant replied, "I shall consult him with you."

51

The Duke of Ryedale handed Davenant the glass of wine he had just poured.

"I must beg your forgiveness for having you followed," the duke said. "I was most reluctant to do so. However, perhaps when I explain the circumstances that caused me to take such action, you will understand. I assure you that neither I, nor this gentleman–he nodded in the direction of the third man present–intended any harm to you or any of your household. Please accept my sincere apologies for any inconvenience it may have caused you."

Davenant inclined his head in acknowledgement. "And I must apologise for bursting in on you like this," he said. "As for having me followed, think no more of it. It is not the first time and probably not the last time that will happen." He lips twitched. "I admit I had flattered myself I was being followed for another more personal reason–but enough of that."

The duke had just finished a late breakfast in his suite at the Ship Inn in Brighton, when his valet nervously informed him that Lord Davenant was in an outer room and insisted on speaking to His Grace: nay, *demanded* to see him at once. What was more his lordship was adamant he would not depart until he had done so.

"Tell him I'm not at home," was the duke's brusque answer. But this order was at once rescinded when the valet added Davenant was accompanied by an acquaintance of His Grace: Mr. Townsend, late of the Bow Street Runners.

Perched on the edge of a chair, his feet in their steel-buckled shoes close together, Mr. Townsend appeared none the worse for having spent the night locked up in Davenant's wine cellar. His only show of discomfort was when the duke requested he take a seat. Unused to such familiarity from a member of the aristocracy, he at first demurred, and it was only the repeated insistence of the duke and Davenant that eventually made him relent.

"A Bow Street Runner!" Davenant said when the two were introduced. "I had not considered that possibility, Mr. Buckles–I beg pardon–Mr. Townsend. For so long I've referred to you as Buckles because of the fine pair on your shoes."

Townsend's ruddy face beamed." No fancy foreign gewgaws for me," he said with a quick glance down at his shoes. "Good British steel! Made in Wolverhampton."

"Your patriotism does you credit, sir, Davenant said."

"And it's a retired Runner, I am, my lord, though as I still likes to keep my hand in, sometimes I takes a special case…like this one."

"To explain how this all came about," Ryedale said as he handed Townsend a glass of wine, "I should tell you that my brother Adolphus had been estranged from my family since his youth. He was a wild boy, born to my father late in life, the youngest of three sons, and therefore unlikely to succeed to the dukedom. He was brought up in wealth and privilege but, as is often the case with younger sons, lacked appreciation of the responsibilities that go with them. Idle. Wasteful. A prodigious gambler. That was my brother. His debts were enormous and there were scandals involving women.

"My father paid the debts and hushed up the scandals. In return Aldolphus promised to mend his ways–but he did not keep his promise. Matters reached a head when, very drunk, he accused another player of cheating at cards and shot and killed him. Father was enraged by the dishonour Adolphus had brought on the family by breaking the law. Nonetheless, my father could not bear to see a son of his hang for murder. He gave him money to flee the country, but disinherited him from whatever was his due. Without exhibiting the slightest remorse, Adolphus left to seek his fortune abroad. We knew not where because all communication between him and my family ceased. My father ordered us never to mention his name again."

The duke shook his head. "Oddly, being cast out by his family may have been the making of him by creating an outlet for his energies. In the only letter I ever had from him–about nine years ago, not long after my father died–my brother said he was now extremely wealthy, far richer than if he had stayed in England. I only hope he came by it honestly."

By that time, the duke went on, he was happily married himself. Although he and his wife had no children, the family line was secure, because his other brother was married and had a son. "Had it not been for a number of family tragedies," the duke said, "I would have no longer concerned myself with Adolphus. But my other brother died in a hunting accident and shortly after his son died of typhoid. My wife, who nursed the boy, also died of the disease." The duke paused and sipped his wine. "After the mourning period for both was over," he said, "I knew it was my duty to either remarry and, hopefully, have a son, or, failing that, find my brother if he was alive, for whatever his past sins, he was heir to the dukedom." Without actually mentioning Georgiana, the duke said, "As you may be aware I attempted alliances with several women of suitable family but without success. I made some attempt to find my brother, but, as I had no idea where he might be, my efforts came to naught. Either he was dead, or he had gone to great lengths to distance himself from his family."

Ryedale got up from his chair and went to his dressing case. From it he took a miniature that he handed to Davenant. It was of a boy–the double of Addy–dressed in the fashion of over forty years before.

"I could hardly believe my eyes when, a few weeks ago in Grosvenor Square, I saw your groom with a boy who bore a striking resemblance to my brother at that age: the climbing boy, the subject of your wager. Under the ridiculous pretext of offering your groom employment, I stopped my carriage to better see the child." He smiled. "I knew your man would decline: his loyalty to you is well known and envied. The boy looked so like my brother. But a foundling? A climbing boy? My nephew? My heir!" He shook his head in disbelief. "If my brother had children, surely they would be wherever he was–not in England. Yet the boy was about the right age. I own my brother may have fathered bastards; but despite his faults, I know he would never have let a child of his be reduced to life as a chimney sweep.

"I did not know what to do. I was in a fever of apprehension. More so when I learned the boy's name was Addy, the diminutive of my brother's name. I knew I would not rest until I learned the truth. I engaged the services of Mr. Townsend, here: a gentleman renowned for undertaking and solving cases of a sensitive nature."

Townsend again beamed.

"He counselled caution," the duke went on, "to do nothing precipitate. He reminded me that although the boy in your care resembled my brother when he was that age, it could just be a coincidence. Your investigation into his identity might, after all, prove him an imposter, or perhaps a child of a family fallen on hard times and forced to send him out to work. The world would have though me foolish, perhaps even mad, for believing such a boy my nephew. Unscrupulous persons might have tried to pass off another boy as my nephew, and I would have been forced to spend much time and money investigating their claims.

"'Twas only after Townsend convinced me that the wisest thing to do was for him to follow you as you made your enquiries and see where they led, that I agreed to this course of action. As a former Runner, he has much experience in following persons without detection. I told him to spare no expense and to watch you day and night. I used any excuse I could to see the boy, so sure was I that he is my nephew. Imagine my horror when I heard your house had been burgled and someone shot! I was terrified it was him."

"I quite understand," Davenant said, "and Mr. Townsend caused me no inconvenience. Indeed, I now realise he has come to my assistance more than once. I have him to thank for giving warning shots on occasions when he thought my house was being burgled."

Townsend's rubicund face beamed yet again. "That were my assistant Cedric who watched your house at night. And it's been a pleasure, my lord. If all my quarry had been as fly as you, sir, my days as a Runner woulda been a lot more exciting. Led me a merry dance, you did. Very impressed, I was by the way you went about matters."

Davenant bowed. After such an encomium he could not bring himself to tell Townsend that, aided by two Piccadilly whores, he had early discovered he was being followed.

"You were wise to heed his advice," Davenant said to the duke. "If had discovered Addy was stolen from a family other than your own, you would have been disappointed, but you would have lost nothing."

Turning to Townsend he said, "You were watching my house night and day, you say, but pray where were you or Cedric when the smuggler broke into my house and tried to kill Addy? The only shots I heard were the one from my own pistol."

His lips twitched in amusement at Townsend's reply.

"Ah well now, that were unfortunate, but Cedric's mother was took sick and he had to leave early," the Runner said.

Davenant put his elbows on the arms of his chair and rested his chin on folded hands.

"Thanks to our friend here," he nodded at Townsend, "you know much of what I have uncovered to date about Addy. But I learned even more on my recent journey to Liverpool."

"So that's where you went!" Townsend said. "Covered your tracks well, you did. All those mail coach seats you bought!"

The duke listened with rapt attention as Davenant told him what he had discovered about Gilden and his family in Liverpool. "I am certain he is Addy's grandfather," he said. "He bought the boy's mourning ring, although Addy bears no resemblance to the portrait I saw of Gilden's stepdaughter, who must have been his mother."

"And the boy's father?" Ryedale's voice was eager. "What of him? Did you learn anything that would lead you to think him my brother?"

"All I know is that as Addy is an orphan, so the father must be dead. The father and Elise lived in Bath after they were married. The boy says his father went on a ship to India," Davenant said.

"If, as my brother wrote, he made a fortune abroad, India would be the place to do it," Ryedale said, excited. "But Liverpool is far from London, where Addy was found, and I don't know if my brother married. Did anyone in Liverpool know the family name of Gilden's son-in-law?'

Davenant shook his head.

Ryedale sighed. "Perhaps Addy's ring was stolen from someone else."

"I think he fantasises about some things, but not that," Davenant said. "He says his grandfather gave it to him; he cherishes it and will not part with it. But if this grandfather is alive, where is he, and why has he not raised a hue and cry about the boy's disappearance? A local smuggler sold Addy to a sweep, so he must come from this area—not Liverpool. I know the families of consequence in

Sussex. I know of one former slave trader in this area, but his grandchild is dead and buried, so it cannot be him. I am also a magistrate. Surely, my servants or I would have heard about a child being kidnapped or missing. However, tonight I will find out more when I see Gil Conway at the Ship in Distress."

"Careful, my lord, from what I hear the Ship in Distress is a dangerous spot," Townsend warned.

"Have no fear. I can take care of myself. No need to have me followed anymore," he told the duke. "I will keep you informed of all I learn."

He smiled briefly. "By the bye," he said to Townsend, "why your interest yesterday in Addys toes?"

It was Ryedale who answered. "Having two toes the same size on one foot is a physical trait often found among my family members."

"If Mr. Townsend had not left in such a hurry, he would have discovered Addy to possess that attribute," Davenant said.

"Then…" began the dour duke, suddenly elated.

"Recall Mr. Townsend's wise counsel," said Davenant, extending a cautionary hand. "Nothing precipitate! I own Addy's likeness to your brother's portrait and his physical trait indicates he is your nephew; but no doubt there are people other than your relatives with this odd configuration of toes. I will not introduce you to Addy as his uncle until I am absolutely sure of his parentage. To do so now, before my enquiries are completed and then discover it was not so, would go hard with him."

Townsend nodded agreement.

"You are both right," Rydale said, "although I feel certain in my heart Addy is my nephew. And I know that in the care of you and your family, he is in good hands. I will remain here at The Ship, entirely at your disposal. Don't hesitate to call on Townsend and me for assistance. Meanwhile, I will send servants to Gretna Green and Bath to enquire about Elise Gilden's marriage and her husband's true identity."

Davenant got up to go. "I shall miss you, my constant shadow," he said to Townsend.

"Call on me any time, my lord. I won't be far away."

Davenant had picked up his hat and cane and was on his way to the door when a thought struck him. He turned to Townsend. "Those buckles of yours were not muddied in my grounds last night?"

"Weren't any mud at all, my lord. Dry it was, very dry, what with all the heat we've had. Gardeners musta been busy waterin' yer flower beds yesterday."

"Yes, that's what, I thought."

Later that day Downsley's head gardener, Abraham Rollins, was surprised to receive a visit from Davenant while working in the kitchen garden. He was even more surprised when his lordship asked him which flower beds had been watered the previous evening and for how long.

52

Davenant stood at the railings atop Middle Street Cliff gazing out at what little of the English Channel was visible in the darkness. It was a night for smugglers to be abroad. The sea was still and calm, the only sound the continual, rhythmic *ssssssh* of waves swishing over the pebbles on the shore below him; while in the black sky the sliver of silver that was the moon made infrequent appearance from behind the clouds. At secluded inlets and lonely beaches along the coast smugglers would be unloading contraband from boats and loading it on the ponies that would carry it inland.

There was more than a hint of autumn in the air, and he was glad he had worn his heavy caped coat for this foray into the unfashionable part of Brighton, the narrow streets and alleys that were not too long ago the fishing village of Brighthelmstone. The nearer he came to the sea, the colder he felt as he walked along Black Lion Street to where the railed cliff top overlooked the beach; but after the oppressive atmosphere of the Ship in Distress tavern, which he had just left, the fresh breeze was a welcome relief.

He had found the dilapidated establishment close to the cliff top at the bottom of Middle Street. He was forced to bend to enter the low front doorway, over which was written:

By danger we'er encompassed round
Pray lend a hand, our ships aground.

The unwelcoming small space that was the taproom stank of fish, tobacco and rum; its blackened beams just cleared the top of his head. Its few customers were obviously fishermen; all of them old men, their faces tanned like hide from a lifetime at sea. On a night like this the younger ones were busy about their business on secluded beaches.

A man playing a concertina abruptly ended his performance and conversation ceased when Davenant entered. Fashionable gentlemen were unknown at the Ship in Distress, and the patrons stared at him with a mixture of surprise and suspicion. One quick glance about the room told Davenant the man he had come to see was not there.

"I am told Gil Conway is a patron of this…ahem…worthy establishment," he drawled. "Perhaps one you can tell me where he is."

No one spoke.

"Come now! Does the cat have all your tongues, or do you fear Conway so much you are afraid to answer?"

Again there was silence.

"Well then, when you see him pray tell him Lord Davenant wishes to speak to him. If he is not here, when I return tomorrow evening…it will go ill for him. Oh, and tell him I don't give a fig for his drunken threats."

Davenant turned from the railings and resumed his walk eastward back to the Castle Inn. He, Georgiana and her husband had gone there to attend an assembly from which he had earlier slipped away. He went alone to find Conway at the Ship in Distress, while Perry and Willoughby remained at Downsley guarding Addy. The day before, a reluctant Henry was dispatched to the Barclay household to protect its inhabitants. The Barclays being Quakers and therefore pacifists, Davenant feared the elderly Mr. Barclay and Joseph Pratt were not capable of adequately defending Bodger and Miss Barclay should an attempt be made on their lives. The Barclays reluctantly accepted reinforcements, unaware that Henry came armed with pistols.

Although Conway had evaded him that night, Davenant felt sure the smuggler was not far away. Their meeting was inevitable: Conway wanted it as much as he did, but for a different reason. He sought revenge for his brother's death. To prevent any further attempts to murder Addy, it was paramount he find out from Conway who hired his brother to kidnap the boy. Unless Conway sought him out before then, he would return to the tavern tomorrow night. In the meantime he would also seek out the dead smuggler's abused wife.

Except for what moonlight there was and the occasional light in a cottage window on the landward side, the cliff top road was dark. There were few people: one or two couples walking arm-in-arm, an occasional lurching drunkard and, just in front of him, four men stood at the railings looking out to sea. Just ahead, where Ship Street met the cliff road, stood the Ship Inn and its bustling yard. Instead of retracing his original route, Davenant chose the well-lit Ship Street.

He got no further.

He was hit on the head with something hard and heavy that sent him sprawling on to his knees. Although a fit man, able to go many rounds in the ring, Davenant was caught off guard, unable to defend himself. His head swimming from the blow, his vision blurred, he could not see his attackers; but as he tried to get to his feet, he was painfully aware of more than one pairs of boots kicking him. Instinctively he reached out for something with which to pull himself up and found himself clutching one of his attackers, who knocked away his hand. Again Davenant struggled to get to his feet, but he was too dizzy to stand. A blur of dark shapes pressed in on him, fists pummelled his body, and his head swam from the nauseating stench of fish, sweat, and something else, something sweet and heavy that assailed his nostrils.

"A-wantin' to talk to me, were yer? Well I got naught to say ter you but this!" the speaker said, giving Davenant a kick in the ribs that sent him sprawling on his face.

Something soft and silky was put around his neck and pulled tight. He tried to pull it away but someone grabbed his hands and stopped him. Tighter and tighter grew the band around his neck as he fought for breath. He was just conscious enough to realise he was being slowly strangled to death by a killer who wanted him to experience the full terror of that realisation for as long as possible.

"Ho, there!" came a voice from the darkness.

But by then he was unconscious.

53

Darkness and silence.

A void. That was all.

He was in the darkness. He was the darkness.

He was in a void. He was the void.

There was nothing. He was nothing.

But then there came a noise—a buzz—faint at first as if far away. Nearer and nearer it came, louder and louder it sounded until it was all about him, like the drone of a bee that hovered close on a summer's day, irritating him and refusing to go. With the first glimmer of consciousness came the thought that he must slap away the bee before it stung him. He tried to raise an arm but could not: his bruised and numb body refused to respond. By then the hum was so close and so loud, he thought he would go mad from it.

But like smoke before a wind, the darkness began to give way to a light that grew larger and larger the nearer it drew to him. And instead of the bee's relentless buzz, the wordless echo of a voice beckoned to him like those of the Sirens who lured Odysseus. Closer and closer came the sound, calling him... calling him...until...

"Praise the Lord! Thou art awake at last!" a Siren exclaimed.

Only half conscious, his head throbbing, Davenant opened his eyes, vaguely aware of Miss Barclay's blue-grey ones gazing anxiously down at him as she dabbed his aching forehead with *eau de Cologne.*

"How art thee now? No, no! Stay still," she said when he winced as he tried to move. "Thou hast suffered a blow to the head and bruising. I am glad thou wert unconscious when the surgeon came; otherwise thee wouldst have felt much pain from his examination. He says the blow to thy head was not as bad as it no doubt feels. Thee hast no broken bones and the surgeon does not think thou hast suffered a concussion, but he wishes thou to remain abed for the time being."

Dazed and confused, his throat sore, Davenant managed to croak, "Where... am...I? Wha...what...happened?"

"Thou art in my uncle's house on Marine Parade. That is enough for now; thee needs sleep not recollection. No doubt your brother-in-law and your man, Henry, will tell thee more when thou art better."

She laid a gentle hand over his eyes. He closed them and was soon asleep

And for the best part of the next day he slept, only vaguely aware of the surgeon's ministrations and Miss Barclay bathing his forehead, or coaxing him to sip drinks that soothed his sore throat.

The following morning, feeling weak and bruised, Davenant awoke fully conscious and anxious to learn what had happened to him. While he sat propped up by pillows, Miss Barclay told him that because he feared it was dangerous for Davenant to go alone to the Ship in Distress, Townsend followed him there and back at a distance. His timely arrival interrupted the attack and the assailants fled. Townsend enlisted the aid of an occupant of a nearby house to go to the Castle Inn and inform Earl Hesston. The earl sent to the Barclay house for Henry's help in moving the injured Davenant to the inn, as he was too ill to be moved back to Downsley. Miss Barclay and her uncle were adamant that he be cared for at their house instead.

Anxious to learn more, Davenant demanded to see Henry. Miss Barclay's refusal was polite but firm. He could not see anyone yet because the surgeon had ordered that he rest. Not used to having his wishes thwarted, Davenant was taken aback by her no-nonsense attitude toward him. Too haughty to plead with her, he resorted to a threat: if she persisted in her refusal, he would get out of bed.

"And I usually remove my nightshirt *before* I do that," he warned, raising the bed covers as if he was about to throw them off.

Shocked, she blushed. "Oh! Thou…thou…thou art…truly incorrigible! I have never met anyone…so…so… "

He nodded agreement as she struggled for words.

"I can only say I pity thy future wife!" she said.

"And I *truly* envy, your future husband, ma'am," he countered with sincerity. "Well?"

Again he made to throw off the sheets. It was an idle threat, he knew: he was too weak to carry it out, but it had the desired effect: Miss Barclay fled. Not long after, she returned with Henry Rollins, his freckled face full of concern, the suspicion of tears in his eyes. After admonishing Henry not to tire the patient, Miss Barclay left them together.

"Give me quite a turn when we brought yer ere," Henry said. "Thought you wuz, dead, I did." He sighed. "Bin in a lot of scrapes, yer 'ave since I knowed yer…but no one ever got the better of yer till now. Shoulda took me with yer, yer should, instead of leaving me here to keep an eye on these Cits and that little perisher Bodger."

"Although touched by your concern," Davenant drawled, "I remind you yet again to curb that vivid imagination of yours. As you can see, I am far from dead! As for someone getting the better of me? I…ahem…I assure you 'twas but temporary." He paused for a moment. "Er…do many know of the altercation?"

"Alter…what?"

"The *attack,* on myself."

Henry hid a grin. 'Is Nibs, who could more than hold his own against a professional boxer, felt embarrassed at having been ambushed.

"No my lord, just your family, me, Mr. Townsend and the Barclays, and none of them'll talk."

"And with those it should remain," Davenant said, looking pointedly at him. "No point in reporting it to the authorities. They can do nothing without proof, although I think we both know who was behind it. After what happened to me, you can see the wisdom of having you remain in this house to protect Miss Barclay and Bodger. "

Henry nodded.

"I gather Townsend found me after he followed me to the Ship in Distress. Did he think me in need of a nursemaid?"

"Good thing 'e wuz there, if yer asks me," Henry retorted, "or yer wouldn't be 'ere now. When he come and got me 'ere, Mr. Barclay—a real gen'leman though he's a Cit—had yer brought 'ere he did, cos yer weren't in any shape to travel to Downsley. Whacked hard with an oar, yer wuz. Found it lyin there. Meant it for yer head, I reckons. Surgeon said yer shoulders got the worst of it cause yer tall."

From a small table near the bed Henry took a large yellow silk handkerchief and dangled it before Davenant. "They tried to strangle yer with this. Got a big knot in it, it has. Here, let me," he said as the weakened Davenant struggled unsuccessfully to untie the knot. As a result of Henry's efforts, the knot eventually gave way, releasing as it did so the coin that it contained.

"Queer way to try and strangle someone, ain't it?" Henry said, with a sniff. "Got a queer smell too."

In silence Davenant studied the handkerchief and coin lying on the bed. It had to be more than a coincidence that whoever tried to kill him had used the same means successfully on the sweep and Sir Thomas Hurley. The same murderer? He sniffed. A murderer that scented his handkerchief with a very distinct, exotic perfume. He frowned. The scent was familiar. He struggled to remember where he had encountered it before, but his brain was still too befuddled to remember.

"Townsend found this, too. Thought it was yours."

"No, it is not mine," Davenant said, examining the gold fob seal Henry handed him, "but I have one like it; one I found on the sweep's body."

Before he could say more. Miss Barclay returned and ushered Henry away, leaving Davenant to doze. Not long after there was a tap at the door. He opened his eyes. Slowly the door opened and Bodger's now chubby, though still pale face, peered around it. When he saw Davenant was awake, he gave a whoop, ran across the room, threw himself on to the bed and burst into sobs. "When they told me I couldn't see yer, I thought yer wuz dead! Scared I wuz that I'd lost a mate."

This demonstration of affection from one as independent and self-assured as Bodger surprised Davenant. Unconsciously, his face softened and he was just about to reach out a hesitant hand to the boy's head when Miss Barclay reappeared. With the promise that he could visit Davenant again, she gently led Bodger from the room

"Although I know thee wouldst deny it, thou inspires affection in others. There are those who care about you," she remarked when she returned.

Davenant said nothing, content to watch her as she moved about the room setting it to rights. The visits of Henry and Bodger had taken most of his energy. He felt lightheaded and drowsy, conditions he attributed to the laudanum and other nostrums the surgeon had prescribed. Despite his weakness, he took satisfaction from the knowledge that Miss Barclay was obviously aware of his attention, for her cheeks flushed more than once, and she avoided coming near his bed until the very end. At last she bent over him to rearrange the pillows, her face very close to his: her blue-grey eyes serious, her nose with its sprinkle of freckles, and her cheeks even rosier than before under his close scrutiny. The warmth of her body with its fragrant aura of fresh lavender was a balm to his aching one and a delight to his senses.

Weak he might be—but not too weak to respond. He covered one of her hands with one of his. "And do I inspire any feelings in you, Miss Barclay?"

"I...I...oh..."

She tried unsuccessfully to free her hand.

"You have certainly shown me a great deal of care in the last few days," he said. "Please accept my heartfelt thanks."

With his other hand he clasped the back of her neck, gently pulled down her head and kissed her. He heard her gasp of astonishment, but she made no effort to move, so he kissed her again, longer this time when he felt her responding. Emboldened by her acquiescence, he was about to kiss her third time when she began struggling to escape his hold.

"Why Miss Barclay, I thought Quakers scorned to fight," he murmured with a hazy smile.

He released her and she stood up, her eyes dark, her cheeks red with embarrassment, or perhaps something else. She opened her mouth to say something, but before she could do so her uncle, Victor Barclay entered with a letter Earl Hesston had given him for Davenant the night of the assault.

This attack on you, following as it does the attempt on the boy's life in London, makes it obvious that Addy is in even greater danger then before, the earl wrote. *Obviously whoever wishes him harm is desperate and will stop at nothing to carry out his purpose. Therefore, after having satisfied ourselves that you were in good hands, Georgiana and I immediately returned to Downsley after seeing you lodged at*

Mr. Barclay's house. I know it incumbent on me to take responsibility for the boy's safety in your absence. I do not question the courage of Perry and Willoughby, but as they are both hotheaded I fear they might, left to their own devices, do something rash in the event of another attempt on Addy's life.

I will send over a servant to Brighton each day to learn of your progress and to receive any instructions you might have for me.

Davenant was relieved. Tedious though his brother-in-law might be, nevertheless, Hesston was trustworthy and responsible. In Davenant's absence, he would do whatever was necessary to keep Addy safe.

"Comforting news, I see," Mr. Barclay said.

Davenant nodded. "Please accept my sincere thanks for all you have done. I am eternally in your debt. I apologise for any inconvenience I may have caused you and your niece, Miss Barclay, who is an excellent nurse."

"Aye, full of good works is Verity," Barclay replied, "and generous, too with her fortune. Uses it to help climbing boys and other poor wretches," she does. "She should marry and settle, but many men find her too independent and a bit of blue stocking, to boot. I sometimes fear she may end her days an old maid." With a penetrating look at Davenant he added. "But there are men who like clever, independent women: our friend Pratt, for instance. The two have an understanding, I believe." He shrugged and smiled. "He is an honourable man, a good Christian, and I've no wish to malign him, but…" He smiled. "I find him a dull fellow. I think Verity finds him so, too, on occasion, although she never says." He shook his head. "Who knows? She is of age, an heiress and her own mistress."

Davenant did not hear him. Tired from the exertion of receiving so many visitors in one day, he had fallen asleep.

54

When Davenant awoke late the following morning, he was disappointed but not surprised to find that the ubiquitous Miss Philmore, Miss Barclay's companion, had replaced her mistress in his sick room. She sat near his bed knitting, her short, round figure in a black dress and a plain white cap. Her plump face broke into a smile when she saw he was awake.

As he was now much better, her charge had delegated nursing duties to her, she explained when he asked after Miss Barclay. "She begs to be excused," she said, adding with a sigh, "such a diligent young lady with *so* many domestic and charitable responsibilities."

Miss Philmore might believe her mistress had other pressing commitments, but he thought otherwise. The virtuous Miss Barclay was no doubt embarrassed— maybe even ashamed—to face him, because before resisting his advances, she had at first returned his kisses. His lips twitched in amusement; he had some cause to be grateful to his attackers for his present infirmities! Had it not been for them, he would not be in his present position; one which enabled him to enjoy Miss Barclay's ministrations and to discover that, despite appearances to the contrary, she was not indifferent to him after all.

Miss Philmore, thinking it incumbent on her to entertain the patient, began to chatter about numerous trivial happenings in her little world; but Davenant, having neither the interest nor the desire to respond to this tedious recital, drowsed off again.

When next he opened his eyes the room was still and quiet, except for an occasional snore from Miss Philmore, who had nodded off to sleep. The headache that had plagued him since he regained consciousness was gone; and his mind was once more clear and alert. His enforced rest must have served to sharpen his wits, for as he lay there with nothing more demanding to distract him than a few snores, he found, without any deliberate effort on his part, that the puzzling oddities, doubts and suspicions that had crowded in on his mind since he began his quest were again to the fore. Only this time, there was a difference; they were no longer a perplexing jumble of individual facts and events. It was as if at a deeper level his mind had used the opportunity occasioned by his indisposition to sort through and bring together those matters with which it perceived a connection.

The recent attack on him, for instance: only Ned, the blacksmith, Earl Hesston, Ryedale and Townsend knew of his visit to the Ship in Distress; and none of them would have gossiped about it. The only way anyone else could have known about it was if they had been outside on the terrace, listening at the open library window to his conversation with Ned. That night the lawns and paths around the house were parched and dusty for lack of rain, but the flowerbeds, including the rose beds just beyond the terrace beneath the library window, were well watered and mucky. Only two people he saw that night had petals and mud on their boots: Ned Ticehurst and Rupert Basingthwaite.

He did not see the faces of his attackers on the esplanade: it was too dark, but he was aware of being kicked by more than one pair of feet. One of the men, he was certain, was Gil Conway, because he knew what Davenant told those at the Ship in Distress. "A-wantin to talk to me, were you, well here I am!" he remembered only too well the fellow saying as he pounded him.

Of the two remaining attackers, one, like Conway, was a seaman, probably one of his gang. How else to account for the overwhelming stench of fish, stale sweat and tar that nauseated him? But there was another odour, too, or rather a perfume: a combination of exotic flowers and musk, a fragrance more in keeping with a fashionable gentleman than unwashed smugglers. He frowned. The perfume was familiar. He *must* know someone who used it, but whom? It was not one he would ever use, subscribing as he did to Brummell's dictate that all a gentleman needed was clean linen and *eau de Cologne*. He had stressed this to Lionel Willoughby's valet when he changed his clothes at his friend's lodgings after visiting St. Giles' rookery.

Now he remembered!

The valet had offered him that very same perfume. Brought from foreign parts, the man said, by Willoughby's lodger: Rupert Basingthwaite.

Of the three with him when Nell and her son were stabbed to death in a riot, only Basingthwaite had blood on him, blood he claimed was from a knife cut to his face by a rioter. But when Davenant saw him later after he had washed off the blood, there were no marks of any kind on his face. It had been Basingthwaite who eagerly volunteered to go with him to St. Giles in place of Willoughby, the latter having been tricked into visiting a dying grandfather, later discovered to be very much alive.

Basingthwaite was present on the two occasions Bodger recognised the voice of the man who questioned him one night in the darkness of the sweep's yard. This recollection reminded Davenant of something he had paid no attention to at the time; during the St. Giles' visit Basingthwaite hardly spoke a word–and never in front of Bodger. If he was the mysterious caller at the sweep's yard, no wonder he kept silent, for fear Bodger would recognise him.

It was Basingthwaite who suggested Sir Richard Hurley's death was reason enough for Davenant to forget his wager, an action that would have ended his efforts to discover Addy's true identity. This astonished Davenant. Whatever was the fellow thinking? Such action would have meant welching on a bet and breaking his word to Addy. No gentleman worthy of the name would think of doing those things.

Loud groans from Miss Philmore interrupted Davenant's thoughts. He looked at her. She was obviously having a bad dream, for she squirmed in her sleep, a movement that sent her ball of wool and needles from her lap to the floor. The ball of wool rolled across the carpet a short way, pulling undone some of the knitting as it did so. Watching, it occurred to Davenant, he might be intent on undoing Basingthwaite's character just because some of the fellow's behavior was suspicious. After all, it was all speculation on his part. Had the attack affected his mind? Had it turned him from a realist into a fantasist, embroidering facts just as Henry Rollins often did?

Perhaps he needed more rest.

He closed his eyes but sleep eluded him; his thoughts about Basingthwaite persisted.

Other than what he appeared–a gentleman of wealth and means–what did anyone know of the fellow? His friendship with Sir Richard Hurley had given *entrée* into the *coterie* of that young man's patron, the Prince of Wales. As such, society, Davenant included, accepted him without question. The prince himself had proposed Basingthwaite for membership of White's Club, and he was a favourite guest of society hostesses. But nothing was known of his past.

An odd couple, Basingthwaite and Hurley. Basingthwaite so charming and of good address, it was no surprise he was such a success in society. Hurley, on the other hand, had been gauche and belligerent, particularly when drunk, which was often. What had the two in common? Harriette Wilson said Basingthwaite was not long returned from the West Indies, an ocean away from Hurley's rural Gloucestershire. How had they come to meet each other? When they parted company, Basingthwaite took lodgings with the good-natured Willoughby; but what need had he to lodge with either Hurley or Willoughby when he was apparently rich enough to rent or buy an establishment of his own?

After helping rescue Addy and Georgiana from the mêlée at the Exeter Exchange, Basingthwaite had become a welcome guest at Davenant House. "Like a member of the family," Georgiana said. As such Basingthwaite was privy to many of Davenant's plans. He knew how important it was for Davenant to question Nell; but while Basingthwaite was close by, she was killed in the riot before Davenant could do so. Basingthwaite had not known that while in a drunken stupor she had mumbled to Bodger that Malloy bought Addy from one of the Conways.

But if Basingthwaite was involved in all of this, what was his motive? What reason did he have to be ill disposed toward a seven-year-old boy? He and Addy were friends; they got on so well together, Basingthwaite always willing to play cricket and other games with him. Addy gave no indication he had known him before they met at Davenant House. And the Duke of Ryedale, who it was certain was Addy's uncle, was on no more than nodding acquaintance with Basingthwaite. A loud snore from Miss Philmore made Davenant open his eyes; he looked about him. His gaze came to rest on the table where Henry left the fob seal. The seal was almost identical to the one he found on the dead sweep; their similarities much too close to be mere coincidence. When they first met at Amy Wilson's 'at home,' Basingthwaite wore so much jewelry, including several fob seals, he thought him a fop. Davenant frowned. The seal was not something a smuggler would own. It must belong to his attacker: the one who wore the unmistakable perfume.

All the circumstances pointed to one man: Rupert Basingthwaite.

Miss Philmore's next snore proved loud enough to jolt her awake. Embarrassed at making such an unladylike noise, to hide her blushes, she bent and picked up her wool and needles. Not wishing to hear more of her chatter, Davenant closed his eyes again and feigned sleep.

Basingthwaite, Basingthwaite, Basingthwaite.

Over and over again the name hammered in his brain.

To obtain positive proof of Basingthwaite's guilt–or innocence–he must dig deeper. Those two gold seals in his possession comprised the key to the puzzle. If he could find a definite link between them and Basingthwaite, he would be well on the way to answering many of his unanswered questions.

He could lie abed no longer; he had much to do. He threw off the bedclothes and leaped from the bed.

Gasping with horror at the thought of what she might see, Miss Philimore turned her face away. However, the elderly spinster's curiosity was such that she could not resist a sly peep in hopes she might see more of Lord Davenant than just his nightshirt.

Sadly for her, Davenant slipped behind a screen to change his clothes, so her hopes were not realised.

55

"*Arundel Castle*…sunk in a storm…in the Atlantic. Cargo…and…all hands lost!" a breathless clerk gasped as he came running through the open door of the Jerusalem Coffee House. The Jerusalem, as usual, was all hustle and bustle, but at this news the din of the patrons' conversations temporarily stilled, punctuated by groans at this news from some quarters of the room.

Fast on the heels of this East India Company clerk came yet another. "*Queen of the North*. Cargo of china. Two days from London."

A few cheers followed this, before the patrons once more resumed their exchanges, the continual hum of their voices interspersed with cries of "What d'ye lack? What d'ye lack?" from the waiters moving among the tables.

Within easy walking distance of the head office of the British East India Company, the Jerusalem in Cornhill was a home away from home for the company's clerks, writers and sea captains, whose business encompassed a commercial empire reaching halfway around the world. There they went to negotiate, transact business, argue and gossip, learn the latest price of tea, the arrival and departures of ships, and the fate of vessels that fell prey to storms, pirates and privateers.

One of the waiters made his way to where Captain Matthew Dawkins sat reading a newspaper at a table near the fireplace. The gentleman who accompanied him, a stranger to the establishment, was the subject of much interest to the patrons. It was neither his height nor the elegance of his attire that held their attention; his air of consequence and haughty gaze combined to give the impression he regarded the commerce that so totally occupied them as beneath him.

The waiter bent and whispered to Dawkins. At first the captain did no more than cock an eye at the hawk-faced stranger who stood before him proud as an eagle in his aerie, his hands resting atop a tall, gold-topped ebony cane. The latter countered with a stare as arrogant as it was intimidating.

Captain Dawkins, however, was not one to be easily intimidated. For the five months or more of the voyage to India aboard his ship, the 900-ton Indiaman

A JACKETING CONCERN

Titania, he reigned supreme over passengers and crew. In over more than twenty years at sea he had, due to a combination of personal cunning, expert seamanship and sheer luck, successfully dealt with privateers, pirates, attempted mutinies, tropical diseases and efforts by the Royal Navy's East Indies' squadron to impress his sailors. In common with many company men, he had also managed through his private dealings to amass a fortune that enabled him to maintain in style two mistresses: an Indian woman in Calcutta, a buxom Dutch widow at The Cape, and his children by them.

But his ship was his real love and even ashore in England he did not like to be too far from her. When not directing loadings, unloadings and refits of the vessel in the East India Dock, he was about her business at the Jerusalem Coffee House. Carrying passengers was a lucrative trade for Indiaman captains, who usually received passengers at their homes to negotiate their fares. Rather than receive his prospective passengers in Kensington, where he lodged with his widowed sister-in-law and her two insipid daughters, he met his at the Jerusalem, where he spent his time when not at the docks. Fares for company officials were set but those of the other passengers were a captain's personal perquisite; and Dawkins had made money from them all: spinsters seeking husbands, missionaries intent on converting the heathen, younger sons seeking their fortune and fugitives from the law, debts and troubles with women.

Dawkins assumed the gentleman wished to book passage aboard the *Titania*. By the look of him the man was rich enough to afford the best his ship had to offer. An aristocrat. Dawkins had seen enough of them to know one when he saw one. Why did he want to go to India? Business? Perhaps to evade the law or other troubles? The captain scrutinised the stranger more closely. Haughty the fellow might be, but there was something in his demeanour that told him here was someone who would never run from anything or anybody, no matter the danger.

The gentleman introduced himself, apologised for the intrusion and begged to be permitted to join the captain at his table. Permission given, the gentleman took a seat and, after a few minutes small talk, with a deft flick of thumb and forefinger he opened the gold top of his cane to reveal a snuffbox. Would the

Captain do him the honour of taking snuff with him? Flattered by this request, Dawkins warmed to the gentleman, eager as he was to welcome aboard his ship this person of consequence with such good manners—and an excellent taste in snuff.

"No finer vessel afloat than the *Titania,* my lord," Dawkins said, his weather-burnished face relaxing into a satisfied smile as he savoured Davenant's personal blend.

"No doubt your ship is a fine one," Davenant answered, "and should I ever desire to voyage east, it would be the one I would chose. However, the reason I have sought you out is not to acquire a sea passage but because of these."

From an inner coat pocket he drew out two gold fob seals and laid them on the table.

"Do you by any chance recognise the inscriptions on them?"

Dawkins took the seals and examined their faces. He frowned then reached for a small dish of butter on the table before him. "If you don't mind," he said, pressing each of the seals into the butter so he could more easily read their inscriptions.

After only two days in bed, and despite the remonstrations of his family and the Barclays that he rest longer, Davenant had declared himself fit. At once he ordered a curricle and horses, and his valet to be sent to Brighton from Downsley; and that morning he and Henry had driven off to London, as fast as short stops for refreshment and changes of horses would allow.

"It's too soon for you to be about," Georgiana pleaded with him before he left. She and her husband had driven over to Brighton with Addy because the boy was anxious to see that his hero was on the mend.

"I want you to take Miss Barclay and Bodger with you when you return to Downsley, where they will be safe," Davenant said when he finished telling her and her husband and the Barclays of his suspicions about Basingthwaite. To Miss Barclay he said, "I beg you and Bodger to accept my humble hospitality."

Miss Barclay's uncle had to return to London on business, and Davenant needed Henry to go to London with him. With only the pacifist Mr. Pratt to protect Miss Barclay and Bodger, Davenant feared for their safety. Basingthwaite was in Brighton, staying at the pavilion. Bodger was in danger and Miss Barclay, too, because she sheltered him. If it were as he suspected, that Basingthwaite had killed Nell, Eddie and Hurley, and was intent on murdering Addy and himself, Basingthwaite not hesitate to harm Bodger, who could identify him.

Since those snatched kisses in the sick room, Miss Barclay had taken care not to be alone with Davenant. Her initial hesitation to his invitation, he felt certain, was because she feared that at Downsley they would be in close proximity to each other. But when she learned he was going to London, she accepted.

"You were to take Bodger to Downsley anyway. Why not go sooner rather than later?" urged her uncle.

Georgiana was delighted at the prospect of having another young woman for company; and if Earl Hesston had reservations about having a climbing boy and a Cit's niece under the same roof as himself, he did not mention it.

Arriving in London at midday, Davenant stopped at Davenant House just long enough to change horses before calling at Rundell, Bridge and Rundell, the jewelers. Believing Davenant intended to act on his notion of ordering enough snuffboxes for each day of the year, Mr. Rundell greeted him warmly. But when Davenant said he only wanted his opinion of the two fob seals, coldness replaced Rundell's fawning manner. Piqued by this request, Rundell took longer than necessary to examine the seals.

"Indian made," he announced at last.

"*Indian?* Are you sure?" Davenant said. "These were both found here in England."

Even more irked by what he considered criticism of his professional judgment, Rundell gave a sigh of disgust. "With respect, my lord," he said, "items of Indian jewelry do sometimes find their way into the English market. Perhaps they were acquired as a memento of that country; there is some public interest in Asian *objets d'arts*. But I'd stake my reputation these were made in India by native craftsmen. The design on the handle: a filigree of entwined lotus flowers and leaves. The elephant head." He gave a derisive sniff. "Made for a foreigner, perhaps, but not an English gentleman." He paused before adding in a stage whisper, "Unless, that is, he had, as the saying goes, 'gone native.'"

Far from clarifying their relevance to his investigations, Rundell's assertion as to the seals' provenance puzzled Davenant even more. Made in India? How could two almost identical seals made so far away end up on a dead sweep's body, and on one of his attackers on Brighton promenade? Despite his expertise, Rundell could be wrong: just because the seals bore Indian motifs did not mean they were Indian made. How to find out for certain if they were? There was one place in London whose business was India: the headquarters of the British East India Company in Leadenhall Street. Someone there might recognise the seals' insignias from letters and documents received there.

"Hopeless," the chief clerk told Davenant when he visited the company's headquarters. "Thousands of pieces of paper pass through these offices each week," he said, obviously having no wish to conduct a paper chase.

It was only when Davenant mentioned he and one of the company's directors had been at Eton together that the clerk suggested he try the Jerusalem Coffee House. "Captain Dawkins is in London. He's there every day. Knows a good deal about India, he does—particularly Bengal."

"How d'ya come by 'em?" Dawkins said, wiping butter off the seals with a handkerchief.

He shook his head in disbelief when Davenant told him. "I wish to return them to their owner...or owners," Davenant explained.

"You'll need to take passage on my ship, then," Dawkins said. "Aye, and then dig six feet down—that's if the jackals haven't eaten what's left of him."

"You recognise the seals, then? But their owner is dead?"

"Recognise 'em right enough," Dawkins went on, "so would everyone in Bengal for that matter, rest of India, too. Ben Chantry. Richest man in Bengal, he was. Founded the ABC Trading Company. This one he used on his business letters," he said, holding up one seal. "Other was his personal one with his initials B C. Found with a dead body in St Giles, you say? A few weeks ago? T'other in Brighton? Strange. Ben died nigh on two years ago. And since he left England over twenty years past, he's only returned twice—for short visits—and they were eight years or so, ago."

"You knew him, then?"

"In a way," Dawkins said. "In his early years dined with him. Drank with him. Went on the occasional tiger shoot with him and others. But know him? No. Not one to get close to was Ben. Had a secret, I reckon." He chuckled. "Plenty of Englishmen in India with pasts they want to forget. Met him aboard my first command over twenty years ago…when he first went out there with the company. Lost touch after a few years, we did, but heard about him. English community in Calcutta ain't large. Everybody knows each other's business and news travels fast. Smart fella, Ben and cunning, too. Soon branched out on his own. Made a fortune, he did: indigo, cotton, saltpeter, opium. Everything he touched turned to gold."

Davenant's eyes widened. "A nabob?"

"Aye. House like a Mogul palace. Army of retainers. Living like a prince came natural to him. My guess is he was born to the purple: the black sheep of an aristocratic family."

Davenant leaned back against the oak settle and tapped his chin with his quizzing glass.

"Kept the match-making mamas at bay, did Ben, though he was never short of female company–if you know what I mean," Dawkins said with a wink. "About nine years ago, we met again when he returned to England on my ship. Said he was going to find himself wife…but he also took back some of his money. He was to return to India with me in the autumn. Who's there to see him off at Deptford? A real beauty. Not more'n twenty and Ben twice that. Met and married her, he had, in a few months…and she already in the family way!" He grinned. "Never one to waste time was Ben. Very upset she was bout his leavin.' Natural I s'pose, in her condition. Wanted to go with him but he'd have none of it. Don't blame him, either. Lots of Englishwomen and their babies die in India. Told me he was going to sell up and retire to England for good."

"Chantry died in India? He never returned to England?"

"Oh, he returned, all right," Dawkins continued. "From what I heard, his wife died not long after the child was born, but she was buried by the time he got back to England. Baby was spirited away by relatives, but he didn't know where. Try as he might, he couldn't find it. Ben returned to India to sell up so that he could go back to England and devote himself to finding his child. Met the second Mrs. Chantry on that trip, he did."

"On your ship?"

"No. Another. I didn't meet her until after they had married in Calcutta. Young, pretty enough…but a flighty piece and extravagant so I heard tell."

"But why did such a grieving widower as Chantry remarry so soon?"

Dawkins leaned his elbows on the table and rested his chin on his hands.

"Five months an' more at sea in close quarters that's why. A sad and lonely widower? A pretty young thing that played the guitar and sang? Tropical nights and starry skies. It's happened before and it'll happen again." He grinned. "I know. I seen it, often. Many a man snared by a husband huntin' spinster during a passage to India. Knew how to get her claws into a lonely rich widower, did that one. Knew how to spend his money, too. She had a brother…bit of a leech, so I gather, though I never met him. Got himself a soft position with Ben's company. Thought herself a leader of society, did the new Mrs. Chantry. No more tiger shoots or wild bachelor parties for Ben. Only a select few invited to the Chantry mansion."

Dawkins sighed. "Like I said, in Calcutta everyone knows your business, so it weren't long afore the word was that Ben and the missus had gone their separate ways. Ben eventually died up country of a fever, though 'tis my guess he died of a broken heart." He held up the seals. "How these ended up where they did?" He shook his head.

Davenant repocketed the seals; but showing no sign of the underlying urgency of his situation, he made no effort to leave. On the contrary, he appeared to have all the time in the world and spent the next hour asking Dawkins about Indian customs and religions of which the captain proved to be a veritable encyclopedia. Of particular interest to Davenant was *Thuggee*, the ritual strangulation of victims practised by followers of the goddess Kali.

Flattered by such attention, Dawkins expressed genuine regret when Davenant finally rose to go.

"I'm sorry I shan't have the pleasure of your company aboard my ship. We'd have lots to talk about."

"Speaking of ships, that reminds me," Davenant said. "Which company ships arrived in London…let us say…two to three months ago?"

"The Jerusalem is the place to come to for that. Names are on that board, over there. Ships from China…and a few since."

"None from India? Calcutta?"

"Several last couple of weeks…but two months ago?" Dawkins shook his head.

They shook hands. Davenant left and Dawkins returned to his newspaper. He had read only a paragraph, when a thought struck him. He summoned a waiter, paid his reckoning and hastened after Davenant.

56

"Cor! This is worser than bein' in a chimley! When's it end?" asked Bodger, who was beginning to wish he had not agreed to accompany Addy down into the crypt of Downsley's ruined priory.

They had been in the dark narrow passage that led underground from the house for only ten minutes, but to Bodger it seemed like forever. The walls, just wide enough apart for the two boys to walk side by side, oozed damp and were covered in slime; and the low ceiling was thick with cobwebs that caught in their hair and tickled their faces. The corona of the Addy's lighted candle penetrated the dark for only a foot or two, so the two boys could only inch forward slowly. And Addy had to cup the flickering flame with his hand to prevent it being snuffed out by the draft. But though the boys found the passage a trial, Puff discovered plenty of smells to interest him in its nooks and crannies.

"Sposin' the candle burns out, now?" Bodger said, trying hard to keep the tremor from his voice. "An' the door back there in the cellar. What if it slams shut? No one knows were 'ere. We'd be 'ere forever!"

"Not much longer, now," Addy reassured him. "It's lighter in the crypt. And there's a door there that leads into the grounds."

They rounded a curve in the passage and into large open space that, although its walls were in shadows, was lighter than the passage.

His confidence restored, Bodger watched as Addy, holding high the candle, looked about him.

"Is this it, then?" Bodger said with disdain. "Nuthin' to be scared of 'ere!" he said with a bravado that belied his shivers.

"Unless smugglers find you here," Addy teased, hoping to frighten him. "Mr. Perry told me smugglers do bad things to people who spy on them. They've been here," he said, indicating coils of rope, empty kegs, some candle stumps and a lantern atop a stone tomb. "Last time I was here there was still some oil in it," he said opening the lamp. With his candle, he lit the lamp and the candle stumps then sat down on a coil of rope.

Not wanting to be too far from his friend in such a dark place, Bodger joined him on the rope.

"How do you like my secret place?" Addy said. "Nobody knows about it... well almost nobody. Lord Davenant, Mr. Perry and Lady Georgiana do."

"'Ow is it a secret then, if they all know?"

"Well they know its here but they've forgotten about it. Mr. Perry showed me the entrance in the cellar and the one in the bushes outside. He said none of his family has been down here for a long time. They buried the dead monks here... under the floor. There! Where the writing is on the stones...and in those big things over there," he added, pointing to several crumbling stone tombs partly submerged in shadows from which pieces of masonry had fallen to the ground.

"Wot's monks, then?"

Addy considered this question. "Well," he said at last, "they wore long clothes and lit candles and said a lot of prayers."

"Monks wuz people!" Bodger said, horrified. "Then this place is full o' dead uns! You're a queer un and no mistake to 'ave a secret place wiv dead uns."

Addy chuckled. "Just their bones, silly! Most of those aren't there anymore. They've been dead a long time." He paused then said cajolingly. "You do like my secret place, don't you, Bodger?

"S'alright, I spose. Long as we can get out easy. Where's t'other door, then?"

Addy pointed to where some well-worn steps were just barely visible in the gloom. "Up there. The steps go up to a door that leads out into the ruins above them. Mr. Perry says the monks brought the bodies from the church that way down here. We can hide here and play without grown-ups watching us all the time. Nobody is going to come here but us, honest."

The mention of grown-ups reminded them of the odd behaviour of the ones at Downsley. Although they had been told nothing of the danger to themselves, they knew something was amiss. Like all children they were sensitive to the mood and actions of the adults around them. They knew only that they were forbidden to play anywhere outside, except on the terrace in full view of the house and with at least one servant present. But that had not stopped Addy from taking Bodger off to his secret place, by way of the cellar, leaving a frantic footman searching for them.

The swift removal of Miss Barclay and Bodger to Downsley, two days after the attack on Davenant, had pleased the boys, even though they sensed something was wrong. Their pleas to be allowed to play elsewhere in the grounds were met with evasive answers in the cheery tones adults use with children when they don't wish to be truthful. "It's like they are playing a pretend game," Addy said, "because even grown-ups can't be happy *all* the time."

Bodger said nothing. Most of the adults he had known were violent and cruel. He was still mistrustful of this new world in which he found himself and unsure how to deal with 'swells' like the Hesstons and their servants.

To the boys there seemed to be too many adults at Downsley. True, they played with them and took them on outings, but they were always close by, watching them whether they were at their lessons or at play.

"We ain't babies," complained Bodger, who was used to taking care of himself.

"Yes," Addy agreed. "We can't have adventures when they are always there?"

"Somefinks up," Bodger said.

"And I know what it is!'

"Wot?"

"The French are coming…and they don't want to tell us, because they don't want to frighten us."

"French?" Bodger asked, puzzled. "Like monks are they? Lightin' candles… an' such?"

"No, silly," said Addy. "They're bad people…very bad people. They took me away from grandpapa and gave me to the sweep. Napoleon is their leader. Bette told me that if the French come, they'd steal something from all the ladies."

"Wot?" Bodger said, intrigued.

Addy frowned. "I don't know. She wouldn't tell me. But what's worse is they *eat* little boys…*like us!*"

Far from frightening Bodger, as this information was intended to do, it elicited only an awed "Cor!" from him.

"Grandpapa told me what Bette said wasn't true, but I think he just said that so I wouldn't be frightened. You see Bette knows about the French… cos she is *French!*"

Bodger's jaw dropped. "Wot we goin' to do?"

Addy got up, picked up the lantern and made his way to one of the tombs hidden in the shadows of a wall.

"This is my secret, secret place," he said. Abruptly he disappeared between the tomb and the wall, and Bodger was left alone in the darkened crypt with only Addy's voice for company.

"When the French come, we'll hide in here," Addy called. "They'll never find us! There's a piece of loose stone back here. If you push it a bit, you can get inside."

The sound of stone grinding on stone echoed through the crypt as he did that.

Bodger shivered but not because he was cold. "Is…is some of them…the monks…bones in there?" he asked.

Addy reappeared, grabbed Bodger's hand and pulled him to the tomb. A small opening, big enough for a child to pass through into the dark interior, was just visible in the lamplight.

"See! Nothing but a few bones and bits of wood in there! But there's room for us. Come on! And Addy, followed by Puff, crawled in with the lamp."

After a moment's hesitation, Bodger crawled in behind them.

The empty tomb's dark confines were warmer than the crypt, and there was enough room for the two boys to stand up and to move about a little.

"See! Nothing to be afraid of!" Addy said, raising the candle. "No bodies, no…"

Puff started to bark.

"Well, only those," he added, as the mice that attracted Puff's attention scuttled away. "All we have to do when the French come is to come down here, get inside the tomb and close the hole."

"'Ow we goin' ter breathe?' asked Bodger, recalling with fear the many narrow flues with little air that he had climbed.

Addy raised the lamp so the roof of the tomb was visible. "See! Up there! The holes? Where the stones are broken. They let in the air, but you can't see into the tomb very easily from the outside."

Relieved, Bodger nodded. "And suppose we 'ave to stay 'ere a long time? Wot we gonna eat?"

"I've got some biscuits in a tin here. I've been taking them at teatime when no one was looking, and I've a bottle of water, too."

"All set, then," said Bodger, satisfied.

"We'd better go back, now," Addy said. "We don't want anyone to come looking for us and find our really, really secret place, do we?"

Bodger nodded. He had just begun to move when a thought occurred to him. "When the French come,' he said, "wot about Lord Davenant an' Miss Barclay an' Lady Georgiana an' Mr. Perry an' all? Don't want nufink to 'appen to them. Where will they hide?"

Addy considered this for several seconds.

"Oh, they'll be all right," he assured Bodger. "The French only eat little boys—not grown-ups."

57

The sun was low in the sky as Davenant drove his curricle across the Middlesex marshland toward the Isle of Dogs, the bulbous peninsular that swells from the north shore of the River Thames, about four miles from London. In a hurry to reach the East India Company docks before they closed for the evening, he had chosen the shorter route there along Commercial Road. Thus he avoided a part of that other London of which the *ton* was unaware: Ratcliff Highway, Shadwell and Poplar with their rookeries, taverns, doss houses, brothels and opium dens patronised by sailors of all nationalities, whores and criminals.

The journey took Davenant longer than he expected because of heavy traffic. Although much of the company's cargoes were moved by water on small craft from the docks to its City warehouse, a good deal of it was also carried there along Commercial Road by slow horse-drawn carts, a steady stream of which impeded the curricle's passage.

The East India docks covered so vast an area that it dwarfed the company's distinctive wide-hulled vessels in the inner and outer docks, so they appeared like toy boats in a child's bath. The establishment was well guarded by the soldiers of the company's private army, and it was only after Davenant presented a note from Captain Dawkins they let him enter. Davenant boarded The *White Rose*, leaving Henry with the curricle to gaze in awe at the workings of an enterprise that was an integral part of England's international trade and a source of its prosperity.

"Dawkins sent you, eh?" said Captain Johnson as he led the way into the ship's great cabin.

Davenant nodded.

Not long after he left the Jerusalem Coffee House, Captain Dawkins caught up with him in the street. *The White Rose*, two months late from Calcutta, had docked a few days ago, Dawkins told him. It had been forced to remain at St. Helena for emergency repairs because of damage sustained in a storm. "Rather than wait for those to be done, some passengers may have transferred to one of the earlier homebound ships from China," he explained

"So you are interested in the passengers we carried during this last voyage," Johnson said. He shook his head. "What a voyage! Been at sea long time, I have, and seen a lot, but this passage…?" Again he shook his head.

"It left much to be desired?"

"That's one way o' putting it," said Johnson, as he thumbed through the pages of the leather-bound log on his desk.

But for the soft rustle of the books pages, the cabin was quiet; the shouts and curses of seamen, the clang of hammers, the buzz of saws and the screech of cargo winches that met him when came on board unable to penetrate the cabin's thick paneling. While he waited, Davenant watched the comings and goings in the dockyard through the cabin's wide window. Beyond it the setting sun sent a shaft of gold streaking across the river's surface, creating strange purple shadows from the ships riding at anchor and the warehouses on the wharfs.

"Mrs. Chantry, you said? Shan't forget that name in a hurry. Are here we are. More'n one entry about her. Widow, she were–young and pretty–her rich husband dead nine months. Airs and graces of a queen! Found fault with everything and everybody. Demanded precedence at the dining table. Said she was now a marchioness, member of one of the greatest families in the land."

Johnson looked at Davenant. "Imagine what its like to have someone like that among a small group of people in a tight space for half a year or more! 'Tweren't as though we didn't have enough trouble! Becalmed in the Indian Ocean for days, set upon by Malay pirates! Give the brother his due though, he acquitted himself well against those devils. Shot a couple and stabbed one with his own knife."

"Really!"

"That's not all. At The Cape the lady ups and tells me her brother is trying to poison her. Hysterical, she was! Well, the brother–if that's who he really was–denied it." The captain looked knowingly at Davenant. "Spent more time in her cabin with her than any brother or servant ought. But for all that, I felt sorry for him: a quiet, pleasant fellow. She treated him like a servant. Forever quarrelling, the pair of 'em. Other passengers and the crew often heard 'em."

"What did they quarrel about?" Davenant said.

The captain shrugged. "Brother told me her husband's death had temporarily deranged her. So I wasn't surprised when she complained things were being stolen from her cabin. Blamed the crew first, then her brother. Said he wanted her inheritance."

"What things did she say were taken?"

The captain thought for a moment. "Oh, jewelery, papers, mementoes of her husband."

"Jewelry?"

"Well, that's what she said." Johnson shrugged. "But after what her brother said about her, I knew she was makin' it up. Only member of crew that went into her cabin been with me for years and is as honest as the days long. And her brother!" He shook his head. "Bent over backwards to please her. Much good it did him. The storm that hit us were a blessin' in disguise I reckon."

"How so?"

"Put her out of her misery. Went overboard in it, she did. What a storm! Three days of it! Waves high as a house! The brother was distraught, of course, but at least he was free of her, poor crazed soul. After what happened to his sister, when we arrived at St. Helena for repairs, the brother didn't want to remain on board. Transferred to the *Maid o' Kent* that arrived day after we did. Homebound from China with a cargo of tea, the ship was. For all his pleasant ways, wasn't sorry to see him go."

Davenant's eyebrows shot up.

"Couple of my lascars swore they saw him push his sister overboard during the storm. That's when talk of demons and evil spirits began. Claimed the vessel was cursed, they did. Made my British tars nervous, too. Nearly had a mutiny. Don't matter what part of the world they come from, sailors are superstitious lot. Course 'twere all nonsense. What brother would do that to his sister? Strange thing was, after he left, the rest of the journey was uneventful." He shrugged. "I'm sure that was just coincidence."

Davenant took one of Georgiana's by now much-creased sketches from his coat pocket.

"Do you recognise anyone?" he said, unfolding it.

Johnson stared at the drawing, his eyes widening in sudden recognition. "Lord above, that's Mrs. Chantry's brother: Mr. Ormerod. You know him?"

"Yes, I know him," Davenant said quietly, "but by another name."

"Blast him!" muttered the night porter at Davenant House.

The Watch, informing everyone it was three o'clock in the morning and that all was well, had just woken him.

The annoyed porter tried get comfortable in his chair once more; but no sooner had he done so than he heard the sound of a horse outside. A furious banging on the front door brought him struggling and cursing to his feet.

"Waddya want this time o' night?" he demanded of the weary, travel-stained rider he found on the doorstep when he finally unbarred the door.

"Special courier from the Duke of Ryedale with a letter for Lord Davenant."

58

To prevent his hat from being whipped from his head, Henry Rollins grasped its brim with one hand and held tight to his seat with the other to stop him being thrown from the curricle as it dashed along the London-to-Brighton road. Yet despite the precariousness of his position in the speeding vehicle, Henry was enjoying himself. His initial ire at being aroused from his bed in the cool, grey dawn with a summons to harness the curricle had dissipated with the exhilaration of the actual ride.

Had the very devil in im did 'Is Nibs, Henry thought, as Davenant deftly overtook vehicle after vehicle in a display of audacious driving skill the envy of every other driver on the road who witnessed it. The horses, too, seemed to sense their master's vivacity, their hooves seeming to barely touch the ground as they raced along.

But Henry's joy was not solely due to the excitement of the ride, for not only had Davenant bid Henry sit next to him, instead of behind in his usual perch, he had also taken him into his confidence. And during this intimacy 'Is Nibs admitted–somewhat ruefully, it was true–Henry had been right about Addy from the very beginning.

They had set off from Davenant House just as the darkness of night was dissolving into the grey of dawn. "For once your imagination actually proved correct, Henry," Davenant said as he took his seat in the curricle. "Addy is, I fear, the victim of what you, in your own inimitable way, described as 'a jacketing concern.'"

Such unexpected praise rendered Henry speechless for at least a minute: a rare happening. And though in deference to his employer he did not say, "I told you so," he savoured that thought with as much relish as does a connoisseur enjoying a rare blend of snuff.

"Newgate seize me!" he said, almost falling from his seat when Davenant named the author of the 'jacketing concern.' "Who woulda thought it? I'm a gen'leman…and a friend of the Prince Regent, too?"

"Gentility does not preclude criminality, Henry. Besides, he is no gentleman—merely an actor playing at being one."

"Well, he must be a good actor, then."

"*Au contraire,* he is but a poor player, unable to perform any other role but the one with which he has deceived society. I have that on no lesser authority than that of my friend Mr. Sheridan, the playwright, whom, you will recall, I visited on our return from the Isle of Dogs, yesterday. And even in his role as gentleman, Basingthwaite has shown himself an inadequate performer."

Sheridan, as usual, was drinking when Davenant called, and had already drunk a great deal; but he was not so drunk that he could not identify from one of Georgiana's sketches the actor who had unsuccessfully sought the lead in his production of 'the Scottish play' several years before.

"Looks like that fellow you introduced to me not so long ago," Sheridan said, "the one who didn't like the theatre. Must have been about nine or ten years ago when he auditioned. I'm certain it was him."

"Scottish play?" Henry said to Davenant. "What's that, then?"

"That, Henry, is how actors refer to *Macbeth,* a play by William Shakespeare about an ambitious Scots nobleman, because they consider it unlucky to mention it by name. The actor in question was unable to maintain the Scots accent Mr. Sheridan required of him and so lost the part.

"Like the chap wot spoke to Bodger when he called at the sweep's yard lookin for Malloy?"

Davenant nodded.

The sketch he showed Sheridan was the same one Captain Johnson identified as that of Mr. Ormerod, a passenger on a voyage from Calcutta, and the brother of Mrs. Chantry. A quick search of Debrett's *Peerage* revealed Chantry as the family name of the Dukes of Ryedale, the younger brother of the present duke being one Lord Adolphus Benjamin Chantry. The remaining pieces of the puzzle fell into place. Lord Adolphus, the black sheep of the Chantry family, known in India as Ben Chantry, the nabob, was the husband of the slave trader's stepdaughter, Elise Gilden—and Addy's father.

"Both the fob seals were, in each case, accidentally snatched from an attacker during the assaults on the sweep Malloy and me. Chantry's widow complained to Captain Johnson that her brother stole from her jewelry belonging to her late husband, a brother subsequently identified from a sketch as..."

"Mr. Basingthwaite!" Henry finished.

"Yes. I recall when I first met him he wore too much jewelry, including fobs. I attributed such a display to him being from abroad and new to society and its ways."

Henry nodded. "Mmmm. Made a lot o' people think 'e wuz a gent."

"Yes. I confess even *I* was taken in by him. The Chantry money made him rich and Hurley's friendship provided him with an *entrée* into society. I do not know the details of Chantry's will, but I assume Basingthwaite believed the fortune would go to the widow, his sister, and she would leave it to him when she died. Although no one can prove it, I believe that is why he did away with her during a storm on the return journey from India. I imagine he had not known Chantry had a son to whom the bulk of the money would go, unless the boy predeceased the widow. When Basingthwaite discovered that he had, he sought out Addy and set about trying to get rid of him."

"And the murders? Nell an' her boy, the Hurley fella and the attempts on you an Addy?" Henry said.

"When Basingthwaite arrived in England he must have discovered that a child stood in the way of the fortune he hoped to gain from his sister's death, so he hired one of the Conways to kill Addy. Instead, Conway pocketed the money and sold Addy to the sweep. Basingthwaite discovered Addy was alive and in my care. At the sweep's yard he learned the boy had been taken there and realised Conway must have sold him to Malloy. Basingthwaite strangled Malloy, and then killed Nell and her son in the riot, so that none of them could identify him to me. He sought out Conway and threatened to give him up to the authorities if he did not get rid of Addy once and for all; that is why Conway broke into my house. Hurley, he killed under the misguided notion that I would not pursue the wager between us if he were dead. I think that was when I began to have doubts about him. No gentleman welches on a wager."

"Then the sooner we get our hands on that bastard, the better!"

"Exactly! Let us hope that once we have him, he will tell us from whence Addy was taken. Recollect, the location of the boy's grandfather is still unknown. Why didn't he raise a hue and cry when Addy was kidnapped? I can only assume that as the kidnapper was a Sussex smuggler, Addy was taken in that county, but I have never come across the name Gilden there before."

By then they were crossing Westminster Bridge, just as the ragged vagrants who had spent the night huddled together in sleep in its stone embrasures were beginning to stir.

"We do not know where Basingthwaite is at the moment," Davenant said. "I left him under Buckles'–pardon, I forget–Mr. Townsend's watchful eye. But last night the Duke of Ryedale sent word that Basingthwaite must have realised he was being watched, for he gave Buckles the slip–and a bump on the head to boot. He must know I have both the seals he lost and if I do trace their provenance, he will be revealed for what he is. When he learned I had gone to London, he headed off there too, by curricle. I've no doubt that to secure Addy's inheritance for himself, he will try again to kill Addy and me to do so. He knows I keep horses on this road and that I will return to Downsley once I learn he evaded Townsend. Both the duke and I think he will lay in wait for me somewhere ahead."

"He'd be mad to try and kill you an' Addy," Henry said. "Couldn't get away wiv it. Too many folks know about 'im."

"Ah yes, but I am the only one with all the pieces of evidence, the evidence that proves his crimes. Besides, I think him now so crazed beyond belief by his mania for wealth and position he is, in truth, mad enough to do anything."

Once across Westminster Bridge, there was no more talk. Davenant, anxious to make as much speed as possible and avoid the worst of the traffic, whipped up the horses and away they went. With the Prince Regent in Brighton, traffic from London to the coast would become heavier as the day wore on, not only with the many daily stagecoaches, but also with the vehicles of the fashionable who always followed the prince to Brighton.

59

As the proprietor of a staging inn, the landlord of the King's Head in Cuckfield was no stranger to the antics of the rich and fashionable young men who challenged each other to feats of driving skill along the London-to-Brighton Road. For wagers and for sheer bravado they raced each other, chased each other and out-manouvered each other in their curricles and phaetons. Their heroes being the drivers of mail and stagecoaches, they aped them in every way: dressing, speaking, whistling and even seeing how far they could spit like their paragons. One of them had even gone to the trouble of having his teeth filed to points to improve his whistle.

Reckless as their behaviour often was, the landlord had a soft spot for these young fellows. They were, after all, a sure source of income for him, just so long as they did not forget to pay their reckoning before they left. They lodged or rented horses at the inn, dined and drunk themselves senseless there and tried, when he was not looking, to seduce his chambermaids. Accustomed though he was to the spirited antics of these gentlemen, even the landlord was taken aback by the request of the one who had arrived by curricle from Brighton late the night before.

"You want to buy *all* my horses!" he gasped when this guest dangled a purse before him after breakfast that morning, a purse whose weight represented twice what the animals were worth.

"A wager with Lord Davenant," the man explained. "You know him?"

"Of course," the landlord said. "Sometimes stops in when he's going up to Lunnon or down to the coast."

"Wagered him he wouldn't be able to reach Brighton within a certain time because of obstacles I'd put in his way," the gentleman explained with a smile. "If you sell me your animals, then he will have to go elsewhere to obtain horses, which will slow him down and increase my chance of winning the bet. Er, does he have any of his own horses here?"

The landlord shook his head. "None of the gentry have at the moment."

"Oh, and by any chance has he been by this way yet? "

Again the landlord shook his head.

Rubbing his chin the while, the landlord studied the would-be purchaser while he mulled over the request: a gentleman, certainly, but one with an odd brownish complexion, a gentleman, whom he thought a little too old for high jinks along the London-to-Brighton Road. Fellow must have more money than sense, too, to pay twice what the horses were worth. Of course, if he sold the horses, Lord Davenant would not be the only person unable to hire them: none of his other customers could, either. But then all they need do was go to the next inn. After all, it wasn't the first time someone had bought up a coaching inn's horses to help them win a bet; Lord Davenant, himself, had done so more than once in his younger days, the landlord had heard. The money would more than make up for any temporary loss of business, and he could obtain new animals in no time at all. Besides, times were hard–and gold was gold, wasn't it?

"You can't have the stagecoach horses," he said at last. "They ain't mine." He smiled. "But the others? By all means. How will you take delivery of em?"

"There's no hurry,"the gentleman said, handing him the purse. "I can see they are in good hands here."

A handshake sealed the bargain and the gentleman then departed in his curricle.

With a few stops at inns just long enough to change horses, and quaff a mug of ale, Davenant and Henry made good time through Surrey, and into Sussex. After they had gone through Horley, Crawley and Hand Cross in the latter county without incident, Davenant began to think it unlikely they would meet Basingthwaite on the road after all. Perhaps he had passed by without seeing them and would shortly find himself in London minus his quarry. Or perhaps Basingthwaite was even now lurking in wait for him nearer to Downsley.

Traffic was much heavier by the time they neared Whitman's Green. Carriages, gigs, phaetons, curricles, whiskies, stagecoaches, wagons and carts travelling in both directions obstructed Davenant's view of the road ahead, and he was forced to slow his pace. Being harvest time, wagons loaded with hay and produce pulled by shire horses and oxen were on the road; and Davenant found himself behind one of these full of cabbages. He was unable to overtake it because coming toward him on the opposite side of the road, drawn by four shire horses was a wagon piled high and wide with hay that occupied most of the carriageway. He slowed and waited for it to lumber by. It was then that he saw what was behind it.

From a small track partially hidden by trees, where he had obviously lain in wait, Basingthwaite shot around the hay wagon in his curricle and drew level with Davenant's stationary vehicle.

Davenant's surprise was momentary.

"He's got a pistol!" Henry yelled.

"So have I!" Davenant shouted, but before he could take it from inside his coat, Basingthwaite fired at him.

Davenant and Henry ducked and the ball went wild. The horses, frightened by the shot, squealed and plunged forward in flight. Struggling to bring them under control, Davenant moved his vehicle into the centre of the road to avoid hitting the cart in front of him, just as Basingthwaite passed by and struck at Davenant with his whip. Davenant jerked his head to avoid the lash; it knocked off his hat, leaving a bloody gash across his forehead.

With the horses so wild with fright it was all Henry could do to keep his seat. Temporarily dazed by the blow, Davenant lost control of his scared horses and the confused animals lurched forward in disarray toward the over-laden hay wagon.

That vehicle's equally terrified horses squealed and reared in the face of the oncoming threat. Davenant tried to swerve, but sitting on such a high perch, his vision was temporarily obscured by the wagon's overhanging hay load that caught about his face. One of the curricle's wheels slammed against the wagon with such force it broke off, the impact throwing Davenant and Henry on to the road. In vain the wagon driver struggled to control his horses, but their writhing had set the vehicle swaying so violently that in a matter of seconds it toppled over under its own weight, engulfing Davenant and Henry under a load of hay.

At the King's Head, passengers from the Brighton Flyer stagecoach were enjoying a refreshment stop before they left on the last stage of their journey to Brighton. The coach's inside passengers occupied the coffee room, while the outside passengers–appropriately enough–sat at wooden tables outside beneath the open coffee room windows. Ready and eager to be off were the four fresh horses that had just been harnessed to the stagecoach in the inn yard.

Satisfied that all was in readiness for the next stage of the coach's journey, the yard porter was just about to enter the inn to quench his thirst when he saw a small cart pulled by a dejected nag ambling into the yard. The cart he recognised as belonging to a local farmer; but it was the two men in it, two men liberally speckled with shreds of hay, which caught his interest. The driver, a tall, hatless gentleman with a cut across his forehead and a decided air of consequence, looked as if he would be more at home tooling the ribbons of a high flyer in Hyde Park rather than a farm cart. Meanwhile, his companion, a short, red headed fellow with freckles, urged on the reluctant horse with frequent curses, all the while doing his best to maintain his balance in the wobbling vehicle.

The outside coach passengers stared with curiosity at this odd sight.

The landlord, recognising Davenant, watched from the inn's open door. He shook his head. What a day! First a gentleman buying up all his horses and now Lord Davenant driving a farm cart and looking as if he had been rolling in the hay with a wench!

"Two of your best horses–*at once!*" Davenant ordered the yard porter no sooner he brought the cart to a standstill.

"We 'as none for hire, sir."

Jumping from the cart, Davenant grabbed the porter by the shoulders and turned him toward the stables.

"Are you blind? You have two dozen or more horses!"

The porter cast a pleading look at the landlord, who came toward them.

Meanwhile, Henry, heeding a call of nature, trotted off behind the inn in search of a privy. It was while he was on his way back to the inn yard that he heard what he at first thought were the grunts and squeals of an animal. Half expecting to see a pig on the loose, he looked about him, but saw nothing. He was about to walk on when he noticed an open ground floor window of the inn and realised the noises came from there.

Cautiously he crept up to the window and peeped inside. What he saw made him chuckle: the flabby, bare buttocks of a man with his breeches down around his ankles protruding from the open door of a tall cupboard. There were two plump arms around the man's neck and a pair of stockinged legs clasped tight about his thighs. A tall hat and a caped coat with a large rosette in its buttonhole lay on a nearby chair: the unmistakable garb of a coachman.

"Reckon as 'ow his idea of a refreshment stop ain't the same as is passengers," Henry said to himself.

"Henry!"

Davenant's shout sent Henry running back to the inn yard, where he found his usually composed employer in a heated conversation with the landlord.

"Sorry, my lord," the landlord said, "but them horses in the stables ain't mine to hire out or sell anymore. Gen'leman who stayed last night bought 'em all this morning! Said he wanted to get the better of you in a wager."

"*All* of them?" Davenant said. "And *you* let him?"

The landlord was indignant. "They was my horses to do as I liked with! And with what 'e paid me—in gold—I could buy them horses twice over."

Davenant's eyes narrowed. "And the name of this horse lover?" he demanded in a voice like ice.

"Er... Bas... er...Basing..."

"Basingthwaite!" Davenant barked. "You damn fool! The man's a scoundrel, a murderer who has just tried to kill me and will try to kill others before the day is out. And you helped him?"

The landlord bristled. "Didn't look like a murderer to me. Real gen'lman 'e was. His money was good, too."

"And how am I supposed to get to Brighton?"

"There's another inn down the road that 'as horses," and with that the aggrieved landlord retired to the inn.

In search of an answer to his own question, Davenant surveyed the surrounding yard. The excitement being over, the coach's passengers had returned to their seats to finish their meal, and the stable hands were going about their business. His first thought was to take a couple of the horses now owned by Basingthwaite, but there were too many hostlers there to prevent him and Henry from reaching the stabled animals and saddling two of them. The only other horses were the four harnessed to the Brighton Flyer. The coachman was nowhere in sight, his seat temporarily occupied by a hostler holding the reins, while two others stood at the horses heads.

Henry followed Davenant's gaze. "If your thinkin' wot I think your thinkin,'" guv, he said with an irreverent grin, "we'll soon be in Brighton."

Davenant looked down at him and his lips twitched.

"Oughtta get rid o' the luggage," Henry said, eyeing the pile roped to the coach's roof. "Without passengers for ballast, it could 'ave us over if we takes a corner a bit sharp like, an' well be goin' fast. Don't want any more tumbles. Had enough for one day, we 'ave."

"We need a knife for the ropes."

"Leave it to me, guv," Henry said, and he darted away.

Davenant hoped he would not be long. They had lost so much time already. It had taken some time to extricate him and Henry from under the overturned hay load, but eventually out they came, hay in their hair and all over their clothes. By then Basingthwaite was long gone; the wagon driver and the other vehicle drivers delayed by the accident had been too busy trying to clear the road to notice which way he went. Then there had been the indignant farmer to placate with money for his overturned wagon and removal of the hay from the road. It took even longer and more money to persuade the farmer to take temporary care of Davenant's stressed horses and what remained of the curricle, neither of which was in any state to continue the journey. And it had taken even more money and a deal of persuasion from Davanent before the farmer agreed to rent him a rickety cart and nag to take them to the King's Head. If that was not enough, Henry, fussing like an old woman, insisted that Davenant have his gashed forehead attended to by the farmer's wife. By then, even the cumbersome Brighton Flyer, had overtaken them.

"Driver's havin' a threepenny standup," Henry announced on his return to the yard. From under his coat he took the meat cleaver he had seized from just inside the open kitchen window. "Still at it they are in a broom cupboard," he added with a grin.

Davenant shrugged. "Far be it for us to interrupt them in their…ahem…labour of love?"

Once more Davenant looked about the yard. Satisfied no one was paying any attention to either of them, he whispered to Henry to go around behind the coach and climb aboard while he dealt with the hostler on the box.

A few minutes later the hostler was wondering how it was he came to be lying on his back in some horse dung on the cobbles. It had all happened so quickly. One minute he had been engaged in conversation with a tall gentleman, the next he had been flying through the air.

"Forgive me, but I'm in a hurry," Davenant called down to him from his recently-vacated seat on the coach's box.

Henry had hacked through enough of the ropes securing the luggage to the coach roof, so that it needed only a couple of pushes from him to topple the trunks and boxes. They thudded to the ground in quick succession; a few broke open, scattering clothes on the cobblestones. Alerted by these sounds, hostlers dashed out of the stable. Their yells and curses bought the inside passengers to the coffee room window and the outside ones to their feet.

Henry, clambering into the seat next to Davenant, noticed the driver's post horn, a yard of tin that gleamed in the sunlight. His eyes wide with anticipation, he seized it.

"By all means," Davenant said to Henry's enquiring grin.

His blast on the horn brought the landlord and passengers spilling from the inn. Red-faced, his shirt hanging loose, the coachman came running from the rear of the building still doing up his breeches. "You can't do that!" he shouted. "That's stealing!"

"Give the passengers whatever they want and send the bill to me at Downsley Priory," Davenant shouted to the landlord.

With that he whipped the horses and accompanied by several more blasts on the horn from Henry, the Brighton Flyer set off in a cloud of dust down the road and was soon out of sight.

60

Phineas Jobbs, the agent for the Brighton Flyer, stepped outside his office in Castle Square, Brighton. Being of a naturally fussy disposition, he was always at pains to assure himself everything was in readiness whenever one of the company's London coaches was due to arrive or depart. Such assiduous attention to detail earned him much favour in the eyes of his superiors: the directors and shareholders of the Brighton Flyer Company, for whom quick turnarounds of coaches were a guarantee of healthy returns on their investments.

Jobbs took out his watch and peered at it through wire-rimmed spectacles. The Flyer was due in about half an hour and all was in readiness for it. Beginning to cluster outside the office were family and friends waiting to greet arriving passengers, and departing passengers with those there to see them off on their journey. Luggage lay stacked, ready to be loaded; and hostlers were on hand to change horses for the return journey.

The hub of Brighton's daily stagecoach traffic, Castle Square was the home of several rival coach company offices. With more than twenty coaches a day between London and Brighton, the square was always bustling with people, the arrivals and departures of coaches attracting the idle and curious. The down coaches brought the latest gossip and news from the London, maybe of a battle won, or lost, by Lord Wellington in the Peninsular. And passengers both down and up were the cause for much interest and speculation. Who were they? Why had they come? Why were they leaving? Catering to the needs of this throng were pie men, muffin men, fruit sellers, and peddlers with cheap trinkets and bottles of a Brighton Elixir (seawater) to sell, as well as beggars and pickpockets intent on catering to their own needs.

Jobbs shooed away some ragged street urchins fighting near his office door while they waited to earn penny or two for carrying passengers' bags. A blind ex-soldier in faded regimentals with a placard identifying him as a 'Peninsular Veteran,' stood by the door rattling coins in a tin cup. Jobbs curtly ordered him to move on. He was just about to re-enter the office, when the blast of a coach

A JACKETING CONCERN

horn stopped him. Surprised, he turned back and took out his watch again.

Could it be? No, it couldn't. The Flyer was not due for half an hour–and neither were any other coaches for that matter.

There was another blast of the horn, another and another and then into the square half an hour early came the Brighton Flyer.

Although he had not expected to see the coach so soon, the agent smiled with satisfaction. His superiors would be pleased at this early arrival: it was good for business.

Cheers greeted the coach as it entered the square and off went the street urchins at the trot to offer their services to the passengers. But almost as soon as they had begun, the cheers died away and the urchins slowed to a stop.

The silence in the square was palpable.

All eyes were on the coach.

But for the two persons sitting on the box, the coach could have been a phantom.

It was empty.

There were no passengers waving from the windows or calling from seats on the roof, and no luggage tied to the back or piled on the roof.

In place of the regular driver sat a hawk-faced stranger, deftly tooling the ribbons; next to him, half sitting, half standing was a small red-headed man blowing the post horn with as much energy as Joshua used before the walls of Jericho.

The coach made two turns about the square before the driver, with unerring precision, brought it to a standstill exactly in front of the booking office. Throwing the reins to a hostler, he jumped down from his seat. After one last blast on the horn–a blast that made those nearby clap their hands over their ears–his companion reluctantly put down this instrument and vacated his perch, too.

At first the dazed Jobbs could only gape at the strange coachman.

"Y-y-y…you're…not the regular driver!" he finally managed.

"Good Lord, I should hope not!" Davenant drawled. "I've no desire to spend my days driving that rattletrap."

"The driver! Where is he?" It was a screech rather than a question.

"No doubt still frolicking in a broom cupboard with a chambermaid," Davenant said, as with studied nonchalance he removed his gloves and used them to brush dust and hay from his coat. Noticing the crowd fast gathering around him he added, "There being ladies present, I will say no more on *that* subject."

When he realised the import of this, the agent's jaw dropped. "You *stole* the coach!"

Davenant stared down at him with icy hauteur. "Implicit in the definition of the verb 'to steal' is the notion that a thief intends to permanently deprive the owner of whatever he has taken from him. I, my good man, had no desire, nor do I have now, to permanently retain that boneshaker behind me. I merely borrowed it. Coach and horses are here—where they should be—safe and sound before your office. More than half an hour earlier than expected, I might add."

He took some money from his pocket and thrust it at Jobbs. "The coach fare for the two of us from Cuckfield."

From all corners of the square a large crowd, eager to learn what happened to driver and passengers, was fast gathering around Davenant and Jobbs.

Fast and frantic, the same questions were repeated again and again.

"What have you done with 'em?"

"Are they hurt?"

"They ain't dead, are they?"

"Yes, where are they?" demanded the agent, who had visions of passengers lying in a roadside ditch with their throats cut. What would his superiors say to that?

Before Davenant could reply, the Duke of Ryedale had elbowed his way through the crowd from the Castle Inn.

"Demned if I expected to see you arrive in this fashion," he said.

"It's a long story," Davenant replied. "I'll explain later. Suffice to say Basingthwaite attacked us on the road. If I mistake not, he has gone on to Downsley. I must prevent him doing any harm to Addy and Bodger. I'll go across country: it's quicker than by road. I need a horse—a good one, *now!*"

"My best! My own. Immediately," Ryedale said. He nodded to a servant, who went off to do his bidding. "I'll follow by road with your man."

A JACKETING CONCERN

A woman grabbed Davenant's arm. "My Ernie? What 'ave you done with him?" she screamed.

Davenant removed the hand from his arm and held up one of his own for silence.

"Your Ernie, ma'am, whom I take it was one of the passengers, is even now being wined, dined and boarded at my expense at the King's Head in Cuckfield, together with his fellow travellers."

With that he and Ryedale pushed their way through the crowd to where a hostler waited with a saddled horse. "The very best and ready for a gallop," the duke assured Davenant.

Unwilling to let Davenant go, the crowd, led by the furious Jobbs, had followed the two men and watched Davenant mount.

Jobbs grabbed the horse's bridle.

"Lord Davenant, eh? Of Downsley Priory? Heard of you, I have! You won't get away with this. Call the constable, I will. See if I don't. Broke the law, you have."

Davenant leaned from the saddle. "Well so has your company. To whit: a negligent coachman, baggage piled above permitted height and an excess of passengers, all of which could cause danger to life and limb. Oh, and I nearly forgot, permitting an amateur to drive a coach. By all means call the constables! And when they arrive send them at once to Downsley Priory. Tell them I have gone there to prevent *murder!*"

With that Davenant broke free of the restraining hand, and horse and rider clattered off across the square, leaving the irate Jobbs and the crowd gawking after them.

61

"The French *are* coming! I *know* they are!"

Addy's stance as he stated this left no room for doubt of his assertion. Eyes narrowed, face determined, fists clenched at his sides, he stood resolute as he delivered his ominous declaration when he and Bodger stopped to catch their breath during a game of tag on the terrace.

Bodger stared at him mystified. He had only a vague notion about these people the French, whom Addy said ate little boys, frogs and snails. They were supposed to live the other side of the sea but, unlike London, where he could see the opposite bank of the river, he could see nothing visible the other side of water from Brighton beach. This troubled him. Out across the water the sea met the sky in a straight line but what came after that? Whenever he looked there was nothing to see. Was that the end of the world? How could anyone, let alone these French live there?

"*The French are coming!*" Addy repeated with even more emphasis than before.

Of that he was certain. How else to explain the behaviour of the grownups since Bodger and Miss Barclay came to stay at Downsley Priory? They had been behaving oddly enough before the two arrived, but since then matters had become much worse. Now he and Bodger could play only in the house or on the surrounding terraces with either one of the house party or a servant present. If they disobeyed, Lord Hesston warned he would confine them to their rooms on bread and water for a week.

"I have no wish to alarm you but Lord Davenant has charged me with your safety until he returns, so you must obey me," the earl said. "To go beyond the house at present is dangerous for you both. There are those who would harm you."

The mysterious those, Addy knew, were the French. Who else could there be to harm them but the French? "I told you they're the ones who steal little boys and eat them. They eat snails, too," he said to Bodger. "They stole me from grandpapa and gave me to the sweep. And now they want to do it again."

"If they eats boys, why didn't they eat yer when they got yer before?" Bodger demanded.

"Well I suppose they weren't hungry then," Addy said, after giving this a few seconds thought.

He and Bodger sat on the grass together. The footman ordered to watch them sat some distance away on a stone bench, boredom and the sun's warmth having combined to lull him to doze.

"What we gonna do then, then?" Bodger said.

"We must hide, of course," Addy answered. "In the old tomb. In the ruins, like we said."

"You ain't fraid wot Lord Hesston'll do to yer when 'e finds out?"

Addy shook his head slowly in defiance. What was Lord Hesston's threat compared to the peril they faced them now? "No. Are you?"

Bodger was both surprised and pleased by Addy's boldness. Defiance of authority having been a way of life for Bodger, the prospect of a week spent on bread and water was better than no food at all–a situation he had often experienced as a climbing boy. But Addy? In his world children obeyed adults and their rules without question. For Addy to be so determined to defy Lord Hesston must mean the French posed a far greater a threat than anything his lordship might do to them. Bodger had faced many dangers in his young life, but none had terrified him to the extent that the thought of being eaten by the mysterious French did.

The boys looked at their watchdog. His eyes closed, the footman sprawled on the bench, his head nodding over his folded arms.

The way was clear.

Although they did not see her, or she them, as they passed by under the cover of the rose gardens bushes, Miss Barclay stood contemplating her reflection in the ever-changing ripples of a fountain's marble basin. Above her, the stone figures of The Three Graces stood hands joined in a circle, the spray shooting high above their heads before cascading over them into the basin. So motionless was she that, but for the intermittent flutter of her white muslin grown in the breeze, she might have been another one of the statues dotted about among the rose bushes.

In the two days she had been at Downsley, Miss Barclay had come to love the beauty and peace of its gardens. As a Quaker, she often sought spiritual solace in quiet contemplation, and for this she found the tranquil rose garden particularly beneficial. And this afternoon she was in dire need of emotional calm. Although outwardly she appeared serene, inwardly she felt a turbulence, the like of which she had never known before. Even in the rose garden there was no respite from it. With nothing to distract her thoughts, the peace of the place only made matters worse, the thoughts and feelings that troubled her surging unchecked to fill her mind. As if to blot them out, she closed her eyes. The sun gently warmed her face and bare arms, a soft breeze toyed with her curls, and the scent of fading roses and rain-soaked earth invaded her nostrils: sensations that only served to intensify her inner turmoil.

In an effort to banish those feelings, she opened her eyes and shook her head. Sternly she reminded herself, as she had done more than once, that she was not attracted to Lord Davenant. And *definitely* not in love with him. He was a friend: that was *all*. Her first impression of him had been wrong. She had thought him a jaded rake, bent on pleasure and violent pastimes such as pugilism—which she abhorred—and a reckless gambler quite happy to use a child in a wager. But in execution of this wager he had shown compassion, kindness, sympathy and generosity. He had been moved by the death of Nell and little Eddie; he had shown in both word and deed a desire to better the life of climbing boys; and he had grown to care for Addy and Bodger, sparing no effort for their well-being and safety. The wager now meant nothing to him; he was prepared to take as long as necessary and do whatever needed to be done, even to the endangerment of his own life, to return Addy to his grandfather and bring to justice whoever was trying to prevent that happening.

Between she and Joseph Pratt there existed a long understanding that they would marry one day. But when she was with Joseph time did not stand still as it did when she was with Lord Davenant, conversing about literature, art, poetry and the affairs of the day. She missed his presence when he went to Liverpool; she missed him now while he was away; and she had been concerned for his recovery when he was the attacked—but *only* because he was a friend, she sternly reminded herself.

And then he had kissed her and she, forgetting she was a lady, had not resisted. Like a hussy, she had responded. Until then, she had never been kissed: Joseph only ever kissed her hand. But Lord Davenant's kisses? She sighed. No wonder her disquiet.

Davenant, she was certain, had kissed dozens of women. No. Hundreds. What was she to him but a passing fancy like a saucy maidservant or an opera dancer? Did he think of her in the same cavalier way he thought of such women? She cringed at the thought. Then anger took over. How dare he think of her like that! Joseph did not treat her in that way; he honoured and respected her—in his own dull way. Dear unexciting Joseph. He had asked her a question before she left for Downsley, a question she had expected he would one day ask her, a question she had promised to answer when she returned. What should her answer be?

No calmer than when she entered the garden, she sighed and opened her eyes. She blinked. She thought she saw something blue among the rose bushes near the gateway in the trellis. It must have been the sun in her eyes, she thought, for the next second it was gone. She had just decided to return to the house, when behind her reflection in the water she saw another.

Agitated, and out of breath from running, the footman designated to watch the boys said, "Master Addy and Master Bodger, miss. I can't find 'em. One minute they were on the terrace, next they were gone. His lordship is very angry," he added, having just experienced Earl Hesston's ire first hand. "Ordered a search of the house and grounds, he has."

Miss Barclay looked back at the terrace. There, Perry was directing staff. "I'm for the cellar," he shouted. "You take the attics, Willoughby."

"Have you seen 'em, miss?" the footman said.

She shook her head, all thoughts of herself and Lord Davenant now gone. "What can have happened to them? Perhaps…Oh, 'tis dreadful to think it… perhaps that man Basingthwaite Lord Hesston warned us of has…"

She could not finish.

"Don't worry, miss. They can't be far. You know boys: always into mischief and no harm done. I must get back to the search, miss. Would you like me to escort you back to the house? His lordship insists you return there—just in case."

"Go on with your search. I'll make my own way back."

The footman ran off. Miss Barclay took one last look about her; there was no sign of the boys. She was about start back for the house when her eye fell on the opening in the trellis, and she recalled the patch of blue she thought she had seen there. She smiled. It had not been a figment of her imagination: it was Addy she saw, Addy, who that morning had been wearing a blue coat.

Downsley's grounds were extensive and the boys could be anywhere in them. But beyond the trellis gateway, the grass sloped down to the ruins of all that remained of the ancient priory: two stone arches rising from tangled undergrowth and a door that led down to a crypt. From other parts of the house, the ruins appeared a picturesque feature of the landscape, but from this side of it they were undetectable. Smugglers had been known to use the crypt, but no one from the house went there, Georgiana had told her, because the loose masonry inside made it unsafe. Although Georgiana did admit that despite the hazard, and unbeknown to their elders, she and Perry had played there when they were young.

Had anyone searched there yet? No one was supposed to go there—but little boys? The footman was right: they were always into mischief. She had learned that in her work with climbing them. The forbidden tempted boys into all sorts of hijinks. It had been silly of her to fear the worst. When she spied Addy in the bushes, there were no strangers lurking about. No doubt the boys were playing a joke on them all. She would search the ruins. If she found the boys there, she would intercede with Lord Hesston for a lighter punishment than he had threatened for causing such an alarm.

She had gone through the trellis gateway and was only a little way beyond the rose garden when she caught a sight of Addy and Bodger, just as they disappeared into undergrowth surrounding the ruins. Lifting her skirts, she ran after them.

"Addy! Bodger! You naughty boys. Come back!" she called.

At the sound of her voice, a man stepped out from behind a nearby clump of trees where he had just tied up his horse.

He watched her go, on his face a satisfied smile

Then he went after her.

62

Scarcely had Davenant reined to a halt before the doors of Downsley, when he flung himself from his steaming mount. So swift and sure-footed had the Duke of Ryedale's horse proved on the ride from Brighton, that at any other time Davenant would have offered the duke a large sum for it. But acquisitions to his stables were farthest from his thoughts as he galloped over the downs.

As he bounded up the stone steps two at a time, the house's doors opened and Georgiana ran out to him.

"Thank goodness your'e here," she cried, grasping the lapels of his coat. "Addy and Bodger? They're missing."

"Missing?"

"This past half hour. Everyone is searching for them."

"My God! Am I too late?" His tone shocked Georgiana. She had never seen him display fear before. Just then her husband, dishevelled and out of breath, appeared. Quickly Davenant told them what had happened on the Brighton road.

"The rest of the story will have to wait," he said. I fear Basingthwaite could have the boys. He had ample time to get here before me. We must find them before he can harm them. Let us pray we are not too late. Extend the search! Hesston, take some men to the village. They could be there, or someone there may have seen them. Ryedale and Henry are on their way by road from Brighton, so if Basingthwaite is on that road, they'll stop him. And from now on everyone goes armed."

He finished just as Perry and Willoughby arrived, flushed from their efforts.

He stared at the members of the house party gathered about him.

One of them was missing.

"Where is Miss Barclay?" he demanded.

Miss Barclay stood before the heavy wooden door leading down into the crypt. She tugged off a creeper that had attached itself to her dress as she fought her way through the undergrowth. The branches, vines and thistles were thick and matted, but where the vegetation crossed the worn, moss-covered flagstones of the path, it was less dense. It had parted easily enough to let her through, and she emerged at the door with only a mosquito bite and a scratch or two for her trouble.

The worn oak door had a heavy, rusted iron handle. With both hands she struggled to turn it. "Addy! Bodger! Are you there," she called.

She gasped in shock when a pair of bronzed hands reached around her and clasped her own like a vice.

"Permit me," a man's voice said behind her.

63

Since he left his life as a climbing boy, Bodger now only experienced the airless black of narrow chimneys in an occasional bad dream; but the fear of the dark that life had given him remained. Although he fought hard to suppress it, that fear was with him now in the dark, damp stone confines of the empty tomb. Even with the light of the solitary candle Addy had lit, the tomb was almost as dark as a chimney.

He had not been frightened when Addy first showed him this hiding place in the crypt: then they had not stayed long. But now? The thought of sitting there for a long time just a puff of air away from darkness frightened Bodger. It took all his usual bravado to hide his fear as he and Addy sat cross-legged, facing each other across the candle.

Addy, who had only once climbed a chimney, had no such qualms. To him the tomb meant safety, certain as he was that his foes, the French, were dangerously close. Happy he and Bodger had reached their refuge without anyone knowing, he sighed with relief. "We're safe. The French won't find us here. No one else will either," he assured Bodger. He pointed to the tin containing the biscuits and to the two bottles of water he had hidden there earlier. "We've got food and water. We can stay here as long as we want."

Bodger shuddered. He racked his brains for a good reason to leave their hiding place; but he could only think of one. He nodded at Puff curled up in one of Addy's arms. "What if he as ter…yer know…go? Us, too?" he said. "Be real smelly, it…"

The sound of voices stopped him. Addy put a finger to his lips and blew out the candle.

"They must be lookin' for us," Bodger whispered.

"They don't know were here. Keep quiet and they'll go away," Addy said.

Never had Miss Barclay felt so alone and as helpless as she did now. Never had she felt herself in such peril as she did now from the man with her at the entrance to the crypt.

"There, all it needed was a turn of the handle and a strong push from me," the man said as the door creaked open. He smiled. "Forgive me if I startled you. I'm a friend of the family. On my way up to the house, I heard you calling for Addy and Bodger. Little devils! Up to mischief, I'll be bound. Saw you going this way. Not a pleasant place for a lady to be by herself, so I thought I would see if you needed assistance."

Her work among the poor in London's slums had given Verity Barclay a sixth sense about when she was in danger from others–and she was acutely aware of that now. In London faithful Joseph Pratt was always there to keep her safe. Dull he might be, but oh how she wished he were there now to deal with this man who stood so menacingly before her. Her heart raced and her breath quickened, for the intuition that had stood her in good stead in the past told her this was Rupert Basingthwaite, the man whom Davenant had warned them all about. His manner and speech might be as courteous as any gentleman making a morning call, but his smile lacked feeling and his eyes were cold. Dismayed by the realisation, she shrank from him. She could not get away because he blocked her path back through the undergrowth, and he showed no signs of moving. The only way she could move was forward–into the darkened crypt.

At her actions a sneer replaced Basingthwaite's smile and a menacing manner his previous affability.

"So, I'm saved the necessity of a formal introduction," he said. "And you, I take it, must be the Miss Barclay those damn Davenants speak of so highly. There now being no need for the social niceties…" He grabbed her arm, his fingers biting so sharply into her skin that she winced. "…we will set about doing what we both came here to do–find those boys!"

"Why?" Miss Barclay managed at last. "What dost thou want with them?"

His voice hardened. "I'm going to kill them: Addy because he has what I want; Bodger because he knows too much. And I'll kill you, too, when you're no longer of use to me."

"Use?"

'As bait. If they're here, I am sure they will appear like magic when I announce…" He raised his voice, "… that I will hurt you, their friend, if they do not make themselves known."

"Kn…kn…know…that voice. Know it…anywhere," Bodger whispered, his own voice shaking. "It's the geezer wot came asking questions in Malloy's yard. Heard it the night Nell died, I did, an' on the beach at Brighton. And he wants ter kill *us*!"

Tears welled up in Addy's eyes and ran down his cheeks. Mr. Basingthwaite! He did not want to believe it. Dear, kind Mr. Basingthwaite, who played cricket with him, wanted to kill him and Bodger–and Miss Barclay, too. His anguished sob was not a loud one and somehow Bodger managed in the darkness to find his mouth and stifle any further ones with his hand.

"What's that?" said Basingthwaite, as he dragged Miss Barclay down the worn stone stairs into the crypt.

"What? I heard nothing," Miss Barclay lied, praying that if Addy and Bodger were somewhere inside, they would not reveal themselves.

After the sunshine outside, she was unprepared for the sudden darkness of the crypt. More than once she stumbled as Basingthwaite pulled her along, because she could not see where she was going. But as her eyes became accustomed to the gloom, she made out chunks of masonry on the stone floor and what remained of the smugglers' activities: some casks, a coil or two or rope and few candle stumps in bottles.

At the bottom of the stairs, Basingthwaite let go her arm to light a candle. She tried to run back up the stairs, but he was too quick for her. He grabbed her and threw her into the shadows. Her fall was broken by one of the tombs at present indiscernible in the darkness. The stone grazed her bare arms and tore the skirt of her dress. Temporarily dazed, she was vaguely aware of Basingthwaite groping about in the darkness for a light. He found the candles and lit them with a tinderbox. Then he ran back up the stairs and closed the door.

Back down in the crypt again Basingthwaite raised a candle and a looked about him. There was little to see except Miss Barclay leaning breathless against a tomb, the smugglers' leavings, chunks of dislodged masonry and the vague shapes of the tombs receding into the shadows.

He grabbed Miss Barclays arm once more. "Those blasted boys. Where are they? You saw them come in here."

"I was mistaken as you can see," she said, trying to prevent her voice shaking. "The grounds are extensive. They could be anywhere in them. Who knows? And if I did know, I wouldn't tell you," she added defiantly.

"Don't play games with me," he snarled. "They're here somewhere. What's behind these tombs? I wouldn't be surprised if…"

"Addy! Bodger! Are you there?"

Davenant's voice from deeper inside the crypt interrupted him.

"I thought he was dead," Basingthwaite said. "No matter." He smiled in a way that made Miss Barclay shudder inwardly and drew a pistol from inside his coat. Then he blew out the candle and pulled her deep into the shadows.

"Not a word from you or…?" he hissed, jabbing the pistol in her back.

Davenant stepped out of the darkness and raised the lantern he carried. What light there was from it left most of the crypt's interior in deep shadow. He shivered: the air was cold and damp. Something tickled his cheek. He reached up to remove it: a spider's web, one of the many in the dark passage he had just left, threads of which clung to his coat unnoticed by him.

"Addy! Bodger! Are you there? It's Lord Davenant. Do not be afraid. You'll not be punished for leaving the house. If you are hiding here, come out and show yourselves."

Addy sighed with relief at the sound of his hero's voice; he would have crawled out of the tomb if the quick-thinking Bodger had not clutched hold of him.

"T'other geezer? One wot wants ter kill yer? He's still out there," Bodger warned in whisper.

Puff, too, heard the familiar voice and was eager to see its owner. Squashed between the two boys, his mouth held shut by Addy, Puff began to squirm in an effort to free himself; it was all the two of them could do to restrain him.

It had been years since any member of the family had gone down into the crypt, or so Davenant had thought. But when he asked the others if there were any possible hiding places they might have overlooked in their search, a shamefaced Perry admitted he had recently shown Addy the secret passage from the house to the old ruins. It was a shorter way to the crypt than from outside, so while the further searches he had ordered went on above, Davenant went down into the passage.

In the lamplight the crypt was just as Davenant remembered it: crumbling tombs, casks, and rope—but there was no sign of the boys.

His twitched his nostrils and sniffed.

A faint smell of burned wax.

He raised the lamp and looked about him once more. On a nearby tomb there were a few candle stumps stuck in bottles. He felt them with his hand. They were warm and so was the wax that had dripped down their sides.

Someone had been there just before he arrived.

Immediately alert, he shot around only to meet Miss Barclay's agonised face and Basingthwaite's mocking smile.

64

"What an unpleasant surprise," Basingthwaite sneered. "I thought you dead on the Brighton road, Davenant. You have a nasty habit of resisting my attempts to kill you—but not this time. Put the lantern down and raise your hands! One false move and I shoot her."

He jabbed Miss Barclay in the back and shoved her to stand next to Davenant.

Inwardly cursing himself for walking into a trap, Davenant set the lamp down on the closest tomb and raised his hands. He had expected Basingthwaite to be lurking in the grounds, not here with Miss Barclay in the forgotten crypt. Those at the house thought she was still in the garden, so he had sent Perry to escort her safely back indoors. Now here she was; her life, like his, just minutes from ending. He had faced death before but never had it been so imminent or as certain as it was now. Damn it! Was there nothing he could do to prevent Basingthwaite pulling the trigger before help came, or he could disarm him without endangering Miss Barclay's life?

There was a small travelling pistol in an outer pocket of his coat. He had not carried it in his hand when he went down into the crypt for fear he might frighten Addy and Bodger if they were there. Now he wished he had done so. Had Miss Barclay not been there, he would have smashed the lamp to throw the crypt into darkness and tackled Basingthwaite. But he dare do nothing while Basingthwaite's weapon was trained on her as well as him.

The tension between the three of them was palpable. But still Basingthwaite had not fired. Instead he continued to watch them with a sardonic smile. Why? Davenant wondered. Was it because of a sadistic delight on Basingthwaite's part to prolong the agony? Certainly anyone who had murdered four people already and attempted to kill two more could have no qualms about killing others. No one knew Basingthwaite was there; all he need do to get away safely was to kill Davenant, the stronger of the two first, then reload and shoot Miss Barclay. The thought of that sickened Davenant. She was putting up a brave front, but her luminous eyes were dark with fear. And he knew it was not just the cold and damp of the crypt that was making her shiver.

And Addy and Bodger? Where were they? Hiding, as Perry thought they might be, in an empty tomb? If so, let the little devils have sense enough to stay where they were. Or were they off outside somewhere playing, blithely unaware of the turmoil their behaviour had caused? Lord, let it be so.

And still Basingthwaite did not fire.

Slowly it began to dawn on Davenant that despite his threats, Basingthwaite was in no hurry to shoot them. On the contrary, he seemed to savour the power he now had over them. His swagger reminded Davenant of Henry Rollins when he had an audience, however small, for one of his tall stories. But then Basingthwaite had been an actor, had he not? Actors loved an audience and Basingthwaite had a captive one now. Basingthwaite wanted him dead, it was true: with Davenant gone there would be no one to prove him a murderer. Once that Davenant and Miss Barclay were dead, he would escape–but not yet– because, full of his own conceit, Basingthwaite could not resist the opportunity to brag. So let him, Davenant thought. Let him show off. Encourage him. Flatter him if need be. Do anything to keep him talking until either one of the search parties discovered them, or he could find a way to safely overpower Basingthwaite. The lives of Miss Barclay and him depended on it.

"Before you dispose of Miss Barclay and myself, permit me to congratulate you,"

Davenant said, doing his best to appear impressed. You fooled society–myself included–into believing you a gentleman of means and consequence."

Basingthwaite grinned in triumph. "Clever, eh?" he said. "Led you a merry dance, too, these past weeks? More than a match for the clever Lord Davenant."

The conceit in Basingthwaite's voice told Davenant he had read him correctly; he was eager to sing his own praises. Davenant, inwardly congratulating himself on being a much better actor than Basingthwaite, pressed on.

"Yes, you really had me fooled. I thought you a friend," he went on, "made the mistake of taking you into my confidence, never realising that all the time you were doing your damndest to foil my efforts to find Addy's family. Played right into your hands, did I not? Until just recently I had no idea 'twas you murdered

Hurley and the others and attempted to kill Addy' and me. How well you concealed yourself behind that gentlemanly façade." Davenant shook his head. "What a performance!" he said with mock sincerity. "A pity you left the theatre. It's the poorer for your absence."

Basingthwaite shrugged.

"It was easy," he said, "and do you know why? Because you and your kind care only for fashion and appearances. I've played the gentleman on stage often enough. It was no different than in life: smart clothes, correct speech, a French phrase here and there, polished manners, flatter the ladies." Then in a sudden burst of anger that made Davenant fear he would shoot, he shouted, "But for that damned Addy, I would be *that* person in life. His fortune mine!"

"Indeed, fate can be unkind," Davenant said with feigned sympathy. "But look at you now! Master of your destiny! How did you do it? What was your secret?"

"Revenge and hatred! A potent mix!" Basingthwaite said bitterly. Revenge against a society that treats as outcasts those who cannot help the accident of their birth. Hatred for the aristocratic father who deprived me of his name and inheritance. My sister Hetty–a flighty, easily led creature–and I were the bastard children of a self-important gentleman just like you. A man whom my mother ran away with, only to discover he did not intend to marry her. However, she was fool enough to love him, and her family having disowned her, she became his mistress. When she died shortly after the death of my so-called father, my sister and I were left destitute. My father's family wanted nothing to do with his bastards and would give us nothing. Do you know what its like to be poor and disowned by your own? I swore then I would one day be rich and powerful, and take my rightful place in society."

His pent up anger relieved, Basingthwaite smirked, obviously eager to boast about how he accomplished his vow. Davenant seized on this change of humour to better the situation for him and Miss Barclay.

"An interesting story. I long to hear more. But first may we make ourselves comfortable?" he asked politely. "May I lower my arms? I am unarmed, he lied."

Basingthwaite shrugged.

"Permit me to lend Miss Barclay my coat. She is cold," Davenant said, lowering his hands.

Basingthwaite laughed. "She'll soon be a lot colder," but he made no attempt to stop Davenant from taking off his coat and putting it around Miss Barclay's shoulders. As he was leading her to a seat on a coil of rope away from Basingthwaites line of fire, Davenant said, "There is a handkerchief in the right pocket, should you have need of it, Miss Barclay," an indirect reference to the pistol in the pocket.

Basingthwaite snorted at this gallantry. But a puzzled Miss Barclay put her hand in the pocket, only to withdraw it as if she had been stung. Blue-grey eyes reproached Davenant. He had forgotten her religious beliefs. In spite of the danger they were in, she would not use the pistol.

"You were saying?" Davenant said, turning back to face Basingthwaite once more.

"Hetty and I were poorly equipped to earn a living," Basingthwaite went on. "She was too pretty to be a governess; in such a position she would have fallen prey to the likes of men like you. For a while I supported us by competing in boxing contests at fairgrounds. That's where I obtained the skills Gentleman Jackson thinks so highly of, but it was no way to live. Our looks enabled us to join a travelling theatre company. My father's only gift to me being his patrician bearing, the roles of gentleman fell most often to me. In London, I even auditioned for Sheridan." He scowled. "Do you know that damned drunkard said I was no actor because I could not maintain an accent?"

"But you professed a dislike of the theatre and stayed away from it," Davenant pointed out.

"Of course. What if my former colleagues had recognised me? And I certainly didn't want it known in society that I had been an actor. *I* was meant for better things!" he said with contempt. "The theatre was but temporary employment. We decided our best hope of prosperity lay in an advantageous marriage for Hetty. Where to find a suitable husband? In England a rich man will keep an actress as mistress, but marry one?" He shook his head. "Europe was out of the question because of the war. But India? There Englishmen far exceed eligible Englishwomen."

'Your sister was prepared to sell herself in marriage for you?"

"Of course. She loved what money buys: jewels, gowns, furs, fine houses, a position in society. Fortune favoured us with Ben Chantry, a nabob and widower. Initially I pretended reluctance." With pretended dismay he said, "How could I leave my beloved sister in India when I must return home alone?" He laughed. "He found me a position with his company so I could remain. I enjoyed all that India has to offer: tiger shoots, dancing girls, opium…"

"And learned the mode of death practised by the Thugee, the followers of the goddess Kali: strangulation by means of a scarf with a coin tied in it," Davenant finished.

"Quiet, clean and very useful," Basingthwaite said. "Worked fine on Malloy and Hurley. Had to use a knife on Nell and her boy, though. Only thing available." He sniffed. "Very messy." He shook his head. "But I digress. While Hetty's marriage was still in the honeymoon stage, at my suggestion, she tactfully persuaded Chantry to make a new will: I was so sure Hetty would get all. She and I then made reciprocal wills, each leaving what we had to the other. It was not until fever took Chantry–I would have killed him eventually, anyway–that we learned from his will of his son in England. He had never mentioned it to us. Apart from a legacy to my sister, the bulk of the estate went to the boy, the whole to go to the survivor if one of them died." His eyes narrowed. "To come that close to a fortune, only to lose it! I wasn't going to let a child stand in my way. We returned to England."

"We?" Davenant said, recalling what the captain of the Indiaman told him. "I was told your sister drowned at sea in a storm."

Basingthwaite looked even more pleased with himself. "Yes, that–and a little help from me. You see, I never intended to share the money with her."

"Your own sister!" Miss Barclay gasped.

Ignoring her, Basingthwaite went on, "The storm was an unexpected opportunity, and I always make the most of any opportunity. The riot at the Exeter Exchange, for instance: but for Willoughby interruption, I would have pushed Addy into the wagon's path and killed him. So instead I…er…rescued him? That put me in your good graces, into your house and close to Addy. Lord, the time I spent playing cricket with Willoughby and the boy, and listening to your sister's stupid prattle while I posed for her sketches. Odd, but I quite liked the boy. Had he not been the stumbling block to my good fortune, I might have become quite fond of him. Your family always being present, I had no chance to remove Addy; but I could learn your movements, be a step ahead of you, and– How shall I put it? –arrange for the removal of those who had information you wanted." He gave a chuckle that made Miss Barclay shudder. "And all the time you were searching for Addy's grandfather, Davenant, I knew where he was–right under your nose, near here," he crowed.

At Davenant's look of astonishment, he went on, "Chantry's London solicitor was naturally eager to track down Addy to give him his inheritance, but he knew only the grandfather's name, not his whereabouts. I, presenting myself as Addy's long-lost uncle and eager to help," he readily gave it to me. "After some effort, I tracked down the grandfather, thus finding the boy. Do you know where? I saw him playing in the garden at *The Beeches.* That silly little castle Addy was always drawing to show you where his grandfather lived and which everyone, including you, dismissed as a childish fantasy! For a hefty price that smuggler Conway was only too willing to abduct the boy and kill him. Everything went as planned–or so I thought. I even went to the boy's supposed funeral. But when I saw Addy with your sister in Bond Street, I knew Conway had deceived me. And then you undertook that ridiculous bet to find the boy's grandfather and prove him a gentleman. You can imagine my rage!

"When I tracked Conway down, he admitted–under duress that he had substituted his own dead son for Addy and sold the boy to a London sweep. It was with infinite pleasure that I threatened to expose him to the authorities for what he had done if he did not help me eliminate Addy for good this time." He shrugged. "He had no choice. If he had spoken out against me, who would they believe: a known smuggler, or a gentleman who moved in the Prince Regent's circle? Blasted fool deserved his sad end."

"D'ya hear that?" Bodger whispered. "He killed 'em, all, and he's gonna kill Lord Davenant and Miss Barclay–an' us, too, when he finds us! What we gonna do?"

A JACKETING CONCERN

Addy did not answer. He was not listening to Bodger, nor had he been listening when Basingthwaite said his grandfather lived nearby. He was scuffling with Puff who, tired of being cooped up, wanted to escape the tomb.

"Help me! Grab his middle!" whispered a frantic Addy, as he clasped the wriggling Puff's snout with both hands to prevent him barking. "If he gets out, were done for!"

Bodger lunged for what he thought was Puff's body; but because the darkness prevented him from seeing where he was going, one hand went wide and the other pushed against Addy and knocked him backwards. Addy lost his grip; Puff slipped free, scrambled through the hole in the tomb wall and trotted off.

Only too aware of their fate once Basingthwaite saw Puff, the two terrified boys could only clutch one another in fear and await the inevitable

65

Time was running out.

Basingthwaite was almost at the end of his tale. And then?

Davenant feigned interest, listening with only half an ear as he watched Basingthwaite for any sign that might indicate he had lowered his guard sufficiently for Davenant to move against him.

If only he had not given his coat with the pistol to Miss Barclay. To let religious scruples dictate her conduct in a situation like this! A quick hand in the pocket: that's all that was needed from her now she was out of the line of fire. No need for her to take the pistol out of the pocket: just shoot through the fabric. But then, out the corner of his eye, he caught sight of her, and he was at once ashamed of these thoughts. Her face was unreadable, but even with his coat covering her she could not stop shivering with fear.

"I thought you wouldn't go on with the wager if Hurley was dead," Basingthwaite was saying. "But his death didn't stop you, did it?" He shook his head. "Pity about Hurley. I quite liked the young fool. Met him in a gaming hell–another of those unexpected opportunities. Damned fortunate him being a godson of royalty. Got me the *entrée* into society I wanted. Dropped him for that idiot Willoughby so I could get closer to you and Addy."

But Davenant was no longer listening to what Basingthwaite was saying, for he had spotted something moving in the shadows behind him. Was it a trick of the flickering lamplight? He blinked. No. He wasn't mistaken. There was something down there on the ground, a vague, white shape coming toward them. And then, just at the edge of circle of light cast by the lamp, there stood Puff.

Davenant heard Miss Barclay's sharp intake of breath. She had seen Puff, too, and knew what his presence meant. Addy and Puff were inseparable; if Puff was there, then Addy, together with Bodger, was back there in the shadows hiding among the tombs.

Basingthwaite was still talking and still had his pistol trained on Davenant. He had not noticed Puff yet, but it was just a matter of time, and when he did, he would shoot Davenant and Miss Barclay, then ferret out the boys and kill them, too.

Puff's presence forced Davenant's hand. With more lives than his and Miss Barclay's at stake, he had to act now. There was no search party to rescue them, no safe moment to disarm Basingthwaite. If he tackled Basingthwaite by the legs, there was just a slim chance—a very slim one—that he could overcome him, if he wasn't killed or wounded in the attempt. On the other hand, if he did nothing, they would all die for certain.

"So there you have it Davenant," Basingthwaite finished.

Before Davenant could make a move, Puff took matters in hand. As he trotted into the light, he saw the tassels on Basingthwaite's Hessian boots. With a joyful bark, he leaped at Basingthwaite, grabbed one of the tassels between his teeth, pulling down and shaking it from side to side in play.

Taken completely by surprise, Basingthwaite forgot Davenant, so intent was he in trying to shake the aggressive dog from his leg. Seizing this opportunity, Davenant leaped at him, clenched hold of the hand that held the pistol with one of his and Basingthwaite's shoulder with the other. In the brief struggle that followed, Davenant forced Basingthwaite's hand above his head, tightening his pressure on the trigger finger to such an extent that the pistol went off, sending its ball ricocheting across the vaulted stone ceiling.

In such a confined space, the shot was like a thunderclap.

Her hands over her ears, Miss Barclay jumped up, and a frightened Puff let go of Basingthwaite's boot and ran off.

Amid the smoke from the shot, Basingthwaite broke free and threw the empty pistol at Davenant. The latter was too quick for him; he ducked, the pistol sailed over his head and landed with faint clink on the floor behind him. In a tackle he had learned on the playing fields of Eton, Davenant hurled himself at Basingthwaite, winding him as the two fell to the stone floor.

Keeping his eyes on the prostrate Basingthwaite, Davenant got up and backed toward Miss Barclay to take the pistol from her. He had gone only a few paces, when Basingthwaite scrambled to his feet. He moved warily toward Davenant, taking off his coat as he did so. "First you" he snarled, "then the boy. If that dog's here, then the boy is, too."

Ashen faced, Miss Barclay hastily moved out the way as the two met. Eyeing each other guardedly, they both struck a boxer's pose and circled each other as they had often done in the ring at Gentleman Jackson's Boxing Academy. Except that this would be no friendly sparring match between gentlemen, but a fight to the death.

Basingthwaite struck first with an uppercut to Davenant's jaw. This prompted a swift facer in return that bloodied his lip. And then the two were pummelling each other in cold fury, each blow more severe than the last as they other continually stumbled in and out the darkness among the tombs, kegs and rope coils.

With her fists clenched at her sides, her breath coming fast, Miss Barclay watched helplessly for what seemed to her like an eternity. The only sounds were the unremitting thwacks of bare knuckles against flesh and Puff's intermittent barks. As both men tired, their faces became more bloodied and bruised, but Basingthwaite was in the worst shape. Motivated by hatred and revenge, he had battled with unthinking abandon that soon depleted his energy. This allowed Davenant, with his more restrained approach, to gradually gain the upper hand. But just as Davenant appeared ready to finish off Basingthwaite, the toe of one of his boots caught against an uneven flagstone. He tripped, lost his footing, and a sock to the jaw from his adversary knocked him hard against one of the tombs and he slithered to the floor.

Taking advantage of this opening, with both hands Basingthwaite bent and picked up a large chunk of the fallen masonry. He staggered toward Davenant with it, intent on crushing his skull while he was still on the ground.

Basingthwaite had reckoned without Miss Barclay.

When she realised Basingthwaite's intentions, the horror of what was about to happen swept away her religious scruples about committing violence.

As Basingthwaite shot past her, she stuck out her foot. He tripped and down he went, his head hitting the stone floor with crack that knocked him out.

Slowly, Davenant got to his feet, leaning against the tomb while he fought to regain his breath.

"Quiet!" he shouted at the barking Puff.

"Is…is… he dead" Miss Barclay asked when he bent over Basingthwaite and checked the pulse in his neck.

"No. Just unconscious."

He stood up and called into the darkness, "Addy! Bodger! You can come out now. There's nothing to fear."

From the look on Miss Barclays face, he thought she might faint. He went and put his arms around her. She sighed and leaned against him. They stood there for some minutes until she looked up and faltered, "I…I…Im sorry. The pistol? I…I… could not…do it. It's wrong to kill. I…"

"I know," he assured her gently. "I know."

She looked near to tears. "B…b…but I had to do…something. He was going to k…k…kill you! I tripped him b…b…but I did not mean to h…hurt him as b…bad as that," she said, looking at Basingthwaite's inert body. "It was wrong of me."

"As I recall the Bible says 'Thou shalt not kill,' but there is no eleventh commandment that says 'Thou shalt not trip someone,'" he said, amused.

Immediately indignant, she retorted, "Dreadful man! Thou mockest me!"

He smiled. "Forgive me, but I do not like to see you so unhappy about saving my life. I hope you do not regret it!" he said as he bent to kiss her.

"Oh you must not. I cannot because…Mr. Pratt and I…" she murmured but she made no effort to stop him.

"Damn Mr. Pratt," he said and kissed her again.

They did not hear the door open.

"Anyone there?"

It was Perry.

After pausing at the open door just long enough for his eyes to adjust to the gloom, he came slowly down the steps, Willoughby close behind him. Halfway down, they stopped. In the weak light of the oil lamp below, Perry recognised the back of his brother's tall figure.

"You all right, Roderick? Willow found a strange horse tethered nearby and we heard…"

His eyes widened and his mouth formed a silent 'Oh' at the sight of Davenant and Miss Barclay in an embrace, and Addy and Bodger watching them while Puff stood guard over the unconscious Basingthwaite.

"Damn it, Willow!" Perry said, exasperated. "I do believe we've missed all the fun!"

66

"You know, Roderick, although you have told us so much about Addy and why that awful Mr. Basingthwaite pursued him and tried to…"

Georgiana glanced down at Addy, who sat next to her, his arm around Puff. Silently she mouthed the words 'kill him' so Addy wouldn't hear. Addy, however, was not listening; his nose was glued to the carriage window in eager anticipation of the first sight of his grandfather's house.

"But what led you to the realisation that it was that dreadful, dreadful, *dreadful* Basingthwaite who was behind Addy's abduction and who committed all those murders?" she said.

"For a long time, I had no idea at all it was Basingthwaite," Davenant said from the opposite seat. "I confess I, like everyone else, was taken in by him. It was not until the last few days, when I was able to establish the provenance of those fob seals he lost during struggles with the sweep Malloy and myself, and my meetings with the two sea captains, that I knew for certain it was him. When I first met him, he had so many gewgaws on his fob chain, he probably didn't notice when he lost the first one at least. However, after our tussle on Brighton seafront, he must have guessed I might have the other. But even if he did suspect I had one of them, I am sure he thought they could not be traced because they were of foreign manufacture.

"There were several odd instances involving Basingthwaite before that, which viewed as isolated incidents were of no relevance. But which taken together and in the light of what I learned from tracing the seals, now make sense. He was not, as would have been expected, with his friend Hurley at the prince's dinner when the wagers were made, because he had gone to the coast to find Conway and blackmail him into doing his bidding. Conway admitted to Basingthwaite that he sold Addy to the sweep Malloy, from whom I subsequently rescued him. What we all thought was Basingthwaite's heroic 'rescue' of Addy at the Exeter Exchange was really a murder attempt by him that was unwittingly foiled by Willoughby.

"When he learned Willoughby was to accompany me to St. Giles in search of the sweep's wife, Nell, it was he who engaged someone to lure him on a false errand to his grandfather so he could go with me instead. He wanted to get rid of Nell because he knew she could tell me from whom her husband bought Addy. That night in the rookery, he hardly spoke at all: he did not dare for fear Bodger would recognise his voice as that of the man who called at the sweep's yard asking questions about Addy. Following the riot, he claimed the blood on his face was from a knife. Yet when I saw him later, after he had washed his face, there was no sign of a cut; the blood must have been from Nell and her son, whom he later admitted to me in the crypt he stabbed to death."

His lips twitched in amusement and he said wryly, "Although when the stabbing occurred I had no idea of his involvement in the mystery, I did have some misgivings about him when he suggested I discontinue the wager because Hurley was dead. He appeared unaware that no gentleman welches on a bet whatever the circumstances. I thought he might be *nouveau riche*—a *parvenu*—there are so many of them about these days. But he was such an amiable, helpful fellow and was of such good address, I overlooked it."

"Dreadful, dreadful, *dreadful* man," Georgiana said. "What will happen to him?"

"By now he is on his way to Newgate Prison, where he will await trial for three murders—four if you include his sister—kidnapping and assault. There is no doubt he will hang. It is indeed fortunate he confessed the murders to Miss Barclay and me; but for his confession, there is no actual physical proof he killed Hurley, Nell and her son. However, the fob seals found with the dead sweep and following the attack on myself, were in Basingthwaite's possession at the time. They are definite proof he committed those two crimes. No doubt I will have to give evidence in court, but I think Miss Barclay will be spared that."

"Hanging is too good for him," said the Duke of Ryedale, who sat next to him. "When I think of what he made Addy suffer, and what he intended to do to him when he caught him…" He looked fondly across at Addy and shook his head.

"And poor, Miss Barclay! What an ordeal for her, too! I feel for her," Georgiana said with a sigh. "And then the very next day to announce her engagement. It is most odd."

Other than apologise to her for what had happened to her while she was under his roof, Davenant had no chance to speak with Miss Barclay privately following the incident in the crypt. In the aftermath, her companion, Miss Philmore, clucking over her like broody hen, had whisked her away to the peace and quiet of her home on Marine Parade, and the safekeeping of herself and Mr. Pratt.

Georgiana learned of the engagement yesterday, when she called on Miss Barclay to enquire about her well being after her ordeal. Pale but composed, Miss Barclay had greeted her warmly and then, during their conversation, announced she and Joseph Pratt had just become engaged. This declaration both astonished and disappointed the romantic minded Georgiana, who had long suspected an attachment between her brother and Miss Barclay. She managed to contain herself sufficiently to offer her best wishes to the couple, but she could hardly wait to return to Downsley and tell her brother the news.

She found him at the desk in the library, where he was putting the finishing touches to the assembly of an ancient clay pot. If she thought the news would surprise or dismay him, she was mistaken; Davenant gave no signs of nursing a broken heart when she told him.

Without lifting his eyes from what he was doing, he remarked in his usual drawl, "There was already an understanding between them, I gather. I wish them joy of the future."

Georgiana, however, was not to be silenced that easily. "Such a strange thing," she persisted, "to suddenly get engaged like that after that dreadful trial in the crypt. A reaction to all that terror, perhaps?"

When Davenant did not answer her question, she added, in hopes to further draw him out, "A thoroughly dependable sort, Mr. Pratt, don't you think, although rather dull? She will have a safe if unexciting life with him."

Davenant was matter of fact. "No doubt, that is what she wants." He turned to look out the window. "There are those who find life itself more alarming than facing a loaded pistol," he said, more to himself than to Georgiana.

The two days after the episode in the crypt saw a flurry of events at Downsley: the departure of Miss Barclay and her companion for Brighton, the presence of constables and magistrates to take statements; the questioning of a truculent Basingthwaite and his departure in shackles to await trial in jail, the first meeting of a thrilled and shy Addy with his uncle, the Duke of Ryedale, Perry's departure for Portsmouth to rejoin his ship and now, at long last, the reunion of Addy and his grandfather.

To give the old man time to deal with the shock of learning that the grandson he believed dead was very much alive, Davenant sent Georgiana to call on Bette, Addy's *gouvernante,* to warn her, so that she could gently break the news to Mr. Gilden they would bring the boy the next day. The morning of their visit, Davenant received a tear-stained note from the grandfather inviting the visitors to stay and dine with him.

Addy turned from the carriage window.

"Lady Georgiana, do you think grandpapa will let me keep Puff in the house now you have given him to me?" And then shyly to the duke, "And may I bring him when I come to your house…uncle?"

"Your grandfather will be so happy to have you home again, dear. I'm sure he will let you keep Puff," Georgiana said.

"By all means bring Puff with you when you come," the duke added. "I have several dogs of my own. One more will make no difference."

Addy smiled with pleasure.

Then almost as quickly as it had come, the smile went from his face. For a couple of minutes he stared down at Puff and stroked the dog's head. When he looked up again, there were tears in his eyes.

"If only Bodger were here," he said wistfully.

None of the four adults in the carriage said anything: there was nothing they could say.

Addy and Bodger proved none the worse for the scare they received in the crypt. Once they knew the danger was past, their boyish enthusiasm reasserted itself; they saw themselves as brave heroes of an adventure rather than victims. And it was with great glee that they watched from the windows of Downsley Basingthwaite being led off to jail. Indeed, their only concern about the entire incident was the prospect of punishment for disobeying Earl Hesston's orders and leaving the house. But everyone was so glad to find them safe and sound that their misbehavior and the trouble it had wrought were forgotten. Georgiana fell upon them with embraces, kisses and tears; Perry and Willoughby slapped their backs and declared them stout fellows; Earl Hesston and the Duke of Ryedale shook hands with them; Henry Rollins, his dislike of Bodger temporarily forgotten, declared they both had 'bottom' and even Davenant was sufficiently moved to give each of them a pat on the head.

But following their deliverance from the crypt, a marked change began to take place in the relationship between the two boys. Amid all the comings and goings at Downsley during the days that followed, no one paid much attention to Bodger, particularly Addy. This was not due to any intentional thoughtlessness on Addy's part; rather it was because of the Duke of Ryedale's attention to his long-lost nephew. So eager was Addy to become acquainted with his uncle and learn about the father he had never known and his new family, he was only too happy to spend much of his time with the duke in Brighton.

Though young, Bodger was a street-wise Londoner, who recognised a 'swell' and the trappings that went with one when he saw them. Though he had no notion of what the title 'duke' implied, he knew instinctively from what he saw of Ryedale and his entourage that here was a 'swell' even richer and more important than Lord Davenant. Then from conversations he overheard among the adults and servants, Bodger learned that Addy would become the duke when his uncle died and would receive not only his uncle's fortune but also those of his grandfather and dead father.

Although he possessed neither the understanding nor the vocabulary to describe it as class division, nonetheless Bodger could see that his friend's new status meant each of them belonged to two very different worlds. The duke had expressed his gratitude to Bodger for his friendship toward Addy; he had also stated a wish to help provide for his future. Other than this, he ignored him, a circumstance Bodger felt sure was because he no longer wished for a close association between his nephew and a climbing boy.

On one occasion, when the duke's elegant travelling carriage, drawn by four matching horses, brought Addy back to Downsley from Brighton, Bodger bemoaned, "You're a real swell cove now, young un. Very high in the stirrups, too. Got no time for the likes o' me, anymore."

There was no doubting the sincerity in Addy's voice. "Oh no, Bodger. Really. We'll always be friends. You'll live here at Downsley. I'll live with grandpapa and we can see each other every day. And when I go and live with uncle, I'm sure he'll let you come and stay for a visit."

Bodger just shook his head and walked away.

That morning Davenant had found a rumpled sheet of paper on the desk in his study.

In printed capitals with many scratchings-out Bodger wrote:

DEAR LAWD DAVENINT:
I AVE GAWN BACK TO LUNNON COS FINGS IS TOO KWIET FOR ME ERE NOW ADDY IS GOIN. THANKS FOR WOT YOU DONE FER ME. TELL MIS BARKLEY THANK YOU TO.
YERS RESPECKFULLY BOGER

At the bottom of the letter was a reference to the twenty-five pounds Davenant held in safekeeping for him.

YER STILL AS ME MONEY. LOOK AFTER IT TILL I CUMS FOR IT.

From one of the outside staff Davenant learned he had seen Bodger in the grounds early that morning hanging about a wagon of produce going to Davenant House in London. A quantity of food was also missing from the kitchens.

Told the news, Addy burst into tears. "It's all my fault," he moaned. "He thought we wouldn't be friends anymore."

Georgiana, whose maternal instincts were aroused, was all for Davenant and her husband going in search of Bodger. "The poor, poor, *poor* little fellow! How will he survive on his own in those dreadful London streets?"

"I am as sorry as you are that he left, for he would have had a safe future here at Downsley," Davenant said. "However, although I will send out a search party, it will be almost impossible to find him now." He shook his head. "He will be too far away. As for surviving on the streets: have no fear. He has already proved he can do that." His lips twitched. "Besides, we have not seen the last of him, I am sure. You saw what he wrote about that money of his, I hold in safekeeping."

Bodger's unexpected departure cast a pall over the occupants of Downsley Priory that only began to disperse when they at last left for the visit to Addy's grandfather, Mr. Gilden. They all thought the excitement of what the trip meant to Addy would distract him from his thoughts about Bodger; it appeared to do that until talk of Puff made him remember again.

At a loss for how to reply to him, the four adults in the carriage were silent until Georgiana caught sight of something among the trees that brought a smile to her face. She tapped Addy on the shoulder and pointed to it: *The Beeches*, the odd little house built like a castle, with the Downs beyond, had him grinning, and jumping up and down in his seat.

"It *is* as Addy says! A castle near where a giant sleeps! Why it's just like Perry and I used to say about the South Downs when we were children; they look just like a sleeping giant sprawled across the land. How could we not have guessed?"

"How come the boy did not recognise the downs as his 'giant' when he saw them when riding out before in the carriage," Davenant said wryly.

"No doubt because until today the motion of the carriage always made him fall asleep," she retorted. Unable to resist a sly dig at her brother, she teased, "Those pictures Addy drew so often are so, so, *so* like it! And to think that in spite of all your efforts to find him, his grandfather lived but a few miles from you."

To hide his mortification at this taunt–mortification he would never admit– Davenant favoured his sister with his customary look of cold *hauteur*. The look remained as the carriage swept up the drive and the house came into clearer view. Pleased as he was to have restored Addy to his grandfather, he could not but be grieved by the knowledge that the old man lived–and would continue to do for some time–in the architectural monstrosity he detested, on land he regarded as his.

The carriage came to stop before the house. A footman barely had time to jump down and let down the steps before Addy scrambled out.

"M'mselle Bette! M'mselle Bette! I'm home! I'm home!" he shouted to the middle-aged woman in a black dress and white lace cap who stood at the open front door. "Such an adventure! And guess what! Now I've an uncle and a dog."

Bette stared at Addy, her eyes wide and unbelieving.

From the carriage's driving seat, Henry beamed as he watched Addy make his way up the stone steps.

"The sweep took me…cos I was naughty," Addy panted as he ran toward Bette. "I made a friend…Bodger…and climbed up a chimney…then Lord Davenant took me to his house…and gave me a ride…in his curricle…and I sat on the Prince Regent's lap and…he gave me a guinea…and, and sugar plums…and Mr. Henry learned me about horses and Mr. Perry taught me knots…and Mr. Willoughby taught me to play cricket…and a bad man…"

He got no further, for by then he was firmly clasped in Bette's arms

"*Mon petit! Mon petit!*" she cried, the tears streaming down her cheeks. "We thought you dead, but you are alive and well. *C'est un miracle!*"

"Is…is…is he…here…yet, Bette?" came a trembling voice from behind her in the house.

With a cry Addy, struggled free of Bette's arms and ran toward the open door shouting, "It's me, grandpapa! It's me! I'm home! I'm home!"

67

It was with a feeling of intense satisfaction Davenant inserted the final shard that marked the completion of the ancient clay pot he had been reassembling painstakingly for several weeks. He leaned back in his chair and admired his handiwork. It gave him almost as much pleasure to view it as did that other demonstration of his talents: the creation of a perfect Davenant Drape. It was a fitting end to a day that had seen him complete what he had set out to do: reunite Addy with his grandfather.

Following the joyful meeting between the two, Davenant and the others had later dined with Mr. Gilden. The old gentleman had been profuse in his expressions of gratitude to his lordship for the restoration of his grandson, praise that Davenant, so undemonstrative himself, found embarrassing. To change the subject, Davenant asked Gilden to explain a remaining piece of the puzzle: Why had he not raised a hue and cry about Addy's disappearance?

"A boy wearing my grandson's clothes, and with his face mutilated beyond recognition, was found dead in a chalk pit the day after Addy went missing," Gilden said. "In the belief that it was Addy, we buried him. After your sister called yesterday with the news that Addy was alive, I had enquiries made. Apparently a distraught woman has been making regular visits to the boy's grave in the churchyard. The curate at the church informed me she was either the wife or mistress of the smuggler."

"Conway, the fellow who was supposed to kill Addy, but who substituted his own dead son instead?" Davenant said.

"Yes," Gilden replied. "By rights she should hang for stealing the clothes Addy was wearing when taken. I don't know what the authorities will do, but I personally have no desire for revenge. I, like her, know the hell of losing a child."

Leaving the grandfather and the Duke of Ryedale together to discuss Addy's future, Davenant, Georgiana, and her husband took a reluctant farewell of Addy and returned to Downsley.

After the frantic last few days following the hectic pace of the previous weeks,

Davenant was thankful to relax at last in the peace and quiet of his study, which was where Willoughby, trailed by an anxious Henry Rollins, found him.

Lost in admiration of his handiwork, Davenant did not hear the door open.

Willoughby cleared his throat. "I say Davenant…" he began.

Davenant looked up at this intrusion of his privacy, his annoyance writ large on his face.

"I've got news for you," Willoughby said with grin, "news that will please you. You haven't caught Gil Conway, so the navy has done it for you—well in a way." To Davenant's enquiring look he added, "One of the footmen just told me. There's a 'hot press' on this evening; navy press gangs are scouring Brighton and the immediate countryside for able-bodied men. The footman said he narrowly escaped one of them himself. Anyway, the word is they rounded up fellas they found at the Ship in Distress, including Gil Conway and some of his gang. The navy isn't too fussy about whom it takes and where it finds them—and smugglers have the advantage of being seamen to start with. It will be a couple of years before Conway returns to England; that's if he isn't killed in a battle before then."

Davenant sighed. Here was yet another reason for satisfaction. "I sincerely hope he lives long enough to return home: I have a score to settle with him."

"That isn't all," Willoughby said. "Henry has something he wishes to ask you."

"What?"

His face looking as if he had lost a shilling and found sixpence, Henry stood twisting the brim of his hat in his hands.

"B…b…beggin' yer pardon, guv, but you aint forgotten…ave yer?"

"Forgotten what?"

"Newgate seize me!" Henry said, aghast. "Yer horses!"

Davenant looked up in some alarm.

"Horses? What about my horses? Is there sickness in the stables?"

"No, guv. It's them greys of yourn," he groaned. "Ain't you looked at the calendar? Today's the last day of yer wager! Been tryin' to remind yer all day, but yer was too busy. I won't live it down, if you lose 'em. It's half past seven o'clock, but there's still time. If yer leaves now, yer could just make it to Carlton House in time. Yer done it before in less."

"Damn it! He's right," Willoughby said. "I'll come with you in my curricle. I've got a few bets riding on your success."

"Well?" said Henry.

68

His pocket watch clutched in one pudgy fist, the Prince Regent sprawled in his chair at the head of the dining table and smiled. He had been in a jovial mood since dinner began but now, just seconds from becoming the new owner of Lord Davenant's greys, he could scarcely contain himself. So certain was he now of victory, he looked ready to burst from high spirits. The mounting tension throughout the evening, rich food, alcohol, and the heat of the room, combined to make him sweat, and the cosmetics he wore to hide the ravages of time and intemperate living ran in rivulets down his chubby cheeks.

There was no clock in the dining room, the prince having no wish to be reminded of time's passing when he immersed in the pleasures of the table. So as midnight, which marked the conclusion of Davenant's wager, approached, the prince took frequent surreptitious glances at his watch.

He sighed. Now at last both hands of his watch rested on the figure twelve and there was no sign of Davenant.

The bulging blue eyes the prince had inherited from his Hanoverian ancestors shone with triumph. The three-week duration of Davenant's wager to discover the climbing boy's identity had ended. Even if Davenant had actually discovered the boy's family, he had failed to reach Carlton House on time. Hurley's estate was the richer by one penny; the prince the new owner of Davenant's greys. The prince had not even a passing thought for the boy Addy, or the deceased Hurley; they were of no importance. Like a child knowing it was about to receive a new toy, he was full of glee that he was about to acquire the animals Davenant had outbid him for at Tattersalls.

Earlier, when welcoming his dinner guests, the prince scented victory when he noticed Davenant was not among them. The guests—the men who attended the dinner at which the wager was made—were pleased about that, too. Most of them had considered the odds heavily against even the resourceful Davenant proving a climbing boy to be gentleman and wagered in favour of Hurley. As the evening wore on and there was still no sign of Davenant, expectation of the bet's outcome reached such a pitch that by the time the serious drinking began following dinner, the guests were behaving like a gang of rowdy schoolboys rather than gentlemen. And foremost in the tomfoolery and had been the prince himself.

Now at last the moment they had all waited for had come.

The prince held up a hand for silence.

The voices and the laughter died away.

"Gentleman," the prince said, "it is now midnight and, as you can see, whatever the outcome of his efforts, Lord Davenant has not appeared."

Loud cheers greeted this.

"Therefore," the prince continued, "he has lost the wager he made with the late Sir Thomas Hurley and also the one made with me." He grinned. "I have won, as indeed have many of you who bet on the wager's outcome."

There were more cheers.

The prince motioned the footmen to refill glasses. "Drink up, gentleman! The night is young." He raised his own glass. "We have much to celebrate."

The talk and laughter resumed and had continued for about ten minutes when the dining room door was thrown open.

"Lord Davenant, Your Highness," a footman announced above the din.

Surprised into silence, everyone stared at the new arrival.

In a dust-covered caped overcoat and boots muddy from driving, Davenant swept into the room, closely followed by the equally travel stained Willoughby.

Davenant bowed to the prince. "Your Highness, I hope you will forgive my unkempt appearance, but I've come post haste from Sussex to be here on time and had no time to stop and change for dinner." He actually smiled. "I am pleased to report that I have been successful in all that I promised to do three weeks ago. The boy, Addy, is all that I wagered he would be, and more. I have been able to restore him to his grandfather: a wealthy merchant. In doing so, I have discovered he is none other than the heir to the Duke of Ryedale."

"Too late, Davenant! Too late!" the prince said, rubbing his hands with glee. "It's past midnight. Those greys of yours? They're *mine*, now. Don't matter whether the boy's a duke or a pauper. You're too late. You lose."

The guests nodded and murmured agreement.

Puzzled, Davenant looked enquiringly at the prince. His Highness folded his arms and gave him a smug nod of confirmation.

In silence, everyone looked at Davenant. But there was no sign of defeat or resignation on his face. On the contrary, although initially surprised, he quickly recovered his usual self-assurance. His lips twitched as if he were about to laugh. Calmly, he took out his own watch and looked at it.

Faithful to his promise to reunite Addy with his grandfather, no matter how long it took, Davenant had given no more thought to winning the wager, and had accepted he would lose his greys to the prince. However, he reckoned without Henry Rollins: *he* had no intention of losing two horses he considered as belonging as much to him as to his 'Is Nibs. Dismayed at Davenant's changed attitude toward the wager, Henry had kept a watchful eye on the calendar, hoping against hope that 'Is Nibs would solve the mystery in time.

All that day Henry had hoped for an opportunity to remind Davenant the three weeks were up at midnight, but 'Is Nibs was too busy engaged with the reunion of Addy and his grandfather and then with the dinner which followed. By the time they returned to Downsley that evening Henry was in despair of ever seeing the greys again. Noticing him so despondent, Willoughby asked him what was the matter, and when Henry told him, he promptly interceded with Davenant.

The reminder there were several hours to go until midnight and the possibility of victory roused Davenant and stirred him into action. He and Willoughby set off at once in their curricles, an overjoyed Henry clinging to Davenant's vehicle as they raced through the evening along the Brighton-to-London Road, scarcely giving hostlers time to change teams when they stopped for fresh horses.

When at last the two vehicles reached London and slowed down to cross Westminster Bridge, several clocks were striking half past eleven. Provided there were no traffic delays, there was just time to reach Carlton House.

"If Your Highness would be gracious enough to indulge me for a minute or two," Davenant said to the prince.

A JACKETING CONCERN

As if he had all the time in the world, Davenant sauntered over to a window and opened it with a flourish that sent a sudden current of cold air into the overheated room.

Watched by the bemused prince and his equally mystified guests, Davenant stood and waited by the open window for a minute or two until borne on the night air, came the distant sounds of more than one public clock just beginning to chime the midnight hour.

With a pout the prince thumped his fist on the table with such force it set the crystal glasses on it tinkling.

"Blast that valet of mine!" he cried. "He's supposed to make sure my watch keeps good time. Damn thing is ten minutes fast!"

Davenant had won both his wagers.

69

Tired but happy, Henry Rollins sat waiting with Davenant's curricle in the courtyard of Carlton House among the line of vehicles belonging to the Prince Regent's dinner guests. It was almost half past two in the morning and, after the rigours of the journey from Sussex and hours waiting for Davenant, Henry was tired and hungry. But weary though Henry was, it did not mar his jubilation. That began when the clock struck midnight ten minutes or so after Davenant entered the house. 'Is Nibs had won his wager: his greys would remain in Henry's tender care. Best of all, it was in no small measure due to Henry's prompting that he arrived just in time—a fact Henry was quick to remind the other waiting drivers who congratulated him when they learned Davenant had won.

Everything was at last as it should be. He, Henry, had been proved right about Addy: he was the real little English gentleman Henry had always believed him to be. Addy was back with the grandfather from whom he had been kidnapped; and he was now the heir to a title and great estates. Miss Barclay—thank goodness!—was engaged to another and no longer posed a threat to the freedom of 'Is Nibs and Henry, so the two of them could continue their bachelor existence together. And, that little perisher, Bodger, was no longer around to aggravate him.

Flanked by footmen with lighted torches, the line of carriages at last began to inch forward toward the house's Corinthian portico. Ahead of him Henry saw Davenant and Willoughby standing before the open front door.

Willoughby took a deep breath. "Lord, the heat in there! Enough to roast an ox! And the prince? What a performance! I'm demned glad its over, aren't you?"

Davenant stared up at the night sky. "To tell the truth, I am rather sorry it is," he said, more to himself than to his friend.

Willoughby shot him a sideways glance. "Oh, you mean the wager, not the dinner. But what is there to regret? You won! You lost neither your reputation nor two very fine horses, and the Regent owes you several hundred guineas. He chuckled. "Won a bit, myself, I did. Had bets at White's and Brookes that you'd win. Now if you are going to be sorry for anyone, be sorry for the ones who lost, including the prince, of course, although he now seems to think it was he who solved the mystery not you."

Willoughby laughed and even Davenant managed a smile.

The restoration of a lost heir, the solving of several murders and the capture of their perpetrator was the stuff of novels brought to life. By morning, the story of Addy's metamorphosis from ragged climbing boy to ducal heir and Davenant's eleventh hour arrival at the prince's dinner, would be being hawked by mercury men and women on every street corner in London. The story would have not only the public's attention but also its admiration: something the prince sought, if only vicariously. By the night's end, and after a great deal of drink, the prince had taken it into his head that he was responsible for Davenant's success.

"'Twas I who actually set the wheels in motion, you know?" the prince spent the rest of the evening telling everyone. "Davenant but followed my lead. As for that scoundrel Basingthwaite? Never did like him. Had my suspicions about him, all along, I did."

"The biggest loser would have been Hurley, not in money of course, but in pride and prestige," Davenant reminded Willoughby. "Poor fool. He wanted so much to discredit me publicly. In light of his murder, it would be ill mannered of me to take such a trivial amount of a pound from his estate. I'll not ask for it. Besides, 'tis I who am really indebted to him."

"Yes," he said to Willoughby's surprised look. "I swear I have never enjoyed myself so much as I have these past few weeks. I cannot but be eternally grateful to the late Sir Richard Hurley."

"Then any entertainment I suggest will seem poor by comparison," Willoughby said with a chuckle. "However, perhaps a little female company? I'm off to visit the love of my life," he said as they went down the steps together. "She has a friend," he promised as he climbed into his curricle.

Davenant shook his head. "This evening the Goddess of Fortune has seen fit to bestow her favours on me; she's more than enough female company for me tonight."

With a final wave to his friend, Willoughby drove off to seek his pleasure.

Davenant's curricle pulled up before the front door of the house.

"So you already know of my victory," Davenant said to Henry, whose grin could have not been any wider.

Henry's deep sigh of satisfaction sent a puff of warm vapour into the cool night air. "Knew you'd do it, I did, guv," he said as Davenant took his seat beside him. He offered him the reins, but as Davenant made no move to take them, Henry let the horses amble across the courtyard to the main gate.

"Home?" he asked.

Davenant appeared lost in thought.

Home. The place where one belonged.

Everyone had one

At long last Addy was back home, and would have now at his disposal several homes belonging to his uncle, the Duke of Ryedale. Georgiana and her husband would leave Downsley tomorrow for their home in Norfolk, their baggage train including a host of childhood toys Georgiana plundered from the Downsley nursery for their expected offspring. Perry, who was more at home at sea than on land, had returned to his ship. And although it was not what most people considered a home, even Bodger had returned to where he felt he belonged.

Davenant's lips twitched. As he told Georgiana, he was certain he had not seen the last of that cheeky climbing boy.

And Miss Barclay? She too would soon be home safe and sound with her new dull but worthy husband. Davenant sighed. Of course he had not been in love with her. Why, he could not even remember what that emotion felt like. She was but a passing fantasy, like all the numerous women in his life: a whim, this time of three week's duration. Yet he was honest enough to admit to himself that it might be a while before he forgot those blue-grey eyes of hers.

And now he, too, could return home to Davenant House, where life would once more return to what it had been before Addy entered it: no mischievous boy sliding down stairs on trays, no nighttime invasions by murderous smugglers and drunken navy lieutenants on leave, no visits from blackmailing chimney sweeps and their geese, no sister reorganising the household, no boarding-party skirmishes on the staircase, no curtain cords tied in nautical knots, no disrespectful parrots, no tradesmen continually delivering feminine fold-de-rols and—*thank God!*—no lap dog attacking his Hessian boots.

Such a blissful prospect.

Or was it?

All that awaited him at home tonight were the impassive marble faces of the Nine Muses, sycophantic servants—and an empty house.

Not such a blissful prospect after all.

At the gateway in the curtain wall, Henry stopped the curricle at the sentry box.

"Home?" he ventured again.

Davenant roused himself. "No," he drawled. "I won tonight. Fortune smiles on me, and the night is young: I intend to make the most of it. Leave me somewhere: White's, Brookes, a gaming hell; I don't care which. Then go home and go to bed. I will not be back until morning."

Under Henry's guidance the curricle moved into Pall Mall and turned west toward St. James Street with its men's clubs and gambling hells—homes away from home for many an English gentleman.

HISTORIC NOTE

From the latter part of the 18th century various acts of Parliament were passed in England–although not always enforced–to restrict the use of young children, usually boys, to clean chimneys. It was not until 1875 that the practice was finally banned.

Britain abolished the Slave Trade in its colonies in 1807, but it was not until 1833 that Parliament abolished slavery.

What might be considered a form of slavery–the impressment of men into service with the Royal Navy–was prevalent during the 16, 17th and 18th centuries, particularly during the Napoleonic Wars. The practice often involved foreigners, including citizens of the United States, their impressment among the cause of tensions that resulted in the War of 1812 between England and America. After the defeat of Napoleon, impressment was discontinued.

The Prince Regent acquired Carlton House as his London home in 1783. Together with architect Henry Holland, he turned it into a palace in the neo-Classical style. In addition to the Gothic Conservatory, where lord Davenant attended a dinner, the prince later added a Gothic dining room, a library and drawing room. The house was demolished shortly after the Prince became king in 1820 and turned his attention to Buckingham House (now Buckingham Palace). The house's contents were dispersed to other royal residences, the columns from the portico now gracing the front of the National Gallery in Trafalgar Square. Carlton House Terrace now stands on the house's former site.

The Prince Regent's fondness for house renovations led to his eventual creation of a seaside retreat, his pavilion, from the former farmhouse he acquired at Brighton on the south coast. In 1811, during which *A Jacketing Concern* is set, the pavilion had not achieved the Indian-style exterior with the domes and minarets created John Nash, and its Chinese interiors, which now make it such a unique landmark.

In 1829 Parliament passed the Metropolitan Police Act, introduced by Home Secretary Sir Robert Peel. This established the first centrally organised professional police force for London, the Metropolitan Police Force. By the

1850s policing was established throughout the country.

Established by a charter from Queen Elizabeth I, the British East India Company rose to account for half the world's trade and also ruled what was the beginning of the British Empire. After the Indian Rebellion, Britain assumed direct control of India in 1858.

A nabob like Addy's father, Ben Chantry, was a man who made a fortune in the East, particularly in India and then returned home to England, often buying himself a seat in Parliament.

Phillip Rundell, the senior partner of Rundell, Bridge and Rundell, built up a successful jewelry and silversmith business, with agencies in Europe, the Near East, India and South America. When the astute Rundell died in 1827, he left a personal fortune of £1,500,000 (£70,000,000 or US$ 87,000,000 today) to a nephew, who in turn bequeathed his wealth to Queen Victoria.

ACKNOWLEDGEMENTS

Writing a novel is a very solitary occupation but even so a writer rarely accomplishes it completely on his or her own.

My thanks for help with my research to the staffs of the Museum of London, England, for answering my queries and providing me with a book of maps of 1811 London; the secretary of White's Club, London; the staffs of the National Library of Canada, Ottawa, Canada; the Central and Centrepointe branches of the Ottawa Public Library; the Redoubt Museum, Eastbourne Heritage, Eastbourne Borough Council, Eastbourne, England; and the Brighton Pavilion and Museums, City of Brighton & Hove Council, England.

My appreciation to my 'techie team:' my brother, Roy Southall, and my stepson, Bruce Cavell, for so patiently helping me when I encountered problems with my computer, and my step-granddaughter and her husband, Sarah and Jeff Washer, for help with my website. Special appreciation goes to my publisher Dana Robinson of Knox Robinson of London and Atlanta.

My gratitude for the ongoing support and encouragement of my sister, Shirley Shakespeare, my friend Ruth Jennings, my brother, Stella, my husband Bill Cavell and my extended family on both sides of the Atlantic.

Lightning Source UK Ltd.
Milton Keynes UK
UKOW04f0828021017
310244UK00002B/438/P